Only Us

only one series

USA TODAY BESTSELLING AUTHOR
KENNEDY FOX

Copyright © 2022 Kennedy Fox
www.kennedyfoxbooks.com

Only Us
Only One series, #2

Cover designer: Designs by Dana
Cover photographer: Regina Wamba
Copy editor: Editing 4 Indies

All rights reserved. No parts of the book may be used or reproduced in any matter without written permission from the author, except for inclusion of brief quotations in a review. This book is a work of fiction. Names, characters, establishments, organizations, and incidents are either products of the author's imagination or are used fictitiously to give a sense of authenticity. Any resemblance to actual persons, living or dead, events, or locales is entirely coincidental.

only one series

SUGGESTED READING ORDER

ONLY HIM
a best friend's brother, second chance,
small town romance

ONLY US
a single mom, friends to lovers,
small town romance

ONLY MINE
a brother's best friend, roommates to lovers,
small town romance

PROLOGUE
NOAH

TEN YEARS EARLIER

"Mmm... yes. You're a dirty girl."

"Yes, I am. Spank me harder, Mr. Plumber."

What the fuck? I groan, then slam my laptop closed. I've resorted to watching porn to get the woman I love but can never have out of my head. I don't know why I try because it never works. Being in love with your best friend, who also happens to be married to your cousin, is the worst kind of torture. I kick myself daily for not telling Katie how I felt before Gabe swooped in and asked her out. That was six years ago, and they're now expecting a baby boy.

It's another Friday night spent alone in my room. My sister, Gemma, is out, and my dad's already asleep. He owns the only garage in town and works long hours. My mother passed away when we were kids, so it's mostly been just the three of us. When I ask him why he hasn't dated, he says it's impossible to replace your soul mate. I know he means well, but I just wish he'd find love again because then I'd have hope of finding someone after I lost my chance with Katie.

Noah: How you feeling tonight?

I text Katie to see if she's still awake. We haven't talked much this week because she's taking it easy since her due date is next month.

Katie: Been having Braxton Hicks on and off, which sucks. It's too soon for him to come, so hopefully, they quit soon, and I can actually get some sleep.

Noah: What does your doctor say about it?

Katie: That it's normal and to monitor them in case it turns into actual labor.

Noah: Are you all set to go to the hospital if it is?

Katie: Well, my bag is packed, but Gabe isn't home tonight. I've been texting him, but he's out with the guys, probably playing poker and drinking.

What the fuck? Is she serious?

Noah: If you need me, call me, okay? I'll be right over.

Katie: I know you will be. Thanks, Noah. I'm gonna try to get some sleep now.

I'm so angry I don't think twice about putting on my shoes and going to my truck. I know exactly where Gabe is, and it isn't at a buddy's house playing cards. For months, I've heard the rumors that he's cheating on Katie, but without actual proof, I can't say anything and risk being wrong.

Though Gabe and I are the same age, we don't have the best

relationship. He moved to town the summer before our junior year and merged himself into my circle. Though Katie is a year younger than me, we were inseparable. However, that slowly changed when she and Gabe got serious. He proposed when she was nineteen, and they got hitched the next year. I pretended to be supportive since she seemed so happy. When they announced they were expecting, I drank for a solid week. Gabe was living *my* dream life with *my* dream woman, and I had to accept it.

I drive downtown and spot his truck parked in front of the Main Street Pub. He's bold to show up there with another chick, but Gabe's been known to be a royal dumbass. Honestly, I don't understand why Katie puts up with it, but I won't stand around and watch him make a fool of her in front of half the town.

As soon as I enter, I spot a blonde hanging all over him. They're seated at a bar top table covered with empty bottles and shot glasses. He holds a pool stick in one hand, and his other arm is wrapped tightly around her waist.

"Gabe." I step toward him and glare. "It's time to go home. C'mon, I'll drive you."

"What the fuck are you talkin' about?"

"I'm talkin' about your pregnant wife who's at home. She's having Braxton Hicks, and there's no reason you should be here." I direct my eyes to the woman who doesn't seem fazed in the least that Gabe's married. Though I have no idea who she is, it's obvious they're more than just *friends*.

"My wife is none of your damn business. She's fine."

I cross my arms over my chest, my blood boiling at what a piece of shit he is.

"You don't deserve her," I spit.

"What'd you say to me?" He stands, wobbly on his feet, then throws the stick down.

"You heard me."

"Yeah, and I see the way you look at her. Better back the fuck off, Noah."

"Alright, time to go. C'mon," I say, reaching out to grab his arm, but he yanks it away.

There are several eyes on us, including his date's.

"You should be ashamed." I look at her, then gaze back to Gabe. "And you should be too. Katie's gonna leave you when I tell her you're sleeping around."

The corner of his lips tilts up in a devilish smirk as he steps toward me. "I can promise you that she ain't going nowhere. She'll be six feet under before I allow that to happen."

I blink hard. *What the hell did he just say?*

There's no point in trying to reason with him, so I shake my head and turn around. Before I can walk away, Gabe grabs my jacket and pulls me back.

I spin until he drops his grip. "Get off me."

"Make me." He pushes my chest, and I stumble back into a couple of chairs. "You aren't going anywhere until we're done."

"Trust me, we're done. You're not worth it."

"Because you're a sissy who can't fight. You let me date Katie when you wanted her. You let me propose to her and then knock her up while you stood there like a pussy." He barks out a laugh, and I'm shocked. He knew how I felt, then asked her out anyway. *Bastard.*

I see red when he charges at me again. "Couldn't man up to date her, and you can't man up now."

His laughter has me seething, and I push him back. "Get outta my face. I'm leaving."

Before I can walk away, he sucker punches me in the stomach, and I bend over, trying to catch my breath. Someone yells at us to take it outside, and his blond bimbo girlfriend laughs.

Just when I can see straight again, Gabe attempts another hit, but I move before his fist connects. He's unsteady on his feet and clearly wasted but completely unfazed. He's a pro at drinking after work and on the weekends, and it's quickly become his favorite pastime. It wasn't always that way, but after the wedding, he changed.

"Get outta here, now!" the bartender shouts. Gabe turns toward him, and I take the opportunity to swing my fist. I deck him in the face and watch as he trips over his feet on his way down. His head smacks the ground so damn hard I swear I hear it crack. The room grows silent as we wait for him to move, but he doesn't. He's out cold.

"Shit." I bend down and see his eyes are closed. "Gabe, can you hear me?"

His girlfriend screams, and a couple of other guys crowd around me.

"Gabe, wake up!" Blondie shakes him, but I stop her.

"Don't. He probably has a concussion."

"You motherfucker, this is your fault!" She jabs a finger in my shoulder.

"I'm calling 911," the bartender says. "Someone better call his wife."

The next hour is a blur.

Gabe's pulse is weak, and he doesn't regain consciousness. When the paramedics arrive, they take him to the hospital in the next town over. I can't bear to call Katie and tell her myself, so I call Gemma and ask her to drive Katie to the hospital while I follow the ambulance in my truck.

Katie's hysterical when the doctor tells her they've put him in a medically induced coma so his brain can heal. It's swelling, and there's a chance he could have brain damage.

Five days go by, and my worst nightmare happens. Gabe's considered brain-dead due to the blunt force trauma he suffered when he fell and hit his head. My body goes from being in shock to utterly numb as I take in everything that's happened. Katie's a mess, his parents won't even look at me, and my sister tries to console me, but I know she's torn between being there for me and comforting her best friend. I don't fault her, though, because

I'm to blame for this. I should've stayed home that night and minded my own damn business.

The morning of his funeral, I contemplate not going, but Katie begs me to attend. My dad tells me I would regret it later if I didn't, so I put on my only black suit and attend the wake and service. I can hardly speak to Katie, but the fact she talks to me is mind-blowing. I'm waiting for her to wake up and hate me.

She clings to me for comfort, but I don't deserve her forgiveness, so I don't ask for it. Seeing Gabe in that maple box with gold embellishments makes me feel sick. It's an out-of-body experience, like none of this is real. How can this be happening? I wish I could wake up from this nightmare.

Gemma told Katie my side of the story—about the blonde and how a fight broke out—even though she never asked for an explanation. Honestly, I think she's still in shock.

I want to explain everything to her but don't even know where to start. I had no intention of hurting him that night and only had her best interest in mind. She deserved better, and her husband should've been home with her that night.

As I watch them lower my cousin's casket into the ground, three police officers walk up and interrupt.

"Apologies for intruding, but we're looking for Noah Reid."

Everyone turns to me, and I nod at the officers. They took my statement at the hospital the night of the fight along with everyone else who was there. I'm not sure what was said, but I told them the truth—he pushed and punched me, so I hit him back.

"I'm Noah," I speak up.

The three of them circle me, then one guy grabs my arms.

"We have a warrant for your arrest for the murder of Gabe Reid." He cuffs my wrists, and the audible gasps echo around me. As he reads my Miranda rights, I look at my dad and Gemma. Then I find Katie and watch her face drop. I'll never forget the look of pure shock, sadness, and fear on her face. I'm in disbelief and horrified that I caused this.

"Noah, stay quiet. I'll meet you down there with our lawyer," my dad tells me. I keep my head down as they walk me to the cruiser and put me in the back. Though I'm mortified, I look out the window anyway and meet Katie's eyes.

"I'm sorry," I mouth to her. She's been crying all afternoon, but a new set of tears falls down her cheeks as she stares at me.

When I get to the station, I quickly learn about the witnesses' statements used against me. Gabe's side chick completely exaggerated reality, but without Gabe to confirm, it's my word against hers. The fact our fight resulted in his death means they can charge me for this.

I'm placed in the county jail until my court date. The lawyer encourages me to take a plea deal because if my case goes to a jury, the prosecutor will push for a harsher charge. When my day to stand in front of the judge arrives, I plead guilty and accept the sentence for a class B felony. My family and Katie sit behind me as the judge reads my charges.

Twelve years for involuntary manslaughter.

My dad and Gemma are distraught, and Katie gives me the saddest, most pitiful expression I've ever seen. I don't know what she's thinking because we haven't spoken since the funeral two weeks ago, but I see the disappointment and pain written all over her face.

Everything in my life changes in the blink of an eye.

She knows I'm the reason her husband is dead.

The reason her unborn son will grow up without his father and why she'll have to raise him alone.

How do I apologize for that? Nothing I say could ever be enough or change things. Instead of helping, I hurt her, and I'll never be able to forgive myself for what I've done.

CHAPTER ONE

KATIE

PRESENT DAY

I LOOK around the two-story house I bought almost a year ago, knowing that one day it'll be the perfect home for my son, Owen, and me. It needed a total remodel, so I've slowly been fixing it up on my days off at the bank. Sometimes, I'll come in the evenings with Owen, but lately, between making dinner, helping with his homework, and getting him into bed by eight thirty, I haven't had any extra time.

Even so, it's been one-hundred-percent worth it. I've invested everything I own into this place and won't stop until it's move-in ready. After tearing down some walls, I hired an electrician to fix the wiring before I insulated and hung drywall. Since I learned from watching YouTube tutorials and made a few mistakes along the way, it took months to get that much done. I'm hoping to do as much as I can on my own and am proud to do it.

Between being a single mom and working full-time, I have limited hours to dedicate to this project, but I'm determined. The flooring has been replaced in a couple of rooms, and I've been buying wood, paint, and other materials as I've saved up the money.

"Knock, knock," Gemma sing-songs as she lets herself in the front door.

"In the master," I call out. This room is almost finished and only needs new windows installed.

I smile when I see my best friend holding two cups of coffee. I grab one and take a small sip. "My hero."

"How's it goin'?" she asks, looking around. She hasn't been here in a while, but she's been busy lately, so I understand.

"Not too bad. Come check out the paint and carpet."

I've decided to leave hardwood in the hallway and tile in the bathroom suite, so the carpet was only needed in this room.

Gemma stands in the doorway. "It looks so good. I can't wait to see the house when it's complete."

I snort. "You and me both."

We walk into the kitchen, where I chat about my plans.

"Are you sure you don't want some help? This seems like such a big project for one person," she says after I describe how I want to restore the cabinets.

"Nah, you and Tyler are busy with the new gym. I'll be fine. I've got Google and YouTube to help save the day. I'll figure it out."

Gemma chuckles. "Well, just holler if you change your mind."

"Do you wanna grab a drink tonight after I'm done here? Owen's having a sleepover with Gabe's parents."

Loretta and Elliot Reid have been very involved in Owen's life since Gabe was their only son. I'm grateful for them because after Gabe died, trying to raise a newborn alone left me exhausted. My mother helps a lot too, which I appreciate. When Owen was a baby, he didn't sleep much, which meant neither did I. I was struggling to be a new mom and a widow. I would've been lost without the support of everyone who stepped up to offer a hand.

"I can't…" Gemma hesitates, and I can tell something's off.

"Oh, why not?"

"Well, I won't be able to drink for about…nine months."

My heart leaps in my throat. "Oh my God. You're pregnant?"

I immediately wrap my arms around her. Gemma and Tyler Blackwood got married over a year ago after her ex-fiancé blackmailed her. He was an awful, conniving man and used threats so she'd agree to marry him. Once all the lies came to light, Tyler devised a plan to get her out of it. Long story short, they've been happily married ever since, and I'm over the moon excited they're adding to their family. They were in love when Gemma was in high school, and it took twelve years for them to find each other again.

"I'm really happy for you guys," I say. "How far along are you?"

"Only ten weeks but I didn't want to wait too long to tell you. Once we got the ultrasound and confirmed everything was healthy, I was just waiting for the right way to announce it."

"That's exciting! I bet Tyler's ecstatic."

"He is. I'm so lucky." She beams. "And I'm thrilled Noah will be getting out next month and can be a part of my pregnancy journey. He's already missed so much over the past ten years. I'm just happy he'll be around for this."

I swallow down the lump that forms in my throat at the mention of her brother. She always treads lightly when it comes to Noah, but I can tell she's eager about his homecoming. I, on the other hand, am dreading it.

"Shit, sorry," she quickly says once she sees my expression.

"No, no, it's fine. Better get used to it, right?" I half-laugh.

Soon, he'll be back and impossible to avoid. Though Gemma and Everleigh are my best girl friends, Noah and I were inseparable for as long as I can remember. Not only was he funny and always down for an adventure but his smile would light up an entire room and cause butterflies every time he looked at me.

When I was younger, I didn't understand what it meant, but I realized I had feelings for him as I got older. Gemma and Everleigh were the only two who knew and kept telling me to ask him out. I was too nervous he'd reject me—or worse, laugh—so I held onto the hope he'd admit he felt the same. When he never did, I assumed he only saw me as a friend. Anytime the opportunity arose, he never made a move, so when his cousin moved to town and asked me out, I accepted. Noah never said a word about it and seemed to approve, so I dated Gabe during my last two years of high school. When Gabe proposed the year after I graduated, I said yes because I thought I loved him. Not the way I had secretly loved Noah, but that was different and unexplainable. It was a love so deep it felt unnatural.

However, those feelings shifted after he was sentenced to prison, and he wouldn't let me visit him. He couldn't even return a damn letter. Years have passed, and I still don't know why he pushed me away. Gemma pleaded with him to respond or let me see him, but he'd give her the runaround. After years of him ignoring me, my hurt turned to anger. If I were to see him today, I don't know what I'd do. Maybe I'd just ignore him for the next decade like he ignored me.

The man I once loved has let me down. Not only did I lose a husband but I also lost my best friend at the same time.

I didn't even get a say in the matter.

"I hope you two can talk it out," Gemma says as I walk around, needing to keep myself busy. "He's going to need as many people on his side as possible. This town hasn't forgotten what happened, and I'm worried for him."

"Well, I've been trying to talk to him for years, Gemma," I remind her.

"I know, Katie. Trust me, I wish I could've talked some sense into him, but he's a stubborn asshole sometimes. Perhaps this will be a new beginning for both of you."

"Not counting on it," I say dryly, wanting to change the subject.

"Katie…"

"I don't want to see him," I admit. "I know I will eventually have to, but I refuse to go out of my way. I've done enough of that."

"I understand, but please just remember Tyler and I had our second chance after he got out of prison. I really believe that can happen for you two."

I snort, nearly choking. "I wouldn't be placing bets on that, babe."

He knew what I was going through, yet he couldn't even spare five minutes to write back. I never blamed him for Gabe's death, never got angry with him for getting in our business, and never wanted him to go to prison for what happened. I knew Gabe was cheating, and the fact his mistress was there that night made the whole situation worse. But to be ghosted by my best friend when I just wanted to support him and make sure he was okay? I was devastated. In fact, if he shows up on my front porch, I won't think twice about shoving him right on his ass.

"Never say never." She smirks.

"I'm too hurt to give him a chance," I admit. "I have too much pent-up anger toward him, and the more I think about it, the madder I get."

"Okay, sorry. I won't bring it up again."

"I know he's your brother, so it's gonna come up, but now you know how I feel about it all."

"So I better warn him to wear a bulletproof vest if he's around you." She's laughing, but I glare at her. "Okay, sorry, I'm done now."

I finish walking Gemma through the house, explaining what I want to do and what colors I want to paint the walls. Owen's an only child, so he'll have his own space upstairs. We barely fit in the place we're renting right now, so I can't wait to give him the home he deserves.

"Just so you know...um, you-know-who will be working with Tyler at the gym. But I hope you'll come and see it once things are ready for the grand opening."

I shake my head at how she tries to avoid using his name. "It's fine, Gemma. Just let me know when he's not there, and I'll come visit. I'm sure Owen would love to see it too." I give her a hug when we reach the front door. "We're very proud of you guys."

"Thank you, I am too. I can't believe it's really happening. With my dad retiring, it feels like the perfect timing."

"Once this house is finally done, I'll actually have time to work out again. Looking forward to that even though I'll probably just hang out at the juice bar."

We laugh, and I tell her to give me every update she gets on the baby. I still can't believe she's pregnant. I wish our kids were closer in age, but that's what happens when one of us gets pregnant before we can even legally drink.

Since I'm kid-free for the night and there's literally nothing to do in Lawton Ridge, Alabama, in January, I finish up at the house, then head home for some solo drinking and Netflix bingeing.

The toxic combination means I'm left to my own thoughts, which have often led me down a path of self-loathing and pity.

Usually after I tuck Owen in, I go to bed, but tonight, I'm sucking down wine and watching a show about a nurse moving to a small town and falling for the local bartender.

"Don't do it..." I slur. "Sex only leads to heartbreak."

Not that I'd really know. I haven't had sex in...a long-ass time. I didn't even think about dating until three years after Gabe passed, and even then, it felt weird and wrong. It was never anything serious, but since I always put my kid and job first, they usually bailed before things could progress. The last time I went out with a man was over a year ago...which was the last time I had sex. But that's what Channing, my vibrator, is for.

After my fourth glass of wine, the TV screen becomes blurry, so I decide to call it a night. I only drink every once in a while, making me a lightweight, but since I don't have to get up early with Owen, I splurge. I'll undoubtedly pay for it tomorrow, but that's future Katie's problem.

As I crawl under the covers, I sink into the bed and seek warmth. I've slept alone for so long now, aside from when Owen crawls in when he has bad dreams, that I'm accustomed to sleeping in the middle. It's probably why no guy has ever wanted to stay with me long. I'm unapologetically independent, and most guys want to feel needed. The truth is, I haven't needed a man for anything in more than a decade.

My eyelids feel heavy, and as I drift off, images of the day they walked Noah out of the courtroom in handcuffs surface. At first, I was in shock he took the plea deal, but the lawyers said he risked a longer sentence if he went to trial. I know he didn't intend to hurt Gabe, but his actions led to his death, and justice was needed.

Gabe's parents were a wreck. Elliot not only lost a son that night but it also tore their whole family apart. The Reid brothers are no longer on speaking terms, and no one dares to mention Noah around Loretta and Elliot. They've completely erased his existence.

They're not happy Noah's getting out early on parole and have made that clear by sending letters to the parole board. Though it hasn't changed anything, I'm concerned about what will happen when he does return. Few people in Lawton Ridge have forgotten, and if Gabe's parents have any say in the matter, they'll do whatever they can to run Noah out of town.

CHAPTER TWO

NOAH

ONE MONTH LATER

Today's the day I've been waiting for. I'm going home, and tonight, I'll be sleeping in my childhood room. It feels surreal to leave this place for the first time in ten years.

Free from this prison.

As I pass through security and walk through the gate for the last time with my one small bag, I don't look back. All I can focus on is my family, who's waiting for me in the parking lot. This has been so hard on them, especially for Gemma. She visited me a lot, and we've stayed close over the years. I know it negatively affected my dad too, but he's tried to be strong for us. I've also tried my best not to be a burden to them and kept how bad things were behind bars to myself. No need to tell them since all it would do is cause them to worry.

In the past year, Dad finally found happiness again with his new girlfriend, Belinda. She's kept him on his toes while he's anxiously waited for my release. He hasn't dated since my mom died and was too focused on raising Gemma and me as a single parent.

When I see Gemma's face break into a smile, I can't stop my own. As soon as they're within reach, we collide and hug each other. It's a moment I've thought about for months—years even—and it's finally here. It almost doesn't feel real.

Gemma bursts into tears as my dad swallows down his emotions. I don't even bother to hide mine.

"I can finally hug you," she whispers, sniffling and rubbing her eyes. "You've beefed up."

I chuckle and shrug, releasing them. "You too," I tease, glancing at her little baby bump.

"Ha-ha." She rolls her eyes.

"You look good, son."

"Thanks, Dad."

I smile at Belinda, who gives me a kiss on the cheek, then I spot Tyler behind them and hug him next.

"Good to see you, man." He squeezes me tighter.

I wipe off my cheeks. "You too. I was just about to say you have no idea, but…" We both chuckle.

Gemma married Tyler not too long ago, and they've visited me every month for the past year. Tyler's also an ex-con, but he spent five years in prison for something he didn't do. However, I'll be relying on him for support to get through these first few months of reintegrating into society. Not sure if my hometown will be very forgiving or accepting of me since Gabe's family's still there. From what Gemma's told me, no one's forgotten that night. I sure as hell haven't.

Given what I did and how it affected everyone, I'm preparing for the worst. Even though my sister and Tyler have reassured me everything will be fine, and they'll help me find my new normal, I'm anxious about it. Since Tyler has hired me to do the construction at the gym he's remodeling, I already have something to keep me busy. It's only a temporary position, but at least it's something, and I'm grateful for it. I hope to have another job lined up by the time I finish this one.

I honestly can't wait to go to work, be around people, and find my footing again. Even though I don't know what people's reactions will be when they run into me, there's one person in particular who probably never wants to see me again—*Katie*.

"Well, let's get out of here and get ya settled at the house," Dad says, beaming wide.

"And eat," Gemma adds. "Belinda made her famous fried chicken, and we bought pie."

"I can't wait. But before we go home, I need to make a stop," I say, looking at Tyler.

"Sure, wherever you wanna go," he tells me as we pile into the SUV. "Just tell me where."

I fidget a little, knowing my sister is about to rip me a new one. "I don't actually know the address, but I'm sure you do."

Tyler looks at me through the rearview mirror, and there's a mutual understanding.

"Wait, where?" Gemma asks, looking over her shoulder at me.

Tyler starts the engine and drives out of the parking lot as my sister continues to stare at me.

"Katie's," I finally answer. "I need to see her before we go home."

"Noah!" Gemma scolds. "No. She specifically said she didn't want to see you, and I'm not gonna be the one who forces her."

"You aren't," I argue, standing firm in my decision. "Tyler's drivin'."

Tyler snorts. "Babe, just let him." He tries to calm her. "What's the worst that can happen? She slams the door in his face?"

"Exactly!" Gemma shouts. "And never talks to *me* again."

"Maybe she won't," I counter, though I know better. Those two are tied to the hip. "I just want to see her. Please. It's been so long," I plead softly, hoping she'll take pity on me.

"Alright, fine. But if she pushes you off the porch or slaps you, don't say I didn't warn ya."

Katie Walker had been my best friend growing up. She was Gemma's friend and always over at the house, and we formed a friendship from there.

Even though I wanted more, I was too afraid of rejection and worried we'd ruin our friendship if it didn't work out. It was more important to have her in my life, so I kept quiet and just enjoyed the time we spent together.

Since I was a coward and too young to truly understand my feelings for her, I didn't say a goddamn thing when Gabe asked her out. In fact, I'm pretty sure I encouraged it. The last thing I wanted to be seen as was the envious best friend or the jealous guy secretly in love with her. I really didn't expect their relationship to last, considering his reputation. Gabe was never the serious type of guy, at least by all the hookup stories he'd text me.

When we were twenty, he proposed, and Katie said yes. It didn't sink in until I saw her baby bump a year after they got married that she'd forever be tied to Gabe.

And I would never have anything more than friendship with her. It was my own fault for never speaking up, and I'll never know if she felt the same. Sometimes, I thought maybe she did, but when she never said anything either, I pushed it to the back of my mind.

So life went on like that until the night Gabe died.

I felt so damn ashamed I couldn't stand to let her see me in prison. Even when she wrote and pleaded to let her come visit, I never wrote back.

And according to my sister, Katie hates me for it.

I don't blame her one bit, but I'd like the chance to at least explain. I know I don't deserve a second of her time, but I've learned a valuable lesson—life is too damn short.

An hour later, Tyler pulls into the driveway of an old beat-up farmhouse that I'm shocked is still standing.

"This is where she lives?" I ask, surprised.

"It needs a little TLC." Tyler chuckles. "She's planning to fix it up."

Fix it up? At this rate, it'd be faster to demolish the whole thing and build it back from scratch.

"She hasn't moved in yet, but she comes here every evening and weekend to work on it," Gemma explains.

Inhaling a sharp breath, I grab the door handle. "Okay, wish me luck. Here goes nothin'." I push open the door and step out. My heart races as I walk up onto the porch to the front door.

Nervously, I knock on the cracked wood, then wait as a million thoughts run through my mind.

Has time been good to her?
Does Owen look like Gabe?
Will she forgive me?

I hear footsteps, and when the door opens, I nearly lose my breath when I see Katie for the first time in a decade.

She's even more stunning than I remembered. Her blond hair is pulled back in a messy ponytail, and dust and dry paint cover her shirt.

"Ka—"

Before I can even finish saying her name, she steps back and slams the door in my face.

I deserved that.

My head and heart drop.

When I get back to the SUV, everyone gives me the most pitiful looks.

"Yeah, she hates me."

Tyler turns and looks at me. "Give her time."

I scrunch my nose. "*More* time? How much more time should I give her?"

"Give her space," Gemma clarifies as Tyler backs out of the driveway. "She'll come around."

I blow out a frustrated breath. Fuck, I hope so.

"Or here's an idea…" Tyler begins. "She needs help on the

new house, and Noah just so happens to be pretty good at fixing shit."

I scoff. "Katie will never hire me."

"She works during the day. She can't say no if she doesn't know…" Tyler grins at me through the mirror.

"Noooo…" Gemma shakes her head. "She'll kill you for sure."

"Actually, that's not a horrible idea," Dad blurts out.

"She might think it's romantic," Belinda adds.

I chuckle at their encouragement.

Gemma shakes her head. "Absolutely not. She wants to do it all herself."

"Well, if she won't give me a chance to talk, then I'll show her how sorry I am instead," I decide and shrug. "Start fixin' things little by little until she notices. She won't be able to slam the door when I'm already inside the house."

"This is seriously a bad idea. How are you guys agreeing with this?" Gemma glances around, furrowing her brows at our dad and Belinda.

"I've pushed her away long enough, Gem. Let me do this," I beg. "I have to win her friendship back."

"Alright, on one condition…" Gemma's shoulders slump as she blows out a breath. "She must never know I knew about this plan. Got it?"

I smile victoriously. "Deal."

Gemma rolls her eyes, then repositions herself in her seat. Though I know it's a crazy plan, it feels good to have my family's support. I'll do whatever it takes to prove to Katie how sorry I am and that I'm no longer pushing her away.

Katie's new house is on the same street as my dad's, which is quite convenient. She probably hates that I'm so close now, but she better get used to it because I'm not going anywhere this time.

"I can't wait to show you your bedroom," Gemma squeals as we make our way inside.

"Why?" I snort, carrying my bag. "It probably looks the same."

"Hey." She smacks my arm. "I spruced it up for ya."

"Of course, you did." I smile, following her upstairs.

"Any chance you upgraded my old nineteen-inch TV to a fifty-inch?" I tease as she opens the door.

"As a matter of fact…"

My gaze wanders around, and I notice everything looks the same except for the new flat-screen TV sitting on my dresser. "Shit, really?" I give her a hug. "You're my *favorite* sister."

She rolls her eyes with a grin. "I even washed all your old clothes and put a couple of new things in the closet. Figured that'd get you through until you had time to go shopping yourself."

"You're seriously the best, thank you."

Gemma smiles. "You're welcome. I'm so happy you're home, and you'll be here to meet the baby." She pats her stomach.

"Me too. Gonna spoil that kid rotten."

"You and Tyler both."

"Damn straight." Tyler walks up behind Gemma and wraps his arms around her waist.

"Gemma, Noah. Come down," Dad calls from the living room.

When we enter, Dad hands me a set of keys. "These are for you."

"Really?"

"Yeah, it's nothing fancy, but it'll get you around town. Let's go check it out."

We walk out to the garage, and I see a blue F-150 single cab. "I fixed it up as best as I could. Should last ya until you can buy a newer one."

I hope Dad hasn't been spending his spare time on this, considering he retired recently. He was the best mechanic in this part of Alabama, and though I'm sure he'll miss parts of it, I can already tell he's enjoying his free time.

I steal a quick hug and grin. "Thanks, old man. It's great."

"Wanna go for a quick drive?"

I hesitate, not sure if that's a good idea. I haven't renewed my license yet, and a ticket is the last thing I need. He climbs behind the wheel, almost as if he read my mind, and waits for my answer. I can't deny my dad for wanting to spend some alone time with me.

"Okay, just a quick trip," I agree and climb into the passenger side.

"I'll give you the updated Lawton Ridge tour." He smirks.

Soon, we're on Main Street, and he's giving me all the details about the new shops.

"That's Everleigh's boutique." He points at a corner shop with the words "Ever After" on a sign. "You remember her? Gemma and Katie's friend."

"Yeah, isn't she Tyler's little sister?"

"Yep. Last I heard, she's single."

I snort, shaking my head. "Slow down. I'm not diving into the dating scene right away." Or ever. No one around here is going to want to date an ex-con.

"I know what you're thinkin', but get it outta your head," my dad scolds. "You have a lot to offer, and any woman would be lucky to be with you."

I stay silent because while I know he's being genuine, I don't believe the words. People around here are judgmental as hell, and even though plenty of them have had their own share of scandals—typical small-town drama like affairs and tax fraud—they don't hesitate to ridicule others.

Swiftly, I change the subject as we make our way back home. Lawton Ridge looks the same with just a few different businesses.

"Just in time, boys," Belinda says as we walk inside the house. "Lunch is ready."

"Great, I'm starving." I take a deep breath in. "That chicken smells delicious."

"Your dad said you loved it, so I made it just for you." Belinda smiles sweetly.

"Don't let this one go, Pops," I taunt as I take a seat next to Tyler.

My dad wraps his arm around her and plants a kiss on her cheek. "Never in a million years."

As we sit and eat, things almost feel normal, but then again, they don't. I'm used to sitting on hard benches or stools and scarfing down my food without really tasting it. If you hesitated, someone would steal it. It was almost always cold and bland, but I needed to get something in my stomach to keep my strength. Not long after I arrived at the facility, some of the prisoners found out what I'd done. Some taunted me about it, some were legit scared I'd kill them with my fists, but others—the ones who were lifers—didn't give two shits. They started fights just to entertain themselves.

I only talked to my cellmate and a couple of younger guys

who came in at eighteen years old. They looked like me when I first arrived—terrified as hell. I wasn't a killer and had only gotten into a handful of fights my whole life, but I had to put on an act just to protect myself. That's all behind me now, though, and today's the beginning of a fresh start.

Being thirty-two years old and starting completely over in my childhood home is an odd feeling, but I'm not taking this second chance for granted. Instead, I'm giving all my energy to rebuilding the life I almost missed out on, and I hope like hell Katie will allow me to be in hers.

CHAPTER THREE

KATIE

AFTER SEEING Noah on my front porch and abruptly slamming the door in his face, I couldn't focus on much yesterday. My first instinct was to smack him for even having the audacity to come to my house, but I didn't. Hopefully, my reaction made it abundantly clear I didn't want to see him.

I don't know what the hell Gemma was thinking by bringing him there, but she's getting an earful from me *very* soon. She texted last night, but I haven't responded yet. I didn't want to say anything I'd regret later since I was so mad.

Seeing his face after a decade took me by surprise. He looks the same but older and more muscular. Minimal facial hair filled his jawline, and his features are more prominent than I remember. He's grown into a man, quite different than when he was twenty-two.

Once I left the house, I returned home and met Loretta and Owen. She loves spending time with him on the weekends, which really helps me when I'm busy remodeling. After she left, we had dinner and watched a movie before I tucked him in for the night.

Now it's Sunday morning, and Owen's watching YouTube on

his tablet while I make breakfast. It's become our routine. Since I'm so busy working at the house on the weekends and evenings during the week, we spend Sunday mornings together and hang out for a few hours.

"Come get your biscuits and gravy, bud," I call out. After I set his plate on the table, I walk to his room to grab his hamper.

On Sundays, I also try to catch up on all the chores I neglected during the week, especially laundry.

Once I've put his clothes in the washer, I head back to the kitchen and see his empty chair.

"Owen!" I shout. "Your food's getting cold."

"I'm comin', Ma!" He finally trails in from the living room with his eyes glued to his tablet.

"You know the rules. Turn it off."

He releases a groan, then looks at me. "Why can't I watch it while I eat? All my friends get to."

I take the tablet and close the cover, then set it on the kitchen counter. "Good for them. They aren't my children, but you are, so I guess you gotta listen to my rules instead." I flash him a wink, but he rolls his eyes with a grunt.

"No fair."

He's only ten, but some days, I swear he acts like a hormonal fifteen-year-old.

"Watch that tone."

"Yes, ma'am."

He dives into his food, and I clear my throat to get his attention. "Where are your manners?" I sit across from him with my own plate.

"Thank you, Mom."

"You're welcome." I smile as I take my first bite. "What would you like to do after?"

He shrugs, which is his usual go-to response. Owen's an energetic kid, but he has his moments. Lately, hanging out with his friends and playing games on his tablet have become the most important things in his life.

"Wanna play one of your new games that Memaw and Papa got you?"

It was his birthday a few months ago, and my parents got him some board games that we've only played a couple times.

He shrugs again.

"What about Pay Day? See if you can beat me this time?" I tease.

I finally get a smile out of him. "Yeah right, but sure."

We continue eating, and I make a mental list of things I want to do this afternoon. Besides laundry, I need to change our bedding, clean the kitchen and bathrooms, and tidy up before going to the new house. I'll probably only get a few hours of work in this afternoon when my mom comes over and hangs out with Owen.

"Can we watch a movie?"

I glance at the clock and figure if we spend an hour playing a game and another hour and a half watching a movie, I'll have time to switch the laundry over between.

"Sure, bud."

He's obsessed with *Star Wars*, so streaming the movies with Disney Plus has been a godsend.

Once we're done, Owen takes our empty plates and places them into the dishwasher. That's one of his chores, and I make sure he stays on it. Besides dishes, his other responsibilities include putting his clean clothes away and keeping his room tidy. It's not always an easy task, but one warning about losing his tablet and he gets it done.

Although being a single parent has had its challenges over the years, there's nothing more rewarding than being his mom and watching him grow into a kind, sweet young man.

As I'm folding clothes, my phone goes off with a text message, and I smile when I see it's from Everleigh.

She, Gemma, and I grew up together and have been best friends for as long as I can remember. We're each other's ride or die, but as we've gotten older, we've gotten busy with our lives—having a baby, getting married, opening a business. We may have chosen different paths, but it's brought us closer together.

Everleigh: Sooo you gonna spill the beans on what happened yesterday, or do I need to bribe you with margaritas and Mexican food?

I snort and curse at whoever told her. Not that I wouldn't have eventually, but it only means the news about what happened yesterday is already getting around our small town.

Katie: There's nothing to tell. But drinks and chips and salsa are always a good idea.

Everleigh: Nothing to tell, my flat ass. Let's talk it out.

I chuckle at the reference to her backside. Everleigh has always been naturally thin, and she got teased for it a lot in school. She didn't fully develop until the last couple of years of high school.

Katie: You'll be able to beef up your ass as soon as the gym is open ;)

Everleigh: Don't change the subject. I'm coming over.

Katie: I'm still at home with Owen. I'll be at the new house around 3.

Everleigh: Perfect. Better be ready to spill the deets.

ONLY US

Katie: Nothing to spill, but okay. See you then!

I shake my head with a grin as I set down my phone and continue folding Owen's shirts and jeans. Once my work clothes finish in the dryer, I'll hang them, then it'll be time to get ready to go.

My mom arrives at 2:45, just as we're cleaning up Pay Day. We managed to play for two rounds, but I let Owen win the second time.

"How's my favorite grandson?" she asks as she sets her bag down and wraps Owen in a hug.

"I'm your only grandchild," he deadpans.

"That's because when your mama had you, I just knew you were perfect. There was no need for another." She flashes me a wink, and I smile.

Owen was six when he started asking about siblings. Several of his classmates talked about theirs, and he wondered why he didn't have any. It broke my heart to realize he'd probably be an only child like I was. Gabe was too, but he had cousins and lots of friends since he attended a larger school district before he moved to Lawton Ridge. The schools are small here, and Owen has no cousins.

"That's right," I interject. "Made perfection the first time around."

Owen's less than amused because he knows we're both taunting him. Considering I spent most of my pregnancy alone, was depressed about my failing marriage, and gave birth shortly after Gabe died, I've associated pregnancy with trauma. Aside from the horrific all-day sickness for nine straight months, the fear I felt while having him has also stayed with me.

However, the moment the nurse handed Owen to me, everything changed. I could still feel sad and lonely, but I had a newfound purpose.

"Alright, you two. Don't have too much fun without me. I'll

be home before bedtime to tuck you in, okay?" I pull Owen into my arms and kiss the top of his head. "Be good for Memaw."

"Helloooooo…" I hear Everleigh sing-song from the living room. "I come bearing drinks and food."

"In the kitchen," I call out.

Tools and notebook paper cover the counter. Every time I watch a YouTube video, I take rigorous notes so I can go back through and read them if I need to.

She comes prancing in with a cheesy grin on her face. "Margaritas for two, guac, chips, and shrimp tacos."

I eye the two to-go cups. "How'd you manage that?" They never allow alcoholic beverages to be taken out of the restaurant.

"Antonio was working, and I laid on the charm." She winks. "Works every time."

"You mean, you flirted to get what you wanted?"

"Perhaps, but look…" She waves one of the Styrofoam cups in the air before handing it to me. "It worked."

I snort. "I guess so. Thanks."

Once the food is laid out, I sip my drink and eat.

"So now that you're all boozed up, you gonna start telling me about Noah? What happened? How'd he look? What did he say?"

"I already told you, there's nothing to tell. I opened the door, saw him, slammed it in his face, and walked away."

Everleigh gives me sad eyes as she takes a large bite of her taco. "Are you ever going to talk to him again?"

"Not if I can help it," I retort.

"Katie..."

"He had every opportunity to reach out, send a letter, or call me...and he didn't. So he doesn't get a free pass just because he's out and *now* wants to talk to me. It doesn't work that way."

"Ya know, before Gabe, I really thought you and Noah were gonna end up together," she says, and I nearly choke on my food.

"Me and Noah?"

"Yeah. You two were so close."

"We were friends, but it was never anything more than that," I tell her.

"Well, it could've been if you would've had the guts to tell him how you felt."

I glare in her direction. "I was fifteen. I didn't know what I felt."

"Yeah, okay." She rolls her eyes, knowing I'm full of shit. "I swear, you two were the only ones who didn't know you both liked each other. Gemma kept pushing him to confess, but he kept chickening out."

"Wait. What?"

She narrows her eyes as she folds her arms. "Noah liked you."

"As a friend," I confirm, trying to end the conversation, but she continues.

"Not from where I stood." She smirks.

Noah and I were always *only* friends. He never gave any indication he liked me more than that. Everleigh continues to stare at me, smacking her lips as she pops a chip in her mouth.

"Noah didn't protest or say a damn thing when Gabe asked me out. If he *liked* me, then why would he remain silent?" I challenge.

"Guess that's something you're gonna have to ask him."

Everleigh smirks like the smart-ass she is. "But I wasn't the only one surprised to see you and Gabe get hitched."

"We were together for three years before we got married, so why would that be a shock to anyone?"

"Because most of us saw how close you and Noah were. Don't get me wrong, Gabe wasn't a bad guy when you were dating, but I didn't see that...*connection*. At least not in the way you had with Noah." She shrugs, and my heart races.

"Noah and I knew each other for most of our lives, so of course we were close, but if anything was going to happen between us, it would've happened before Gabe moved to town."

"Perhaps if you'd give him a chance to talk, you could ask him yourself. He sure has a lot of explainin' to do."

"He doesn't deserve my time, Everleigh. I waited years for him to get the stick outta his ass, and he just expects me to accept him with open arms the day he gets released? Fuck that."

"Hey, I'm all about making him grovel. That man better beg on his knees, but eventually..." She shrugs with a smirk. "Give him a second chance. Or at least five minutes of your time. Either way, he's back, so you won't be able to avoid him for long."

I know she's right, but that doesn't mean I'm going to give in anytime soon. I don't know how I really felt about him back when I was a teenager, but if he wanted to be more than just friends, why didn't he say anything? I'm not sure how I would've responded, but it would've been nice knowing the truth.

"You're overthinking right now, aren't you?" Everleigh interrupts my spinning mind.

"No."

The corner of her lips tilts up. "I've known you a long-ass time and know when you're lying, so nice try."

"So, who are you dating now?"

Everleigh scoffs at my subject change. "I wouldn't call it dating per se..."

"Alright, who're ya banging then?" I tease, sucking down the rest of my margarita.

"Well…there's only one guy at the moment. I don't double dick."

I nearly choke. "Everleigh!"

"What? I'm just sayin'. One dick at a time. I mean, *usually*."

We burst out laughing, the alcohol clearly taking over. At this rate, I'll get nothing done at the house tonight, but it was totally worth it to spend time with her.

CHAPTER FOUR

NOAH

After settling back at home, I spent Sunday making a list of everything I needed to get done before my first day of work at the gym on Tuesday.

I eat breakfast with my dad, then we head to my truck that I've named Violet after the character in the *Willy Wonka and the Chocolate Factory* movie. When the remake came out, Katie and I watched it together for twenty-four hours straight. I haven't watched TV in a long time, but I can still remember the lines word for word.

As he drives me to the DMV to renew my license, I look over and see Everleigh's boutique. It's not open this early, or I might've been tempted to go in and say hi. Surely, she doesn't hate me. Well, no more than Katie anyway.

However, I need to focus on my to-do list: get a new license, buy some new clothes, get a cell phone, open a checking account, and meet with my parole officer. It's surreal that I have to do these things. While I'm excited about my fresh start, I'm not looking forward to the inevitable stares and whispers. Tyler warned me about how he was treated when he returned, but I have a feeling it'll be much worse for me.

My dad walks home instead of waiting for me. It's not far, plus I know he likes the fresh air, so I don't argue. I don't blame him for not wanting to sit in here.

As I wait in line and glance around, I feel eyes boring into me. Strangers stare like they know my story and what I did. No one says a word directly to me, but they don't have to. I know exactly what they're thinking. Aunt Loretta and Uncle Elliot have made it clear they didn't want me coming back here. They have every right to hate me for what happened but being behind bars wouldn't change anything. Gabe's death was an accident, and I did my time. Now I just want to live a simple life and right the wrongs that I can.

"How can I help you, Mr. Reid?" the clerk asks before she even takes my application. Of course she knows who I am, perks of small-town gossip.

"Hello, ma'am. My license expired, and I need to get a new one." I hand her my application and study her as she types.

"You'll need a quick eye test, and once you pass the online exam, you can get your picture taken."

It takes over an hour to finish everything, but it's all worth it when she hands over my new license.

"Thank you, ma'am. Have a good day." I smile as I shove my wallet into my back pocket.

"Mm-hmm." The corner of her lips turns into a scowl, and it's obvious she hated being cordial to me.

Next, I go to the store for some work clothes and boots. Nothing fancy, just jeans and shirts that can get dirty while I paint or rip out carpet. I grab some nicer ones too, just in case.

After I finish shopping, I get a new cell phone because my dad generously put me on his plan. After all this time, it feels strange to have a phone with a nice camera and so many features. Things have really changed in a decade.

There's only one more stop to make, but I decide to grab something to eat first. Belinda owns the deli, and I know she'll be welcoming, so I stop in for a sandwich. I nearly inhale it as soon as it's placed in front of me.

"How's your day goin' so far?" she asks as she takes my empty plate.

"Alright, I guess." I shrug, not wanting to tell her how cold or downright rude people have been. Even the worker at the clothing store kept her eye on me like I was shoplifting or going to cause a scene.

Belinda pats my hand and smiles. "It'll get easier. I remember when Tyler returned, and though you have different circumstances, the town eventually accepted him."

"Guess we'll see. One can only hope," I say as I pull out my wallet.

"It's on the house." She shoos me away.

"Absolutely not. I don't want any special treatment. The last thing I need is rumors spreading that I'm getting handouts or taking shortcuts."

She frowns but doesn't argue. I pay the bill and leave a tip. Once I say goodbye, I walk outside and stare at the bank across the street. I've been putting it off all day, but there's nothing left for me to do other than open an account and deposit some of the money I had before I went to prison.

If it wasn't for Gemma, I wouldn't even know Katie works there.

Maybe I won't see her. Not that I don't want to, but I have a feeling she'd be pissed after the way she reacted the other day.

She got a job promotion last year and is a loan officer. Gemma says she has her own fancy office, so I might be able to avoid her completely.

Inhaling a deep breath, I walk across the street, then step inside the small lobby. Only two tellers are working, and one chair sits in the waiting area.

"How can I help you, sir?" the young woman asks. She might not actually know who I am. Her name tag says Missy.

"I'm looking to open a checking account."

"Have you banked with us before?"

"No, well…yes. Years ago."

"Okay, no problem. I'll see if a banker is available to help set that up for you. You can take a seat while you wait."

"I appreciate that, thank you."

I turn around and am immediately greeted with a death glare.

Katie.

And she looks less than happy to see me.

"Hi—"

"What're you doin' here?" she nearly hisses. "Coming to my house uninvited wasn't enough?"

"He needs to open a checking account," Missy interjects. "But Jasmine isn't answering her phone."

"I just sent her on break," she grumbles, then looks at me. "You'll have to come back in an hour when she returns."

"There aren't any appointments on your schedule, Katie," Missy says, and I can hear the smile in her tone. "Perhaps you can help set him up."

Katie grinds her teeth, an awful habit she's had since middle school, and I hold back a smile at how frustrated she is. I need to give that teller a high five. She's obviously on my side.

"I'd really appreciate it," I speak up. "I've been running errands all day and would like to get this done as soon as possible."

"Fine," she snaps, narrowing her eyes. She walks down a hallway, and I quickly follow but flash the teller a wink before she's out of sight.

"We have two types of checking accounts, Mr. Reid." She slaps a brochure in front of me as I take a seat. "I assume the traditional, but—"

"What're the perks of each one?" I smugly ask as she sits behind the desk.

Katie shoots daggers at me while plastering on a professional smile. She gives me the spiel on each type, and after pretending to think about it for a moment, I decide on the traditional.

"Just as I expected," she mutters to herself as she logs into her computer.

"I need to see your ID please."

"Just got a new one, actually," I say, hoping she'll hold an actual conversation with me. "The DMV got a remodel since I last saw it."

She grabs it without a word and starts typing in my information.

"I need your social security number too."

"On one condition."

"Excuse me?"

"Give me five minutes. That's all I'm asking."

"You're wasting my time. I'm at work," she barks.

"I know, and I tried to go to your house, but…"

"Well, you weren't invited."

"How's Owen doing? Heard he's athletic."

Katie quickly stands. "You can leave and wait for Jasmine."

"I'm not leavin'," I argue. "Not without a new checking account."

"Then tell me your damn social."

The corner of my lips tilts up in amusement. Katie was always so easy to rile up as a teenager, and it doesn't look like anything's changed.

Deciding to comply, I give it to her and watch closely as she finishes on the computer.

"Here's your account number," she says, handing me a card.

"Thank you." I slip it into my wallet.

She folds her hands over her desk and speaks in her professional tone. "Is there anything else I can do for you, Mr. Reid?"

"Well, actually, yes…"

"Any other banking needs," she clarifies.

The edges of my lips tilt up into a knowing smirk. Should've figured she'd say that.

"Then no. Appreciate your help."

Katie stands and walks out of her office. I follow her to the front doors as she waits for me to leave.

"I am sorry, Katie. Truly. Give me five minutes to explain," I plead one more time.

"Have a lovely day," she sing-songs before walking off.

Fuck.

Even though she's being stubborn and won't even grant me the time of day to tell her my side of the story, I'm not giving up. She doesn't owe me anything, especially after the way I've hurt her, but I'd like to be able to apologize properly.

Once I meet with my parole officer, sign the paperwork, and schedule my upcoming appointments with him, I go home. After I'm inside, I put away all the clothes I bought and hang out with my dad until Gemma and Tyler come barreling over.

"Hey kids, what're ya up to?" Dad asks.

"Just stoppin' in to say hi and see Noah," Gemma replies, leaning down and giving me a hug. "How was your first day in civilization?"

I snort. "Fine, I guess. Got all my shit sorted out."

"Oh awesome." She takes the seat next to me as Tyler heads into the kitchen.

"I smell Belinda's cooking!" he shouts as he walks away.

"It's been taunting me for an hour," I groan as my stomach growls. I notice Gemma's all dressed up and pinch my brows. "Weren't you at the gym today? Lookin' a bit fancy."

"Oh, no. I work at Everleigh's boutique part-time. She's been nagging me for years to help her out, and once the garage closed, I had the time between gym stuff."

"You didn't tell me that. I would've stopped in."

"It's a newer position. It'll probably only last through the summer." She clears her throat, then turns toward me. "Speaking of which, Katie stopped in during her lunch break today."

I lift a brow, knowing she's about to tell me something I won't like. "Oh yeah?"

"Yep, told us all about how you came into the bank and demanded she open you an account."

"Demanded is a pretty strong word." I cross my arms over my chest, getting a little heated at her accusation. "What else did she say?"

Gemma makes a zipping motion across her lips. "That's girl code. Sorry, bro."

I roll my eyes, frustrated. "I asked her to give me five minutes to talk, and she walked away."

"It's gonna take more than just askin'," she tells me. "She nearly ripped me a new one for the little stunt you and Tyler pulled on Saturday. So I'm staying out of it."

I bark out a laugh. "When have you ever stayed out of anything in your life?"

"Hey!" She smacks my arm. "I can mind my own. Nothing I say is gonna change her mind. Believe me, I've tried. But it's what you get, Noah Reid. You wouldn't budge either when I asked you to let her visit on her behalf."

"And I had a good reason for that, which she won't let me explain," I counter.

"Doesn't matter. She doesn't want your excuses. You're gonna have to win her back another way."

"Yep," Dad agrees. "Katie's independent and strong-willed. She's had to be for the last decade, so you're gonna need to do a lot more than just sweet-talk her."

God. Now my father is adding to this. Just great.

Belinda making an announcement that dinner is ready right now would be perfect but no such luck. Tyler comes strolling back in with a piece of bread in his mouth.

"You ready to work tomorrow?"

"Hell yeah. Can't wait, honestly."

"You'll be working with Smith," he tells me.

"Smith? I thought I was workin' with you."

"I'll be there," he confirms. "But Smith takes the lead on most projects since he's experienced. It's good for you too, so you can have a potential reference for a future job."

"Okay, sounds good."

Belinda picks that moment to let us know dinner's on the table, and we all rush into the dining room. Dad grabs the plates, and Gemma sets the silverware. Tyler brings out the glasses, and I stare at the four of them.

"What can I do?"

"You can sit and enjoy," Belinda muses.

"Hey, what did I say at the deli?"

"Hush. This isn't the deli. This is home."

I smile, then notice the way my dad looks at her, and it grows even wider. There's so much adoration between them, it makes me damn happy.

"Alright, y'all. Dig in," Belinda says after she says grace.

We chat about old memories and plans for the gym. It still doesn't feel real to be eating at home with my family, but I am, and I'll never take it for granted again.

CHAPTER FIVE

KATIE

It's officially been eight days since Noah returned and knocked on my door, and even less since he strolled into the bank. When I saw Gemma at the boutique and told her what happened, I let it be known that he better be glad he left in one piece. I'm harboring a decade full of emotions, so my reactions when he's around are more than valid.

After Owen and I finish eating lunch, he helps me clean up, then goes to his room.

As I wash the dishes and wipe down the counter, my mind wanders back to the past several years and how strong I've had to be. Juggling work, my son, and paying for everything. Anything I need, I do my damn self. Sometimes I resent Gabe for cheating and leaving me to do everything on my own, but then I feel guilty as hell about it because of the way he died.

Grief is weird and makes you second-guess your feelings. I loved Gabe, but once I got pregnant, things shifted between us. He didn't look at me with the same twinkle in his eye. Instead of dealing with it, I ignored it. I'd made up my mind I'd figure it out after the baby was born.

I honestly feel as if I'm broken, and I'm meant to be single for the rest of my life. Most days, I'm okay with it. At thirty-one, I live in a small town where everyone knows my business and am in the process of remodeling an old house, all while trying to give Owen the best life that I possibly can. It makes dating nearly impossible, so I gave up on it years ago.

After the kitchen's cleaned, I vacuum and try to pick up the house before tomorrow. Heading to Owen's room, I find him lying on his bed listening to music.

"Laundry time," I tell him, and he immediately huffs. I lift an eyebrow in warning because this is our Sunday tradition. He puts his tablet on the bed and opens his closet door. Clothes are halfway off the hangers, socks litter the floor, and shoes are stacked on top of each other. Owen grabs a few shirts he had stuffed in the corner.

"This is it?" I ask as he hands me hardly anything. "What about everything you wore all week to school? Your basketball uniforms?"

"Mom," he whines, and I step around him, looking for myself.

I give him a smile. "I'm going to put these in the wash, and I need you to bring me the rest. Got it?"

He nods, and I walk away. I'm certain he's back to stuffing things under his bed because he knows how I feel about things being on the floor. I might not be able to give him everything, but the least I can do is teach him how to clean up after himself. I'm raising a gentleman who will eventually make some woman happy and treat her like a queen.

As I'm in the laundry room, Owen enters with a full basket, grinning sheepishly. "I found them."

"Mm-hmm, interesting. Where were they?"

He laughs before he walks away. Raising a boy has been...an *experience*.

As soon as I start the washer, my cell phone rings, and I see it's Loretta.

"Hey, sweetie! Happy Valentine's Day!" she says.

"Same to you."

Even though it's Sunday and I typically work at the house, I spend every Valentine's Day with Owen no matter what. It's been our tradition since he was born.

"I was wondering if we could stop by this afternoon. We got Owen some Valentine's gifts."

I blow out a laugh. "How much candy?"

"Honey, you know how it is. Just have to spoil my grandson."

"Loretta," I say, smiling. "We'll be here. Feel free to stop by anytime you'd like. Not too late, though, because he'll be bouncing off the walls after eating the sugar."

"Great! We'll be there within the hour. See you soon."

I end the call, and Owen walks into the living room. "Was that Mimi and Pawpaw?"

I nod. "Yes, it was. They're gonna stop by and see you today."

"Yay!" he squeals. He loves Gabe's parents so much, and I'm lucky they've stayed a part of Owen's life. They faithfully support me, and I honestly don't know what I would've done without them, my parents, or my friends.

Within thirty minutes, a knock rings out on the door. Owen hurries and answers it. As soon as he sees his grandparents, he squeezes Loretta tight. Elliot enters behind her, carrying a red bag with a heart on it.

Owen's hopping from foot to foot as Loretta hugs me.

"Looks so nice in here," she says, glancing around the spotless room. I try my best since it's the one thing I have control over in my life.

"Owen helped." I flash a wink. He's old enough to have responsibilities, and he gets excited when others notice.

"Good to see you." Elliot smiles, then wraps his arms around Owen.

I offer them some sweet tea while they give Owen his gift bag. As I'm in the kitchen putting ice in glasses, I hear Owen's excitement. When I return, he's still pulling out velvet hearts full of candy in all different sizes, and I know I'll be dealing with a hyper kid tonight.

Owen's pile on the floor consists of a remote-control car, endless candy, and some small holiday-themed games.

"Oh, you two..." I sigh. "You didn't have to do all of this."

He gives them kisses and thank you's and positions himself between them on the couch. You'd think he hasn't seen them in months by the way he's acting, but he sees them several times a week. They love having him around, but so do my parents, so they take turns picking him up after school and watching him until I get off work around five. My mom and Loretta alternate on the weekends when I'm working at the new house.

"Can I have a sleepover at Mimi and Pawpaw's tonight?" Owen asks with a grin.

I shake my head. "Not on a school night, bud."

He flashes me his big puppy dog eyes, the same eyes his dad used to give me when he wanted to get his way. "Owen," I warn.

Loretta laughs and pats his back. "You know the rules, honey. Maybe if you're good this week, you can next Saturday."

Owen rips open one of the velvet boxes and pops a piece of chocolate in his mouth. He talks and chews. "I'll be good!" he declares.

"Manners, Owen. Don't speak with food in your mouth," I remind him.

"Yes, ma'am," he says, covering his mouth. "Want one?" He holds the box out toward Loretta and Elliot, but they shake their heads.

"I've had so much sugar this weekend I'm surprised I'm not a candy heart right now," Loretta laughs as she tells Owen.

"Candy hearts are nasty, Mimi."

"They're my favorite," she gushes.

"They *are* gross," Elliot agrees with Owen, then looks at Loretta with a devilish grin.

"More for me then!" she exclaims, taking a sip of her tea.

After Owen puts batteries in his remote-control car and drives it all over the house, Elliot and Loretta say their goodbyes.

"He really can come stay next weekend if you'd like to get some uninterrupted work done on the house," Elliot tells me as we walk them to the door.

"I know. I really appreciate it. I'm sure he'd love that too!"

Owen runs up and gives them another hug. "Love you!"

"Love you too," they say. "Be good for your mom. Don't eat too much chocolate, even if it is Valentine's Day." Loretta flashes him a wink, then turns toward me.

"You know…" She lowers her voice. "It's been years since you've had a serious relationship, Katie. You should get back out there and date again."

All I can do is laugh. "With all my spare time?" I tease. "They say you find love when you're not looking for it. And well, I ain't lookin'." I shrug

She gives me a smile. "You're right, but it'd be okay if you did," she says genuinely. "Bye, Owen! Mimi and Pawpaw love you!" Loretta blows a kiss as they walk to their car.

Owen nods with a big cheeky grin. "See you this week!"

"Thank you again," I tell them as we wave. Once they're out of sight, I shut the front door. Owen's already bouncing around the house, but I can't even be mad about it.

"Want some, Mom?" He holds up one of the chocolates.

I snag a piece and pop it in my mouth, then immediately scrunch up my nose. "Eww!" I hurry and swallow it. "What flavor was that?"

Owen thinks it's the funniest thing as I try to wash down the disgusting taste. He grabs the key and tries to match it with the one I had.

"It was coconut raspberry," he explains, then finds another one in the batch and eats it. "Mmm, it's good, Mom!"

I laugh at how he's struggling to eat it just like I had. "Mm-hmm. I can tell by the look on your face."

He quickly realizes how gross it is and runs to the kitchen. I hear him being dramatic as he spits it in the trash. Owen returns and pretends to scrape his tongue. "You're right. That was disgusting!"

"I always loved these chocolates and never looked to see what kind they were. I wanted to be surprised. However, I'd learned to take a small bite before eating the whole thing because I didn't want to commit to the ones I ended up not liking. Your grandma would find half-eaten chocolate every year."

Owen snickers. "You're funny."

"You are," I say, reaching over and poking his side. Immediately, he flinches, and I wiggle my fingers in a tickling motion.

"Noooooo," he screeches, moving away from me. I motion with my eyes to clean up his mess, and he reluctantly does.

"Thank you," I say, grabbing the empty glasses to take to the kitchen. After a while, I tell Owen to take a bath as I cook dinner.

When he's out of the tub, I make our plates, and we sit at the table. "All your homework is done, right?" I ask, just as I do every Sunday night. Instead of checking for myself, I give him the responsibility to make sure it is. I've tried to teach him that his grades are his and not mine, so he has no one to blame but himself if he does poorly. Of course, I'll always help if he asks for it, but for the most part, he's good about finishing his assignments and turning them in on time.

"Yes, ma'am," he tells me with a grin before taking a huge bite of his cheeseburger. As we eat, he tells me about his latest school project. Then asks how long until summer because he wants to go to Disney World like a few of his friends have gotten to.

"We'd have to plan that months in advance, sweetie. Maybe next year," I say, though a trip like that would cost me most of what's left in my savings. I've always wanted to surprise him, but right now, all my extra money is going into the new house.

Once our plates are cleared and the kitchen is clean, Owen and I watch *Be My Valentine, Charlie Brown*. He snuggles in close to me, and I soak in these little moments with him since he won't want to much longer. Eventually, he'll grow up and move out, then I'll have to adopt a few dogs and cats to keep me company in that big ole house I bought. I squeeze him just a little tighter, knowing his teenage years are right around the corner.

Owen laughs at Lucy and Charlie Brown as I'm lost in my thoughts. Gabe would've loved spending time with Owen. Though years have passed, it'll never erase the pain of my son not having a father to bond with and have these special times with him. Though he doesn't have a dad in his life, I try hard to make sure he doesn't feel any less loved.

When the movie ends, Owen brushes his teeth, then I walk him to his room. After he climbs into bed, I sit on the edge and admire the features he shares with his dad.

"Love you, sweetie," I say as I cover him up, then hand him his stuffed bear my mom got him for Christmas last year.

"Love you too, Mom."

"Sweet dreams. Good night, my love." I kiss his forehead, then turn on his night-light.

On the way to my bedroom, I realize how secluded it feels to sleep alone. It's been my life for so long now, so I should be used to it, but Valentine's Day only reminds me that I'm still single.

CHAPTER SIX

NOAH

I<small>T'S BEEN</small> over two weeks since I was released from prison. I've wanted to go to Katie's house and beg her to listen to me on more than one occasion, but I know it's a bad idea, considering how frustrated she was with me at the bank.

It's another Monday, so this morning, I decide to do something special for my sister and Tyler. There's a donut shop that Gemma's always adored that makes special pastries. I park my truck in the side lot at the gym, then walk into the donut shop.

Years may have passed, but Lawton Ridge is a time capsule. I take in the cool breeze and breathe in the fresh air. It's crazy how everything looks the same—the buildings, businesses, and town square. Before my life drastically changed, this was the last place I expected to be long-term because it was so boring. But now I realized how much I took that for granted because I can't imagine ever leaving again.

The woman who owns the shop greets me with a smile. I lean over the glass case and look at everything. Food like this wasn't available in prison, so I feel like a king as I choose a dozen different cake donuts. If I remember correctly, Gemma's favorite is the blueberry, so I get an extra six of those.

After I pay and grab the box, I turn around and notice a woman and man staring at me. Another couple whispers, but they look away when I make eye contact. I don't even have to hear what they're saying to know they're talking about me. I wish the gossip didn't run rampant because it makes starting over even harder.

My blood pressure rises and my face heats, so I get the hell out of there as quickly as I can. It felt like the walls were caving in on me.

I try to shake it off as I walk the few blocks back to the gym. Since I've been back, I've tried to ignore the way people have acted around me, but I can't seem to let it go today. A man wearing a dark hoodie walks down the sidewalk and meets my eyes. He glares at me with intent right before his shoulder slams hard into my body. He mutters, "Murderer," under his breath as he passes. I turn to look at him, but he keeps going.

My heart pounds, and I swallow hard. Though he's taller than me, I'm five seconds from beating his ass. Instead, I inhale a deep breath and continue toward the gym. I don't need trouble finding me right now.

If that would've happened ten years ago, I probably wouldn't have walked away. Prison changed me, and now I'm a different man who has a lot more to lose.

Was he a friend of Gabe's?

I walk inside with a fake smile plastered on my face even though shit like this eats away at my conscience. As I cross the large open room, I try not to smash the cardboard with the force of my grip. Tyler notices, and I give him a smile and open the box.

"I brought donuts for everyone. Where's Gemma?" I glance around but don't see her.

Tyler studies me before meeting my eyes. "She'll be here any minute."

He continues staring, and I forgot he's even more observant than my sister. "Everything okay?"

"Honestly, no," I admit. After I get my thoughts together, I explain what happened at the bakery and with the guy on the street. "It makes me feel awkward in social situations. Like this town would be better off if I weren't here."

Tyler shakes his head and places his strong grip on my shoulder. "You know, when I returned, people whispered about me in the grocery store and everywhere else they'd see me. They'd call me a convict under their breaths. I didn't think I'd even be able to find work with my past. Thankfully, your dad took a chance and hired me. Otherwise, I don't know what I would've done."

He smiles, then continues. "After a while, they got over it. People stopped talking shit and moved on to the next big thing because you know it's something different every week. The same will happen for you too. They'll get over it," he says confidently. "Or I'll kick their asses."

I chuckle, but my blood starts pumping again as I think about all the unfairness he experienced.

"You didn't murder a family member. Or your best friend's husband. Or a man who was about to be a father." I sigh, brushing a hand through my hair because those aren't easy things to admit aloud. "Our situations aren't the same, Tyler. I know why you're saying that and being encouraging, but I'm not convinced it'll ever get easier for me. You were helping a friend and got framed. Every single day I sat behind bars, I knew I was paying for the consequences of my actions and wishing I could take it all back. I never wanted my cousin to die. I didn't want Katie's husband not to be there for her or their son. I stole that from them. Everyone in town knows it too."

"It was an accident," Tyler stresses. "Bad things happen to good people."

"It doesn't take away the fact that my aunt and uncle lost their only child and refuse to talk to my dad. You and Gemma won't have them in your baby's life because of me. People treat me like I'll break into their houses and kill their family. It makes me want to pack up my shit and leave, then start new where no one knows who I am."

Tyler looks at me with pity, which I hate, but I just laid a bunch of shit on him. I take a bite of a donut as Tyler processes my words. "I understand where you're coming from, Noah, but leaving won't fix *you*. The burden is carried inside wherever you go. You'll still have to work through that. Being out of prison takes some getting used to, but I know you'll eventually adjust. Things would be different if you went down to that bar that night with the intent to kill him. You just wanted him to go home to his pregnant wife. I know you'd take it back if you could, but you can't, so you need to work through that guilt. You deserve good things to happen to you, and you can't let people who whisper about you ruin it. You're a *good* son. A *good* brother. A *good* person. And not one damn person in this town will convince me otherwise. Not even you. The next few months will be the hardest, but I'm here for you, man. I promise you that."

I appreciate Tyler so damn much and get emotional just thinking how I'd get through this without him. I knew it wasn't going to be easy, but I hadn't really known what to expect.

Just as Tyler and I finish our conversation, Gemma arrives. Immediately, she spots the box of goodies and makes a beeline toward the counter with a smile on her face. Leaning over, she peeks inside, then turns to us.

"Who's responsible for my sugar rush today?"

Tyler lifts his hands. "It wasn't me."

Gemma smirks, then grabs a chocolate-filled one. "Thanks, bro. You know exactly what I like."

I look at the donut, then back at her. "I thought you liked the blueberry ones."

"Oh, I love *all* donuts. I'm not picky!" She nearly devours it in three big bites, then goes for another. When I give her a look and laugh, she glares at me.

"Hey, I'm eating for two here." She points at her little bump.

Tyler playfully rolls his eyes. "Don't blame it on the baby. You would've gone for seconds regardless."

She shrugs, taking another. "Don't judge me, or I just might take this whole box," she says, then walks away laughing.

Gemma has a way of lightening my mood. There's no way I can tell her what happened today. She's already concerned I'll move away even though I wouldn't leave when she's expecting.

Every person I've ever loved is here. I want to be in my niece's or nephew's life. It's important for me to make up for all the lost time. Plus, my dad's not getting any younger. Though now that he's busy most days with his girlfriend, I still want to be around for him.

After Tyler and I snag a donut for ourselves, I look over today's list of tasks. The building's old, and it's gonna take a lot of manpower to get it where it needs to be on time. I'm happy there's a lot to do. If I was sitting at home doing nothing, I'd probably go crazy.

Thankfully, most of the walls are prepped since Smith had started before I was released. The drywall is hung, and all the nail holes have been spackled. This week, I'll be painting.

I grab my supplies as Smith walks me through the list of things that still need to be done. He's experienced in this stuff, and I'm happy he's taken me under his wing. Learning from him has been a nice advantage of working here.

Based on his list, he suspects the grand opening will be in three to four months.

I've made a silent commitment to bust my ass and help make that happen sooner.

I'll work extra hours and put in as much time as I possibly can to make sure they open ahead of schedule. There's still a lot to do, like the plumbing and some electrical. Tyler wants to install a juice bar, which I think will do great since the gym is downtown. There'll also be a boxing ring and a yoga studio. We still have to lay the flooring, hang all the mirrors, create an office space, and put together the workout equipment once it's delivered. When the walls are painted, we can start tackling the larger items, so I spend most of my day on that.

I climb up and down the ladder with my brush and listen to music to clear my head. Eventually, we break for lunch, then afterward, I pick up where I left off. It takes me nearly all day to apply the first coat on the long wall from the front doors to the back. Once I'm done, I stand on the other side and review my work.

Tyler walks up. "Wow. You did a good job."

I nod with a proud smile. "Thank you. Means a lot."

"Yeah, man. Keep it up," he says, patting my shoulder before taking off.

After I wash up, I tell Tyler I'm heading out and will see him in the morning. He thanks me again, and I walk out beaming—a much different feeling than I had when I arrived this morning.

I get in my truck and exhale all the tension I'd been holding in my shoulders. For the first time in a decade, someone appreciates me, and I'm making a difference.

On my way home, I slow down as I pass Katie's house. I imagine her tearing down drywall or remodeling a bathroom alone. The thought makes me smile because she's not a contractor, but she's always had a strong spirit. Katie could do anything she put her mind to, and that hasn't changed. I continue home, remembering Gemma said to give her time. After ignoring her the way I did, I have a lot of explaining to do.

I'm willing to do that, and hopefully, she doesn't make me wait a decade because she's the only person I want to see.

CHAPTER SEVEN

KATIE

I'm a nervous wreck and have been since I woke up this morning. An uneasy energy swarms through me, and I've already changed my clothes three times. Today's Jerry's retirement party, and Gemma's confirmed Noah will be there. Now I have no choice but to be in his presence.

Belinda planned a big party at the event center downtown so people can stop by to eat and congratulate him for finally retiring after forty years. From the sounds of it, everyone in Lawton Ridge will be there at some point.

I put on my earrings and check to see if Owen's dressed. When I walk into his room, he's lying on his bed playing with his tablet.

"Ready to go?" I ask, leaning against the doorframe as I scan his floor of dirty clothes.

"Yep," he tells me, then slips on his shoes and walks past me. Raising a boy means he doesn't give a shit what he looks like, which is both a blessing and a curse.

When we're in the car, I turn on the radio and try to keep my mind focused on the music. Other people will be around, so I won't be able to tell Noah to go straight to hell if he tries to speak.

to me. I'll have to play nice for the sake of not creating a scene, but I won't make it easy for him, just as he didn't make it easy for me.

After we park and walk inside, I'm shocked by how much food is laid out. But I shouldn't be, considering Belinda loves to cook. Balloons fill the ceiling, reminding me of the iconic high school dance scene in a movie. As I'm scanning the room, I see Gemma and Tyler standing by the punch bowl. I place my hand behind Owen and guide him over toward them.

"Hey, Owen," Tyler says, holding up his hand and giving Owen a high five.

"Hey!" Owen slaps his palm. He's always liked Tyler.

Moments later, Everleigh walks up with an extra bounce in her step. She gives me a hug, squeezing me tight. "Katie! Oh my God, I've missed you so much."

I laugh at her antics because we hung out last week.

"What am I? Chopped liver?" Gemma scowls.

"Oh, be quiet," Everleigh tells her with a playful eye roll. "I see you like four times a week."

She grabs a plate, then starts stacking it full of food.

"Mom, can I get some?" Owen asks.

"Sure, but only take what you're going to eat. Don't be wasteful," I remind him. He slides in beside Everleigh and follows her lead. Owen grows excited as he places different colored squares of cheeses and mini sandwiches on his plate.

Ruby walks up with her fiancée, Stephanie.

"Well, there you are," Gemma says, pulling her into a hug.

"You know I wouldn't miss this party for the world. Free food." Ruby smirks.

Belinda comes over and wraps her arms around Ruby and greets Stephanie.

"I didn't know you were coming," Belinda admits. "You never RSVP'd."

"Sorry, my bad. I wouldn't miss Jerry retiring for anything!" Ruby says. "Where is the man of the hour anyway?"

"Let's go find him," Belinda says, pulling Ruby and Stephanie away.

We go to one of the round tables where Owen sits and gobbles up his food. Tyler chats with him about basketball and when they can play together again. As I look around the room, I see a few ladies who work with me at the bank and a couple of cashiers from the grocery store. Even the city mayor is here, but thankfully, I don't see Noah yet.

As I pass the buffet on my way to the restroom, my palms become sweaty. Just as I make my way to the hallway, he walks through the door. It's as if everything around me freezes as our eyes meet, and my heart races as he studies me. I snap my gaze away, keep my head up, and walk into the ladies' room. I lean against the door and suck in a deep breath, trying to calm my nerves.

At one time in my life, Noah was my everything. He ripped that away when he decided he didn't want to see or talk to me anymore. I was lonely as hell and needed him the most. I'm not sure I'll ever be able to forgive him for how he treated me—like tossed-out trash on the curb.

I give myself a pep talk, then walk back out to the party. I try to find my courage with each step I take, knowing it's inevitable that he'll try to speak to me again. The last thing I want to do is embarrass him at his father's retirement party, but if he knows what's good for him, he'll keep his distance.

As I'm closer to the table, I notice Noah's chatting with Ruby. I sit beside Owen as he finishes his food. I ignore everything else around me as Gemma explains to Noah our friendship with Ruby and how we all became close.

"But then I found another job out of town and ruined it all," Ruby adds with a laugh.

"I offered you one at my new gym, but you refused," Tyler

chastises with a raised eyebrow, then glances at Stephanie with a grin.

"She's mine now," Stephanie says. "And I'm not *ever* letting her go."

Ruby smirks and looks at Stephanie like she's her whole world. "They're just being dramatic," she tells Noah. "We're only thirty minutes away."

"That's too far," Gemma whines, sticking out her bottom lip.

Noah listens to them go back and forth, then glances over at me as if he wants to say something. If he tries anything, it'll take every bit of strength I have not to tell him off. Once I furrow my brows at him, he breaks eye contact with me and interrupts their conversation.

"Well, it was really nice meeting you two."

Heat hits my cheeks as he glances at me one last time, then thankfully excuses himself. I let out a relieved breath.

"You alright?" Gemma asks as if she can read my mind.

"Perfect," I say, then turn to Owen. "Did you get enough to eat?"

"Can I get more punch?" He grins.

"Sure. I'll get you some," I say, grabbing his cup and going to the line. I decide to get myself some food too while I'm here. As I'm scanning the goodies, I glance over my shoulder and see a blonde walk up to Noah. She's overly nice and so loud I can hear her laughter echo off the walls. As I'm pouring a cup of punch, I watch them, then finally recognize her from Owen's school drop-off. That's when I notice her son is standing next to her.

She reaches over and touches Noah's arm, then flips her long hair as she giggles like a lovestruck teenager. Jealousy immediately courses through me at how close she's standing to him. It's obvious she finds Noah attractive by the way she keeps gazing up and down his body as if she's memorizing every inch of him.

She leans closer, flirting with Noah even though a room full of people are watching. The thought infuriates me as I fill another cup of punch for myself. I get Owen's attention and wave him over to help because there's no way I'll be able to carry all of this without spilling it.

When he's close, I bend down and keep my voice low. "Doesn't that kid go to your school?" I ask him.

"Yep. That's Anthony. He moved here a couple of months ago and is in my class."

"I thought so," I say with a smile.

"Can I go say hi?"

"Sure," I say. He takes his punch from me, then crosses the room.

As soon as I'm back at the table, Gemma moves her chair closer to mine.

"Who's that woman?" she whispers.

"I don't remember her name, but her son is in Owen's class."

Everleigh butts into our conversation. "Oh, that's Brittany Townsend. She works at the deli with Belinda."

Gemma and I turn toward her as she pops a grape in her mouth. "How the hell do you know everybody in town?" I ask.

"Lawton Ridge covers a five-mile radius. Everyone *should* know everyone, Katie."

I scowl at her sassy response. "Everyone knows everyone who's always lived here. She hasn't, and she doesn't come to the bank."

Everleigh laughs. "I'm surprised you haven't seen her working at the deli. I think she started a month ago or so."

I shrug. "I'm a single mom. I make a lot of slow cooker meals and eat a lot of leftovers, so I rarely go to the deli unless I forget to pack my lunch."

Gemma snorts. "I don't think that's a single mom thing. I think that's a super organized OCD thing."

I laugh with a shrug. "Perhaps."

"Don't be modest. You're a great mom, and I can only hope I'm half as good a mom as you."

"You will be. Honestly, you just figure it out as you go. Most of us don't know what the fuck we're doing," I admit truthfully. "I'm a professional at winging it."

"Well, you make it look effortless," Everleigh adds. "Knowing me, I'd forget to feed my kid."

I snort as I watch Owen chatting with Anthony. "Trust me, you won't. Between them crying or yelling 'Mom' a hundred times a day, you'll happily stuff food in their mouths to shut them up."

"Probably why Tyler and Noah keep bringin' pastries to the gym every morning," Gemma says, chuckling.

"They're trying to keep you from talkin' their ears off." Everleigh laughs.

After I'm done eating, Owen returns, and I notice Jerry is finally alone. I take the opportunity to give him a hug and tell him congratulations.

"Thanks, Katie. I'm sure Gemma thought I'd be working forever."

"Well, you probably would've if it wasn't for Belinda talkin' some sense into you." I nudge him.

Jerry gives his famous hearty dad laugh that I always loved growing up. "You're right. She's made me realize there are more important things in life than working every day, and this old man needed a break."

"You deserve it. I'm so happy for you."

"Thank you. Now, I'll get to be a full-time grandpa." He beams wide as more people walk up, so I tell him goodbye and go back to the table.

Gemma stands before I can take a seat. "I think we need some more juice for the punch bowl. Can you help me grab them from the fridge?"

"Sure." I tell Owen I'll be right back before following Gemma toward the kitchen.

"You doin' okay?" she asks. "You look a little stressed."

"I'm fine. It's just weird seeing Noah here. Especially when I didn't even want to see him the *first* time." I glare at her because she knows what she did.

"Yeah, I know. That's why I wanted to check on you. It's gonna take a little getting used to for everyone. But with that being said, maybe you should give him one more chance, Katie. He still cares about you."

I let out a frustrated sigh. "I'm sure he *does* since he refused to see or talk to me. That sounds like something you do when you *care* about someone," I say sarcastically.

She gives me a small smile and heads out of the kitchen instead of going to the fridge.

"Wait, don't we need more punch?" I ask, confused.

"Nah. Just wanted to get you alone for a moment to check on you without other ears around." Gemma gives me a wink.

"Should've figured," I say. "Thanks, I appreciate it."

"Anytime. And if you ever want to bust his balls, feel free to do it, okay? He kinda deserves it."

I laugh. "I'm just glad you're on my team."

"I'm team Katie *and* Noah," she corrects.

"Oh God. Don't even start with that again! We're not fifteen anymore," I scold but laugh at the memories.

Gemma glances over her shoulder, then leaves. I take a moment to myself before following. When I finally walk through the door, I nearly run into Noah. His hands grip my arms, holding me steady on my feet. We look at each other in shock, and it takes everything I have to push past him.

Before I get too far, he gently grabs my elbow and pulls me back.

"Katie, please talk to me," he begs in a deep, rough voice.

Shaking my head, I pull away from him. "No thanks. I have nothing to say to you."

"*Please*," he pleads again, this time in a husky whisper.

"I've been begging to talk to you for ten fucking years. So *no*, Noah, you don't get my time when it's convenient for you. Should've thought about that when you refused to let me visit or write me back. I waited around for you long enough, and I'm not wasting any more time on you."

He looks as if I slapped him, the same reaction I imagine he had on my porch when I slammed the door in his face. It hurts to see him this way, but he left me no choice.

Without another word, I walk across the reception hall and tell Owen it's time to go.

After we say our goodbyes, I notice Noah's staring at me, but I keep my eyes forward and walk out with as much dignity as I can.

CHAPTER EIGHT

NOAH

THOUGH IT'S BEEN four days since Katie and I had a run-in, I can still feel her verbal slap. I know I don't deserve her attention, but I'm not giving up. If she wants to cuss me out after I've explained my side of the story and apologized, then I'll walk away peacefully. But until then, I'll fight for just five minutes of her time. Our friendship was strong before, and it can be that way again if she'd give us a chance.

When I got home that night, I found a box of pictures and old yearbooks. After pouring myself a glass of whiskey, I went through them. Pictures of Katie and I goofing off, taking road trips and hikes, every homecoming and prom. We always exchanged yearbooks first, and in her freshman one, I almost confessed my feelings but chickened out. That's the summer Gabe moved to town, and they started dating.

I find the first one of mine she ever signed and smile as I read her handwriting.

My dearest Noah,

Thanks for helping me get through my first year of high school. Though

I had Gemma and Everleigh's support, you made sure I had fun at football games and sent me flowers so my Valentine's Day wasn't lame. Can't wait to hang out all summer and make even more memories :-)

Love,
"Your Girl" for life (haha)

I snort at how she ended her message as the memory of our inside joke surfaces. We were together so much that people assumed we were dating, so I would openly call her my girl. After correcting it the first ten times, we stopped and let them think whatever they wanted. When she didn't say anything about it, I figured she was sick of telling people we were only friends, but I wonder if she secretly felt the same as me.

I find another box in my closet filled with folded-up notebook paper. Katie and I exchanged notes all through middle and high school. They were mostly about silly kid stuff and what we were gonna do after school that day. We'd both gotten caught a handful of times by teachers for writing them in class, but it never stopped us. Sometimes I'd draw funny things just to see her smile and hear her laugh.

Though it's been years, I wonder if she saved any that I sent her. I have a feeling she had a burn party on my behalf, but a part of me knows she'd never do that, no matter how mad she was.

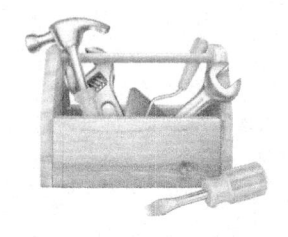

I've been distracted as hell at work for the past two days, and

I need to get my head on straight so I don't make any mistakes on the job. It's the middle of the week, and as we get closer to the re-opening, there's more stress to get everything done and the equipment built on time.

As I drive closer to the gym, I notice Sheriff Todd parked out front. Tyler and Smith are outside, but I can't see what's going on.

Once I hop out of the truck, I rush over and notice the broken glass on the sidewalk. The big front window is completely smashed in.

"What happened?" I ask as all three men stare at me. "Everyone okay?"

"We're good. Someone threw a brick into the window sometime in the middle of the night," Tyler confirms.

"Gonna see if the business across the street caught anything on their security camera, but until then, I'll get this vandalism report filed so you can get it fixed as soon as possible," Sheriff Todd says.

Tyler thanks him, and we watch him drive off.

"I'll start cleaning this up inside," Smith says before walking off.

"Why would someone do this?" I ask. "Someone against you opening?" There aren't any competitor gyms in town, so that wouldn't make a whole lot of sense.

"No, actually…there was a note wrapped around the brick." Tyler looks down, and it's obvious he's not telling me something.

"What'd it say?"

He inhales sharply before slowly exhaling. "Umm…"

"Tyler," I press. "Just tell me."

He finally meets my eyes, then frowns. Reaching into his back pocket, he pulls out a piece of paper and hands it to me. When I open it, I read the word *MURDERER* written across it.

Guilt immediately surfaces, and my shoulders drop. "I'm so sorry. This is my fault."

"No, it's not."

I wave the note in the air. "Clearly it *is*. Someone's obviously not happy I'm working for you. I'll cover the expenses."

"Noah, stop. You're not paying for it. That's what I have insurance for."

"I insist. It wouldn't have happened if I didn't work for you. I'm a risk to your business."

"You're not risking shit. I couldn't have gotten this much done without you. Fuck whoever did this. Got it?" Tyler pats my shoulder.

I blow out a frustrated breath. He's being much more reasonable than I deserve.

"At least let me help clean up."

"Fine, but wear your work gloves. I'll get the broom."

I look around the area and am glad that no other businesses were vandalized.

"I'm gonna look for another job out of town," I tell Tyler when he returns. "I can't be the reason Club Blackwood suffers."

"Absolutely not," he retorts, handing me the broom. "We aren't letting whoever did this ruin a good thing. You're a hard worker, and I need you as much as you need this job."

"You're sure?"

"Fucking positive. We'll get security cameras installed. We won't let them win."

"Thanks, Tyler. I appreciate you so much."

"It'll get easier, I promise."

I nod, though I'm not sure I believe it.

"Once you're done, we'll get some plywood and cover the hole until I can get it fixed."

"You got it, boss."

After Tyler walks inside, I sweep up the glass from the sidewalk and parts of the street. Whoever threw it had good aim and strength. Perhaps Gabe's dad hired someone, or he did the dirty work himself. I wouldn't doubt it, honestly.

Tyler, Smith, and I board the window. I try to shake off what happened, but it's heavy on my mind as I work.

"Hey," Gemma sing-songs as she strolls in around noon. Though she doesn't look pleased about what happened this morning, she's still glowing. I know she's over the moon excited about the baby, and seeing how happy she is makes me happy.

"Hey, sis. What's goin' on?" I ask, wiping off my hands.

"I came here to kidnap you for your lunch break."

I arch a brow and grin. "Really? What's the occasion?"

"Nothing. Can't a sister want to spend time with her brother?"

"Sure, alright. Lemme just wash up, and I'll be ready."

Ten minutes later, we're sitting at the deli and chatting with Belinda. She works the lunch rush, then lets her employees stay till closing. Gemma said once she and Dad started dating, she's worked fewer hours to spend more time with him. I think the love they have for one another is incredibly sweet and cute.

"I can't tell you how good it is to see you two in here again. Brings me back to when y'all were in high school and would come in with Everleigh and Katie."

My smile drops at the mention of her name, and Belinda immediately notices. "I'll get your orders in and will be right back."

"Thank you," Gemma says.

I meet my sister's eyes. "How've you been feeling lately? Everything going okay so far with the pregnancy?"

She places her hand on her belly. "I'm doing really well. I'm blessed to have no problems."

"Absolutely. So when are we gonna find out if I'm getting a nephew or a niece?"

Gemma laughs as I add sugar and cream to my coffee. "Well, I think Tyler and I have decided to wait to find out, so it will be a surprise for everyone."

"That doesn't shock me at all. You've always loved

surprises." I take a sip of my coffee. "Alright, so what's the real reason you dragged me out of work today?" I pop a brow.

"Just wanted to see how you were doing. After Katie left the party Saturday, you were pretty quiet."

"Well, that's mostly because only five people will talk to me, so…" I shrug, then spot Brittany behind the counter waving at me.

I wave back, and Gemma looks over her shoulder.

"Make that six…" Gemma grins, then leans forward and lowers her voice. "I saw the way Brittany was giving you bedroom eyes."

Nearly choking on my coffee, I cover my mouth. "Bedroom eyes? What the hell are you talkin' about?"

"You're so out of the game, you don't even know when someone's flirting with you."

"That's not true…I mean, yeah, it's been a long time, but she wasn't."

"You mean like she's *not* right now?" Gemma snorts. "She just flipped her hair while giving you a sultry look."

"Christ, you watch too many romance movies."

"Prove me wrong then. Invite her over here." Gemma arches a brow, challenging me, but it doesn't matter because Brittany's already on her way.

"Hey," Brittany says with a big smile. "How're y'all doin'?"

"Doing just fine, thank you. How 'bout yourself?" I ask.

"I'm good, thanks. Just wanted to say how nice it was to see you last weekend." She stares at me intensely, and I wonder if Gemma's right. "Anthony's been talkin' about you nonstop. He's hoping to take you up on the offer to play baseball with him sometime."

"Of course. I'm a little rusty, but I'm sure it won't be a big deal."

"Okay, great." She pauses, and the silence between us grows

awkward. "Well, I'm sure I'll run into you again soon, and we can figure out the details."

Before I can respond, Belinda walks up with our plates. "Alright, kids. I'll get y'all a Coke refill and be right back."

"Oh, I can do that." Brittany grabs our glasses, then returns a minute later.

"Hope you two enjoy your lunch." She gives me a wink, then walks back to the counter.

I take a large bite of my sandwich and see Gemma smirking at me. "What?"

"I think I just witnessed the start of something..."

"Huh? What're ya talkin' about now?"

"Jesus, Noah. What'd she have to do for you to ask for her number...skywrite a message?"

"Why would I ask for her number?"

"Uh...to ask her out. Didn't you see all the signs? The flirting, the eye batting, the giggling. Then the way she brought up her son playing baseball with you. Could it be any more obvious she's interested? I'm only shocked she didn't lean over and touch your bicep."

I furrow my brows. "You think she was hinting for me to ask for her number?"

"I was two seconds away from giving her *my* number. That's how thick she was laying it on."

"Well, I'm not looking for a relationship anyway, so it's best I don't give her the wrong idea."

"You gonna stay single forever?" she challenges.

"I hope not, but..." I shrug, not finishing that thought.

"Look, I've always rooted for you and Katie, you know that," she says, which is true. Gemma knew I had a crush on Katie and encouraged me to tell her, but I refused. "But Katie might need a little...push of encouragement."

"A *push*? What do you mean?"

"Goodness, Noah. Did they not have enough oxygen circulating in prison or something?" she scolds, and I roll my eyes. "Perhaps if she saw another woman pining over you, she'll remember what an amazing guy you are and what a great friendship you two once had. Maybe she'll be scared to lose you and finally admit her own feelings..." She shrugs with a devious look on her face.

"Ohhh...you want me to play into some high school bullshit? Got it." I grunt, shaking my head. "I'm too old to play games, Gemma."

"It's not a *game*, per se. It's showing her that you have a lot to offer. If she acts jealous or mad that you're seeing someone, then you'll know how she really feels."

"I'm not gonna lead someone on just to see if Katie gets jealous."

"It's not leading her on if you're innocently playing baseball with her son." Gemma smirks as if she's just come up with the most brilliant plan of her life. "And what's the worst that could happen? You could actually like Brittany, or Katie could finally get her head out of her ass. Either way, it's a win-win for you."

"I think your pregnancy hormones are sucking the life out of your brain cells because you've lost your goddamn mind," I retort, finishing my sandwich. I'm ready to get back to work and avoid continuing this pointless conversation.

Gemma snickers. "Mm-hmm. Just wait and see, big brother."

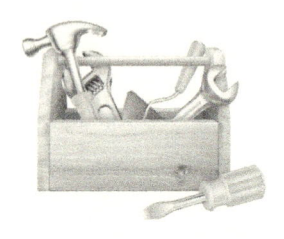

Once I'm back at the gym, I get right to work and lose myself in my thoughts. Though I gave my sister shit for her not-so-great idea, I wonder how Katie would react to seeing me with another woman. I didn't date much in high school, mostly because I was always hanging out with Katie. The rare times I did go on dates never led to anything serious.

As I glance around and look at the wood currently covering the front window, guilt floods me again. Tyler will never blame me, and I appreciate that more than I can say, but I feel like even more of a burden now. The last thing I'd ever want to do is damage the reputation of his new business, especially before it even opens.

Not to mention, no thirty-two-year-old man wants to be living at his parents' and starting over. The guilt of Gemma visiting me every month was so intense that I nearly told her to stop coming even though I knew she wouldn't listen.

They don't exactly give you therapy in prison, and going-back-into-civilization counseling isn't something offered, so the anxiety and depression I feel on top of everything else leads me to believe I've developed some sort of PTSD. The trauma of what happened to Gabe and me landing in prison affected everyone in my town, especially my dad and sister. I've lived with the guilt of that night for ten years, and no one, not even my family, can convince me I deserve a happy life when I took another. Falling in love and starting a family would be a dream, but a part of me doesn't believe I've earned it while the other part desperately begs for a fresh start.

Honestly, it's like living in a broken home inside my head. One side of my thoughts always blames the other, and they're always fighting. It's quite exhausting, which is why it's best to keep myself occupied so I don't have time to think about it.

Dad's suggested I find a therapist before I was released, and I've been thinking about it though I'm hesitant. I was never good at expressing my feelings or sharing my thoughts, which is exactly why Katie never knew how I felt.

A part of me always wondered why that was.

It brings me to thoughts of my late mother, who I lost at a young age, and I wonder if having a woman figure in my life would've helped me be more open. My father did the best he could raising us alone, but he wasn't expressive either. We didn't discuss deep personal issues, and my sister was the quiet one out of us all. It wasn't until she started to visit me in prison with Tyler that I saw her outgoing personality.

"We're wrapping up for the day," Tyler tells me just before five. "Wanna get a beer?"

I grab a towel and wipe off my hands. "I'd rather not go to a bar tonight, but thanks for the invitation."

"I understand. Come over to the cottage then. Gemma's been texting me for the past two hours about how good it smells. She made pot roast."

Chuckling, I nod. "Alright, sure, thanks."

"I'll lock up, and we'll get outta here. Smith, you ready?"

"Ready, boss."

The three of us head outside, and I watch as Tyler locks the door.

"Stop beating yourself up, man," Tyler says as he catches me looking at the boarded-up window. "I already called insurance, and a new window will be installed tomorrow, along with security cameras."

I nod and hope this is the only incident I have to deal with, but a part of me thinks that's too good to be true. For some reason, this feels like a warning shot.

CHAPTER NINE

KATIE

"Hey, buddy…" I tap my knuckles against Owen's door. "Dinner's ready."

"Okay. Be right there, Mom."

"I think you need to clean this room…" I say, glancing around at the Lego pieces and other random toys on the floor.

He furrows his brows. "It is."

I snort, then pick up a piece of clothing. "Oh, is the floor your new hamper?"

His face turns red as he takes the dirty underwear from my hand and tosses it into his basket. I turn as Owen follows me to the kitchen.

Since it's Friday, I'd usually be at the other house working for a couple of hours, but I couldn't get a sitter, and after the long week I've had, I was content with staying in with Owen.

"So, tell me about school today. Anything fun happen?"

"No, school's boring." He groans as he twirls the spaghetti around his fork.

"Even recess and lunch?" I tease.

"No, those are fun."

"So..." I linger, trying to ease into the conversation naturally. "Do you play with Anthony during recess?"

The image of Brittany all over Noah hasn't left my mind, and even though it shouldn't bother me, I'm annoyed by how much it does. I may be mad as hell at him, but I still care.

"Yeah, we play sometimes. We have to sit alphabetically at the lunch table, so he's kinda across from me."

"Ohh gotcha."

"He doesn't have a daddy, like me," he blurts out, and I'm taken off guard.

"You guys have talked about that?" I ask, shocked.

"Just a little. We had a class project where we had to make a family tree."

I furrow my brows because I had no idea about this. "Why didn't you tell me, Owen?"

He shrugs, gazing down at his plate instead of at me. "I don't know."

I've talked to him about Gabe his whole life but haven't told him everything about the night he died. I don't want him to feel any of the resentment and anger I have, so I try to only talk about the good memories I shared with his dad.

"You know we can talk about your daddy anytime you want," I say. "I know he'd be here if he could, baby."

He wasn't always a great husband, but I have no doubt he would've made an amazing father. He was always good with kids.

"I know."

Owen doesn't bring it up again while we eat, and once we're finished, I serve ice cream for dessert. He talks about his favorite game, Roblox, and shows me all the cool things he's built on the iPad. I love that it encourages him to be creative, though I don't really understand it, honestly. But it has opened a dialogue for online safety and strangers on the internet.

I spend the rest of the evening relaxing on the couch with a glass of wine as I scroll through Pinterest. I love looking for inspiration and have several boards and pins of house ideas. I'm not the best decorator, so I've been saving things for when it's time to finally get furniture and décor.

"Alright, baby. It's time for bed. Get jammies on and brush your teeth, please," I tell him at nine. I let him stay up an extra half hour on the weekends.

He slowly walks down the hallway with the iPad in his face, and I chuckle when he nearly runs into the wall. "Turn it off, Owen. You're gonna hurt yourself."

"I will!"

If I had a dollar for every time he said those words, I'd have enough to retire.

I clean up the living room and kitchen while I wait for him to get ready for bed. My mom's going to watch Owen tomorrow so I can get an early start at the house.

Once I'm done, I head to Owen's room and tuck him in. "Love you, sleep tight." I kiss his cheeks.

"Night, Mom. Love you too."

I slide my hand underneath his pillow and grab the iPad. "Nice try."

He groans as he rolls over and closes his eyes.

Taking the iPad with me, I close his door, then make my way to the bathroom to wash my face.

As soon as I'm getting into bed, my phone rings, and I see it's Gemma.

"Hey, it's kinda late. Everything okay?"

"Katie! Oh my gosh. No! I need your help."

Her frantic voice has me sitting up and my heart racing. "What is it?"

"Noah needs a place to stay for a few days. Can he stay at your new place?"

"What? I don't understand. Why can't he stay at your dad's?"

She blows out a frustrated breath. "Someone threw a pipe

bomb through the living room window and spray-painted MURDERER on his truck."

"Holy shit," I exclaim in disbelief. "Are y'all okay?"

"Luckily, it didn't go off. Must've been defective or maybe just another warning, but after the brick incident, it's looking more like someone is trying to intentionally hurt him."

Gemma told me about the window a couple of days ago, which I'm still shocked someone would do that.

"We're worried about his safety, Katie. Plus, my dad's and Belinda's. Not to mention, the cottage is right behind them, so it puts us all at risk. He needs to go where no one knows where he is."

"Why can't he stay at a hotel in another town until things die down?"

"Because we still want him close by, and honestly, he can't afford it. Sheriff Todd is here filing a report and gathering evidence, but I'm terrified whoever keeps doing this will come after him again. They know what he drives, so Dad's planning to move Noah's truck somewhere else."

"Gemma." I sigh. "You're putting me in a tough spot."

"Look, I know you two have your issues right now, and I get it. But you don't need to do anything besides let him inside. It'll only be for a few days until we figure something else out."

"I'm supposed to be working on the house this weekend."

"He'll stay out of the way, I promise."

I snort, knowing damn well that's a lie.

"There's nowhere for him to sleep. I don't have any furniture yet."

"We have an air mattress, and you have electricity and water, so he'll be fine."

I squeeze my eyes closed and blow out a breath. "Fine, but *only* a few days, Gemma. Of course, I don't want anything to happen to either of you."

"Thank you, thank you, thank you! We'll come over tomorrow morning."

"I'll be there by ten."

"Perfect. He'll have his things packed and ready. Though the cameras on my cottage don't show the front of the house, we're going to check anyway in case we can see something. It's most likely the same person who vandalized the gym, so hopefully, if they don't see his truck, they'll stay away from the house."

"Where're ya gonna keep it?"

"Not sure. Dad hasn't decided yet."

"What does the sheriff think?"

"He believes it's someone with a vengeance. Though, whoever it was did a half-ass job building the bomb. If they intended for it to go off, they could be charged with intentional homicide. Photos were taken, and they gathered evidence."

"I hope they find whoever's responsible for this soon because it's total bullshit," I say honestly. "Please stay safe, okay?"

"I will. Thank you again."

"You know I'd do anything for you...even when I really don't want to." I groan, thinking of the things I can pack for him.

She chuckles. "I know."

After we hang up, I grab a couple of duffel bags and put extra blankets and pillows in them. I don't know what he's going to need, so I grab everything I can think of—towels, soaps, snacks. Though I hate to admit it, I still have a soft spot for Noah and don't want anything bad to happen to him. It'd devastate Gemma and Jerry, and I'd be lying if I said I wouldn't be sad too.

Once I have the bags ready for tomorrow, I check my phone and see a message from Everleigh.

Everleigh: Oh my God, did you hear what happened??

Katie: Yes, it's horrible. I can't believe someone's trying so hard to hurt him.

Everleigh: You mean KILL him! That bomb could've exploded and destroyed the entire house for all we know.

That thought sends a chill down my spine.

Katie: They better find out who it is soon. I can imagine Tyler's ready to swoop up Gemma and take her away.

Tyler's always been an amazing partner to Gemma, but he's been super protective ever since she got pregnant. He's already a take-no-shit kinda guy, but if he thinks his wife or family are in danger, he won't think twice about getting revenge.

Everleigh: Oh, he's pissed. I called him after Gemma texted me, and he was nearly screaming in my ear. I told him to calm the fuck down so he wouldn't stress her out.

Katie: Yeah, she sounded pretty upset on the phone, which is how she sweet-talked me into letting Noah stay at the new house for a few nights.

Everleigh: Yeah, I might've suggested that…DON'T BE MAD!

Katie: OMG, EVERLEIGH! I'm going to strangle you!

Everleigh: You love me, and you know this is the right thing to do. It hides Noah for a few days and keeps his family safe until they have time to investigate. Sheriff Todd has to interview the neighbors to ask if they saw anything.

Katie: Y'all owe me margaritas.

Everleigh: Don't worry, they'll be bottomless :)

I swear, my friends are going to be the death of me.

After an hour of tossing and turning with my thoughts racing about Noah, I decide to get up. I go to my closet and look for an old shoebox I stuffed in the back. We used to write notes to each other during school, and for whatever reason, I kept them. Hell, I know why I did…I was crazy about him, even if we were only just friends.

Everleigh and Gemma would pass notes to me during class too, but not as much as Noah did. Sometimes, they'd be serious things, like how he struggled in a class or how he missed his mom. Other times, it was stupid drawings, jokes, or he'd ask silly questions.

Katie,

If you could only take one thing with you to a desert island, what would it be (besides me, of course)?

I read the note and laugh, remembering how I responded.

If I could only take one thing with me, it'd be a How to Survive on a Deserted Island book, so I had a better chance at living since I know you'd be useless.

Noah knew I was only teasing, but I bursted out laughing when he read it. He frowned and scowled at me.

After school that day, we made a whole survival guide as if we'd actually get stranded.

He was in charge of gathering wood for a fire and branches to build us a shelter. Then he'd hunt, and I'd cook.

We had planned out an entire scenario, and it was moments like those when I thought maybe he did have feelings for me. We were acting like a couple at our pretend island. According to Gemma, Noah did have a crush on me, but I still don't believe that. If Noah did, he was really good at hiding it.

I find another box with all kinds of keepsakes Noah gave me. Birthday cards, super special notes he'd written me, movie theater stubs, dried petals from the flowers he'd gotten me for Valentine's Day, so I didn't feel left out freshman and sophomore year. There's a decade of memories inside, and though our friendship is long over, I can't find it in me to throw these boxes away.

Once I finish going through them, I put on the lid and tuck them away because that part of my life doesn't exist anymore.

CHAPTER TEN

NOAH

TWO HOURS PREVIOUSLY

After a long day at work, I'm looking forward to relaxing at home with my dad and Belinda. I don't even care that he keeps his old British TV shows on all night because it's paradise compared to when I was locked in a cell.

Though I had time outside and in the lounge since I wasn't deemed a high-risk inmate, it wasn't much, and I could never truly relax. Not until the day I left.

"How's the gym remodel goin'?" Dad asks as I sit down with a beer.

"Really good. If it wasn't for the delay in delivering the equipment, he'd be able to open earlier than expected."

"I can't wait to see what he does with it," Belinda chimes in.

"It's gonna be pretty awesome. Besides the boxing ring, we're gonna build a juice bar and serve protein smoothies and healthy drinks. Then a nice studio for classes and a stretching area with punching bags."

"And y'all are gonna get it finished in a few months?" Dad asks.

"Definitely. We're working hard, and if we need to pull some weekend shifts, I will. Smith is quite experienced, so that keeps us on task."

"That's Tyler's other guy, right?"

"Yeah, he—"

Suddenly, the sound of glass shattering rings through the air, then a loud thud echoes, and I duck as I wait for whatever is happening to stop. Belinda shouts, and I hear my dad asking her if she's okay.

Standing, I immediately look around and notice what went flying through the large bay window.

"Holy fuck, is that a…?"

I study the pipe as the clock counts down, and it beeps loudly.

"Get out. Now!" I pull my dad's arm, and he holds onto Belinda as I rush us out the front door.

Expecting to hear an explosion, I run across the street and keep them behind me as we stand on the sidewalk.

Nothing happens.

What the fuck?

Then I spot my truck that I parked on the street. The word MURDERER is spray-painted across the side.

Goddammit.

"Oh my gosh…" Belinda sees it too.

"I'm calling the sheriff," Dad says.

I nod, reaching for my phone. "Good idea. I'm gonna call Tyler and Gemma."

The bomb might've been defective, or there could be a delayed response, but I'm not taking any chances.

My heart races, and I'm short of breath, but it's taken me a minute for this to sink in. Did someone just try to bomb our house? That would've killed us.

Soon, Sheriff Todd arrives, and he's calling in backup from the next town over, along with the bomb squad. Red and blue lights illuminate the street, and the entire neighborhood watches from the sidewalk. While the bomb squad takes care of things, the sheriff asks if I have any idea who might be doing this. I honestly don't know, but I tell him of two people who have a vendetta against me. *Gabe's parents.*

Then I tell him about the one guy who slammed into me and called me a murderer, but I have no clue who he is. I can't give him much of a description either since he wore a hoodie covering his head.

"It's defective," one of the bomb squad members comes over and tells us. "It was set to go off as soon as it flew through your window, but whoever did this didn't do a very good job building it."

"Thank God," Gemma mutters.

"Will you be staying here for the night? After traumatic things like this happen, sometimes it's safer and helps with peace of mind to leave after everything's properly secured," he suggests.

"Not sure yet. We'll figure it out," Dad says. He glances at Belinda, who's on the phone and is clearly shaken up. "Thanks for everything."

Sheriff Todd writes a report and tells us he'll file it in the morning so Dad can get insurance to cover the expenses. Once again, I feel fucking terrible.

"I'm so sorry," I tell him and Belinda. "I'm so relieved you two are okay."

"It's not your fault," Belinda says, ending her call.

"Not at all," Dad adds, but I know it is.

"Are y'all gonna go somewhere?" Gemma asks.

"Well, I just talked to my sister and let her know what happened. She has a spare room, but there's only a full-sized bed." Belinda frowns, then glances at me.

"Take it," I demand. "I'll figure something out. Plus, it's probably best I stay close and watch the house tonight. But tomorrow I'll need to find somewhere else to go for a while.

Perhaps if this asshole thinks I moved out, it'll keep you both safe. I can move my truck so it's not in front of the house."

"You have nowhere to go," Tyler says.

"And you can't afford a hotel." Gemma gives me a sad look. "Though I wouldn't want you in the next town anyway. That's too far."

I shrug, trying to calm myself. My body is still in shock. "It might be my only option."

"Let me see what I can do…just give me a minute," Gemma says, pulling out her phone and walking off.

"You're sure about this?" Dad asks.

"Absolutely. You and Belinda go pack and stay at her sister's. I'll be fine here," I reassure. "I just need someone to help me drop off my truck somewhere in the event it's being tracked."

"I'll work on removing the spray paint." Dad pats my back. "It'll look good as new in no time."

I manage to smile. "Thanks."

"We can keep it in the back parking lot of the deli. There are security cameras too."

"That's a great idea," Dad agrees.

Five minutes later, Gemma returns with the biggest grin. "All sorted out. You're gonna stay at Katie's new house."

My heart jumps into my throat, and I'm sure I heard her wrong.

"Wait, what?"

"Yep, it took some sweet-talkin', but she can't say no to me so…" She shrugs, clearly proud of herself. "Pack a bag because you're going first thing tomorrow morning. But tonight, you can sleep on our couch."

"Okay, I'll be over after I board up that window," I say, hardly believing any of this.

Once again, I feel like a burden to everyone who has to adjust their lives for me. I'm determined to figure out who this coward is and put him through hell. It's one thing to come at me because of what I've done, but you leave my family the fuck alone.

My blood boils at how they're harassing others to get to me. I wonder if they hope I'll lose my support system since they're being targeted by association. This person highly underestimates the people I've surrounded myself with because nothing will change how protective they are of me. Tyler, for one, is someone I trust with my life. Though we've got to know each other when he accompanied my sister during their short monthly visits, seeing him nearly every day for the past month has cemented our friendship.

"You sleep okay?" Gemma asks when I make my way to the kitchen.

I stretch my arms over my head and crack my back. "You need a new couch. Preferably a longer one."

She snorts and nods. "Whenever we move, we definitely will. Just for *you*, brother."

Tyler strolls in after his shower and cups Gemma's face before kissing her. She clings to him, and it lasts for a solid thirty seconds.

I clear my throat loudly. "Can we keep it G-rated, please? I don't need a visual on how you knocked up my sister."

Gemma glares, and Tyler laughs. "Sorry, man."

"If you need a tutorial, there are plenty of websites I can show you," Gemma taunts.

"Nah, just send him to PornHub. Plenty of...*educational* videos there." Tyler chuckles as he brews a pot of coffee.

"Yeah, watching that while at Katie's house is really gonna make things less awkward," I say, groaning. "Are you certain she's okay with this?"

"No, but oh well..." Gemma smirks. "Just stay out of her way, and she won't even know you're there."

"Sounds easy enough. She's dodged and ignored me every time we've run into each other, so it shouldn't be an issue." I sigh, walking around the counter for a mug since the coffee's ready.

"Or use the opportunity to help her. She'll never admit it, but she doesn't really know what she's doing," Gemma says, grinning. "She watches videos and reads up on it, but it slows her down."

"She won't speak to me, so I doubt she'll let me near her tools."

"Wait...is that a euphemism for something?" Gemma waggles her brows.

"Hormones," Tyler mouths with wide eyes, signaling for me not to challenge her.

I suck in a breath. "I'm gonna take a shower and get ready to go..."

"We're leaving in thirty minutes," Gemma announces as I walk down the short hallway to the bathroom.

Once I'm under the stream of hot water, it doesn't take long before visions of Katie surface. I've thought about her every single day of my life, so today's not any different. My cock gets hard as I picture her heart-shaped face and ruby lips. I always adored her spitfire attitude. It's why I fell for her in the first place.

Before Gabe showed up, we used to have movie nights every

weekend. We'd sit on my bed, share a large bowl of popcorn mixed with M&Ms, then fall asleep together. I almost had the courage to kiss her one night, but then something in the movie had her bursting out with laughter, and Coke spewed out of her mouth. It sprayed all over my chest, and she couldn't stop giggling.

Of course, I laughed with her, but as soon as I took off my shirt to wipe off the mess, I saw the way her eyes stared at my chest. Katie licked her lips and quickly averted her gaze when she realized I'd caught her.

That was when I should've made my move, but I fucking chickened out. The self-conscious part of me took over, so instead of kissing her, I created more space between us.

Didn't stop my fantasies every time I took a shower.

"You ready?" Gemma asks as I stroll into the kitchen with my duffel bag and air mattress.

"Ready as I'll ever be, I guess."

"Eh, don't worry," Tyler says. "What's the worst that can happen? She poisons you and feeds you to the gators?" He chuckles, patting me on the back.

"Just promise me you'll at least look for my body…" I groan.

To be on the safe side, we walk through the backyards to Katie's. It's just down the block, so it's not far. The asshole harassing me might be watching my dad's place, so it's best if they don't see where I go.

"If you need anything, just call, okay? I don't want you out of work for long, so I promise you we'll find whoever it is," Tyler reassures me.

"Yes, and let me know if you need me to bring you anything to eat. Katie's a good cook and all, but she doesn't have a fridge yet, so I think your choices will be limited," Gemma tells me.

"I'm sure I'll manage."

Gemma walks with me, and soon, we're at Katie's back door. I knock and nervously wait.

CHAPTER ELEVEN

KATIE

Noah's the last person I want to be around, but I'd do anything to keep him safe regardless of how mad I am or how awkward it will be. He desperately needs somewhere to disappear to, and I agree that my house is the perfect haven, even if it's inconvenient for me.

My focus will still be on finishing the house so Owen and I can move in. I haven't gotten used to Noah being back in town, and it's been harder than I ever imagined. Working on the house has been my escape for the past year. I've lost myself within those walls on more than one occasion, and now Noah will be in my safe space.

I'm not sure how to feel.

He'll undoubtedly use this opportunity to talk to me about everything, and honestly, I have nothing more to say, nor do I want to hear his excuses. After I put on my remodeling clothes, I cook Owen and me some eggs and bacon. After we eat, I pack the car, and we head out.

My fingers tap against the steering wheel, and I'm a nervous wreck to face him again. Owen doesn't notice, which I'm thankful for, but I still need to talk to him about Noah living there temporarily. After I park, I turn around and grab his attention in the back seat.

"I've gotta tell you something before we go inside," I say.

Owen furrows his brow. "Okay, what?"

I swallow hard. "Well, there's gonna be a man staying here for a little while."

"Who?"

"It's Gemma's brother, but it's really important you don't tell anybody that he's here," I explain.

"Why?"

"Because bad people are trying to hurt him, so I want to keep him safe, which is why it needs to stay a secret."

Owen's eyes widen as he tries to understand. "Why do they want to hurt him?"

It's a question that's way too complicated to answer. I haven't explained to him exactly what happened to his dad other than he had an accident and passed away. I've never said who was responsible or gave any details to what happened that night. I've been waiting for him to get older so maybe he'd comprehend it better. I haven't lied to Owen, but I haven't given him every detail. He's still too young to know the full story.

"Well, that's hard to explain. I don't know why anyone would want to hurt him. Gemma asked if her brother could stay until things were safe for everyone, and I said yes. But it's very, very, *very* important that you don't tell anyone. Not Mimi, Pepaw, Memaw, or Pawpaw. Nobody. It would put him in danger if anyone knew. Do you understand?" I tell him directly and clearly, then wait patiently for his response.

He nods. "I won't tell anyone."

"Not even your teachers or friends at school," I add.

"I promise." Owen holds out his pinky finger, and I hook it with mine. He pinky promises and swears to keep it to himself.

"Is he here now?" he asks.

"Not yet. He'll be arriving soon, though."

We get out of the car and go inside.

I turn on one of the space heaters to warm up the place. As I walk through and make mental notes of what I want to do today, I can tell Owen is already getting bored.

"Memaw will be here to pick you up for basketball practice in thirty minutes," I remind him. "Not too much longer, promise."

Owen forces a smile, but I can see right through him. Once this place is finished, he's going to love it, but right now, all he sees it as is work. He'd rather play with friends than help me, so I don't force him if he isn't interested. He sits on a stool in the middle of the living room and kicks his legs out as he plays on his tablet.

I hear a knock on the back door, and my heart races in anticipation.

"Hello," I greet Noah and Gemma. She smiles wide, and I glare in return. "C'mon in."

"Thank you..." Noah says, walking past me with his arms full of stuff. "For letting me stay here."

I swallow hard, avoiding his eyes. "Mm-hmm."

The tension between us is so thick I almost feel bad for Gemma standing awkwardly between us.

"Well, uh...where do you want me to go?" Noah asks.

"A thousand miles north?" I smirk.

"Let's just get you settled into the master bedroom," Gemma interjects.

"Are you sure she won't kill me in my sleep?" Noah mumbles under his breath.

"No, I mean..." Gemma shrugs with a grin. "Probably not."

"If I was gonna kill you, I wouldn't do it in my own house. Unless of course, I can get the concrete truck out here sooner."

Gemma chokes back a laugh, then quickly clears her throat to cover it up. "She's kiddin'," she tells Noah as she grabs his arm and leads him through the house.

I arch a brow. "Or am I?"

When they get to the kitchen, Noah stops and stares at Owen.

I walk around them and kneel beside Owen and speak to him. "This is who I was talking about."

Noah's mouth falls open and closes. I brought Owen with me to the retirement party, but we didn't stay long, and Owen was busy with his friend Anthony. This is the first time Noah's gotten a close look at Gabe's son.

"Hi, I'm Noah," he says nervously.

"I'm Owen."

Noah smiles, then shakes his little hand. "It's nice to officially meet you."

"My mama told me not to tell anyone you're here. I'll keep it a secret. I promise," Owen says.

"Thank you."

"Since you don't have any appliances, I told Noah I'd bring him food, or he can sneak over to the cottage, so you won't have to worry about him much," Gemma says. "You won't even know he's here."

I grunt, crossing my arms. "Doubtful, but alright."

Gemma smacks my arm and looks at me with a warning. "Do I need to bring a rifle?"

"For me or her?" Noah quips.

Gemma rolls her eyes. "Okay, well as much as I wish I could stay and witness this grand reunion, I have a new business to get up and running, so I'm gonna trust you'll get yourself settled in." She pats his arm. "Call me if you need anything, okay? I'm just down the block."

"Might wanna check on me if you don't hear from me in a few days…" Noah taunts, flashing me a look.

"Oh c'mon…" I narrow my eyes at him. "Now y'all are just being dramatic, and I have a ten-year-old who gives me enough of that."

Gemma gives me a hug goodbye and thanks me again.

As soon as she walks out the back, I hear a door close from the front.

Panic fills me. "Oh shit, that's my mother. Of course, she's early. You've gotta hide. *Right now*," I urge Noah. "She's here to pick up Owen for basketball practice." I point at the staircase, and Noah quickly bolts upstairs. My heart races a million miles per minute as she knocks on the door. I put a finger over my mouth, and Owen pretends to zip his lips.

"Come in," I say, and my mother enters.

She's dressed prim and proper and looks around at the progress I *haven't* made, but at least I've taught her to keep her opinions to herself.

"Ready to go to basketball practice?" she asks with a cheeky grin.

He smiles and nods. "Yep! Coach said we'd be practicing three-pointers today." He grabs his small duffel bag with his shoes and bottle of water, then gives me a side hug before walking toward the door.

"I'll probably take him to get something to eat afterward, then bring him back here, unless you'll be at home?" Mom asks.

"I'll be here," I confirm. "Wanna try to make some progress on the guest bathroom."

"Good deal," she tells me before leaving.

Once I hear the car back out of the driveway, I exhale in relief. My phone vibrates, and I see a text from Everleigh.

Everleigh: I want to schedule a girls' day in two weeks on Saturday. A spa day for a pregnancy gift for Gemma. You in?

Katie: Abso-fucking-lutely.

I'll need to find a sitter. After we have massages and mani-pedis, I'll be useless, so I won't work on the house that day either. Honestly, though, I can't remember the last time I relaxed.

I hear the old floorboards creaking on the second floor, and soon, Noah's feet touch the bottom stair.

He glances at me with dark brown eyes, then looks around. Noah's gaze trails over the unfinished walls and hanging electrical wires.

"You are literally in over your head," he mumbles.

I grind my teeth. "How the hell would you know? I'm not the same twenty-year-old Katie you once knew. And if I'm being honest, it's actually none of your damn business," I snap.

Noah's lips tilt down. "I'm sorry. I wasn't trying to offe—"

"Just keep your thoughts to yourself. I'm doing you a favor. If I want your opinion, I'll ask for it."

He flashes a cocky grin that makes me want to punch his stupid face in.

"Yes, you are, and I'm grateful for it. I was just going to say, I could help you with some of this, Katie. This is a huge project to undertake."

"No, thank you. I don't need your help. At least not anymore. When I did, you pushed me away, so I'm not taking your pity offer now."

"It wasn't a pity offer," he says, then chuckles softly to himself. "You were always so damn stubborn. Should've known that'd never change."

Narrowing my eyes at him, I'm over this conversation and want to get to work. "Follow me, I'll show you the room," I say, keeping my tone flat as I head down the hallway.

I open the door to the master and go in. By the expression on his face, I'm positive he's in shock I actually have a liveable room in this house.

"This is really nice," he admits, which is nice to hear considering how long I've worked on it. I ripped out the old carpet, repainted the walls, and installed crown molding around the ceiling. I still have a small list of things to finish in here, though. The entire house still needs new windows and lighting fixtures.

"Where should I put my bed?" he asks, holding the air mattress bag.

I nod toward the opposite wall. "Probably best you stay away from the window since I don't have any curtains in here."

"Alright." Noah walks over and sets it down with his small duffel bag.

"I packed some things for you too."

"Really?" he asks, surprised.

"Yeah, they're in my trunk. I grabbed some extra blankets and pillows, in case you needed them. I also have bottled water in a small cooler in case you get thirsty. There are paper plates in the kitchen, though, if someone brings you food or whatever." My voice lingers, and now it's awkward. "I'll just go grab them."

"Great, thank you again," he says sincerely as he blows up the mattress.

I quietly make my way outside, and it feels like I'm gulping in the fresh air. It could be because I've been holding my breath since the moment he arrived. It takes me two trips to bring it all in. I take a moment to notice how muscular and fit he is as he arranges his area. When the pump stops, I clear my throat to get his attention.

"That's all you have to eat?" I blurt out when I notice his bag of snacks.

Noah nods. "Yeah, I'll be fine. Don't worry about me."

"Alright well...I have *a lot* to do today, so I'm gonna get started," I tell him as I bounce between my feet.

"Anything I can help you with?" He cocks a brow.

I inhale sharply, not wanting to snap at him again. "As I said before, I don't want your help."

"Well, you just said you had *a lot* to do, and I'm basically doing nothing, so..."

His arrogant smirk has my blood boiling. Yeah, he's gonna *stay out of my way*, my ass.

"How about a quick house tour then?" he asks when I don't respond.

I let out a sigh. "Fine, as long as you don't make any more negative comments."

"Deal."

He follows me out of the bedroom, and I swear I can feel his eyes burning through me.

After I show him the guest bathroom, dining room, and living room, we make our way to the second floor, which is awkward as hell. Silence lingers other than the hum of a small space heater.

"This is *a lot* of house," Noah finally says once we're back downstairs. "But I see why you bought it. Has a lot of potential."

"It really does," I agree. "I envision myself growing old here and hopefully playing with my grandkids someday, but anyway, I really only get the weekends to work on it."

"So no time to date then, I assume?" He crosses his arms as he moves closer.

My heart drops into my stomach, and I take a step back.

Whether it's due to shock or anger is yet to be determined.

"Do you honestly think that's an appropriate thing to ask me?" I snap. "We're not having this conversation. You aren't here to chat, got it? This is a favor to Gemma and your dad. *Not* for you." My cheeks heat, and I somewhat feel bad for blowing up at him, but I have a decade of pent-up anger inside me.

Instead of being insulted or walking away with his tail between his legs, the motherfucker smirks. "You haven't changed a damn bit, Katie Walker."

My last name is Reid, which he knows.

Noah chuckles. "It was always so damn easy to rile you up."

I want to be so angry with him for pushing me away, but I also still miss him more than I want to admit. Having him here is a reminder of everything I lost.

After six hours of working, my back aches, and my stomach growls. Before I left this morning, I put a roast and potatoes in the slow cooker so I wouldn't have to cook dinner. Though I'm not happy Noah's here invading my space and head, I won't let him go hungry. He stayed out of my way for most of the day. Later, I find him reading a book on his bed.

"I'll be right back. I'm going to grab dinner and bring it here."

When he looks up at me, it's almost as if time stands still and we're teenagers again. It's the same look he used to give me that melted my heart every damn time I saw him.

"Okay."

I only live ten minutes away, so it takes me no time to round up everything. I freshen up in the bathroom before I grab a few drinks and the slow cooker, then bring it out to my car.

Shortly after I return, my mother shows up with Owen. I hurry and meet them outside, not giving her the opportunity to find Noah bunkered inside. She grabs Owen's bag from the trunk and hands it to him.

"How was your day?" I ask.

"It was good. We had milkshakes after practice." Owen grins.

"Lovely, nice and sugared up for dinner." I chuckle.

"What are grandmas for?" My mom smirks.

"I'll see you later this week. Thanks for taking him to practice and hanging out with him so I could work."

"No problem. You know I love doing it, even if he can be exhausting at times." She smiles at Owen before engulfing him into a hug. Once she's in her car, we both wave goodbye, then head back toward the house.

"Is Noah still here?"

I place my hand on his shoulder as we go inside. "Yes. He'll probably be here for at least a week."

His lips tilt up. "I didn't say anything to anyone."

"That's good."

The aromas from the roast and potatoes float through the air as we walk to the kitchen. Owen sets up the small card table and folding chairs I keep in the closet for when we eat dinner here. I put the food on three plates as Owen sets out the forks.

"Can I help with anything?" Noah asks as he watches.

"You can grab the roll of paper towels from under the sink," I say.

Once we all sit, we dig in. Owen asks Noah a million questions, and I let him because it fills the silence.

"So, what's your last name?" Owen asks.

Noah looks at me as if he's asking permission, and I nod.

"It's Reid, like yours."

Owens scrunches his nose in confusion, then glances at me. I confirm with a nod. "We have the same last name? Does that mean we're related?"

I clear my throat. "Yes, he's your daddy's cousin, which makes him your second cousin. Jerry is his dad, and my friend Gemma is his sister."

Owen looks immediately confused, then frowns before looking at Noah. "I never met my dad. I've only seen him in pictures, but I wonder what he was like. If he played basketball like me or if he was good at video games." Owen's eyes lower to his lap, and I reach over and squeeze his hand. Before I can say anything, Noah clears his throat and grabs my attention. He gives me a look as if he's asking for permission to talk about him. I offer a quick nod and pray it won't make Owen feel worse.

"Your dad *loved* basketball," he says, and it immediately grabs

Owen's attention back to him. "And you look so much like him when he was your age. I'm certain he'd be incredibly proud of you."

Seeing Owen's mouth tilt up into a sad smile breaks my heart. "He's right. I know Daddy would be amazed by your good grades and by how nice you are to everyone and how you always help me. He'd be so proud because I know I am."

Owen's smile grows bigger, but I notice how hard Noah swallows. I've talked about Gabe around Owen since he was a baby, so this is nothing new, but it's a first for Noah. I know how much it hurts Owen that his friends have a dad, and he doesn't.

We finish eating as Owen talks about his day and tells Noah about his school and friends. It's sweet how open he's being, but it also reminds me how desperate he is for male companionship. Though he has his grandfathers, Tyler, and even Jerry in his life, it's not the same as having a father.

Once everything is cleaned up and packed to leave, I tell Owen to wait for me in the car.

"We're gonna go. Do you need anything?" I ask Noah as he stands against the wall with his arms crossed.

He looks up at me with sad eyes. "I'm good, Katie. You've done enough." I can hear the pain in his voice, but I don't ask him what's wrong because I know it has something to do with the conversation he had with Owen about Gabe.

I nod and start to walk away when he stops me. "Wait, there is one thing."

Turning around, I meet his gaze.

"Can I get your number just in case?"

"Yeah, sure," I say. After we exchange them, I realize how chilly it's gotten. Since half the house still needs new insulation, the cool night air sneaks in. "One more thing. There's an extra space heater in the hall closet if you need it."

"Thanks. Good night."

Meeting his dark brown eyes once again, I think of all the things I want to say but don't. "Good night, Noah."

I turn off the living room lights before I lock the front door. As I drive home, I feel guilty for leaving Noah in my big, empty house. Though I wasn't happy about him coming in the first place, it's the best I can do for him, yet I hate that he's alone. I also hate to think how prison has probably made him used to it.

After I get Owen in bed for the night, I close my eyes and fall asleep with Noah on my mind.

CHAPTER TWELVE

NOAH

The sun rises, but I don't want to climb out from under the covers that kept me warm all night. Luckily, Katie had a space heater, so that helped. I stretch and stare at the high ceiling as I think about yesterday.

It was surreal talking to Owen about his dad and seeing how much he looks like Gabe.

Owen's facial expressions are just like Gabe's, especially the way his lips curl up when he smiles. He even has his eyes. It looked like Gabe's ghost was sitting at the table with us.

I get out of bed and go to the bathroom, then get dressed. Wanting to feel useful in some way, I walk through each room and take note of what Katie still needs to do. Once I'm in the living room, the front door swings open.

I'm shocked to see a smiling Katie carrying a brown bag and two cups.

It's completely unexpected, considering how yesterday started out between us. Not to mention, she basically loathes me.

"Good morning," she tells me.

"Mornin'."

She hands me one of the cups. "I didn't know how you take

your coffee anymore, so I just got it the same way as mine with cream and sugar."

"Thank you. I appreciate it." I take a sip and enjoy how warm it is. Prison sure makes a person appreciate the small things in life, such as a good cup of coffee. Katie looks at me the same way she used to when we were teenagers, then beams as she opens the bag and pulls out two bagels. She's in a good mood today, and I've missed seeing this side of her.

"There's cream cheese in the bag," she informs me, handing it to me.

"You're amazing." I cover mine in cream cheese, then take a bite. "Where's Owen today?"

"Loretta and Elliot took him to church and will have him until this evening. I'm hoping I can make some progress here while he's with them."

I haven't talked to them since before the accident, and they ignored me at the funeral. No telling how many bricks they'd shit if they knew I was staying at Katie's house or that I had dinner with Owen. I hate that she has to keep secrets from them, but it's for the best.

"He's a good kid, Katie. You've done an amazing job with him," I say, meaning every word.

Her shoulders slightly relax, and she smiles gratefully. "Thanks, it wasn't always easy."

I nod in response, though I can't imagine what she's had to go through while juggling work life and single mom life.

"Alright, well, on to bathroom duty." She taps on her phone. Moments later, someone's giving monotone instructions on how to remove a toilet and a sink. The video is long and boring. I try to keep my opinions to myself, as she's asked, and quietly eat my bagel.

"What?" She looks at me.

I shake my head and chuckle. "Nothing."

She stops the video. "No, you want to say something. I can tell. Go ahead."

"You're sure?"

"Yes," she snaps.

"Well…" I hesitate. "While I'm here, I'd like to help you, Katie. It'd be a lot easier and faster than watching that."

She acts as if she's contemplating my offer, but she's still too damn stubborn to agree.

I continue before she can tell me to fuck off. "If I'm being honest, not having anything to do is making me feel useless. I know you can do this on your own, but I want to repay you somehow. It would be my way of thanking you for letting me stay here. You've fed me dinner and even brought coffee and bagels today. I'm using your electricity, water, and everything else. It'd make me feel a lot less guilty for being an inconvenience."

She lets out a sigh.

"I'm just trying to offer my skills as a payment for your kindness and using your resources. A fair trade. I don't want to take advantage or get handouts. Not from my family, and especially not from you."

Her face softens, and I can see that old twinkle return to her eyes. She studies me for a brief second before speaking. "Okay, I understand that more than you know. When I was younger and struggling, I wanted to repay them by doing whatever I could—cleaning, running errands, cooking dinner. I didn't like the idea of getting free handouts either."

A hopeful smile touches my lips.

"Alright, you can help, but you still have to keep your negative comments to yourself."

I chuckle because whether she realizes it or not, she knows me better than anyone. "Deal," I agree.

"That means you're on bathroom duty with me today."

"Great. Time for us to rewatch that video and follow the tutorial from Mr. Monotone."

Katie grabs one bag of tools and asks me to carry the other.

"I'm not sure where we should start," she admits from the doorway, then moves to the side.

I look around. "Well, first off, is there anything you want to save in here?"

Katie looks around at the Pepto Bismol-colored toilet and bathtub. Her eyes trail along the gaudy tile on the walls and floors. "I don't think there's anything worth salvaging, do you?"

"Hell no," I say, loving how she asked for my opinion. It's proof my words actually got through to her.

"I think we should remove the toilet, then work on tearing out the counter, cabinets, and sink. Then the bathtub, wall tiles, and flooring. I think if we go in that order, we'll be able to have an empty space for you to paint. Then we can rebuild from the bottom up."

Katie grins. "That sounds like a solid plan."

"What do you envision in here?"

"I'd like a big shower with glass doors. This bathroom will primarily be for guests, and there'll be a huge tub upstairs if they want to soak or something."

"Expecting a lot of visitors?" I ask and internally slap myself for crossing my boundaries.

She snorts. "Not really."

Quickly, I change the subject. "Most people take showers anyway."

"Speak for yourself. There's nothing like a tub full of scorching hot water and a bath bomb paired with a glass of wine after a long-ass day."

I imagine her naked body but quickly push it away. "Can't argue with that."

Katie pulls out a few wrenches and sizes them against the bolts holding the toilet to the floor. I turn off the water valve and flush down the remaining. After she finds the correct size, she uses all her strength to loosen it but fails, nearly hitting her knuckles against the porcelain.

"Let me try," I say in a near whisper, not wanting her to hurt herself. She gladly moves out of my way. I kneel and position the wrench over the rusted bolt.

"Shit," I grunt.

"I didn't think it'd be that hard," she admits.

"Me either. Do you have any WD-40?"

"Hmm, maybe. I'll go check." She walks out, and I keep trying to loosen it, but it won't budge. Moments later, she returns with a can, and I spray each one. I work them the best I can, using both hands until I finally get one off. Thankfully, the others aren't nearly as hard. Once that's done, I remove the tank and set it to the side. Then I wiggle the toilet until it's off the wax ring.

"This thing has been here for so long it's basically glued to the floor."

"I think it was installed in the sixties. So yeah, definitely older than either of us. Probably would've had to hire someone."

I give her a smirk, glad that I was able to help, so she didn't.

I carry the toilet and tank and place them next to the front door. It's heavy, so I'll bring it outside once it's dark. The last thing I want is for anyone to know I'm here and to put Katie in a dangerous situation.

Gemma promised to let me know if anything else happens, but so far, everything's been quiet. It makes me think whoever was trying to attack me has been watching and knows I'm no longer at home.

Katie gets a paint scraper and removes the gunk from the floor, then we clean the area.

"That's one thing off our list," Katie says, then looks at the counter. "What will be the easiest way to remove that?"

"I think just by diving in." I open the cabinet and turn off the water valve. I twist the knob, then gently pull the cabinet door toward me. It nearly crumbles in my hand.

Katie gets a crowbar and pries out the rotten wood. She hands it to me, and I wedge it under the sink and easily pop it out. I grab a small hand saw and cut the piping. With a swing of a hammer, Katie crushes the counter to pieces. We laugh as she puts all her strength into it, and it brings up a memory.

"Do you remember that time we snuck into my mom's paint studio and decided to create masterpieces on canvases?" I ask, and she glances at me with a smile.

"Of course I do," she says as we clean up our mess. "We were covered in paint by the end."

"Yeah, my dad wasn't happy about trying to get it out of my jeans. But ya know, that was the summer I realized I had a super mad crush on you. I remember it clear as day."

Katie stops, and her eyes glue to mine. "What are you talkin' about?"

I swallow hard, somewhat shocked by her reaction. "Yeah. Katie, I mean, I thought it was obvious how I felt."

Clearly not.

She blinks, and I watch as she opens and closes her mouth. "How you felt? Wait...what do you mean you realized you had a crush on me?"

"Well, I mean, I always knew but hadn't acknowledged it. That was the summer I almost crossed the line and kissed you."

She shakes her head. "Are you messin' with me? You wanted to...*kiss me*?"

I snort and shake my head. "You must be the only person in Lawton Ridge who didn't know."

We sit in silence as my heart races in anticipation of her next words.

Eventually, she speaks up. "Noah, I just... I don't know what to say."

"Then don't say anything," I say honestly. "It was a million years ago."

Her arms drop to her side, and her brow furrows. "You never said anything."

"I know," I say somberly.

She eventually snorts. "You're kidding. You didn't like me that way."

Shock washes over me as I study her reaction. I was certain it was painfully obvious how much I liked her. I went out of my way to make sure she was happy. All I ever wanted to do was spend time with her. Even though I was only thirteen, I knew deep in my heart she was the woman for me.

"I'm not. I'd never joke about that. I honestly thought you knew but didn't see me that way and just never said anything," I admit.

The mood grows awkward as I finish sweeping the floor. I'm not sure what else to say or how to change the subject. Instead, we start working again. Katie removes the molding and wrinkled wallpaper like a pro, and I help keep the space clean.

We both take a deep breath and look at the bathtub.

"We've completed a lot already," she says with a pleased smile.

"So what you're saying is you're glad I'm here?"

Katie smirks. "I *am* glad you're here. Will say it took you long enough."

We take a quick water break and eat leftover bagels for lunch.

"So what's next on the list after the bathroom?" I ask as we stand in the kitchen.

"I'm not sure yet," she says around a mouthful. "I'd like to finish the first floor, then work on completing the upstairs. The only problem is Owen's room is up there, and I want it to be done sooner than later so if we move in before everything's done, he has somewhere to sleep. I need to make a list and stick to it, but I get overwhelmed and get off schedule. I'm paying a mortgage note and rent at my place plus double utilities, so things are tight. Moving would make it easier to save money for new furniture and décor."

"Yeah, that makes total sense. When are you hoping you can move in?"

Katie lets out a sarcastic laugh. "Well, the flooring needs to get done, and I need to order the windows so then we could at least have the bedrooms done. In a dream world, the house would be completely done by the end of the year. Realistically, I think it's going to take me a few years due to my work schedule and needing to save up for all the appliances on top of everything else."

"Well, if it means anything, I promise to help you with whatever I can," I say. "Seriously, just put me to work."

"Thanks, Noah. I appreciate that, but you don't have to worry about me. I'll eventually get it done," she tells me.

"I'll always worry about you, Katie. No matter what. I worried about you at fifteen, and I worry about you at thirty-one." I chuckle, but it's true. Even when I was locked up, I thought about her constantly.

Soft eyes meet mine, and I take the opportunity to mention the past again. "Earlier, when I admitted I had a crush on you... There's actually more to the story. It wasn't just a crush. I was in love with you for years. If I could go back in time and tell you, I would. Keeping it to myself is one of the biggest regrets of my life because when Gabe showed up, I lost my opportunity."

I see tears well on the brim of her eyes. I can only imagine how hard this is to hear.

"I don't know why I'm telling you this, but I don't want to keep it inside any longer. The last thing I want to do is have something happen to me without you knowing the truth."

"Wow." She releases a breath. "Why didn't you tell me all those years ago?"

"Rejection, mostly. I was scared I'd ruin our friendship if you didn't see me that way. There were countless times when I thought it was the perfect opportunity, but I kept chickening out. I tried during our movie nights or summers hanging out together, but I was a coward. I'd thought up so many different scenarios to say something, but I'd talk myself out of it. I was too scared of your reaction. Guess I figured it was better to have you as a friend than to potentially lose you forever."

"Noah," she whispers.

"I think back and wonder what would've happened if I had told you. Maybe my life wouldn't be like it is today. Maybe Gabe would still be alive, and I wouldn't have gone to prison. Maybe you'd be my wife, and Owen would be my son."

Tears stream down her face as I continue.

"I blame myself and will harbor a lifetime worth of guilt. I wish I would've found the courage to admit how in love with you I always was. At times, you'd look at me, and I felt the chemistry between us. But we never talked about it, and I just assumed it was one-sided."

Katie takes a step back and leans against the kitchen counter. "I-I can't believe this…"

"I'm sor—"

"It wasn't one-sided, Noah," she interrupts, keeping her eyes on mine. "I didn't know how to tell you either, especially because you were older and seemed way too cool to like a girl like me. I used to dream about you making a move and kissing me. I was way too scared to say anything, or I guess, even hint I wanted you to. Then Gabe came along, and when he asked me out, you didn't say anything. I thought maybe you'd fight for me if you had liked me that way, but you approved. You seemed happy for us, so I figured you saw me like a sister. I'd convinced myself that I'd imagined you flirting with me, and it was nothing more than a stupid teenage crush."

"I thought that's what you wanted and was trying to be supportive. I was jealous as fuck, but as long as you were happy,

I'd get over it. The truth is, I never moved on and couldn't. Knowing Gabe had the woman of my dreams and was purposely taking you for granted made my blood boil. If you were mine, I would've given you the world. I would've been home with you when you were dealing with pregnancy sickness. It fucked me up knowing he was cheating on you." I brush a hand through my hair, frustrated that I let so many years pass before saying anything. Shaking my head, I blow out a breath. "I should've just told you."

Katie takes two steps forward, closing the gap between us. I tuck loose hair strands behind her ear as we gaze at each other. When she leans into my touch, I slowly inch forward and wait. Emotions soar through me as her lips seek mine, and our tongues tangle together.

I know it's wrong, but at this moment, it feels so damn right to be kissing the woman I've wanted for as long as I can remember.

CHAPTER THIRTEEN

KATIE

Our lips crash together, and teenage me is screaming inside. Having him like this shouldn't feel so safe, so right, or so natural, but it does. It feels *perfect*.

I'm burning from the inside out as I moan and wrap my arms around his neck, pulling him even closer. I'm being greedy and desperate, but I don't give a damn. One kiss broke down barriers that have kept us apart since we were teenagers.

Noah's hand lowers, then grips my ass. I shouldn't like this. I shouldn't enjoy tasting his lips this much. I need him more than air, but I can't deny how the confusion hits me like a punch to the gut. I fight an internal battle with my head and my heart.

His hardness presses against my stomach, and my body wants to lose control. This time, I know the feelings are mutual. There's no denying it.

"Fuck," his soft lips whisper against mine. I swipe my tongue against his, deepening the kiss because he feels like home.

"Noah," I moan when he squeezes my breast. No man has kissed me with such intensity in…well, *ever*. Not even Gabe, and the fact that I'm comparing the two disgusts me.

What the hell am I doing right now?

His mouth trails to my ear, and I arch my back, pushing away all the lingering thoughts in my mind.

"You're so goddamn beautiful," he whispers, causing electricity to shoot down my spine. "I've wanted to kiss you for so long."

"Me too," I groan as he fuses our lips back together. Noah cups my face and tilts my chin up, twisting his tongue in deeper as I fist the fabric of his shirt. His fingers thread through my hair, and I release a throaty moan at how good it feels to be touched by him. My breathing increases, and though I don't know where this is leading, I don't care.

That is until I hear a car door slam outside.

I pull away, anxiousness and panic soaring through me. "Fuck." I step back, putting space between us. "That's Loretta and Owen."

Noah's eyes widen as I adjust my messy ponytail. Adrenaline spikes through me at how reckless I've been. "You have to hide right now," I tell him eagerly.

It won't matter if he's here or not because my lips are swollen and my face is flushed. My body's going to give it away before I even get a word out. This can't be how Loretta finds out Noah is here. Hell, she can *never* know.

Seconds later, Noah shuts himself in a hallway closet full of old lighting fixtures and spider webs. I feel awful that he has to hide away like an unwanted stray cat after everything he's been through. If it wasn't for her own judgments and her impact on my son's life, I wouldn't give two shits what she thought. However, it'd hurt Owen more than anything.

I pick up my coffee cup, hoping to seem normal as the door swings open. Loretta enters with a wide grin, and Owen follows her. I put on the act of my life as the floodgate of guilt opens. Devastated wouldn't even begin to describe her reaction if she knew what I was just doing and with who, and I already know there's zero chance she'd approve of our relationship.

There's a lot of hostility in the Reid family. My heart races, and turmoil twists inside me as my thoughts circle in a tangled web. I'm torn between my loyalty to Gabe's family and the way I've always secretly felt about Noah. When she comes closer, I try to ignore my beating heart. Loretta looks me over from head to toe, and I hope my face doesn't give me away. I take another sip of coffee.

"Hey, sweetie," she says. "Were you able to get a lot of work done today?"

"Yep, I focused on the bathroom. Got the toilet and cabinets knocked out, pretty much everything other than the tub and tile."

"That's incredible!" Loretta beams.

Owen's all smiles as he sets down his Bible and bag on the table that's still set up from when we had dinner with Noah.

"How was church?" I ask him.

"It was good." He sits on one of the folding chairs and yawns, already bored.

Loretta takes her attention off me and looks around, giving me a moment to relax and breathe.

"Oh wow, you've done a lot more since I've been here," she tells me, but I know it's bullshit. Not much has changed in the past two months. No monumental progress has been made, at least nothing she'd notice.

She turns to me. "Want to give me a quick tour?"

"Oh, there's not much to show. Just the bathroom," I blurt out eagerly, pointing toward the toilet and trash bags by the door. I let out a nervous laugh.

"Do you need some help carrying all that to the front for trash pickup?" she asks. "I could get Elliot out here to assist you."

One thing I appreciate about Loretta is how she's always offering to help. I don't know if it's because she's trying to overcompensate for her son cheating on me while pregnant or because it helps her cope with his death. I've always felt like it was a way for me to forget how badly he treated me. It wasn't her fault, though. Gabe made his own choices, no matter how his parents brought him up. The fact he was sleeping around on his pregnant wife has been swept under the rug and replaced with demonizing Noah.

"No, thanks. Granted, it was heavy getting it to that point, but I can manage," I say even though Noah did that. "I'm gonna get my cart from the garage and load all the trash on it. Don't want to kill my back or either of yours in the process!" I give her a smile.

"Alright, show me this bathroom then," she says.

My adrenaline spikes when we pass the closet as I lead her to the guest bathroom.

"This is fantastic progress, Katie. I can almost imagine what it'll look like when it's done. The space is much larger than what I remember."

It's hard for me to envision anything in here with the bubble gum pink tiles and tub.

"Yep, so this is it. I plan to take the rest out soon. Once I get the tile off, I can paint and put the flooring in. Hoping to within the next few weeks." I lean against the doorway, hoping she doesn't ask to see the master bedroom since it has the air mattress and blankets. She'd inevitably ask too many questions, and I'd have to lie to her, which I'd hate.

"Mom, can we go home?" Owen asks with an exaggerated yawn.

"He nearly fell asleep at dinner." Loretta grins. "He and some of the other boys were running around outside in the parking lot afterward and got worn out. We had lunch, then went to the park."

"Wow, okay. I should get him home then. I still need to make dinner, and he needs a bath."

"He's sweaty too," she admits as we enter the living room. "Make sure he cleans under his arms."

"Mimi!" Owen whines, and I laugh.

She gives him a kiss on his forehead. "I'll see you sometime this week after school."

A thud from the hallway grabs all of our attention, and my breath hitches. *Noah.*

"What was that?" Loretta asks, placing her hand over her heart.

"I-I'm not sure. Let me go see," I say, rushing to the hallway. I walk past the closet, knowing damn well the noise came from in there. I hurry and move to the bathroom, then Loretta steps into the hallway.

"What was it?" she asks.

I put on a fake smile. "Oh, the broom fell."

"Oh, thank goodness," she says, coming toward me. She's beside the closet door now.

I keep my eyes on her, hoping Noah stays still long enough for her to leave. I'm sure he can hear how close our voices are.

"Right!" I grab the broom and lean it back against the wall, hoping my acting skills are believable. "I was guaranteed by the previous owner that this house wasn't haunted." I let out a choked laugh. "Perhaps they were wrong."

Her eyes soften as she walks toward me, then grabs my hand. "If you ever want help here, don't hesitate to ask. We'd be happy to lend a hand."

"I know," I say. "You've done so much for me already, and I kinda want to do as much as I can on my own."

"If you change your mind, just ask." She squeezes my hand. "Elliot and I adore you both, and once this house is finished, it's going to be beautiful."

"Thank you. I'm trying my best," I admit, swallowing down my panic. She gives me a sweet smile combined with a hug before saying her goodbyes. I don't move an inch or even breathe until I hear her car reversing out of the driveway.

"I'm sorry," Noah whispers when I open the closet door.

"You almost got us busted," I scold. "And I nearly had a

panic attack when she followed me over here." I inhale a deep breath before releasing it.

Seconds later, Noah inches closer and palms my cheek. It takes all the willpower I have not to sink into his warmth and give into what we both want.

"Owen's here," I remind him, then take a step back. The added space is needed, but I immediately feel the loss.

The moment passes just as quickly as it came.

"Mom!" Owen yells. Noah follows me into the living room, and I try to act as if we didn't just share a heated moment. Immediately, Owen's face lights up with excitement.

"You're still here!" he says.

"Sure am." Noah offers him a boyish grin. "How was your day?"

"It was good. But tomorrow's Monday." Owen frowns.

Noah chuckles. "Back to school?"

Owen sighs, and I notice he gets antsy. "Yeah, ugh."

Noah and I look at each other, and though there's an awkwardness between us, I try to act normal in front of Owen. There are so many things I want to say, so many questions I still have about the confessions we admitted earlier. Losing control was dangerous and exhilarating, but I'm not sure it can happen again. Over a decade of pent-up emotions poured out of us today. It's a dangerous game to play, and there's a lot to lose—not just for me but for Owen too.

We need to discuss what took place and figure out what it means or where we go from here. I'm not sure how to even start the conversation, but things will get even more tense if we don't talk it out.

Owen yawns, and I check the time, realizing it's close to five.

"We probably should get going since you have to take a bath after dinner," I tell him, flattening down his hair that's a mess from playing.

"But Mom," he whines, and I know it's because he wants to

hang out with Noah. It makes me happy and breaks my heart at the same time.

"We have to be up early," I remind him.

He pushes out his bottom lip.

"I'll be around for a while," Noah promises him. "Probably will be around working on the house every now and then too."

Owen's face lights up. "Really? Maybe I can help too."

Shocked, I immediately beam. "Who would've thought all it took was Noah to get you interested."

Noah chuckles, and Owen crosses his arms over his chest. "I am sometimes," he says, and he puffs out his little chest.

"You do." I throw him a wink. "Go put your stuff in the car, and we'll get going."

"Bye, Noah." Owen gives him a wave, grabbing his Bible and bag.

I linger for a moment, not really sure what to say. "Let me know if you need anything, okay?"

"I will. Good night."

"Night," I say and force myself to walk away.

On the drive home, I try to process what happened earlier. I feel silly for not believing Gemma and Everleigh in high school, but he didn't make it obvious—not to me, at least. Had I known, maybe things would've been different, but it doesn't matter now. What happened can't be changed. All we can do is move forward, even if I don't know what that currently means.

CHAPTER FOURTEEN
NOAH

I never thought I'd have the guts to confess my feelings to Katie. However, something came over me yesterday, and I couldn't stop the words from coming out. Once they did, though, I felt a huge wave of relief because it's finally out there.

The last thing I anticipated was for her to admit they weren't one-sided and to *finally*...kiss her.

Decades of dreaming and fantasizing about that very moment couldn't do justice for how it actually felt.

Pure fucking heaven.

Like everything in the world made sense.

The axis that'd tilted had straightened.

Katie's soft lips tasted like the sweetest honey, and hearing her moan my name nearly had me losing control.

As much as I wanted more of her, I knew we had to slow down. Good thing Loretta showed up because I'm not sure I would've had the restraint to actually stop.

This puts Katie in an awkward position, and it makes me feel horrible, especially since she has to lie to Gabe's mom. Not to mention, Owen's in on it too. But the consequences of anyone finding out could mean the difference between life and death.

As I stand in the shower, I replay every second of our kiss. My cock hardens as I squeeze my eyes closed and recall the sweet sounds she made as my tongue danced with hers. I stroke my shaft with images of her floating in my mind, and I pump faster as the release builds. Soon, I'm muttering her name on my lips.

"Fuck," I hiss as I catch my breath. The number of times I've jerked off to Katie is embarrassing, but I don't care. It feels like I've waited an eternity for this chance with her.

After I get out, I wrap a towel around my waist and check my phone.

Katie: I'm on my way over with lunch.

Just as I'm about to text her back, I hear her clicking heels against the floor as she walks toward me.

"Noah?"

I step out of the bathroom and meet her gaze as she walks into the master.

"Hey," I respond sheepishly.

Her mouth falls open as she stares at my damp bare chest. She swallows hard, then meets my eyes.

"Uhh, hi. Hey. Sorry, I texted but—"

"No, it's fine," I interrupt her adorable rambling. "I just saw your text. I was in the shower."

"Yeah, I, um…see that. I'll just meet you in the kitchen." She gives me a nervous smile as she stumbles backward. "Come out when you're ready."

I smirk, holding back a laugh at how frazzled she is. "Sounds good. I'll be there in just a second."

After she closes the door, I put on some clean clothes. Once I'm decent, I find her standing at the counter.

"I hope tacos are okay," she says, handing me a paper plate and a can of Coke.

"Tacos are perfect." I grin. "Especially if you made them."

She lowers her eyes, but the corner of her lips tilts up into a smile.

"This is so good," I say after a couple of bites. "Definitely not the tacos I was getting in prison."

"Guess you probably had to change your palate, huh?"

I nod. "The first few months were rough. It wasn't all horrible, but it definitely wasn't anything to rave about. I was just lucky to eat."

"Well, you know Lawton Ridge isn't gonna let you go hungry now that you're back."

"No kidding. Between you and Belinda, I'm living my best life." I flash her a wink, and her cheeks heat.

"This might not be the best time to say anything, but I need to get something off my chest," Katie says.

"Alright, go ahead," I tell her, though her tone makes me nervous.

"Um…well, last night." She pauses, licking her lips. "We should talk about what happened between us."

I swallow down the last of my food and wipe my hands. "Okay, no problem," I reply hesitantly.

"I'm not sure I'm ready," she blurts out. "I mean, I've thought about kissing you since I was fifteen, and it was definitely a…kiss to remember."

"But?" I arch a brow because I know there's more.

"But I'm still upset with you for pushing me out of your life. Also, I don't know how to feel about this. Learning you've had feelings for me and the guilt I have because of Gabe leaves me very confused. Honestly, it's a lot to process." She pauses briefly, and her features soften. "More than anything, I want you to be safe, so you can stay here as long as needed. However, I think we should stay within the friendship boundaries."

Nodding, I pinch my lips together because as much as it hurts to hear, I'll respect her decision. "I understand, Katie. It's a lot for me to process too. I don't want you to do anything you aren't comfortable with, especially if you're unsure. But I would like the opportunity to explain why I acted the way I did."

"I-I'm not sure I'm ready for that conversation yet," she confesses. "Eventually."

"Of course." I stand and walk to her with open arms. "Is it okay to hug you?" I smirk.

"Yeah." She beams.

Wrapping my arms around her, I feel her warmth and don't ever want to let go. When I finally release her, I kiss the top of her head. "You being shorter than me was always an advantage."

She chuckles and looks up at me. "Why's that?"

"Because anytime I hugged you, I felt like your protector. Plus, getting to kiss your forehead was the highlight of my teenage life."

Katie snickers and playfully pushes me away. "Now you're just laying it on thick."

Laughing, I shrug. "Apparently not thick enough. I'm shocked you had no idea."

"Well, Gemma and Everleigh always said you did, but I never believed them."

"Gemma kept pushing me too, but..." I swallow hard. "By the time I actually hyped myself up to say something, I was too late."

"If I had any inkling that you felt the same, I wouldn't have dated Gabe," she admits earnestly. "You weren't fazed when he asked me out. I thought my best friends were just messing with me, or they just didn't want me to date Gabe."

"I was a coward," I admit. "I acted like it didn't bother me because I thought Gabe was purposely trying to get a reaction out of me. We'd always compete with each other, and I didn't want to give him one more thing to beat me at. Plus, you seemed happy. I realized I couldn't stay hung up on you, so I started dating what's-her-face."

"Claudia," she answers. "I thought you liked her?"

My shoulders rise and fall as I pinch my lips together. "Liked her enough to use her, I guess."

"Noah!" she scolds.

"I needed someone to join me for our double dates!" I defend. "Otherwise, I was the awkward third wheel, and there was no way I could do that. Not to mention, Gemma kept trying to set me up with her other friends too. So it was a win-win...*at the time.*"

"I'm learning so many new things about our teenage years."

"It feels like a lifetime ago," I say.

"It *was* a lifetime ago," she reiterates. "Now I'm a widow, have a ten-year-old son, a half-demolished house, and a career to focus on."

"You have your shit together more than you realize," I tell her.

"Kinda, *maybe*. But adulting sucks. Zero out of ten, would not recommend." She bursts out laughing, which causes me to do the same.

Moments later, I help Katie clean up, and we say our goodbyes. Once she's gone, I go back to looking at all the paper she has scattered on the counter and try to make sense of her scribbles.

"Noah!" Owen shouts my name as soon as he barges through the front door.

"Hey, buddy," I greet him with a high five as soon as he sees me. "What're you up to?"

"We brought dinner," he tells me, then I see Katie rushing forward with her hands full. "And dessert!"

"Hey, let me help." Quickly, I grab the slow cooker and carry it into the kitchen.

"Thanks," she says breathlessly, setting down a bag from Belinda's deli.

"I didn't know you guys were coming tonight. You know you're not responsible for feeding me. Gemma or my dad can bring me something." I pause, then lower my voice so only Katie hears me. "Though I do enjoy seeing you." I wink, and I swear she blushes.

"Well, it's hard to cook for only two, then the leftovers usually go to waste. Plus, Owen wanted to see you, so…" She shrugs.

"It smells delicious. Can't wait to try it."

After we're seated at the table and start eating, I mention the pieces of paper I read today. "So you haven't told me a whole lot about your plans for the house. I tried to read your chicken scratch, but I think I need a detailed list."

Katie glares. "That's because I'm writing notes as I watch videos, and they talk so damn fast, I can't always keep up."

"Ever hear of typing?" I snicker. "Okay, well, I saw one of your drawings, and I think it's a pantry?"

She immediately lights up. "Yes, the pantry of my dreams."

I snort, taking another large bite. "I'm very invested in what you consider the pantry of your dreams."

"You can make fun of it all you want, but it's gonna be amazing. I'm turning one of the closets into a floor-to-ceiling pantry that'll have plenty of storage. Wood shelves along all sides that are wide enough for wire baskets and Tupperware. I need to find a contractor for it, though, because it's beyond my skill level. But I already have the paint for it in the garage. "

"What color?" I ask.

"Like a robin's egg blue."

I scrunch my nose, trying to imagine it.

"Hold on, let me show you my Pinterest board."

"Really? People still use that?" I chuckle.

Owen giggles as he shoves potatoes in his mouth. "Mom's obsessed with Pinterest!"

Katie furrows her brows. "I am *not*! It just helps me visualize my ideas."

Moments later, she shows me her screen and scrolls through dozens of images. "Okay, this one here. This is how I'm hoping it'll turn out."

I grab the phone and study it. It doesn't look that hard. Most of the aesthetic she's after is in the wire baskets and white brushed jugs.

"It looks really nice, Katie," I tell her honestly, then wonder if I could actually do this for her. I could easily get it done while she's at work, and I doubt she'd notice.

Plus, she wouldn't have to hire someone, so it'd save her some money.

"So besides the pantry, what else are you thinkin' for the kitchen?"

"I want to restore the cabinets. It's far too expensive to get new ones built, so I'm gonna sand and paint them. I just need time to do it."

"My offer to help is still on the table. You can boss me around all you want…"

Katie nearly chokes on a piece of chicken and scolds me with her eyes.

After we're done eating, I help clean up. "So Owen, what do you think about the house? Are you excited to move into a new place?"

"Yeah, but it's taking literally forever!" He groans, and Katie laughs at his dramatics.

"I'm hoping to have it done before he graduates high school," she teases, though I remember her mentioning the end of the year as a dream goal.

"I doubt it'll take that long, especially if you let me take over some of the big items on your task list."

"I appreciate that, really I do, but I want to try to do as much as I can myself."

"Great, I'll be married before it's done." Owen sighs, and I burst out laughing.

"It's safe to say he got your personality."

"And attitude," she adds.

"So what did you bring for dessert?" I ask, remembering Owen mentioning it.

"I picked up a pie from Belinda's. She texted me and said she made your favorite."

"Sweet potato?" I ask excitedly.

Katie laughs. "Yep. Brought whipped cream too."

I press a palm over my chest. "You two spoil me."

"I saw your truck in the back parking lot," she says softly. "I'm so sorry about what they did to it."

"Don't worry. I'll clean it off, and Violet will look as good as new." I smirk. "Hopefully, anyway."

"Who's Violet?" Owen interrupts.

"My truck," I confirm.

He giggles. "You named your truck?"

"Of course."

"How'd you think of that name?" he asks. "I thought your truck was blue."

"It is, but Violet is a character from *Willy Wonka and the Chocolate Factory*. You ever seen that movie?"

Owen's eyes light up as a soft gasp escapes Katie's mouth.

"Mom *loves* that movie! We've watched it eighty bazillion times."

I chuckle at his exaggeration, though, knowing Katie, it might not be.

"Wait, hold up," Katie interrupts. "You named it after her?"

I flash her an amused smirk because I know where her head is going. "Yeah, she was my favorite character because she reminded me of you."

"What? How?"

My eyes nearly bug out of my head. "Are you kidding? You were always chewing gum! Plus, you were sassy and talked a lot like she did."

Katie covers her mouth when she laughs as Owen gets up to use the bathroom.

"Oh my God, that's right. To be fair, I always secretly hoped you'd kiss me one day, so I wanted to be prepared with fresh breath."

"I thought you did that because you didn't want me to kiss you...like a barrier of some sort," I admit.

"Wow...our communication skills kinda sucked, huh?" She shakes her head in disbelief. "Though, I would've been too nervous and choked on my gum or something."

I smile because it's definitely something teenage Katie would've overthought. Owen returns, and I finish our conversation.

"Well anyway...that's how Violet got her name," I tell him.

"I wonder how many times we saw that movie together," she says.

"Between the original and the remake, hundreds at least."

"Did you even like it that much?"

"I liked it enough to watch it with you," I say swiftly. "Some of my favorite memories were when we were together watching movies. Didn't matter what it was. I just wanted a reason to be around you."

We both stay silent as we stare at each other, neither saying what we truly want to say.

"Willy Wonka freaks me out!" Owen exclaims. "He's weird looking."

Katie and I laugh because we've had similar conversations about that character too.

The three of us finish eating, then dive into dessert. It's delicious and reminds me of several heartwarming memories from our youth.

Once the table is cleared, I help Katie organize the notebook paper that's sprawled all over the counter. Owen plays on his tablet, and I watch Katie walk around the house with her phone like she's making a list of things to do. Maybe my words got through to her, and she's actually writing things down for me to help with.

Although we've briefly talked about our past, I know our friendship isn't back to normal yet, but considering she hasn't recently slammed a door in my face or told me to fuck off is progress. It almost feels like we're friends again, but it won't be until I tell her the whole truth.

"Alright, buddy. It's time to go home and get you ready for bed."

Owen immediately groans, and Katie raises her brows.

"Plus, I gotta sign your agenda and pack your lunch for tomorrow."

"Ugh."

"Maybe I'll see you again this week?" I say to Owen, hoping to distract him. "Only if you're good for your mom, though."

Katie smirks, and Owen groans again. "Alright, fine. Maybe I'll talk Mom into doing pizza tomorrow night," Owen whispers to me.

"Maybe we can both talk her into it." I flash him a wink.

"Go buckle up in the car. I'll be there in a second," Katie tells him. We watch as he heads out, then moments later, Katie's standing in front of me.

"I know what I said at lunch today, and I don't want to send you any mixed signals, so I hope it's okay that we eat with you. It's been the two of us for so long that—"

"I love having dinner with you both," I interrupt, bringing a finger to her lips so she'll stop talking. "Plus, I'm very grateful for you, and I love your company."

"I just don't want to cause any confusion," she states. "Regardless of the hurt and our past, I enjoy spending time with you, and Owen does too. Though he's just met you, you've made quite an impression on him already."

I feel bad knowing Owen's probably craving male attention since he's been without it his whole life. He has his grandfathers, but it's not quite the same as having a father figure to talk to and play with.

"I have a lot of making up to do, for both you and Owen, so seriously…come over anytime. This is your house, after all."

She chuckles with a nod. "Right. Okay, well, I will see you tomorrow then."

I lean down and press my lips to her forehead. "Good night, Katie Bug."

She looks up at me with bright eyes. "I haven't heard that nickname since high school."

Smiling, I shrug. "And a decade later, it still suits you."

CHAPTER FIFTEEN

KATIE

TEN DAYS LATER

Life has been crazier than usual, but I don't mind. I'm trying not to overthink how I feel—how I've always felt—about Noah. The reality that we had feelings for each other and didn't do a damn thing about it has been a lot to process. I'm fighting a constant battle with my emotions over this. Of course, after I spilled my heart and revelations to Gemma and Everleigh, they gloated, and I got them telling me, "I told you so."

It doesn't help me much because now they're encouraging me to "go for it." I wish a decision like this was easy, but it's not *only* about me anymore. I have a son to think about and how dating Noah will impact him too.

On top of that, I'm well aware of how this could affect my relationship with Gabe's parents. Loretta and Elliot have always been there for me, and they'd never support Noah being in our lives. They understand I'm best friends with Gemma and have been for two decades, but they still act as if she doesn't exist. If they knew what was going on, Owen would lose his relationship with them, and I'd never forgive myself if that happened.

I don't like deceiving them. However, it's necessary for Noah's safety right now. Until he finds out who's threatening his life, he can't go home. I don't think Loretta or Elliot are behind the brick and bomb, but I can't exclude them just yet. If I had to guess, it's probably someone close to Gabe who doesn't approve of Noah being back and is seeking revenge.

So until the risk is gone, Noah will stay at my house, and I'll continue bringing him lunch and dinner. The couple of times I couldn't, Belinda or his dad made sure he ate. However, I enjoy doing it, and Owen loves having him around too.

Lately, Owen's been a different kid, and there's no denying Noah's positive effect on him. They talk about school, sports, and fun summer activities they can do together, such as hiking, camping, and even taking a road trip to the coast to swim in the ocean. However, I don't have the heart to tell Owen it might not happen.

When I visit on my lunch breaks, Noah and I end up reliving our high school days. As we talk about our past, all the memories and details I'd forgotten resurface. Our time together typically ends with us laughing our asses off at the shit we'd do. Since Lawton Ridge is so small, the teachers knew our parents and grandparents, which meant nothing could be hidden. When we got into trouble, they'd conveniently run into our parents somewhere in town and rat us out.

When Noah and I got caught sneaking out of study hall, Ms. Landry gave us detention. Instead of giving our parents the slips, we signed for each other and turned them in. We would've gotten away with it had she not mentioned it to my mom at a barbecue. I was grounded for an entire month.

However, leaving school and driving around with Noah was worth it. Though we often fought over the radio, he'd eventually give in and was forced to listen to me belt out the lyrics. The memories of driving around with the windows down, listening to music are unforgettable.

"You finally got laid," Missy blurts out as she walks into my office uninvited.

"Excuse me?" I ask, ignoring her as I finish typing an email.

"You've been smiling nonstop for over a week and haven't yelled at Yolanda in days. She screwed up so bad the other day we had to stay late, and not a peep came out of you, so I've come to the conclusion that you're gettin' laid. The question is, who's the lucky guy with the magic penis?"

My fingers stop as I narrow my eyes at her.

"So because I'm in a good mood, I'm automatically having sex?"

"In my experience, yes. And by how you've been prancing around, I'd say it's happening frequently. You're gettin' regular dick without a doubt. So whose is it?" She waggles her eyebrows at me.

I pick up my cold mug of coffee and take a sip, trying to pretend she's not there. "*Prancing* around?" I muse. "I have no idea what you're talking about. I'm not getting *anything*...except annoyed."

"Did you get a new vibrator? Because that could also explain your sudden mood change."

I half choke, half swallow my drink before setting it down. "You Gen Zers are too comfortable discussing your sex lives."

She points a finger at me with a gasp. "So there *is* sex happening! I knew it."

I stand. "No. Been going solo for a long time. Now, if you'll excuse me, I'm going on my lunch break."

"Well, whatever it's worth, I've never seen you happier." She smirks as I playfully shove her out of my office.

"Go do your job before I fire you."

She cackles because she knows I can't, but either way, I wouldn't. She's a great teller and has excellent people skills.

I didn't have the chance to prepare any food ahead of time, so I walk to the deli to grab something for Noah and me.

When I enter, Belinda immediately greets me. She knows the situation, but we don't talk about it outside of our circle, so the conversation stays light.

"I can ring her up while you finish," Brittany says as she comes toward me from the kitchen.

"Two soup and sandwich combos," Belinda tells her.

"Two, huh? Must be hungry today," she says in a sugary-sweet tone that's so fake. I want to roll my eyes but refrain.

"I'm getting one for a coworker," I answer, reaching into my wallet for my card.

Brittany smiles as she swipes it, then hands it back.

"How's Owen doin'?" she asks while Belinda bags my items.

"He's fine, thank you."

"My Anthony has been beggin' me to set up a playdate. I know you're super busy with work and your house, but maybe I could take Owen off your hands on a Saturday? I'm sure the boys would love to play baseball and video games."

Belinda finally hands me my food and grins. "There you go, darlin'. Hope y'all enjoy."

"Thanks, you know we will." I turn toward Brittany. "I'm sure Owen would love that, but I'll have to find a good date and get back to you. His grandparents take turns seeing him on the weekends."

"Sure, no problem. Just have Owen tell Anthony when and we'll set something up."

"Will do. Bye now." I go to my car parked behind the bank and try to ignore the weird vibe Brittany gives me. Not to mention, I'm still bothered by the way she was all over Noah at the retirement party. She barely knows him. Hell, she doesn't know me either.

The last thing I'd do is allow Owen to go anywhere with that woman. Perhaps I'm being petty, but my gut instincts tell me otherwise.

As I drive to the house, the excitement I feel when I see Noah returns.

"Hey," he immediately greets. By the dust on his jeans, I can tell he was messing with something around the house. "Let me take that. It smells delicious."

His hands brush mine as he takes the bag from my grip, and I smile up at him. "Belinda's cookin'."

"Ahh, perfect." He unpacks it as I grab silverware and paper plates.

"I talked to Tyler this morning," he says as we sit at the table.

"Any news?"

"No, but I spoke to Sheriff Todd afterward, and the investigation is still active. Thankfully, there hasn't been any other suspicious activity."

"That's good. Guess the plan to move your truck and disappear worked."

"Yeah, it's hard to target someone who's not around." He shrugs.

I reach over and cover his hand with mine. "They're gonna find out who's behind this."

"Hopefully, but a part of me worries it won't solve my problems. The stigma of being an ex-con will follow me for the rest of my life. If it's not this person throwing bricks and bombs through windows, it'll be someone else."

I feel sick to my stomach and am more worried for Noah than I want to admit.

"I know it's easier said than done, but positive thinking goes a long way. Many have rebuilt their lives under worse circumstances."

"I want to, but what happened didn't just affect me. It affected the whole town." He blinks, then meets my eyes. "Especially *you*."

"I wish you would've let me be there for you," I say softly.

"You didn't give me a choice. You took that from me."

"Katie, I know." He sets down his sandwich and inches closer.

"And if you're ready, I'll explain everything. It won't change a damn thing, but maybe it'll help you understand that it wasn't you, it was me."

I swallow hard because while I do want answers, I haven't been ready to hear them. But it's time, especially if we're going to repair our friendship.

Slowly, I nod. "Okay, I'm ready."

I take a bite of my sandwich as he swallows down a spoonful of soup. He lowers his eyes briefly before meeting mine, and I can see the remorse and pain behind his gaze.

"After the incident, I was overwhelmed with shame and didn't want anyone's pity. Going to prison wasn't punishment enough, but losing you would hurt me the most. I assumed you'd be disgusted with me and what I'd done, but I should've known better. You weren't even mad at me. Instead, you cried on my shoulder at the funeral and clung to me like I was your life support. I didn't deserve it. Once I was behind those bars, I went numb. I craved your touch and allowed my thoughts to self-sabotage everything. I quickly went into a downward spiral of anger and depression. Images of Gabe on the floor unconscious consumed me while the memories of him hooked to the ventilator fighting to live haunted my dreams. It was impossible to sleep or eat, and when you sent me that first letter, I couldn't understand why you didn't hate me. I despised myself and thought I didn't deserve your friendship."

Noah licks his lips as I take in his words. The pain in his voice and how low he thought of himself hurts my heart.

"When you sent me the second letter with a baby picture of Owen, the realization that you'd be raising him as a single mom hit me so hard, I lost control. I got into a fight with my cellmate over something so damn stupid, I ended up getting into more trouble. It's probably why my dad has suggested I talk to a therapist more than once."

"What were you fighting over?" I ask to break the tension.

"Honestly, I don't even remember. I just wanted him to hit me. I needed to feel physical *pain*."

I swallow hard. "Noah."

"I felt dead inside, and that was the only thing that made me feel alive, even if it was only temporary. What I did to you wasn't right by any means, but ignoring your letters and denying your request to visit was how I punished myself. It was selfish, and I realize that now."

"You wanted to suffer?" I ask softly, trying to understand.

He nods sheepishly. "Yes, I deserved it. You were giving me a get out of jail free card, and after what I'd done to you and Owen, I couldn't accept it. After years of pushing you away, I was too embarrassed for you to see me at rock bottom in a jumpsuit and unshaven. I didn't even want Gemma and my dad to visit, but I knew that I couldn't stop them."

"You never have to be embarrassed about anything in front of me," I ensure him. "Ever. No matter what. I thought you knew that?"

"I did," he confirms. "But it didn't matter because I was ashamed and mortified. Though I'm in love with you, I knew I'd never deserve you, and I thought if I pushed you away enough, you'd move on and find true happiness. I'd hoped anyway. I thought when I did get out, you would've gotten remarried and moved on, making the temptation to kiss you disappear."

My heart nearly bursts out of my chest, and I blink hard as I repeat his words in my head. "Did you just admit that you're in love with me?"

He tilts his head and furrows his brows. "Yeah, I-I thought I made that pretty clear when we kissed."

I hold up my hand and shake my head. "No, no. You said you had a *crush* on me and *were* in love with me. As in, past tense."

The corner of his lips tilts up slowly. "I've been in love with you, Katie Walker, since I was fifteen years old, maybe even younger. That's never changed and never will. I tried for years to forget those feelings, but it was useless. My heart can't not be in love with you."

I blink to keep tears from falling, but they roll down my cheeks anyway. The ache in my chest feels like it'll combust at any moment.

"I really want to kiss you right now…" I whisper. "But I'm so conflicted," I choke out, hating that I'm crying in front of him. Doing what my heart says shouldn't be this complicated, but it always has been when it comes to Noah.

Noah kneels next to me, and I turn slightly while wiping my cheeks.

"I know exactly how you feel, Katie. There's absolutely no pressure, and I don't expect anything from you. As long as I have your friendship, I'll die a happy man."

I chuckle softly as I stare into his deep brown eyes. "You have nothing to worry about. It's exhausting trying to stay mad at you, and I don't want to harbor that anger anymore."

Noah smirks at me as if I've just hung the moon, and my cheeks heat. "What?" I ask.

"Only took…five and a half weeks." He winks, and it's then I realize what he's implying.

"Oh my gosh." I laugh, then playfully push his arm. "Was this an evil plan to get me to admit I'm no longer mad at you? Is there even someone after you?" I tease.

He snorts, then stands and kisses my forehead. Butterflies surface in my stomach as a shiver slides down my spine.

"Yes, unfortunately, but at least one good thing's come of it."

He sits in his chair, and I suddenly miss his closeness. These conflicting feelings are tearing me up inside.

"Well, whoever they are won't win against us. Not this time anyway," I reassure him. "I'm glad we're starting fresh."

"Me too. It's a new beginning, and I'm ready."

We finish eating, and as we're cleaning up, I mention something weighing on my mind. "Do you remember how we used to pass notes to each other in middle and high school?" I ask.

He chuckles smoothly. "How could I forget? Those got me into trouble just a couple of times."

I laugh and nod. "Me too. I actually found a box of our old notes a few weeks ago."

"Really? That's funny, I was looking through some of my old yearbooks. Should've known you wanted me by how you signed it."

"What'd I write?"

Noah's eyes gaze down my body as we stand next to each other in the kitchen. I do the same to him, except I'm imagining what's underneath his clothes.

"You put, 'Your Girl for life' and then 'ha-ha' in parentheses."

My eyes widen, and I smack my forehead. "Oh my God, that's embarrassing."

"Are you kiddin'? I cherished it. Might've jerked off to the fantasy of you whispering that in my ear."

"Noah!" I swat his chest. "You were too young for that."

He barks out a laugh. "You can't be serious. I was sixteen. I'd been doing it for years at that point, mostly to images of you."

"Stop, oh my God." Now I know my face is beet red.

He smirks, grabbing a paper towel and spraying some cleaner on it before going to the table. "Wouldn't be surprised if Owen is taking extra long showers."

I release a groan and inhale a deep breath. Owen having a father would come in handy right about now. He needs a man to talk about this kind of stuff with. I don't even know what I'd say. Is it time for the birds and the bees talk?

"Katie, I can see the dials spinning in your head." Noah moves in front of me as if he knows exactly what I'm thinking. "Owen only has a few years before he's a full-blown teenager. Do you remember all the trouble we got into at thirteen and fourteen years old?"

"Half of those ideas were yours!" I scold.

He cackles. "Yeah, and the other half were yours."

"I guess I didn't realize how fast he's growing up. I kinda forgot that he'll need a man to talk to him about puberty and girls. He won't want his mom to tell him what to expect."

"You're right," Noah agrees. "But luckily, he has a lot of people in his life, though. There's me, Tyler, and his grandfathers. He might've already had the talk with one of them."

"You think so?" My heart races at the idea.

Noah shrugs. "Only one way to find out. Also, he has access to the internet, so it's likely he's already stumbled across something on his tablet."

"Ugh," I say.

I check my phone and realize I'm going to be late returning to work. Our conversation is all I'm gonna be thinking about for the rest of the day. If we'd restored our friendship years ago, where would we be today? I wonder if we'll ever be able to get back to how things used to be or if we'll always have this lingering *what-if* between us. "Shit, I gotta go. My break is over."

"No worries, I'll finish cleaning up here and look through your list for anything else I can do."

"Thank you," I say.

"For what?"

"For sharing with me what you went through and why you acted the way you did. I can't pretend to have any idea how being in prison was for you, but please know I'm here for you. I always have been. You don't need to hide from me anymore," I tell him sincerely. "Please, don't push me away again. I don't think I can survive it twice."

Noah closes the gap between us and cups my face. He lowers his forehead and presses it to mine as our breaths entangle.

"You deserve the best, even if the best isn't me, but I'll never make that mistake again." He pulls back slightly until our eyes meet. "I can promise you that."

CHAPTER SIXTEEN

NOAH

It's been one week since Katie and I opened up to one another. Though I was nervous, I'm happy I gave her a glimpse of what I went through and how I felt. I think we've found common ground, and it feels nice for the truth to be out in the open. Understanding where her head and heart have been opened my eyes. Her feelings are valid, and I should've never ignored her while I was in prison.

The elephant that's been sitting on my chest, smothering me for the past decade, is finally gone. I can finally breathe again, even if I'm not sure what our future holds. If all we can be is friends, I'll take it, although it's not what I want.

After Katie showed me all the ideas she had from her Pinterest boards, I started working on the pantry. It's been five days, and she hasn't noticed, so I'll be excited to surprise her when it's finished.

After I saw what she envisioned for the kitchen and how excited she was about completing it, I decided to focus there next. Katie has a lot of tools here, but she's missing key things like a circular saw. Dad brought his tools over, and I salvaged some old wood and supplies I found in Katie's garage. After I sanded and stained the wood, I measured and cut the boards, then got to work building her dream pantry. It took four long days to finish, and my dad's coming over this morning to look at it before I show her. He has an eye for these things, and I want his opinion.

Dad calls to let me know he's on his way.

"Hey, stranger," he says when he walks in, then looks around the place. "I've always loved this house. It has character."

I lead him to the kitchen. When he sees what I've been able to accomplish in such little time, his face lights up.

"I removed the cabinetry here and rebuilt the shelving. And look…" I reach forward, showing him the slide-out drawer I added at the bottom for storing pots and pans.

"Noah, this is incredible." Dad flashes a cheeky grin. "You did an amazing job. And this blue color, it looks good."

"Katie already had it picked out. She's still deciding if she wants to keep the countertop or replace it."

My dad runs his hand across the old linoleum that has a weird yellow tint to it. "I bet she upgrades."

"Eventually, I'm sure. But at least now, she won't have to pay someone thousands to build this," I say, taking a step back to admire my work.

"It's gonna hold a ton of food and storage. You could start a business doing this, son. Not everyone can whip up a pantry in less than a week with limited supplies."

"I was highly motivated," I admit, appreciating his genuine words. "I know how much it means to Katie to have this, and now she won't have to pay anyone to do it."

"Well, you'll be glad to know there haven't been any more threats. I got the red spray paint off your truck, and it's waiting for you at the house. You should come home and go back to work. I'm sure Tyler could use your help. Plus, I miss seeing you," he admits, and I immediately feel guilty. He's barely seen me since I've been released.

"Thanks for doing that, Dad. And you're right. It's been long enough, I suppose. I'll let Katie know after I show her this that tonight will be my last night. Hopefully, she'll like it so I can continue to help her on my days off. She could hate it, though, considering I didn't exactly tell her my plans."

"She's gonna love it," he reassures me with soft eyes. "And I'm sure she's happy to have your experience. She's been working on this house for a while."

"I hope you're right." I try to shake off the nerves of the anticipation.

Dad's phone rings, and when he pulls it out of his pocket, I see it's Belinda calling. He answers it, softens his tone, and walks through the living room. I hesitantly follow him onto the front porch and look around outside. I've been inside for two weeks, but I'm still nervous someone's after me.

When he's off the phone, he glances over at me with a smile. Seeing him this happy after all this time gives me hope for my own future. "She wants me to have lunch with her today," he tells me.

"You gonna propose soon?" I ask, giving him a nudge.

Dad laughs and shakes his head as we walk to his truck. "You can meet us at the deli around twelve if you're hungry," he offers.

"Appreciate it, but I wanna do some finishing touches before tonight."

"Alrighty. See you soon, right?" He pops a brow.

"Yep. Probably late tonight." I wave goodbye as he cranks his truck, then reverses out of the driveway.

When I go inside the house, I clean up around the place. I sweep up the sawdust and get rid of the scrap wood. At some point, I take a break to eat and call Gemma.

"Hey!" she says in a high-pitched voice after the first ring.

"You can't be *that* excited to talk to me," I tease.

"Of course I am. You're my favorite brother."

"I'm your only brother," I remind her.

"Oh yeah, almost forgot," she says with a laugh. "What's goin' on? Hold on." Gemma pulls the phone away from her ear and yells Tyler's name. "It's Noah!"

I hear shuffling in the background.

"Am I on speakerphone?" I ask.

"Yes," Tyler says loud and clear.

I roll my eyes. "Well, since you're both here, just thought I'd let you know I'd like to come back to work on Monday. I mean, if you still want me around," I offer, giving Tyler a pass, especially after the window incident.

"Of course we do. You can come in today if you're free," Tyler tells me.

It makes me laugh. "Thanks, man. I'm busy today but looking forward to returning. You two should see what I built for Katie."

"Uhh," Gemma hesitates nervously.

"Don't worry. We discussed it, and she was okay with me helping. Now, I did kinda take it upon myself to build her a pantry, but she showed me pictures of what she wanted," I explain. "And I nailed it based on her Pinterest board."

"And if you didn't...say goodbye to your balls," Gemma warns.

Tyler laughs. "Yeah, I wouldn't want to cross her, especially since she's learned how to use power tools and hammers. I bet she has a helluva swing."

I snort. "I'll send you a picture, and you two can be the judge of it."

"Has she seen it yet?" Gemma asks.

"Not yet. I'm showing her today after she gets off work." I run my fingers through my hair, hoping she doesn't kill me.

"I'm sure she'll like it," Tyler encourages. "Send over that pic."

"I will. And if I disappear after today, you know Katie did it,"

I joke. "Dad said things have been really quiet, so I'll probably be home later tonight. I'm excited to work again and help y'all finish the gym."

"Hell yeah," Tyler says.

"Anyway, I'll let y'all go. See you sooner than later," I say, not wanting to linger on this call much longer.

After I hang up, I send them some pictures. Gemma replies instantly, telling me she loves it and wants one in their future house. I go to the bedroom and pack up my belongings. After I undo the stopper in the air mattress, I fold the blankets, then stack the pillows. Letting out a breath, I realize how much I'm actually gonna miss being here. It wasn't ideal, but it gave me the opportunity to see and speak with Katie every day.

Things will probably change after I leave, but hopefully, we won't take two steps back from how far we've come.

I keep myself busy until I decide to hop in the shower. Just as I'm putting on some clean clothes, Katie's car pulls into the driveway, and my nerves get the best of me. Though I'm confident I made it as perfect as I could for what she wanted, I'm still worried she'll be upset. Though the house has a chill, I feel as if I'm sweating.

Moments later, the front door swings open, and Katie enters with Owen trailing her. As soon as he sees me, his face lights up with excitement.

"Noah! You have to see my writing project!" He pulls something out of his backpack.

"Yeah, buddy. Let me see," I say, grabbing the notebook he hands me. He's bouncing on his feet as I flip through the hand-drawn comic book pages. "Whoa! You did all of this by yourself?"

He nods with a proud smile. "Yeah! I love superheroes but wanted to write one with a kid my age."

"I'm impressed," I say honestly. "The detail is really good. You've got some mad skills, Owen."

ONLY US

Owen stares up at me. "You really think so?"

"Dude, I'd never lie about something like this. You're talented," I say, reading through the pages until I hit the end. "Wow. I guess it's true that not all superheroes wear capes."

"It's based on a true story." Owen puffs out his little chest.

Katie pats his back. "Enough tall tales."

"Mom! What if I were a superhero and could save people from the bad guys? If my dad would've had someone to save him…"

The mood changes immediately, and it feels like all the air has been sucked from the room. Based on Katie's reaction, I'm not alone. She clears her throat, keeping her smile locked in place. "You're right. Now let's eat dinner. Go set the table," she urges.

As Owen's busy, I stop Katie. "Real quick, I have something to tell you."

"Is everything okay?"

"I think so. I mean, it might not be after you see what I did. Close your eyes."

She furrows her brows, but she doesn't argue. I carefully lead her into the kitchen while she covers her face.

"Ready?" I whisper close in her ear, and she shivers.

She nods, and I open the door. I tell her to look, and she blinks hard.

"Noah," she whispers, opening the door wider and peeking inside. "It's exactly how I imagined. How did—" Before she finishes her sentence, Katie wraps her arms around me and hugs me tight. Her breasts press against my chest, and her mouth is so close to mine as she thanks me, I'm tempted to kiss her again. Her eyes flutter closed, and I can almost taste her lips again.

"Mom?" Owen calls, and his feet shuffle across the wood floors. Katie immediately puts space between us, but her breasts continue to rise and fall as her pulse throbs in her neck.

"Yeah?" Katie walks toward him as he enters the kitchen.

"I think we left the food in the car," he says, then grins at me.

"You're right. I'll go grab it," she says. Owen walks out, and when Katie turns, her gaze nearly pierces through me.

She wraps her arms around me, and my hands slip around her waist. I pull her close and feel her hot breath on my neck. We're so damn close.

"Thank you so much for building this. I love it. You really didn't have to do any of this. It seems like so much, almost *too* much."

Heat rushes through my body, and as if she noticed our closeness, she puts space between us. Immediately, I feel the loss of her warmth and body pressed against mine. I clear my throat.

"I wanted to do this for you. And I want to keep helping you, if you'll let me."

She flashes a sexy smirk and nods before walking away. I'm thankful for the separation because I need a moment to catch my breath and readjust myself. I head to the table, and as soon as she returns, I smell the fried chicken.

After Owen passes out the napkins, we fill our plates, then dig in. So many stolen glances are shared between Katie and me that the sexual tension is almost unbearable. Though we're keeping up with small talk, all I can imagine is kissing her again, having her melt into me once more, and it makes me wonder if we'll ever have a real chance of being together.

Once we're done eating, I help clean up. Katie goes back to the kitchen, and I follow her while Owen plays with his tablet. As she looks over everything again, I lean against the counter and watch her run her hand across the freshly painted wood.

"You were right. The paint color actually looks really nice," I admit.

"I still can't believe you did this. It's too much."

The way her face lights up as she looks around makes it all worth it.

"It's not enough." I lower my voice. "There's something else I need to talk to you about, Katie. I'm going back home tonight. It's time."

She nods and gives me a small smile. "I figured it was coming."

"I can't stay hidden forever, or whoever is doing this wins. I served my time already and can't continue being a prisoner. The police still have an open investigation, and my dad said nothing else has happened."

"You're right," she tells me. "You deserve to get back to normal."

I step forward and take her soft hand. "I still want to help you on the weekends, if you'll let me. Getting this house finished before the end of the year is doable with a little elbow grease."

She grins and nods. "I'd like that." I kiss her knuckles, and she tucks her bottom lip into her mouth.

"You're amazing. I don't deserve you," I say, meeting her eyes.

"Why would you think that?"

"Because you let me be a part of your life again after everything I did and how badly I hurt you."

She sucks in a shallow breath, and we stare at each other as the tension between us rises. A thump sounds in the next room, and we rush toward it, only to see Owen picking up his tablet from the floor.

"Whoops."

"Did it break?" Katie asks.

"Nope!" he says with a grin, flipping the screen around.

Katie turns back to me. "Oh, before I forget, I have a girls' day planned with Gemma and Everleigh tomorrow. Owen's going to my parents."

"Do I have to?" he groans.

I smile at him, getting an idea. "You can hang out with me tomorrow. I mean, if your mom says it's okay."

Katie tilts her head at me as if she's unsure.

"Yeah, we're related, so it should be fine!" Owen immediately tries to convince Katie. "Pretty, pretty please, Mom!"

"Are you sure?" She glances at me.

"Absolutely. Just drop him off in the morning and enjoy your girls' day."

A wide smile sweeps across her perfect lips. "Okay, deal. I'll call my mom and let her know."

Owen's over the moon.

"Do you want a ride home so you don't have to carry everything back?" Katie asks.

"Sure, that'd be awesome."

Owen follows me to the bedroom and helps me grab my stuff.

"Tomorrow is gonna be so much more fun now," he tells me. "You like Marvel movies?"

"Love them. Which is your favorite?" I ask.

"I love the *Avengers*!"

He's so excited that all I can do is laugh even though I have no idea what that is, considering I've been locked up. We'll have a good time, and I'm actually looking forward to hanging out with him. Seeing what it's like to entertain a ten-year-old all day will definitely be interesting.

"Go take that stuff out to the car, then buckle in," Katie tells Owen. I grab the rest of my things and head out while Katie locks the door.

Within minutes, we turn into my dad's driveway.

"Thanks again for everything," I say.

"You're welcome. Thank you for my dream pantry." She smiles at me with hooded eyes.

Turning, I look at Owen in the back seat. If he wasn't in the car, I know I'd press my lips against hers. The moonlight casts a bright glow across his face.

"See you tomorrow," I say to him.

I offer him a high five, and he returns it. "Yes!"

ONLY US

It's not lost on me how big of a step it is for her to leave Owen with me all day. I also realize how much is at risk, and I'm determined not to fuck this up.

A smile touches my lips as I walk inside because she loved the pantry, and I got to keep my balls after all.

CHAPTER SEVENTEEN

KATIE

"Did you brush your teeth?" I ask Owen. He's been up and ready to go for over thirty minutes. Typically, he's dragging ass in the mornings, but not today. I'm happy he's amped to hang out with Noah, but I'm a little nervous about it. Noah's not exactly experienced with kids, but I anticipate they'll be fine.

As soon as I enter the living room, Owen bounces off the couch and grabs his backpack. Last night, he stuffed it full of DVDs and board games. He even has his basketball waiting by the door.

"I'm ready!"

I laugh at his tone as we go to the car. On the way to Noah's, Owen talks nonstop about the plans he's made today, and I'm an anxious wreck about it, especially when it comes to Owen bringing up his dad. I trust Noah, but this is new territory for me. Owen's only ever been left with my parents, in-laws, and close friends.

As we pull into the driveway, Noah walks outside. I roll down the window, noticing how good he looks in his tight T-shirt and dark wash jeans. He looks and smells as if he just got out of the shower. Owen can't unbuckle himself fast enough and rushes out of the car.

"You're sure about this? I can still call my mom and—"

He chuckles, and I'd be lying if I didn't enjoy the sound of it. "Katie, we're gonna have a blast. We'll be fine," he confirms, the smile never fading. "Gonna order a pizza and shoot off fireworks in the street."

My eyes widen, and he bursts out laughing. "Go have fun. Relax," he says, tapping the top of my car.

I shake my head. "Just make sure you give him back to me the same way I left him."

"Tell Gemma I said hey," he offers with a wink. "And try not to talk about me *too* much."

I scoff and roll my eyes, but he already knows how Gemma and Everleigh are, so there's no denying it.

"Be good, Owen," I say. "Love you."

"Love you, Mom. See ya later!" Owen waves, and I back out of the driveway.

It takes me no time to arrive at the spa. The quaint red brick building has been completely remodeled. As soon as I walk inside, I'm bombarded by my best friends.

"Yay, you came!" Everleigh says as Gemma pulls me into a hug.

"Mimosa?" Everleigh asks, and I have a feeling she's already downed one.

"Absolutely!" I barely get out as I'm handed a fluke.

Gemma pokes out her bottom lip. "I can't wait till I can have alcohol again, even if it's just a little!"

"It's okay. I'll drink for two," Everleigh taunts.

Her antics make me snort.

"I'm sure you will," Gemma says.

Soon, we're shown to the back to change into soft robes and slippers. The mimosas are flowing through my bloodstream, and I feel relaxed as hell as I lie on the massage table.

Gemma's in the middle of me and Everleigh and clears her throat. "So we have some things to discuss."

"Oh yeah?" I ask, playing stupid, but I know exactly what she's referring to.

"Spill it!" Everleigh demands. "You haven't given us a proper update." I'm relieved we're out of town, and the massage therapists don't know who we're talking about.

I sigh. "What do ya wanna know?"

"*Everything*." Gemma grins.

"Okay, I have a question for both of you first." My heart hammers in my chest as I delve into this conversation. "Was it really stupidly obvious that Noah had a crush on me when we were younger?"

Everleigh bursts into laughter. "I'm sorry, it's the mimosas, but also that's hilarious you ask. Yes, of course, *undeniable*."

My face contorts, and Gemma notices. "You really couldn't tell?" she asks.

"Well, no. You both knew I thought I was friend-zoned," I admit. "He was my best friend, but it's not like he ever made a move."

"I literally told you he did!" Gemma throws back.

"Yeah, but he never acted on it, then Gabe came along and..." I trail off as the woman puts her elbow into my shoulder.

"Honey, you're tense," she says, and I try to relax.

"So let me guess...he finally admitted it, and you were shocked. How'd you respond?" Everleigh asks.

I suck in a breath. "I told him the truth and admitted how I always felt about him too and..."

"And what?" Gemma asks.

"And then we kissed," I say with a grin, remembering how it felt to have his lips on mine.

Gemma gasps.

"Finally!" Everleigh shouts.

"But we were interrupted and had to finish talking about it

later. Then we talked about why he pushed me away while he was locked up. It was great hearing the whole truth, but I just don't know how to feel. I'm conflicted because of Gabe's parents," I admit.

"Well, what does your heart say? Deep inside, none of that logical bullshit," Gemma asks.

I think about it as my massage therapist works out the knots in my neck. I'm scared to death to say my true feelings out loud.

"I've always been in love with Noah, and I guess…if things were different—"

"Things are different *now,* and you have the opportunity to create your future, so do it. If your feelings are mutual, what's stopping you now?" Everleigh interjects.

"Exactly," Gemma adds. "Giving Tyler a second chance was one of the best decisions of my life. I ran from him and my heart so damn much and wasted a lot of time. Who gives a shit what anyone has to say? It's about *you* and what makes *you* happy while doing the best you can for Owen. Anything else is just outside noise."

My emotions begin to bubble. "But Loretta and Elliot…"

Gemma turns her face toward me, and I meet her eyes. "They'll get over it. There's no way they'd ever give up seeing their grandson. I know my aunt and uncle better than that. They might not agree and be angry about it, but Owen is the only piece of Gabe they have left. Now, you might get guilt-tripped and yelled at, but you can't allow them to control you. Following your heart is all you should worry about."

"She's right," Everleigh says. "I know it's cliché as hell, but you only live once. And you deserve to be happy. We support your decision and know how good the two of you would be together."

"And I will selfishly always be Team Noah and Katie!" Gemma reminds me.

"Me too, and then after you and Noah get married, we'll all be sisters," Everleigh exclaims. "So make it happen, pronto!"

I snort. "But what if it all goes wrong?" Losing Noah twice would not only destroy me again but it'd affect Owen too.

"And what if it all goes right?" Gemma counters. "Then you get the happily ever after you deserve, and Owen will have a man in his life who cares about him more than anyone else could."

Though it seems amazing, it's almost too good to be true.

Their words drift through the room just like the mimosas in my bloodstream. I close my eyes and inhale a deep breath. "You're both right, but I don't even know where to start."

Gemma chuckles. "It starts with you giving him a chance."

A smile touches my lips, and it's decided, just like that. My heart has always beat for Noah, and though I loved Gabe when we were together, it hadn't felt right.

"Not to change the subject or anything, but have either of you been to the deli lately?" Everleigh asks. "I went a few days ago, and Brittany was working, so we started talking. Then she started asking about my boutique, which is fine, but then it turned to Tyler's gym and how Smith and Noah were doing there. Of course, I was vague about Noah, but her sugary-sweet tone threw a couple of red flags."

Our massage therapists place warm stones on our bodies, then leave the room, giving us much-needed privacy.

"Yes!" I shriek. "I went two days ago, and oh my God, she gave me the strangest vibe. She was asking why I was buying two meals, then proceeded to talk about Owen. I don't know. She's probably trying to be nice, but my gut says something is off with her. "

Gemma lets out a long sigh. "I'm sure she means well. She's still kinda new around here and is probably just trying to make friends since we're close to her age. She asks about Tyler and me all the time."

"I am *not* listening to your judgment calls when it comes to people," Everleigh says. "She's weird as hell."

I snort. "You're terrible. Maybe she's an introvert."

"Uh, no...Gemma's an introvert, you're an extrovert introvert...but Brittany has *I'll sell your soul if you cross me* vibes," Everleigh says. "And I'm clearly an extrovert, which is why I'm the life of the party."

I burst out laughing, which actually kinda hurts when I'm lying on my chest. "Yes, clearly."

"Oh my God..." Gemma groans. "Because I make one bad judgment call on someone, now I'm bad at judging everyone?"

Everleigh and I say yes at the same time.

"Plus, she was strange at the retirement party too. She doesn't even know Noah, yet she was obnoxiously flirty with him," I say.

"Do I hear a hint of jealousy?" Gemma teases. "I think she's just friendly and doesn't know boundaries. Prove me wrong."

Our massage therapists return and tell us to put our robes on when we're ready. We're escorted to the next room for our manis and pedis, plus more mimosas, but I pass because I have to drive after this.

By the time our spa day is over, my body feels like it's made of spaghetti noodles, but it was a much-needed day of relaxation. After we hug goodbye, I head to my car and am grateful to have spent time with my best friends.

As I drive to Noah's, I think about what they did all day. Owen packed enough things to keep them busy until next week. My thoughts drift to my conversation with Everleigh and Gemma and giving Noah a chance. If following my heart was as easy as they made it sound, I wouldn't be in this predicament.

Once I get to Noah's and knock on the door, I hear them laughing. It warms my heart, and when Owen lets me in, I see his messy hair and chocolate-filled face.

"Back already?" Noah asks, sitting at the kitchen table.

"Are y'all having fun?" I ask, noticing they're playing Jenga.

"I'm fixin' to whoop him," Owen gloats, plopping back down at the table, then pulls out a log. The stack sways, but it doesn't fall. Noah moans and pulls one out, causing them to scatter across the table.

Owen stands up with his arms in the air in victory. "Woohoo!"

Noah laughs. "Good game, bud. Beat me fair and square."

I help them clean everything and stack the blocks back in the box. "Get your stuff together, please."

Owen groans, but it only takes one look for him to do what I say. As he's stuffing things into his backpack, he tells me about everything they did today.

"You must be tired." I turn to Noah with a small smile.

"Exhausted." He chuckles. "But we had tons of fun."

"Yeah! Can we do it again sometime?" Owen asks.

"We'll see," I say, then turn to Noah. "Thank you again."

"Anytime. It was no trouble at all," he says. "He's a good kid."

Once Owen zips his backpack, we say our goodbyes and make our way outside. Noah stops me as Owen climbs in the back of the car.

"Hey," he says, leaning against the doorframe.

"Yeah?"

"Do you have any plans for your birthday next weekend?"

I tilt my head at him, almost shocked he remembered. "Not exactly. Working on the house, I guess?"

The sexy smirk that touches his lips has my heart fluttering. "I'd like to do something special for you. I mean, if you'd like."

This is my opportunity to give him a chance, and I'll be damned if I pass it up. "Sure. I'd love that."

"You can bring Owen if you'd like or..."

"I'll get my mom to watch him. It won't be a problem, especially since she was pissed she didn't get him all day today."

There's a sparkle in his eye. "Great, don't eat beforehand. I want to cook you dinner."

"I'd like that a lot," I admit as a blush hits my cheek, and I don't know why I'm suddenly nervous.

"I'll grab your favorites. Steak and potatoes." He winks.

"It's a date then," I say, the word feeling foreign on my tongue. I take one last glance at him before I go to the car. As I reverse onto the street, I notice he's watching me. I give him a quick wave before driving away.

I'm happy Owen fills the space by telling me about all the games they played, movies they watched, and snacks they ate because my mind is reeling on the way home. I can't remember the last time I celebrated my birthday or had anyone make a big deal out of it. Sure, Gemma and Everleigh, plus my parents try to do something special, but it's never been a special date.

I'm floating on cloud nine as we walk inside the house. Owen gives me a hug. "Thank you for letting me hang out with Noah."

"You like him?" I ask.

He nods feverishly. "A lot. He's super cool."

I laugh. "Good, that makes me really happy. Now go get your dirty clothes together so I can get them in the washer."

He sticks out his bottom lip but doesn't argue. I go to the kitchen, replaying the conversation I had with the girls today.

My doubts have kept me from giving in to what and who I want.

I pull out my phone, then text Gemma and Everleigh, filling them in on my thoughts and Noah's plans for my birthday next weekend. I already know how they'll react, but when I get their responses, I smile.

Gemma: FINALLY! Get knocked up so we can have kids the same age.

Everleigh: That would be AMAZING! But then y'all have to have more when I'm ready to start.

I snort.

Katie: Jesus, no one said we're having sex.

Though the thought has crossed my mind a few times over the past few weeks. I realize this could be the beginning of something amazing. I know I'll eventually have to figure out what giving Noah a chance truly means before rumors fly like airplanes.

CHAPTER EIGHTEEN
NOAH

AFTER BEING GONE for two weeks, it felt really good to be back at work. It's only been five days since I've returned to the gym, and I'm on high alert when in public. I constantly look over my shoulder and double-check my surroundings. The trauma of what's happened has affected my anxiety, and a couple of days ago, I finally booked an appointment with a therapist. I won't go for a few weeks due to their availability, but I think it'll be good. Even if I don't like talking about my personal life to strangers.

Though I miss seeing Katie during her lunch breaks and at dinner, I'm hoping that will change after this weekend. I'll never pressure her to make a decision about *us* even if she's conflicted, but I want her to know where I stand.

Throughout the week, we've texted but have both been so busy with work that I only saw her once when she stopped by the gym during her lunch break. She took me by surprise when she kissed me goodbye, and it took every ounce of my strength not to lose control. I hadn't expected it but was more than happy to kiss her again. We've been talking about our date this weekend, and although she told me she's still processing me being here, we've definitely grown closer since then.

"How's it goin'?" Tyler asks when he walks in the studio after his meeting. Smith and I have been hanging mirrors all morning.

"Good, almost done." I wipe the sweat off my forehead.

"If y'all wanna take your lunch break, go ahead. I have some calls to make."

"Oh my God," Gemma squeals as she enters. "It's looking so good!"

Tyler wraps his arm around her and grins. "Just the way you imagined it?"

She looks up at him. "Even better."

Leaning down, Tyler kisses her.

"Alright, let's keep it PG," Smith groans. "I don't wanna get sick before I even eat."

I chuckle at the disgusted expression on his face. Though we're not close, I've learned a lot about him while being here. He lives a bachelor lifestyle and prefers it like that.

"Don't be that way, Smith," Gemma teases. "There's still someone out there for you."

With a scoff, he grabs his stuff and walks toward the door to leave. "Nah, hard pass."

I smirk and shake my head when he's out of sight.

"So a little birdie told me you're making dinner for Katie tomorrow night." Gemma beams.

"Yep, gonna celebrate her birthday." I have about ten of them to make up for.

"Hope you know how lucky you are that she forgave you so fast." Gemma crosses her arms. "So don't screw this up."

"Thanks for the confidence, sis."

Tyler chuckles, then mouths, "Hormones."

Gemma smacks his arm. "Oh shut it. I'm on your side, Noah, but Katie's my best friend, and I don't want her to get hurt again."

"Trust me, I don't deserve her kindness and definitely don't deserve her, so I'm willing to do anything to make up for the pain I've caused. Hurting her is the last thing I've ever wanted. I won't make the same mistake twice, and I'll do anything to prove that to her."

"I have no doubt you two will figure it out." Tyler pats my shoulder.

"I'm just worried that I could be putting her and Owen in a dangerous situation, considering there's a target on my back, so I'm not telling anyone," I explain.

"Yeah, Aunt Loretta and Uncle Elliot would lose their shit." She rolls her eyes. "But don't worry about them. This is between you and Katie, and that's all that matters. On the plus side, Katie's parents are supportive no matter what, so you won't have to worry about them."

I nod because I'd like to keep it that way. If people knew we were hanging out again, it'd be the talk of the town. It's the last thing either of us needs while we figure out what our future holds.

"Alright, go enjoy your lunch so we can start the flooring this afternoon," Tyler says.

I grab the sandwich I packed and hang out in the back while I text Katie.

Noah: Just wanted you to know I'm thinking about you and can't wait to see you tomorrow.

She must be on her break too because jumping dots appear immediately on the screen.

Katie: Been thinking about you too and really excited for our date :)

After I told my dad about my plans for this weekend, he booked an overnight trip with Belinda at a romantic bed and breakfast in Mobile, the next town over. Now we'll have the house to ourselves, and the thought makes me feel like a nervous teenager.

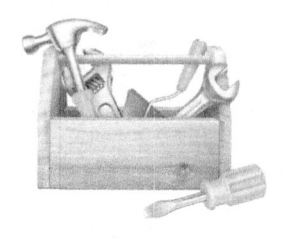

I'd be lying if I said I wasn't anxious as hell for today. Though I'm eager to make Katie's birthday special, it won't make up for the decade I was gone, but hopefully, it's a start. After I shower, I send her a text.

Noah: I couldn't wait till later to say Happy Birthday!

Katie: Thank you :)

Noah: Can't wait to see you! I'm about to hit the grocery store to grab the food for our dinner. Anything particular you'd like me to get for dessert?

Katie: Surprise me!

Noah: You got it... see you soon ;)

Tonight is all about her, and I'm ready to spoil her. If I'm being honest, I want more than just one evening with her. I want forever, and by the way her eyes soften when she looks at me, I think she might want the same.

Over the past few weeks, I've been contemplating what to get her. Anything materialistic doesn't seem right, and we never bought each other those types of gifts when we were younger. It was always something sentimental or homemade. After thinking about it, I came up with an idea and can't wait to see her reaction when I give it to her.

Heading into the grocery store, I grab two sirloin steaks and a couple of baked potatoes. After looking at the dessert options, I pick a Tiramisu since she used to be crazy about it. Hopefully, she still is.

The wine section is a lot larger than it used to be, so it takes me a minute to find something that'll pair with our meal. After grabbing a Cabernet, I stick it in the cart and think about what else I need.

"Noah," someone calls out, and when I turn around, I see Brittany with her son, Anthony, behind her.

"Hey." I smile. "How're y'all doin'?"

"Great, just picking up some snacks for the park this afternoon. Anthony's been askin' when you'll be free to play baseball with him." She pins me with a stare, putting me in an awkward position.

"Oh, right. Well, I'm busy today but maybe next weekend?" I suggest to appease her.

Brittany beams. "That'd be great. We should exchange numbers, so we can plan a time." Before I can say a word, she pulls out her phone. Gemma claims Brittany wants me to ask her out, but that's not happening. Even if I wasn't head over heels in love with Katie, I wouldn't be romantically interested in Brittany.

"Sure," I say hesitantly, then we add each other to our contacts.

"You can call me anytime. I haven't seen you at the deli in a while."

"Yeah, got super busy with work."

"I noticed your truck was parked behind it for a while. Belinda said someone *vandalized* it," she says with a gasp.

Nodding, I respond, "Yeah, probably some punk kids, no biggie. My dad was able to clean it."

Brittany smiles, then peeks into my cart. "Steaks and wine? What's the special occasion?"

"It's Katie's birthday, so I'm making her dinner," I respond, watching her reaction.

"Oh wow, didn't realize you were such a chef. Katie's a lucky woman."

I chuckle. "Nah, I'm not. Just trying to repay her for helping me with something. We're just friends," I emphasize, so news doesn't get around that Katie and I are spending time together. Though it's no one's business anyway.

"Really, *just friends*? Interesting." She bats her eyes and looks at me like she wants to devour me.

"Well, I gotta go so I can get home. It was nice seeing you. Bye, Anthony." I smile sheepishly at the two of them, then take off.

I feel her eyes on me until I walk out of the aisle and wish I hadn't given her my number. Hopefully, I can create some boundaries, so she doesn't assume I'm interested.

Once I'm home, I spend the afternoon marinating the steaks and tidying up. I offered to pick Katie up, but she's dropping Owen off at her mother's, and it's on the way.

Just as I'm grabbing two wineglasses from the cabinet, I hear a knock on the front door. I quickly set them down and rush toward it.

"Wow." My eyes light up when I see Katie. "You look stunning." She's wearing a sparkly dark blue mid-thigh dress with a shawl around her shoulders.

"Thank you," she says as her cheeks tint. "You look quite handsome yourself."

I take her hand and escort her inside, then shut the door behind us. Bringing her knuckles to my lips, I place a soft kiss on them. "Happy Birthday, Katie."

Her eyes zero in on my mouth. "You really didn't have to go through all this trouble," she mutters as we walk hand in hand through the living room, and I love that she squeezes mine in return. "But dinner smells amazing."

Pulling out her chair, she takes a seat. "Are your dad and Belinda here?"

Her noticing we have the house to ourselves makes me smirk. "They went on a romantic weekend away in Mobile."

"Oh," she says, and I think I see a twinkle in her eye.

"I was just about to pour the wine. Want some?" I ask as she settles in.

"Yes, please."

Once I fill our glasses, I raise mine. "To my best friend who captured my heart over fifteen years ago."

I clink my glass with hers as Katie sucks in her lower lip, then she takes a sip. Right now, I wish I knew what she was thinking.

Once I've set the food out, we dig in.

"Do you remember all the birthdays we've spent together?"

She nods with a smile. "I remember the year Everleigh thought it was a brilliant idea to sneak into the old firehouse. Then as we ran from the sheriff, I tripped, and you literally picked me up and carried me."

Chuckling, I nod. "Oh yeah, and you twisted your ankle and had to ice it for a week."

"Of course then I had to tell my mom the truth because she wasn't buying that I slipped down the stairs."

"And your mom told my dad, which got Gemma and me grounded for a month," I add.

"Yeah, but it was still the best day ever hanging out with my best friends," she confirms, then takes another bite of her food. "My God, this is so good." Katie moans.

"I can't even tell you how long it's been since I've had a good steak," I respond.

We continue talking about all the trouble we used to get into.

Katie laughs so hard she nearly chokes, which causes her to laugh even harder. By the time I bring out the dessert, she's wiping tears off her cheeks.

"You gonna make it?"

"I-I think so." She swallows down the rest of her wine, then clears her throat.

I can't stop admiring her beauty and how good time has been to her. The woman sitting in front of me is the same girl I fell in love with, and there's no doubt she's the only one I want.

"Before we have the Tiramisu, I wanna give you your birthday gift."

"Noah...you didn't have to get me anything."

"I technically didn't." I flash her a wink, then grab the box from the coffee table. "I made it."

I hand it to her and hold my breath as she opens it.

She releases a small gasp, then looks up at me. "Is this the scrapbook I made you for graduation?"

"Yep, except I added some pages of my own."

She grins as she opens the cover and the first page makes her burst out laughing. "We look like babies."

"We were."

She gazes over her senior prom picture. Gabe was supposed to take her, but he got drunk on a fishing trip and slept off the buzz in his truck, so I took her. When Gemma texted and told me, I refused to let Katie go alone, so I went to dinner with them. It was one of the best nights of my life. I was so damn close to confessing my feelings to her that night, but then Gabe showed up, and I lost the courage.

"We had so much fun," she says, meeting my eyes.

"I'm glad you did."

She furrows her brows. "You didn't?"

I shrug. "It was a long time ago."

"I had the time of my life dancing with you," she says defensively. "I thought you—"

"I did too," I interrupt. "In fact, I almost got lost in the moment and kissed you. Was gonna spill the truth about how I felt until Gabe arrived and ruined it."

She stares at me, speechless, and I feel bad that I've brought him up when this is supposed to be our time together. "I'm sorry, I shouldn't have said—"

Katie stands, then pulls me to my feet in front of her. "Tell me now."

I swallow hard, gazing into her gorgeous green eyes.

"Tell me what you wanted to say that night," she demands. "I want to know. I want to hear you say it."

Gripping her waist with one hand, I brush a strand of hair behind her ear. "I know this is the worst timing, and I apologize for that, but I can't hold it in anymore." I drag my fingers across her jawline, then pluck her bottom lip with my thumb. "I'm in love with you, Katie Walker, and if you give me a chance, I'll spend every day proving how much you mean to me. If I were ever lucky enough to call you mine, I'd cherish you the way you deserve."

I clear my throat as she intently stares at me, frozen in place.

"Then I would've cupped your face like this…and so very slowly moved in…then brushed my lips against yours until—"

Our mouths collide as she places her arms around my waist, and I slide my tongue between her soft lips. Katie releases a whimper and arches her back as she melts into me. My fingers wrap around her neck, then slowly tangle in her hair.

The taste of her is something I'll never get enough of, and I hope I never know what it's like not to kiss her again.

Sliding my hands down to her ass, I quickly lift her, and she wraps her bare legs around my waist. There's no denying she feels how hard I am, and when she presses into me, I release a deep throaty groan.

"Fuck, baby girl." I walk to the loveseat and sit with her straddling me.

"Baby girl?" she whispers as she grinds against my cock. "I like that."

"Yeah?"

"Mm-hmm." She wraps her arms around my neck and leans in. "I like it *a lot*, actually."

I smirk and bring a hand to her cheek. "Now tell me what your response would've been."

Katie leans back slightly. "Truthfully, I probably would've slapped you for deciding to finally tell me when I had a boyfriend…"

The sass in her tone has me rolling my eyes.

"But after the initial shock, I would've said, 'Noah, it's about damn time, but you're too late.'"

My heart drops into my stomach as she smiles with amusement.

"Then I would've admitted that I've been in love with you for years, and it was the kind of love you don't just ignore or walk away from." She cups my face and stares into my eyes. "As hard as it is to admit, I would've left Gabe had I known. Even then, I knew I deserved better, but after I suffered a miscarriage, I felt tied to him."

"You what?" My eyes widen in shock. "When?"

"The summer before my senior year. I took a test, and it was positive. By the time I went to my first doctor's appointment, I had miscarried."

"Why didn't you ever tell me?"

"I planned to once it was confirmed, but after I lost it, Gabe made me promise to keep it between us. I'm not sure why, but he was adamant about it not being anyone's business but ours and promised to make us a family. It's why we got married so soon, and why I'd gotten pregnant again so quickly."

"Wow…" I blink hard. "I wish I'd known, so I could've been there for you. It must've been an emotional roller coaster."

"It was, but it was something I figured out on my own. You

were working at the garage a lot, and we hadn't been hanging out as much because of our schedules. It didn't take much convincing from Gabe for me to stay quiet about it."

"Well, either way, I'm sorry."

"I think it's why I stayed with him through the emotional abuse and his cheating. He promised me he'd change, and we'd be a family, and a part of me believed I owed him that for the baby I'd lost."

"You're braver than you give yourself credit for."

"I think you mean cowardly."

"There are lots of words I associate with you, but that's absolutely not one of them. You were young and in love. People do stupid things for love, trust me."

"I thought I was in love, but I should've known better when the only person my heart fluttered for was you. Even after years of being friends, I'd get butterflies in my stomach. Sometimes I'd sweat so bad, I'd have to change my shirt." She laughs, then blushes. "Oh my God, I can't believe I just admitted that."

"I wanna know everything about you, embarrassing or not." I swipe a piece of her hair and tug.

A mischievous twinkle flashes in her eyes.

"What?" I ask, gripping her waist when she rocks her hips again.

"I used to masturbate to thoughts of you. Then I'd scream your name into a pillow."

Swallowing hard, I lick my lips. "Jesus Christ, Katie. Do you have any idea how many times I've jerked off to dirty thoughts of you? Basically, my entire adolescence."

"So I wasn't the only one with a naughty mind?"

"Hell no. You should show me," I encourage. "Show me how you touched yourself."

Katie doesn't hesitate but instead confidently stands. Our gazes lock as she slowly unzips her dress, teasing and tempting me at the same time. I watch in amazement as it falls to her feet and she steps out of it. I scan down her body, admiring the goddess standing in front of me.

"Fuck, I want to rip off your panties right now." I adjust myself and narrow my eyes on her chest.

"No, sir...only watching, remember?"

I release a groan and sit back as she slides her hand down her stomach. The pure willpower she holds over me is monumental. I'd do anything to be able to touch her.

"Alright...I'm here for the show." I smirk.

Her fingers dip into her panties, then she spreads her legs slightly as she releases a soft moan. I wish I could see what she's doing underneath the fabric, but by her little breathy sounds, she's rubbing her clit slow and steady.

"I bet that feels good, doesn't it?"

"So good," she confirms with her eyes shut. "I'd picture your big hands touching me as you lay next to me, whispering all the dirty things you wanted to do."

Goddamn. She's going to make me fucking bust in my jeans.

"Well, I'm here now, baby. Let me tell you..."

She purrs, opening her eyes. "Do it with me," she says, lowering her eyes to my hard-on. "Then tell me."

Fuck, yes. I unbutton my jeans and lower them to my ankles, then slide down my boxers. My cock throbs in my palm as I stroke it a few times.

Katie's eyes widen as she takes in the view, then she blinks a few times.

"First, I'd ease my finger inside nice and slow..."

"W-what?" She blinks again. "Oh...right. Yes..." She grins. "Go on."

I chuckle at how flustered she's become.

"I'd slide my tongue up your neck as I push in deeper until I fill you completely." I watch as Katie moves her hand down farther and enters herself. "Then I'd pull out and thrust in hard, over and over, until you squirted."

"Oh my God…" Her head falls back, and I pump my cock faster.

"Yes, just like that," I tell her when her hand moves rapidly. "Then I'd trail down your body, kissing every inch of you before I pull your throbbing clit between my teeth."

Katie's breathing accelerates as her breasts move up and down.

"Massage yourself, baby," I demand. "Imagine it's my tongue."

Her eyes flutter closed as she obeys, spreading her legs wider and circling her nub.

"Faster, Katie." I pump my cock to the same rhythm and can feel the buildup pulsating through me.

"I'm so close…" she murmurs.

"Good girl. Keep going."

"Finish me off. *Please*." She opens her eyes and pleads. "I want you."

CHAPTER NINETEEN

KATIE

I DON'T KNOW what's come over me, but I keep going. I like how Noah looks at me like he's going to devour and swallow me whole. My entire body buzzes as I nearly drown in my own pleasure.

"Massage yourself, baby. Imagine it's my tongue," his deep voice commands.

The dirty words and his sultry tone encourage me to widen my legs, then rub my clit.

"Faster, Katie."

I do as he says, but it's almost too much. "I'm so close…" I whisper.

"Good girl. Keep going."

I desperately crave his hands on me. Noah's been the star of my wet dreams since high school, and now that I've had a preview, I need all of him.

"Finish me off. *Please*." I see his thick cock in his palm. "I want you."

"Katie…" He groans, inhaling a deep breath. "We don't need to rush. As much as I want you too, we can take our time."

Adrenaline unravels inside me as I loop my fingers in my panties and take them off.

"We've waited long enough, don't you think?" I taunt, then kick off my heels. "But if you're content with just watching…"

As I return my hand between my legs, Noah studies me intently. The vein in his neck pulses, and I'm certain he's about to lose control. Quickly, he throws his jeans, then slides his boxers back up.

"Get over here, now," he demands, holding out his hand.

I walk toward him, and he swiftly wraps his arm around my waist. Gently, he pulls me onto the loveseat and climbs over me.

"You have a filthy side, don't you?" He smirks, rubbing his knee against my pussy.

"You bring it out in me," I admit.

"Is that so?" He lifts a brow. "What other secrets are you hiding from me?"

I grin, placing my palms over his shoulders and arching my back into his touch. "You're gonna have to keep goin' to find out."

"You're sure about this?"

"Yes," I say without hesitation. "*Please*."

"I don't do one-night stands, Katie. I haven't slept with a woman in a decade, so if you give yourself to me, that's it. You're mine. *My girl*."

Fighting back the emotions swirling inside me, I bite my lip and nod. "I wanted to be *your girl* in ninth grade when people assumed we were dating, and I want to be yours now."

"Even though no one can know we're together?" he asks, and the guilt immediately rushes through me. I wish I didn't have to keep him a secret, but I will.

"Absolutely," I confirm.

He breaks out into a smile, then brings his lips to my ear. "Good because I'm all in, no matter what."

Thank God.

He presses a kiss to my neck, and I shiver under him. "Yes, more of that...*a lot* more of that."

"As much as I'd love to taste your pussy right now, we can't here. I mean, we could, but..."

"Yeah, no...let's go to your room," I say urgently, laughing. "That's where we were in my fantasies anyway."

Noah chuckles as he stands, then helps me to my feet. "You're bad."

"Where did you envision it happening?" I counter as I pick up my dress and slide it back on.

"Oof, where to start..." I take his hand as we make our way upstairs. "My passenger seat, the bed of my truck, under the bleachers..."

I bark out a laugh. "The bleachers? You've watched too many teenager movies from the eighties."

When we walk into his room, he shuts the door, then pushes me up against it. "But the place I dreamed of most was having you in the shower...the hot water staining your skin red, the steam surrounding us, the slap our bodies would make as I took you from behind. That got me through some hard times," he muses.

"Mm...that imagery alone might make me come," I tease, sucking in a shallow breath. "I think we could turn that one into a reality."

"I'll make a list so we can check it off." He smirks, bringing his hand under my dress and finding my pussy. "You're so wet for me."

I tilt my head back and moan as he takes control. "Yes."

He rubs my clit before sliding down and thrusts his fingers inside me. I gasp at how amazing the intrusion feels. Noah captures my mouth, and I widened my legs as he fills me deeper.

"Baby girl, you're so tight." He pulls out, then pushes in two digits. "I have a feeling I'm gonna embarrass myself when I finally get inside you."

Wrapping my hands around his neck, I pull him in for an intense kiss. "I thought we weren't going to be embarrassed with each other anymore, remember? Because if that's the case, don't look at my stretch marks and cellulite."

Noah chuckles. "Fair point, though I love everything about you, even the things you think are imperfections." His fingers slide up my slit before he brings them to his mouth and sucks. "You have any goddamn idea how long I've dreamed of tasting you? Fuckin' hell." He growls.

"Don't stop," I plead. "More."

"I want to see all of you." He unzips my dress and unclasps my bra, then admires every inch of me as he undresses me.

"Now you," I say eagerly, reaching forward to touch him.

"I'm all yours, sweetheart."

I lower his boxers, and when his cock springs free, I stroke him. His eyes roll to the back of his head as he fists my hair. "Totally worth the wait."

Grinning, I lower to my knees to put him in my mouth, and the moment I do, Noah releases an animalistic groan. "Katie, baby. *Fuck*. That feels way too good."

Though it's been a long-ass time since I've done this to a man, it feels natural and right with him. I glide my tongue along his velvety soft skin, and he shakes against me.

After a moment, Noah lifts me back to my feet and playfully throws me on the bed. I yelp in surprise as I bounce on the mattress, then move to the middle. He towers over me, and our tongues tangle together in a heated kiss.

I'm close to begging him to get inside me when he spreads my thighs and dives between them like a starved man. As he sucks my clit and fingers my pussy, my breathing goes ragged. It only takes seconds for an orgasm to build, and then I'm screaming out my release.

"Mmm…" He buries his face in me, then licks his lips. "I could stay here forever."

"Shut it and get up here." I laugh.

His mouth crashes against mine as he palms my breast and pinches my nipple. "I can't get enough of you," he whispers.

"I need you inside me now," I demand. "Bare."

Noah raises a brow. "You're sure? Tyler gave me a big-ass box of condoms, the fucker."

I snort. "I'm on the pill and used condoms after Gabe."

Noah scowls and furrows his brows. "I don't like the idea of other men with you."

Sucking in my lower lip to hide my amusement, I thread my fingers through his hair. "Trust me, you've always been the only one I've wanted."

Leaning in, he captures my bottom lip, then winks. "Is that why you nearly squeezed my head off with your thighs?"

Rolling my eyes, I adjust myself under him until I can feel his hardness against my clit. "*Fuck. Me.*"

Noah's gaze hardens as he positions himself at my entrance and slowly pushes in. My back nearly flies off the bed at the thickness and the delicious way he's stretching me. Emotions flood me. It's impossible for me to put into words how much I love him and how long I've been waiting for this very moment.

"You have no idea how good you feel," he whispers hoarsely when he thrusts the rest of the way.

I wrap my legs around his waist and match his rhythm. "It's heaven."

Noah sucks on my neck and ear as we pour over a decade's worth of unrequited feelings into this moment. He kisses every inch he can, and as I near my climax, he rubs my clit and pushes me over the edge.

"Oh fuck," I breathe out, panting.

"Sweetheart. I'm not gonna last much longer."

"Come inside me, Noah," I tell him.

"You're sure?" His eyes meet mine, and for a moment, we're suspended in time. When I said I wanted *all* of him, I meant it.

"Yes, positive."

Noah latches on my neck and sucks my collarbone. The sensation of his body on mine sends shivers down my spine, and the urge to have more of him erupts through me.

"Deeper," I say with a smirk. "*Much* deeper."

He lifts both my legs and rests them on his shoulders. "Better grip the sheets, baby."

Noah towers over me, and goes so deep, I come again. The moment I arch my back, Noah groans, and releases inside me.

"Holy shit," he groans in my ear. "So goddamn good."

We lay together, catching our breath as he holds me in his arms. After a moment, he turns on his side and looks at me.

"Now I'm not trying to sound arrogant or anything, but I think you can successfully say this has been your best birthday yet."

I immediately blush and laugh. "Take me in the shower, and it just might be."

"I think we can make that happen."

The day after my birthday, I could barely walk up and down the stairs. I felt like a college student doing the walk of shame, but Owen had a sleepover at my mom's, so I took advantage of every minute alone with Noah. And soreness or not, it was hella worth it. I wanted to stay with him all weekend, but I had to get home before Owen returned.

"Good mornin'," Missy says as she cheerfully enters the break room. It's Wednesday, which means I've successfully made it through half of the week.

"Morning." I sip my coffee, needing it to bring life into my soul.

"Late night?" she asks, and I nod.

Since the weekend, Noah and I have stayed up texting or talking on the phone, so neither of us has gotten much sleep. I won't see him again till Friday night when he comes over for movies and popcorn. He promised Owen they could watch *Star Wars*. I hope to explain that he'll be seeing a lot more of Noah. While Owen doesn't need to know the details of my dating life, he'll have to keep this secret to himself—for a little while at least. Besides Gemma and Everleigh, only Belinda, Jerry, and my parents know. And I'll keep it that way to protect my son. Of course my best friends were ecstatic and excited for us. I'm close with my mom, so I wouldn't be able to lie to her even if I tried. Eventually, I told her the truth that Noah stayed at the new house and explained how we ended up together. She knew my marriage to Gabe was rocky and had mentioned me dating again, though at the time, I wasn't interested. She's always liked Noah and is happy for us. Ultimately my in-laws will find out, and though they won't accept it, they'll have to get over it. I would love it if they could welcome Noah into our lives permanently, but I'm not holding my breath.

Fortunately, there haven't been any more threats to Noah, so hopefully whoever had a vendetta against him has moved on. "Meeting. Ten minutes. Conference room," Cheryl pops her head in and reminds me.

"Great," I mumble, then take another long drink.

"My, my, my...either you've bought a super-charged vibrator, or you really are gettin' regular dick. You could hardly walk Monday."

I nearly cough and spew my coffee. "You watchin' me or something?"

She shrugs unapologetically. "Not much else to do here."

"Your job," I emphasize.

She shrugs again. "So you gonna finally confess who's giving you a good ole pussy beatin'?"

My eyes widen as I push off the table. "I'm going to my meeting."

"If you need an ice pack for your fanny, just holler."

I force back a smile as I leave. She's seriously a handful.

After lunch, I suck down another cup of coffee before going to the waiting room to grab my next customer.

"Katie," Brittany calls from the lobby.

Just great.

I wave. "Hey."

Though I continue to walk, Brittany catches up to me and stops me.

"Hey, real quick. Can I ask you somethin'?" There's a fake sweetness in her tone.

"Sure." I stand straighter.

"I'm not tryin' to get into anyone's business, but I just wanted to make sure you and Noah Reid weren't dating."

I furrow my brows. "Excuse me?"

She licks her lips. "Well, we made plans for him to play ball with Anthony, but some rumors are swirling that you two have history. Didn't want to step on any toes if you're a thing."

Well shit. What rumors? I'm tempted to ask, but I keep my poker face.

"Noah and I are just friends," I say as if I've rehearsed it a hundred times. "We've only ever been friends."

She releases an exaggerated breath. "Okay, phew. Then I don't have to feel guilty that we exchanged numbers last weekend."

I force out a smile. "Nope, guess not."

"To share a little gossip myself, I'm hoping he'll ask me out on a date. Wouldn't we be the cutest couple ever?"

My heart races, and my body feels like it's on fire. By some higher power of strength, I manage to keep calm and amuse her with an agreeable smile. "Definitely."

Before this painful conversation continues, Missy calls Brittany forward. She gives me a toothy grin and says goodbye.

I finish my shift with annoyance flowing through my blood. Though Brittany's clueless about Noah and me, it irritates the hell out of me that we can't make it public. Aside from what the Reids would say, I'm sure half the town would pass out from shock. People knew we were close growing up, but considering he's the reason I was a widow at twenty-one, they'd never understand why I'm with him.

Keeping us a secret is hard when chicks like Brittany openly chase after him.

Noah: I miss you. Can't wait to kiss those delicious lips again ;)

I check my phone after I tuck Owen into bed and take a breather on the couch.

Katie: Which pair?

Noah: BOTH.

I snort, imagining it.

Katie: I ran into your #1 fan today. She's one restraining order away from forming her own group—an "I heart Noah Reid Club."

Noah: Do I hear jealousy in your text tone?

Rolling my eyes, I hate how he knows me so damn well.

Katie: Nope. Just thought I'd give you a warning. She asked if we were dating because you two exchanged numbers, and she's hoping you'll ask her out.

Noah: Oh boy.

Katie: Is that all you have to say for yourself? You gave her your number?!

Instead of responding, his name pops up on the screen as my phone rings.

"Fangirls Unite, which crazy bitch can I direct your call to?"

Noah barks out a laugh. "Not gonna lie. Kinda like you being the jealous one for a change."

"Is that so?" I snark.

"Quite refreshing actually."

"Oh my God." I groan. "You're loving this."

"You're too easy to rile up, baby girl."

"Hey, no sexy talk. I'm still mad."

He chuckles. "Trust me, I didn't wanna give it to her, but she cornered me at the grocery store when I was buying your birthday dinner. Anthony was there, and she keeps asking me to play with him. It's not like I could tell her I plan to bang my girlfriend all night and every weekend until the end of time, so…"

His voice lingers, but my breath hitches.

"Hello?" he says into the silence.

"Did you just call me your *girlfriend*?"

"Well yes, that's what you are until I make you my wife."

At that moment, I swear my heart stops as I nearly burst into tears. It's different hearing him call me his girlfriend and especially *wife*.

"Katie. Are you having an internal meltdown? Should I come over?"

"Yes," I blurt out. "Wait, no. I mean…" I clear my throat. "No, I'm not having a meltdown, just a little frazzled."

"Thank God I didn't say the L-word." He chuckles.

I roll my eyes because he's already confessed he's been in love with me. Though no telling what hearing those three words will do to me. "What if I bring Owen with me to play with Anthony, and I can use the excuse of having to take him home to bow out early? That way, it'll be crystal clear we're hanging out as friends."

"Except I don't want Owen around her."

"He'll be with me," he reassures. "I'd never let anything bad happen to him."

I suck in a breath and sigh. "I'll think about it."

"Alright, my stubborn girl," he taunts. "Now tell me what you're wearing and climb into bed so I can whisper dirty things to you."

Heat rushes to my cheeks, and I can't stop smiling. Just like the past three nights, we stay up late talking and teasing each other.

I don't remember ever being this damn happy.

CHAPTER TWENTY

KATIE

Gemma: Swing by on your lunch break. I wanna show you the gym's progress. I'll feed you pizza!

I SMILE when I read her message. Of course she'd persuade me with food.

Katie: I have my Friday conference call at 1.

After I hit send, I add an eye-rolling emoji.

Gemma: That gives you an hour if you leave in 15 minutes!

I sigh, unable to deny my best friend.

Katie: Alright fine. Ya twisted my arm. See you soon.

Gemma: YAY!

I finish the email I was writing, then log off my computer. Once I'm in the lobby, I see Loretta and wave.

"Fancy seein' you here," I say as she looks around nervously. "You okay?"

"Oh yeah, sweetie. I'm fine. Just someone giving Elliot and me a hard time, so it's got me a little flustered, but it's nothing you need to worry about."

I tilt my head and try to read her. Loretta's a tough cookie and is always vocal about her feelings, so this is strange.

"What is it? Anything I can do?"

"No, dear. We're handling it, and it'll be over with soon." She nervously smiles just as Missy calls her forward.

"Loretta, your withdrawal is ready. Sorry it took a few extra minutes."

My eyes widen at the hundreds stacked on the counter. Then I notice the duffel bag Loretta's carrying.

"You and Elliot goin' on a gambling trip?" I tease.

She brushes me off with a laugh as she places the cash in her bag, then walks toward the exit.

"Bye, sweetie. See you tomorrow," she says, and I wave.

I go to Missy and ask to see the withdrawal slip. It's none of my business, but something fishy is going on, and it could affect my son.

"She's never taken out that much at once," Missy says quietly as she hands it to me.

"Twenty grand?" I whisper-hiss.

Missy shrugs.

Something is *definitely* going on.

I don't have time to think about it because I need to leave for the gym. It's a short ten-minute walk, and when I enter, a beaming Gemma hugs me as tightly as her preggo belly allows.

"Just on time!"

"Well…I was promised pizza, so…" I tease.

"Plenty of it on the table," Tyler says around a mouthful.

"You eat while I show you around," Gemma says before grabbing me a slice and putting it on a paper plate.

I glance around for Noah, wondering where he is but don't ask. Even though Gemma knows we're together, we're still keeping our relationship on the down low. Tonight we have plans to hang out with Owen, but I was hoping to get to see him here too.

"And of course, my favorite room: the studio." Gemma does a ta-da motion, and I smile wide at her excitement.

"Wow…it looks so good, babe. My yoga pants that have never gone to yoga just might now."

Next, she shows me the room where the boxing ring will go. It's not up yet, but the area is mostly finished.

"Gemma, your phone's ringing. It's your OB," Tyler calls out.

"Oh, shoot. She's got my test results. Be right back." Gemma rushes in the other direction.

As I finish my pizza and set the plate down, I spot the locker rooms. Instead of waiting for Gemma's guided tour, I take it upon myself to peek inside.

From behind, an arm wraps around my waist, and before I can scream, a hand covers my mouth.

"You look beautiful," Noah whispers in my ear, then lowers his warm mouth to my neck.

My chest rises and falls. "You scared the shit out of me. I nearly junk-punched you." I spin around and pull him close. "That was mean."

He flashes a shit-eating grin. "I couldn't help myself. You know how many times I've wanted to slam you up against my locker and kiss the fuck outta you?"

I arch my brows, licking my lips. "Should we do a little fantasy play?"

He groans, biting his lip. "Don't tempt me, baby."

Lowering my hand down his jeans, I feel his erection and rub it with my palm. "Looks like you're already tempted."

Noah's head falls back with a groan. "You have any idea how much I've missed you? Every minute away from you feels like an eternity."

My heart gallops in my chest as my body shivers. It's hard not seeing him every day like before, but between work and taking care of Owen, there's not a lot of free time.

He cups my face and presses his lips to mine.

"I've missed you too," I tell him. "I can't wait to get you alone tonight."

"We're alone right now." He smirks, then glances around. "C'mon, there's a room back here that's private." Noah takes my hand, and I follow.

He leads me into a fitness room that only has a table and cabinets. Once we're fully inside, Noah shuts the door, then locks it.

"What're you up to?" I muse.

"Getting a few minutes with my girl." He winks. "Have I ever told you I fucking love when you wear those pencil skirts?" Noah's eyes trail down my body and back up before he locks them with mine.

Heat rushes to my cheeks at the way he's admiring every inch of me, making my panties ready to combust.

"You do?" I taunt.

Noah grips my waist and pulls me to his chest. "Are you wet?"

His cock presses into my stomach, and I hum out in response. "God, *yes*."

It feels so wrong sneaking around, but as Noah's fingers trail down my arm, leaving goose bumps on my skin, I don't care.

"You know how many times I dreamed of touching you? Kissing your skin. Feeling your hands on me. Fuck, you'd drive me wild without even realizing it," he says in a deep drawl. "I was turned on every fucking day and couldn't do a damn thing about it."

"Show me what you wanted to do," I demand.

"Yeah?" The corner of his lips tilts up. "You sure?"

"Yes."

Without missing a beat, Noah spins me around and pushes me into the table. "Spread your legs," he growls in my ear. "These fuck-me heels have been in my fantasies since I returned."

Looking over my shoulder, I grin at him and watch as his eyes go dark with anticipation. I don't know how much longer we have until Gemma or Tyler come barreling in, so I widen my legs, giving him permission.

Noah kneels behind me, palming my thighs and pushing up my skirt until it's over my ass. His fingers loop into my panties, and he swiftly drags them down to my ankles.

I give him as much access as I can when he squeezes my ass cheeks, and his tongue dives into my pussy. My chest is nearly flat against the table as he sucks me from behind, flicking my clit and thrusting his tongue in and out.

"Oh my God," I moan at how good it feels.

Just when I think it can't get any better, he drives two digits inside me and goes deep and hard.

"Come on my fingers," he demands.

We don't have a lot of time, so I ride his hand and cover my mouth when the orgasm hits. Noah slides out of me and latches his lips, licking my release.

"Fuckin' heaven, baby girl."

He helps put my panties and skirt back into place, and when I spin in his arms, I notice he's still hard as hell.

"Let me take care of that." I fist my fingers in his shirt, ready to pleasure him.

"Later." He flashes a wink. "That way I can sink deep inside you and watch your face as I come."

His words have my eyes nearly rolling to the back of my head.

Hell yes.

"There you two are," Gemma scolds when we finally make our way to the front.

Tyler snorts, shaking his head. "I recognize that sex hair."

My eyes widen as Gemma swats him. "That's my brother. Please stop talkin'."

Quickly, I flatten my hair as my cheeks go crimson.

"I better get back to work," I say awkwardly. "Thanks for showing me around. Everything looks incredible."

"Should be up and running in about six weeks," Tyler says proudly. "Just waiting on some final pieces of equipment and the boxing ring."

"And hiring more people," Gemma adds.

"That juice bar is gonna be a hit." I smile, giving her a hug goodbye.

Before I walk out, Noah pulls me aside and kisses me.

"See you tonight for movies and popcorn." He winks.

When he comes over to visit, Noah parks a block away, then enters through the back door. Though I hate we have to be a secret, I'm also enjoying keeping our relationship status within our inner circle only. The moment people find out, I'll be bombarded by rumors, so it's nice to enjoy this quiet time.

"How was your pizza?" Missy asks as I walk through the doors.

"It was…" I tilt the corner of my lips. "Hot."

I go to my office and shut the door for my conference call, which is boring as hell. The end of my shift can't come soon enough. Owen's been bouncing off the walls excited to watch *Star Wars* tonight, and I'm eager to hang out with Noah. Though he typically stays till one or two in the morning, it never seems like enough time.

After work, I pick up Owen from my mother's, and he immediately begs me to stop by the bakery.

"Please, Mom? We can have cupcakes for dessert! And it's not a school day tomorrow."

I sigh and give in. "Alright, just one, though."

As we walk to the car, my phone rings with Noah's name.

"Hey," I answer.

"Hey. Just wanted to give you a heads-up that I'm gonna be a little late. Brittany called and said she's stranded with a flat on some country road ten minutes outside Mobile and needs a ride back to town."

Agitation rolls through me.

"She can't call a tow truck? Or someone else?"

"She said she tried but was given a two-hour window, and she doesn't want to sit out there in the dark. No one else answered, I guess. She's with Anthony and doesn't have a spare."

I have a hard time being mad, knowing she's with her son in the middle of nowhere on the side of the road.

Though I suspect this is just a ploy to get Noah's attention, I know it won't work. There's no harm in him helping her out either.

"Alright well, just please be careful. Text me when you're on the way back."

"I will. Once I drop them off, I'll go home and shower, then be right over."

"Sounds good." We hang up, and I drive to the bakery that's next to the deli.

Once we park, Owen rushes in and leaves me behind.

"Owen Gabriel Reid," I scold when I finally catch up to him. "You don't run across parking lots like that."

"Sorry," he mumbles while scanning the display case.

"Hey, Alexandra," I say as soon as she greets us.

"Hey kiddo, what're ya in the mood for today?" she asks Owen.

"Alllll of them." He nearly drools.

"One," I remind him.

While he decides, I order two for Noah and me.

When he finally decides, Alexandra packs everything, and we say our goodbyes. As we exit, I spot Jerry and Belinda leaving the deli.

"Hey, you two." I smile.

"Hey, kiddos. What are you up to?"

"Just gettin' some cupcakes for dessert," I explain. "What about you?"

"Brittany had to leave early for some family emergency, so I had to stay later than usual," Belinda says.

I furrow my brows, confused. "In Mobile?" I ask.

"Um, I don't think so. Her vehicle wasn't working, so someone picked her up." She shrugs.

"Wait, what?" My heart races.

"Yeah, she left it over there and said she'd pick it up tomorrow." I look over and see the same color SUV as hers parked there. My mind instantly reels. Needing to double-check for myself, I walk over and notice the back window decal that I've seen at school drop-off.

Peeking inside, I glance around and see something on the floorboard in the back. I try my best to make out what it is and realize it's a can of red spray paint.

The same color spray paint that MURDERER was written in on Noah's truck.

What the fuck? Why would she be after Noah?

Without making Jerry panic, I try to keep calm, but it's hard. I'd like to think I'm overreacting, but my gut tells me otherwise. The strange way she's been acting, the odd questions she's asked, it's all a little too convenient. The fact that Noah's driving to her right now without knowing what her intentions or motives are makes me feel sick.

"Can you take Owen home with you and watch him till I get back?" I rush over to them, then hand Belinda the box of sweets.

"So sorry to spur this on you, but I'll be right back. It's really important."

"Everything okay?" Belinda asks.

I force a smile. "Yeah. It will be once I figure something out."

I kiss Owen's head and tell him to be a good boy. Jerry nods and ensures it's no problem. They're confused as hell, but I can't say anything until I know what's going on. It might just be a coincidence, but I doubt it. Brittany's given me a weird-ass vibe since the way she acted at the retirement party. She's militantly tried to get Noah's attention, which makes this even more suspicious.

As soon as I'm in my car, I gun it and drive to the interstate. I call Noah, and after five rings, it goes to voicemail.

"Ugh, c'mon. Pick up," I beg, hitting his number again.

Voicemail again.

I text him.

Katie: Call me ASAP. It's urgent!!!

No response.

My heart races so hard, I can barely breathe.

It's already getting dark, and I don't know exactly where she said she was, so he could be anywhere.

As I continue driving, I keep calling, but after a while, it goes directly to voicemail without ringing.

Fuck, fuck, fuck.

I take the exit ramp that leads to the country road before Mobile. Slowing down, I do my best to scan the area in the dark. When I come close to an intersection and see two pairs of headlights in a ditch, my heart sinks. There aren't any ambulances or police cars, which means it might've just happened.

"*Noah...*" I let out a strained whisper.

As soon as I park on the gravel, I pocket my phone and run over.

One truck is facing the wrong direction and has been hit on the driver's side. From what I can make out, it's blue like Noah's. The closer I get, I know it's his. I continue stumbling forward, trying to gain control as my adrenaline rushes.

"Noah!" I scream, smacking the front fender. The door is completely dented in and won't open. The glass is smashed in, so I can hardly see inside.

I rush over to the passenger's side, and after a few attempts, I manage to get the door open. The airbag is deflated, and I notice he's limp against the seat.

"Noah, baby...do you hear me?" I take his hand and shake him, noticing the blood trailing down his face.

He lets out a low groan, and I exhale a breath of relief that he's still alive.

"Stay with me. I'm calling 911."

As soon as the dispatcher answers, I explain the situation and beg them to come as soon as possible. Noah's breaths are short and staggered, and I'm worried he has a concussion or his lung collapsed.

"They're on their way, ma'am," she reassures me.

"I think his legs are stuck. The whole door is bent in," I tell her.

"Keep him talkin' and see if he can open his eyes," she directs.

"I'm going to set the phone down for a second so I can get closer," I tell her.

"Noah, can you hear me?"

He squeezes my hand lightly. "Katie..." he mutters just above a whisper.

"Yes, it's me."

Tears fill my eyes, and I try my best to stay strong for him and not cry.

"You're gonna be okay, baby. The ambulance is on its way."

"Katie…" he says my name again weakly, then squeezes my hand, this time a bit harder. "I love you."

There's no use fighting the tears because as soon as he says those three beautiful words, they fall down my cheeks uncontrollably.

"Noah." I stare at him as he struggles to open his eyes. "I love you, too. I always have."

Once the words leave my lips, he releases my hand.

CHAPTER TWENTY-ONE

NOAH

EARLIER

"Hey, Tyler," I say, searching for him around the gym.

"What's up, man?"

"I gotta see my parole officer next week. Is it okay if I take a half-day Tuesday?"

"Yeah, no problem. Just let Smith know."

"Will do. Thanks, man."

After Katie's and my risky rendezvous in the back, I haven't stopped smiling. Though we were together just an hour ago, I already miss the fuck outta her and can't wait to see her again.

"What're your plans this weekend?" Gemma asks as we pack up.

"Fuckin'..." Tyler responds before I can.

"Babe!" Gemma scolds him. "As happy as I am they're *finally* together, I don't need that image in my brain!"

I chuckle, shaking my head. "We're watching a movie with Owen tonight, then I'm gonna help her with the house tomorrow and Sunday. Hoping to help more so she can get done sooner."

"But still fuckin'." Tyler laughs, dodging a hit from Gemma.

"Well, I did tell her to get pregnant soon so our kids can be the same age," Gemma muses, and my heart races at the thought of Katie carrying our baby. After she told me about her miscarriage, we've grown closer than ever, and I love that she trusted me with that information. I'm not sure my sister knows, so I don't say anything.

"You're gonna scare the shit outta him now," Tyler tells her. "Good thing I got you that big box of condoms." He smirks.

"You didn't!" Gemma's eyes widen.

Tyler shrugs, then looks at me. "You're getting a free preview of the pregnancy hormones. You sure you wanna go through this?"

"Alright, time for me to go." I snicker. "You two have a good weekend."

Gemma hugs me before I leave, and I wave at Tyler before walking out to my truck.

Just as I start the engine, my phone rings, and Brittany's name pops up on the screen. Considering she's gone out of her way to confront Katie at work, now's a good time to make it crystal clear that I'm not interested in her that way.

"Hey," I answer.

"Noah? Oh thank God. I've called ten people already, and no one's answered. I'm so sorry to bother you, but I can't find anyone else to help me." Her strained tone concerns me.

"What's the matter?"

"Anthony and I were about ten minutes from Mobile when my SUV started shaking. I pulled over and realized my tire is completely flat. I forgot to get a replacement spare the last time this happened, and now we're stranded. I called a tow truck, but they can't come for two hours, and it's almost pitch black out, so I don't want to wait out here with my son. Is there any chance you'd come and pick us up? I'll pay you gas money and for your time," she rushes her words out, and I can tell she's freaking out.

"Not necessary. I just left work, so I can head that way now. What road are you on?"

After Brittany gives me directions, I call Katie and let her know I'll be late.

"She can't call a tow truck? Or someone else?" she asks, and I know she's not any happier about this than I am.

"She said she tried but was given a two-hour window, and she doesn't want to sit out there in the dark. No one else answered, I guess. She's with Anthony and doesn't have a spare," I explain.

Katie releases a sigh.

"Alright well, just please be careful. Text me when you're on the way back."

"I will. Once I drop them off, I'll go home and shower, then be right over."

We say goodbye, then I head Brittany's way.

Once I get off the exit ramp, I take a right and go toward Mobile. I haven't been there since before prison, and I'm reminded of the time Katie and I went to their famous fall festival. I'd just gotten my license and wanted to hang out with her alone. Though Katie was only fifteen at the time, her parents adored me and allowed her to come with me. I remember it clear as day—the perfect weather, a band playing on a stage surrounded by hay bales and pumpkins, and the sweet smell of caramel wafting through the air. I had hyped myself up all week to finally confess my true feelings and ask her to be my girlfriend.

Then I got cold feet.

I shake my head just thinking about it because I even had the perfect opportunity and blew it.

Katie literally took my hand and held it during a hayride.

I'm so stupid.

Laughing to myself at the idiocy of my teenage years, I turn down the music and reach for my phone to call Brittany. I think

I'm getting close to where she said she was, but I don't see any hazard lights flashing.

I click on her name and wait for her to pick up, but it goes to voicemail after three rings. I try again but have no luck.

Well, shit. I hope her phone didn't die.

Just as I'm about to text Katie, I hit a bump in the road and lose my grip. My phone flies to the floorboards on the passenger side where I can't reach it.

"Fuck."

I try to reach for it, my other hand sliding down the wheel as I struggle to find it. I hear it ring with Katie's ringtone and decide I better pull over to grab my phone and call her back. I peek in my rearview mirror to see if anyone's behind me so I can slow down and pull over. The phone goes off again, and this time, I'm anxious as hell that something's wrong since she knows I'll be right back. Just as I put on my blinker to turn at the intersection, something smashes into me.

Metal scrapes against metal, the airbag deploys, and I smack my head. Confusion envelops me as a metallic taste fills my mouth, and blood drips from my head. I can't seem to physically move, and darkness eventually takes over.

I'm not sure how much time passes before I hear a door open. Katie's voice instantly soothes me, though I don't understand what she's saying. She grabs my hand and shakes me, but the pain makes me groan.

"Stay with me. I'm calling 911."

I immediately wonder about the other vehicle and who's inside.

"I think his legs are stuck. The whole door is bent in." I hear her say. Oddly enough, I can't feel below my waist. The only pain is the throbbing in my head.

"Noah, can you hear me?"

I don't have much energy, but I try to squeeze her hand. "Katie," I murmur.

"Yes, it's me."

I hear the tears in her voice and hate how worried she sounds.

"You're gonna be okay, baby. The ambulance is on the way," she reassures me.

"Katie..." I repeat, squeezing her hand with a little more strength. Though I feel my mind losing focus and I'm not sure how much longer I'll be able to stay awake, I try to open my eyes to look at her. "I love you."

"Noah. I love you, too. I always have."

I smile for a beat before everything fades away.

I don't know how long it takes before I become alert. When I try to open my eyes, my head throbs, so I don't attempt it anymore. Whispers around me grow louder as I try to move my body.

"You were supposed to kill him! I paid you for a job, and you didn't do that job," a woman snarls.

"I T-boned him with an F-250! That should've taken him out or at least put him in a coma," a man grits.

"If you'd listened and been going faster..."

"I would've risked missing him completely if I was going any faster, Brittany," the man hisses. "I nearly killed myself trying to do this job."

Brittany? What the fuck? No, that can't be right.

Why would Brittany want me dead? I only just met her.

"You did *not*. I was right there waiting for you with the car and watched the whole fuckin' thing. Plus, I didn't pay you *twenty grand* to play it safe. Now look. He'll probably make a full recovery, and this will have been for nothing." The anger in her voice sends a chill down my spine, though it's nice to hear I'm not in a life-threatening condition.

I keep my eyes closed so they don't know I can hear them, but I'm tempted to knock the shit out of whoever this guy is.

"Stop worrying. I never fail at a mission, and I won't fail at this one. Just because it didn't work doesn't mean we can't try something else next time," he reassures her.

"Next time?" She barks out a laugh. "This is your final chance. The brick and bomb didn't send a clear message, so the *next time* better be a success or else," Brittany orders.

"You have my word."

CHAPTER TWENTY-TWO

KATIE

I FEEL like I'm moving at hyper speed as I follow the ambulance to the hospital. It took them nearly twenty minutes to find us, and I felt relief when I finally heard the sirens. Noah's blood is on my hands and clothes, but I don't care. The paramedics tried to calm me down, but nothing they said registered because shock took hold. I wish Noah wouldn't have answered Brittany's call and ignored her ass.

Brittany.

I grip the steering wheel tight with one hand as I call Jerry with the other. When he answers, I can tell he's smiling, but when I croak out that there's been an accident, it quickly fades.

"Which hospital?" he asks. I hear keys jingling and know he's already out the door.

"Mobile General Hospital," I say.

"I'm on my way now," he tells me. I hear Belinda in the background asking what's wrong. "I'll bring Owen with us too unless you want me to take him to your mother's."

"It's fine. He can come. Thank you so much," I reply, and the call ends. The next logical person to contact is Gemma, and my heart races as her phone rings. When she answers, the strength I had when I spoke with Jerry quickly vanishes. I try not to cry so my vision doesn't blur while I'm driving, but I fail. I talk a million miles per hour as I explain exactly what happened.

"Oh my God!" she shrieks.

"I thought he was dead," I whisper. "I can't lose him, Gemma. Not now. Not when we've decided to finally be together."

My emotions bubble to the surface, and my words come out in sobs.

"He's strong, Katie. My brother's a fighter. If anyone can survive an accident like that, it'll be Noah. Tyler and I are on our way now. I'll let Everleigh know too. I know you're upset," she says. "Please be careful."

"I will, I promise. We're in town now and should be at the hospital in five minutes," I tell her.

"Okay, I'll see you soon."

When I pull into the parking lot, the ambulance goes to the emergency room entrance. I park in the visitor's area, then run inside and explain the situation to the woman at the front desk. Since he's just arrived, she hasn't received any patient information yet and asks me to sit in the waiting area.

The hospital has a certain smell to it, and it brings me back to the night of Gabe's accident. While I've been here a few times over the years, those memories never go away. I find myself staring at the wall, drowning out the surrounding chatter and the TV in the corner. Nothing else matters besides Noah right now.

The doctor finally comes out. He explains what's going on, then asks me questions about Noah's health history, mostly things I don't know.

"They just took him back for a CT scan, and once we have the results of that, we'll let you know. He's banged up but remaining stable. As soon as we have more information, I'll come find you."

"Thank you," I say. "Other family members are on their way now."

He gives me a smile, then returns through the double doors.

When I sit down, I just keep thinking about the what-ifs. What if I wouldn't have searched for him? Would he have survived? For all I know, he'd still be unconscious and bleeding in his mangled truck. There's not much traffic on those country roads so there's no real way to know, but not one car passed while I was there. My mind goes crazy with all the horrible scenarios, and I try to push it all away. The reality is I could've lost Noah tonight, and the thought makes me sick to my stomach, almost to the point of dry heaving.

I try to suck in air, but it feels like the ceiling is closing in as my mind reels. The only thing that brings me back to reality is the sound of Belinda's soft voice. Owen rushes to me and wraps his arms around me.

"I'm fine," I tell him, knowing he was probably worried. I never randomly leave him with anyone. In this instance, I had to follow my gut.

"How is he?" Jerry asks with concern written on his face.

"Not sure. They just brought him back there. As soon as there's an update, they said they'd let me know." Owen sits next to me as Belinda pulls me in for a hug. Just as she lets go of me, a frazzled Gemma and Tyler rush through the door.

As soon as she's close, Gemma pulls me into her as close as she can. "You okay?" she asks when we break apart.

"I will be once I know he's fine," I admit.

"He will be," she confidently says.

Everleigh arrives, and we sit in the waiting room, but no one really says much. Owen has his tablet and headphones, which keep him occupied. Although he's next to me, he leans in as close as he can until we're touching. Having him here brings me comfort. As Gemma and Everleigh ask me a myriad of questions, I lose track of time.

"So what the hell happened?" Everleigh finally asks.

I keep my voice low, trying to put all the pieces together. "Noah called and said he was gonna help Brittany because she had a flat and didn't have a spare. She was stranded on the side of the road with Anthony and needed help."

Everleigh gives me the side-eye. "Why didn't she call someone else? Why him?"

"Exactly," I mumble. "I asked, and he said he was her last resort. Anyway, we were getting pastries for our movie night, and I saw Belinda, who explained Brittany had left early. Her SUV was parked behind the deli."

Gemma looks as confused as I feel. "I thought she had car trouble?"

"Apparently, she had a rental," I say. "I'm not buying any of this. There's something deeper going on, and while I hate to admit this..." I glance over at Owen, making sure his headphones are still on, and drop to a whisper. "I'm not convinced Brittany is solely responsible for this, but I think Loretta is paying her to do her bidding. Brittany's a single mom struggling to get by. Today, Loretta conveniently withdrew twenty thousand from the bank. I don't think any of this is coincidental."

Gemma places her hand on her chest over her heart, and I don't want to upset her any more than she already is because of the baby. "You think they're conspiring against Noah together?"

I nod, unable to meet her eyes.

Everleigh clears her throat. "Looks like Imma need to stab two bitches then."

It's the only thing that makes me smile. Before we can continue our conversation, the doctor interrupts us. Jerry stands and greets him. We wait with bated breaths as he informs us of Noah's condition.

"He's doing fine. Noah has a concussion, some bruised ribs, and a lot of cuts and scrapes. We'd like to keep him overnight for observation. He's been given medication for the pain, and we're in the process of moving him to another room. I believe the nurse said he's going to room 327, but it might take some time to get him transferred. In the meantime, do you have any questions for me?"

"No, sir, I don't think we do," Jerry says after he looks at us, and we shake our heads.

"Not many people have walked away from such a severe accident. From what I've heard, his slow speed, along with the side airbags, helped with the impact. He's lucky to be alive."

"Thank you, Doctor. I'm happy to hear my son will be okay. We're thankful," Jerry says.

The doctor gives a slight head nod. "If you have any questions, please don't hesitate to ask."

"We will." Jerry lets out a long breath and sits when the doctor is out of sight. "Good. My boy's gonna be fine."

I relax slightly, feeling better.

"Noah being moved to a room is a good sign," Gemma says, and Everleigh agrees.

"Yeah," I let out. "That's positive news."

Thirty minutes pass before we're told we can go upstairs to Noah's room. I'm nervous as we step onto the elevator because I know what he looked like when I found him. When the doors open on the third floor, my anxiety spikes, and Owen grabs my hand. He's such a good kid, very empathetic, and I couldn't be prouder to have him as my son. I'm positive he doesn't fully understand what's going on, and I make a mental note to explain the accident to him on the way home.

Jerry opens the door, and when he and Belinda enter, I can see the foot of Noah's bed. It brings back the bad memories of seeing Gabe on life support, but I keep it to myself.

"Go ahead," I tell Gemma. "Go see him."

She tilts her head at me. "We'll go in together," she says. She and Everleigh wait for me to gain my composure as I try to be strong.

After a few minutes, we enter the room together. Noah's sleeping, but his breathing is steady. His eyes are black, and there are gashes on his arms and scratches on his face. His hair is matted in places from the blood, and it hurts my heart to see him lying there so broken. Owen looks up at me, and I place my hand on his shoulder, then bend down and whisper in his ear. "He's going to recover."

Belinda keeps her hand tightly secured in Jerry's as he talks to Noah, letting him know we're all here and thinking about him.

"Has he been awake at all?" Gemma asks the nurse, who smiles sweetly.

"Oh, I don't think so. He's on a lot of morphine right now too, so I don't imagine he'll be awake until morning." She adjusts Noah's oxygen and types something into a laptop, then leaves.

The more I look at him, the more visibly upset I become. Owen stands close, but I notice he hasn't lifted his head from his iPad. I can't imagine how hard it is for him to be in here too. Everleigh is on the other side of me and wraps her arm around my waist. "It's gonna be okay," she whispers.

"I know," I say, hoping she's right.

Gemma moves closer to Noah and takes his hand in hers. Her voice drops to a near whisper. "You're gonna make it through this, bubba." His hand stays limp in hers.

After an hour, Jerry and Belinda decide to go. Gemma, Tyler, and Everleigh hang around for a little longer, then say their goodbyes too. Then it's just Noah, Owen, and me in the room. It nearly breaks me to leave him here alone, but it's a long drive home on old country roads, and it's getting late.

I swallow hard and lean over, whispering in his ear. "I'm gonna come see you tomorrow. Please stay strong, Noah. I love you."

I pull away as tears fall down my face, and I give him a kiss on his cheek before we leave.

"Bye, Noah," Owen says, patting Noah on the shoulder.

Owen doesn't say much on the way home, but I explain what happened the best way I can.

"He's going to be fine, right?" Owen finally asks.

"Yep, he'll pull through. Might take a little while, though," I tell him as I keep my eyes on the road. I'm a nervous wreck on the way home because I know how dangerous it is to drive these roads at night. There is no shoulder, and deer will often run out in front of vehicles. Though my mind is running a million miles per hour, I keep my eyes on the road and focus. When I finally turn into my driveway, I let out a relieved breath. Tomorrow when I visit Noah, I'll take Owen to my mother's. He was supposed to go to Loretta's, but no way in hell am I letting her close to my son, not until I know her involvement.

I slept like shit and woke up exhausted. After I showered last night and calmed down a bit, I called my mom and explained what happened. She was upset but also happy that Noah will recover. After I get dressed, I cook us breakfast, then drop Owen off at my parents' house. Before I leave, Owen hugs me tight, and I make sure to tell him how much I love him. This accident has really shaken him up, but I've tried to put on a happy face even though it's hard as hell. Over scrambled eggs this morning, I made sure to keep our conversation upbeat while also answering his questions truthfully.

On the way to the hospital, I go over everything that's happened, but none of it makes sense. Is Loretta capable of doing something so horrific and using Brittany as an accomplice? I'd like to think not, but I don't know.

I replay last night and the conversation Noah and I had. The truck that slammed into him was big, and thankfully, it missed his door and hit closer toward the front fender. I wonder if this was an accident or intentional. Too many questions run through my mind, and by the time I pull into the parking lot, I'm wound tighter than a ball of yarn.

I go straight to Noah's room and smile when I see Jerry and Gemma.

"I'm sorry, I didn't realize y'all were here," I say.

Gemma grins. "Katie! I was just telling Dad I need to eat *right now* before I get hangry."

Jerry laughs and looks at his watch. It's barely past eleven. "She did, but I was hoping Noah would be awake," Jerry says. "He's been sleeping all morning."

"Dad. Food. Now," Gemma says, and they stand.

Jerry grins. "If he wakes up, will you let us know?"

"I sure will," I reply with a laugh because Gemma grows more impatient with every passing second.

"Bye!" Gemma happily exclaims as she heads toward the door with Jerry behind her.

Once Noah and I are alone, I move the chair next to the bed and sit. I grab his hand and squeeze tight, then close my eyes.

"Katie?" At first, I think I'm imagining him saying my name.

When I look at Noah, his eyes are open. A smile instantly hits my lips as I lean over and hug him.

"Noah," I croak out. "You're awake. Oh my God. I'm so happy. How do you feel?"

"Like a giant pile of shit." He tries to reposition himself and moans with a painful expression.

Immediately, I feel bad for him, but I'm thrilled he's talking to me. "You bruised some ribs and had a concussion. The doctor said you'd be really sore for a while," I explain.

Noah stares at me, then looks around the room with furrowed brows. "Was Brittany here?"

His question shocks me. "No. I haven't seen her. Before I showed up, Gemma and your dad were here, though. They just went to grab some lunch."

"You're sure Brittany wasn't here?"

"I can't be positive, but I think Gemma or your dad would've said something if they saw her. No one has heard from her since yesterday. I'm not sure if she ever found a ride or got a tow back to town either. Enough of that, though. When you're home and feeling better, we need to discuss some things regarding her. I just don't want to talk about it right now."

"Yeah." He blows out. "I agree. I just...I could've sworn she was in my room."

Curiosity fills me. Is it possible she stopped by before Gemma and Jerry arrived? Absolutely.

Considering he's awake and talking, the last thing I want to discuss right now is Brittany.

"I was worried about you, Noah. I thought..." My voice cracks, and I choke up. "I thought I was going to lose you."

With a tight squeeze of my hand, he tries to reassure me. "I'm not going anywhere, sweetheart."

His words make me smile, but I also know we can't control every situation. "I was scared. The blood and the way your truck looked. I just...I thought the worst."

Sucking in a deep breath, he turns his body toward me, and I stand to help adjust his pillow.

"It happened so fast," he says.

I can't even imagine what it was like. "They said the truck hit you off-center, and if it would've been two feet to the right, you probably wouldn't have walked away."

He tries to suck in a deep breath but winces instead. I give him all the time he needs, and before I say another word, my phone dings. Pulling it from my purse, I unlock it and see a text from Gemma.

Gemma: Belinda just met us for lunch and said Brittany showed up for her shift today and acted like nothing happened. No comment about yesterday. Do you think she knows about Noah's accident?

Katie: If he was going to pick her up and never showed, wouldn't she question it? All of this is strange AF.

Gemma: Yeah, I agree. Belinda did mention she was driving a rental car and had her SUV towed.

I narrow my eyes and reread the message.

Katie: If you wanted your story to be believable, wouldn't you tow it somewhere too? I'm not buying this, but I'll figure it out. Also, your brother's awake now.

Gemma: I agree. Something weird's going on, and I'll tell Dad about Noah. Yay! Please tell him I love him and I'll see him soon. I'm sure we'll be back after we eat. We're just down the street at a cafe grabbing a sandwich.

Noah clears his throat. "Who's that?"

I give him a smile and lock my phone. "Gemma. Just letting her know you're awake. They're eating, then they'll be back. She said she loves you."

"Tell her I said it back, please," he says and sucks in a ragged breath. "Were they worried?"

"Yes, we all were. You had a room full last night. Even Owen was stressed," I say.

Sadness meets his eyes. "I'm sorry. I hate that I've put y'all through this."

"You're alive, and that's all that matters. It was a wake-up call, I think. A reminder that life is short, and we don't always get second chances. Not that I ever have, but I promise I won't take a moment with you for granted, Noah. I just kept thinking...what if I lost you?"

"Might be broken and bruised, but I'm here, baby."

I lean over and press my lips against his, and the emotion pours through me. When I move back to my chair, I meet his eyes again. The nurse enters, and she's pleasantly surprised to find Noah awake.

"Good afternoon, Mr. Reid," she tells him. "I'm Tracy, your nurse. How's your pain level today?"

"I'm okay," he tells her. "Could use some water."

She nods. "I'll bring some. Anything else?"

"I don't think so, thanks."

Tracy leaves and eventually returns with a small pitcher of water and some ice chips. "Press your call button if you need anything."

"Thanks," he says, and she leaves. I pour a glass of water as he tries to sit on the edge of the bed and put his feet on the floor. "I feel like I got my ass beat."

I hand him the cup, and he drinks it in a few gulps, so I give him more. "Last night, I just remember wanting to talk to you. You called, and I dropped my phone on the passenger side floorboard."

Staying silent, I just listen.

"Then the crash happened, and I saw my entire life flash before me," he says, and I can tell sitting upright is taking a lot out of him. When he drinks all the water he wants, I help him lie down.

"What else do you remember?" I study him.

"You showing up and me telling you that I loved you. Then you said it back." His gaze pierces through me.

A smile touches my lips and grows wider. "I do love you."

"I meant it, Katie. I love you so damn much. It was one of the last thoughts I had before everything went black."

"You mean more to me than words can express."

I move forward and kiss him. Emotion pours out of me in waves, and I sink toward him when his tongue swipes against mine.

"Lie down with me," he says, holding me close. The hospital bed is small, but somehow, we manage it.

Noah chuckles. "Maybe I should get into more accidents."

"Maybe I should kick your ass?" I look up at him with a smirk.

"I might like that." Noah wiggles his brows. "I've missed you."

"Same," I admit. "I'm happy you're awake."

"There's no other person I'd rather see right now than you," Noah says. "You're so damn beautiful, Katie."

CHAPTER TWENTY-THREE

NOAH

I'VE ONLY BEEN HOME for twenty-four hours, but it already feels like a lifetime because I can't do much. The doctors stressed that I needed to take it easy, and Dad said he'd make sure I did. Now that he's retired, I'm positive he will. The ride home from the hospital was absolute torture because I felt every bump and pothole. It took a while for me to make it upstairs and get settled in bed, and I've been in here ever since. For most of the afternoon, I've been in and out of sleep, but I called my parole officer and let him know what happened. He was gracious enough to reschedule our meeting as long as I called and checked in with him regularly. When Katie got off work, she brought Owen to visit, and I assured him I was fine.

This morning, I woke up with aches in muscles I didn't even know existed. Getting comfortable enough to fall asleep was nearly impossible, but the pain meds helped, even if they don't last long. Doing basic tasks like showering or brushing my teeth seems to take every bit of strength I have, but I manage. The last thing I want to do is ask my dad for help regardless of how many times he's offered. I think this accident shook him up as much as it did Katie and Gemma.

After I'm ready, I go downstairs and attempt to make myself something to eat but settle for toast. I slap some butter and jelly on it, then go to the living room and sit on the couch. Though I turn on the TV, I'm not listening because I'm too lost in my thoughts.

I know what I heard at the hospital, and I'm positive Brittany was there with a man. The only thing I haven't figured out yet is her motive to kill me. Hearing that she's responsible for breaking the window at the gym and the pipe bomb that was thrown through my dad's window makes me fucking sick. All this time, she's probably been busy trying to impress me to make it easier to take me out. Too many scenarios float through my mind as my cell phone rings.

I don't recognize the number, but I answer it anyway.

"Noah Reid?" a man with a deep voice asks.

"Who's speaking?" There's no way in hell I'm admitting this is my number when I'm on someone's hit list.

"It's Detective Sanderson. I've been reviewing your case and wanted to touch base with you. Heard you were released and are at home, so that's good news."

I let out a relieved breath. After I was awake, the detective asked me to explain my side of the story. The meds have put me in a brain fog, and it slipped my mind that he'd call. "Yeah, thanks. Happy to be home and resting. Did you find out anything new?"

"Not exactly. I did some digging on the F-350 that hit you and contacted the registered owner. Apparently, he sold the truck a week ago to a guy who paid cash. The title hadn't been transferred yet. While the guy fully cooperated and gave me a copy of the bill of sale, the name and address the buyer listed was fake."

"Damn." I huff, remembering what I heard Brittany and that guy say. I knew it was going to be a dead end.

"This happens a lot, actually. You'll see people buy vehicles, then not file the paperwork to transfer because they can't afford it, forget, or have warrants. I can't tell you how many accidents I've seen like this where the driver fled because of an invalid license on top of drinking and driving. They'll do anything to avoid a DWI or being arrested," he explains. "Considering the speed at which you were hit, the guy would almost have to be drunk to walk away from a crash like that. I contacted all the surrounding hospitals in a one-hundred-mile radius, and no one checked in with injuries that could've resulted from that crash. Unfortunately, the truck wasn't insured either."

Unless the person driving was a professional who has experience crashing vehicles. But I keep that to myself until I have substantial evidence. The last thing I want is for Detective Sanderson to think I'm paranoid. "So where do we go from here?" I ask.

"We're keeping watch for anything out of the ordinary with this case, but since there weren't any witnesses, it's unlikely we'll find out who's responsible unless they come forward. Wouldn't hold my breath on that one, though. If someone thinks they can get away with something like this, people will typically stay silent and pretend it didn't happen. I'm finalizing the report so you can turn it into your insurance company and start the claims process. Sorry I didn't call you with better news," he tells me.

"It's fine. I appreciate your time, Detective."

"No problem. You hear anything at all, let me know," he says right before we end the call.

I set my phone on the couch and lean my head against the cushion. It's not comfortable, but no position in my current state is. I'm pissed off and frustrated that I'm so banged up and bruised. I reposition myself and lie on my side until my dad comes back from eating breakfast with Belinda.

A few hours later, Gemma and Tyler come over for lunch and bring pizza. I take the opportunity to tell them what Detective Sanderson said.

Disappointment covers Gemma's face.

"It's okay, Noah. I had full coverage on the truck," Dad says. "We can get it replaced."

"Thanks, Dad, but it's not about that," I tell him.

"Karma needs to work her magic," Gemma says matter-of-factly.

Tyler quietly listens as we continue. When there's finally a break in the convo, he speaks up. "What do you think about this?"

I glance at him. "I think it was done with intention."

All eyes are on me.

"Think about it. The gym. The bomb. Murderer being painted on my truck. This accident. After all of that, I don't think any of it's coincidental."

Tyler nods as though he understands. It's not an assumption, though. It's my reality, even if it's a harsh one.

Silence lingers, then Dad speaks up and changes the subject. "Can't believe the grand opening is in six weeks. It'll be here before we know it."

"I know, I'm so excited," Gemma exclaims. "There's just so much to do still."

With a grin, Tyler grabs her hand. "We'll get it done."

Immediately, my old friend guilt returns, and Gemma notices. "What's wrong?" she asks, studying me.

I let out a breath. "I'm upset I won't be able to help you guys, knowing the opening is soon. Every day I'm not there puts you further behind. It's frustrating as hell that things keep happening to me that are affecting everyone in my life," I admit.

"Noah, it's fine. You taking two weeks off won't hinder us that much. When you're better, we'll have the rest of the back-ordered equipment in, so there will be plenty to do."

"Two weeks?" I scoff. "I won't need that long. Probably just a week to recover."

"You gotta stop doing that," Gemma snaps. "You have to listen to the doctors. If they said two weeks, it's for a reason."

I roll my eyes, but I know her concern comes from a place of love. "We'll see. Once my muscles no longer ache and I can walk better, I'll be there. Don't want to put anyone in a bind."

I snag another slice of pizza as Dad mentions the weather. "Supposed to be warm this weekend."

Tyler laughs. "Eighty degrees. Not looking forward to summer if that's the temperatures we're getting in the spring."

"No shit," I say. "Summer's probably gonna be brutal."

"Don't put that into the universe. I've heard how horrible being pregnant in the summer is. And I'll be huge at that point." Gemma groans, and it makes me laugh.

After we're done eating, Dad cleans up, and we say our goodbyes. Once Gemma and Tyler are gone, Dad lets me know he's going to take a nap.

"If you need anything, you holler, alright?"

"Okay, thank you," I say, knowing damn well I won't ask for help.

I take another pain pill, then slowly make my way upstairs. Once I'm in my room, I climb into bed and spend the rest of the afternoon trying to get comfortable while watching TV. All I can think about is seeing Katie later when she gets off work.

A couple of hours pass, and soon, my door is being swung open. Katie immediately rushes toward me with a plastic bag in her hand. She sets it on my nightstand, then nearly topples me. I wince when I feel her weight against my body, and she apologizes, but it doesn't stop me from holding her close. I paint my lips across hers, wanting more of her.

"God, I've missed you," I admit when she repositions herself and snuggles next to me.

"Missed you too. How was your day?" She studies my face, trying to read me.

"Better now that you're here," I say, stealing another kiss. "Did Owen come with you?"

"Yeah, he's downstairs with your dad. Wanted to be alone with you for a few minutes because I can't stay long." She grins.

My eyebrows raise. "I'm gonna need more than a few minutes," I add with an eyebrow waggle, and she smacks me.

"I wish," she says, licking her lips. "Thought we'd talk about what's going on and what I've found out so far."

I sit up a little straighter, ready to listen, but before she starts, I rehash what Detective Sanderson said.

Shaking her head, she lets out a huff. "That's bullshit."

"I know, and it has me more convinced it was premeditated."

She sucks in a deep breath, then goes into detail about what happened the night of the accident. Then tells me about Brittany's SUV being at the deli, the rental car, and how she showed up to work the next day.

"Honestly, she never mentioned what she was driving," I explain. "I just assumed, but that's an important piece of information to give someone if you're stranded."

"Unless she never intended for you to meet her," Katie mutters. "And it was just a ploy to get you out of town."

I nod. "At the hospital, I had asked you if she was there because I heard her in my room talking to another man. She listed all the things she had paid him to do and was adamant about wanting me dead. Even threatened that he'd better not fail the next time."

Katie's eyes are wide, and she nervously chews on her bottom lip. "I'm convinced Loretta has something to do with this. She took twenty thousand out of the bank the same day of the accident. She was nervous and fidgety about the situation, too, and told me she would take care of it. I know what you heard, but I feel like Brittany's the middleman, and Loretta is really calling all the shots."

I try to take this all into account. "That's a lot of fucking money to be withdrawing at one time."

"Exactly. Especially in cash because it's not traceable. I don't know what happened to that money unless she delivered it to Brittany to help take care of a problem she was having," Katie says. "Plus, the way Brittany's always acted around you. The fact that she guilted you into exchanging numbers and has been pushy about you hanging out with her son is odd. I wonder a lot about her motive, especially if she wants you dead. You going directly to her would just make her job easier."

I let out a deep exhale. "If I can give hard evidence that this was planned, then we have a fighting chance. Right now, it's our word against theirs. I know my aunt, and she won't go down without a fight."

"I know. Also, I looked inside Brittany's SUV at the deli and saw a can of red spray paint on her floorboard. While it's not concrete evidence, it's a link. Honestly, though, I can't seem to shake the way Loretta was acting at the bank. It was awkward."

I grab her hand and kiss her knuckles. "We're going to get through this, Katie. I promise."

"We will as long as you stay safe. There have been too many close calls, and I'm worried that something terrible will happen. I love you so much, and I can't lose you again," she says.

Pulling her close, I can tell she's worried as hell as I slide my lips against hers. "I love you too. I'm not going anywhere, sweetheart. I promise."

When we break apart, I smile. "They're too stupid to pull this off. Look how many mistakes they've already made. It's like Tweedle Dee and Tweedle Dum are trying to scare me. We just have to ensure you and Owen stay safe, and I don't let my guard down. Justice will be served; I can guarantee you that. With all the attention on what happened and what's been happening, I imagine they'll lie low for a while to figure out their next move."

"You're right. A lot of people were talking about the accident today, and news has traveled fast. Oh, I got you shepherd's pie," she says, changing the subject.

"Really? I haven't had that in forever."

She grins. "I know. It's Belinda's famous recipe too."

As if my stomach understands, it growls. Katie checks the time and sighs. "I should get Owen home. He has homework, then needs to eat dinner and take a bath."

"Okay, thank you," I say. "You're too good to me."

"Just wait and see how good I am to you when you're better," she teases with a wink.

"Damn," I say, adjusting myself. "Hopefully, I recover sooner than later."

CHAPTER TWENTY-FOUR

KATIE

I CAN'T BELIEVE it's already been a week since Noah's accident. Over the past few days, we've texted and talked as much as we possibly can. Noah's been a lot more angsty and irritable than usual, and I'm worried he's going to overdo it because he's growing bored. Since he's still recovering, I've tried to keep his mind on other things that don't involve the accident or work. I'd be lying if I said I hadn't sent him a few scandalous pictures when I got out of the shower last night. The thought has me smirking as I drink my second cup of coffee this morning.

Missy walks by with a lifted eyebrow, and before she can say anything, I shoo her away. As she continues toward the break room, I hear her chuckle. There's never a dull moment when she's around, something I can be grateful for considering the bank is boring most of the time. After I spend an hour on a call explaining interest rates in great detail to a customer, I finally pull my phone out of my desk drawer and see a text from Everleigh.

Everleigh: Brittany just left the boutique, and something is going on with her.

I check the time and saw she sent the message ten minutes ago. Considering it's a Friday and she launched new spring items today, I know she's probably busy. I text her back anyway.

Katie: What happened?

Fifteen minutes pass before she replies, and I swear I checked my phone every thirty seconds.

Everleigh: Sorry, Mrs. Beverly came in here talking my ears off about the weather. Anyway, Brittany was here acting strange. She was being overly nice, almost to the point where it seemed sarcastic. Her eyes were shifty, and she seemed nervous too.

I think back to the way Loretta acted at the bank, and it sounds eerily similar.

Katie: Did she say anything?

Everleigh: She asked if I'd heard from Noah.

I send a tirade of angry face emojis.

Everleigh: There was something venomous about the way she'd look at me, like her mask was melting off her face when I said he was fine and would fully recover.

Katie: It's because she's fake as fuck. And really wishes he was dead.

The more I think about this, the more annoyed I become.

Everleigh: Not to mention she tried on fifty different

things and bought a key chain. A fucking key chain! It's like she did that shit on purpose so I'd have to fold and rehang everything even though we're busy as hell this morning.

Katie: Wow. I'm pissed for you right now.

Everleigh: She better never step foot in here again, or I might punch her in her face. Anyway, I gotta go. Super busy!

Katie: Don't let her ruin your day! Sell all the things.

Everleigh: Thanks! Margaritas soon…please and thank you.

Katie: Deal!

Another hour passes, and I've had too much time to think about what Everleigh said. By the time my lunch break rolls around, I'm livid. I leave the bank with my phone in hand and find myself entering the deli on a mission.

Belinda's carrying a tray of drinks and smiles when she sees me. "Hey sweetie, didn't know you were stopping by today."

"I'm not staying long," I tell her as Brittany appears from the back. Her eyes meet mine, but it's like there's nothing behind them, almost as if she's dead inside. However, her lips curl up into an evil grin, and I'm tempted to slap it right off her face as she walks toward me. "Need a menu?" Her voice is sugary sweet, and it takes all of my willpower not to roll my eyes.

"Quit the shit," I snap, my heart rate increasing. I'm not a confrontational person, so I'm not sure what comes over me, but there's no turning back now. "I want to know why the hell you lied to Noah and everyone else."

The room grows quiet, and Belinda waves for everyone to mind their own business. I'm sure it won't take long before the news spreads across town about this, but I don't care. The only thing I have to lose right now is Noah, and I'll be damned if I allow that to happen. We've been through too much to get where we finally are.

Brittany acts stunned and places her hand over her heart, making sure those still being nosy see her award-winning act. "I'm not sure what you're talkin' about, Katie."

A sarcastic laugh escapes me as I take a step closer and lower my voice. "I want to know exactly what happened last Friday, and I'm giving you one chance to tell me your goddamn self."

Her expression hardens first, then fades to concern as she leads me outside. I cross my arms over my chest and keep my stance wide.

"You want to know what happened last Friday?" she asks.

I nod.

"I needed a ride back to Lawton Ridge, and the only person who could help me was Noah, but he didn't show up. I ended up having to call a wrecker to give me a tow and didn't find out about his accident until the next day at work. How's he doing? Okay, I hope."

Remembering what Noah recalled at the hospital, I narrow my eyes at her. If she was there, then she knows the answer to that question already. Plus, she already asked Everleigh earlier today. This act is pathetic. "He's fine."

"Oh great." Her inflection rises. "I've been worried sick about him all week, and no one would really give me any information. I couldn't help but blame myself about the whole thing because he was coming to my rescue."

Worried sick? Give me a damn break. "Why'd you lie about your SUV?"

A laugh escapes her. "Lied about what, exactly? I was having issues with my SUV and rented a car that didn't have a spare. A repair shop in Mobile came and picked it up the next day so they could fix it."

"On a Saturday?" I question, not believing a single word that comes out of her mouth. Most repair shops close early on Saturday, if they are open at all.

"What is this really about, Katie? Are you concerned I'm gonna steal Noah away from you or something?"

I swallow down the knot that quickly forms in my throat. "Give me a break. You know what this is about, and so do I. You're more involved in this than you're admitting. I'm sure you have a reason there's a can of red spray paint in the back seat of your SUV too. The same color that vandalized Noah's truck."

Her entire demeanor changes, and she grows more defensive in her stance. "Are you accusing me of that?"

I let out a heavy breath. "It's a weird coincidence, don't you think?"

"Not that it's any of your damn business, but that paint was for a project Anthony was doing. In fact, I have more colors in there too if you need a complete inventory of everything I have in my SUV," she says. "You should really learn to mind your own business, Katie."

"Were you at the hospital on Saturday before your shift?" Our eyes lock, and for a moment, I see something behind her glare. Is it anger? It feels more dangerous, almost deadly, as if I said something she hadn't thought of. If she spoke so freely about Noah in his hospital room, I'm sure she assumed no one would ever find out. Too much time passes as she awkwardly stares me down, and I wonder if she's about to crack and spill the truth, but I couldn't be so lucky. "When's the last time you spoke to Loretta?" I ask with venom in my tone.

"You're actually insane," she finally says, shaking her head. "Get help, or that jealousy is gonna eat you alive." Brittany gives me a pointed look before going back inside the deli, shaking her head and muttering something under her breath. I think I hear her call me a crazy bitch, but it could be my imagination.

A few seconds pass while I try to regain my composure. Either she's guilty and has perfected gaslighting her victims or maybe I really am losing it. While I'm hungry and probably should've ordered something to go, I return to work with no food. Thankfully, I keep snacks at my desk that should hold me over until dinner.

As soon as I enter my office, Missy waltzes in. "Who pissed in your soup at lunch?"

I narrow my eyes at her. "I'm not in the mood."

She chuckles. "Tonight, I give you permission to have all the D in all the right places. You need something to loosen those muscles so you chill the hell out. Seriously though, you look like someone just told you Christmas is canceled this year."

The thought of getting to spend the holidays with Noah makes me smile.

"Okay, well maybe you aren't dead inside." Missy gives me a wink before leaving me to my Cheetos and beef jerky.

By the time my shift is over, I'm emotionally exhausted. I texted Noah and gave him a short summary of my day. Of course, he was concerned, and I promised him I'd explain everything later tonight. I've replayed what happened at the deli at least a thousand times and can't seem to shake how Brittany acted. It's easy to blame jealousy, but I think it's because I struck a deep nerve. If I had to guess, I'd say the money has motivated her, and Loretta has a lot of it.

When I arrive at my parents', Owen throws a fit and asks to stay, and my mother doesn't help either. Considering I don't feel like arguing, I cave, kiss him good night, and make my way home. As soon as I'm inside, I make a grilled cheese, then grab a giant bag of chips and some bean dip. Since Owen's not home, I'm not cooking a full-blown meal.

I sit on the couch, pick up my phone, and text Noah between bites.

Katie: Owen's staying at my parents'.

Noah: Is that an invitation?

I chuckle.

Katie: Doctor's orders were for you not to have any physical activity for two weeks.

He sends over an eye roll emoji.

Noah: So what you're saying is instead of calling and telling me about what happened today, you're gonna come over?

Katie: I'd be lying if I said the thought hadn't crossed my mind.

Noah: Perfect. I'll be waiting for you then. Text me when you leave and make it sooner rather than later.

My cheeks heat as I finish eating. I hadn't planned on seeing him in person tonight, but it's a nice surprise. After I take a shower, I change into some comfortable clothes. Before I leave, my phone rings.

When I see it's Loretta, I'm tempted to reject the call, but considering I've been in a mood all day, I answer.

"Katie. My God, I can't believe you answered," she says with an edge to her tone. "We need to talk. The way you've been ignoring me is upsetting, and I miss my grandson. I don't thi–"

"Loretta. I'm not letting Owen see you until you explain what the hell is going on. I'm not stupid and wasn't born yesterday. Right now, I've lost my trust in you, and I don't want him around you. Something strange is going on, and I need the truth."

I hear her suck in a deep breath. "The truth about what exactly?"

"The twenty thousand you withdrew from the bank," I snap, hoping she'll tell start talking.

She hesitates. "What does that have to do with anything?"

"Because I want to hear it from your mouth, not anyone else's," I admit, my adrenaline spiking and heart racing. I've never been this tough on Loretta and have mostly done whatever she's asked because she's been such a big help to me. But I can't allow this suspicious activity to continue, especially if she's responsible for Noah's accident.

"Katie, I don't think this is any of your business or concern, but if you're going to keep my grandson from me over it, then you're forcing me to explain," she says.

I swallow hard. "Alright."

"This is extremely personal, so I expect you to keep it to yourself, but Elliot has been gambling again. The tenth anniversary of Gabe's death has hit him hard, and he's out of control. If I didn't withdraw the money, he would've spent it, and we don't have a lot left in our savings. So I moved it and am keeping it hidden. He can't find out about it. I didn't want to involve you because I know you don't like to lie and keep secrets," she says.

My anger with her slightly melts away because I remember how bad Elliot's addiction used to be. Even though he got help, I understand that certain events can trigger the need to feel those endorphins. After Gabe passed away, it was bad before it got better. I feel like a giant asshole for forcing her to tell me, but I'm also cynical. She knows I won't be able to confirm her story without going to Elliot, and I would never do that.

Would she admit that she paid Brittany to set up Noah? No.

"I'm sorry to hear that," I offer.

"I miss seeing Owen every week. I miss his laughter and eating cheeseburgers together on the weekends. Can you please reconsider?" she nearly begs, but I have to protect him at all costs.

"I'll think about it," I finally say.

"Thank you," she mutters. "Just let me know."

"I will, thanks." I end the call and stare at the ceiling, trying to calm down.

If I were pettier, I would've mentioned Noah and the accident and brought up Brittany to gauge her reaction. It's something I'd need to do face-to-face, though, because she's not great at lying. Eventually, she'll learn that Noah and I are together, and while I'd like to tell her first, I'm not ready yet. When she knows, she'll have to accept my decision. I can't continue trying to make everyone else in my life happy without considering my feelings. I grab my keys and head out the door without giving her words a second thought.

When I finally arrive at Noah's, he opens the door wearing a sexy smirk.

"There's my sweetheart," he tells me. Pulling me close, he drags his soft lips across mine.

"Hey, Katie!" Jerry says from the living room when I enter.

"Hi!" I say, and he smiles big. "Belinda made some chocolate cake if you want some dessert."

"Thanks for the offer, but I just had dinner. Though it's tempting, I don't think I can eat another bite of anything."

We stand awkwardly in the living room and talk about nothing before Noah leads me upstairs to his room.

"So tell me everything," he says after we sit on his bed. His arm brushes against mine, and I can feel the warmth of his body.

I explain what happened at the deli and what Brittany said.

He laughs. "I can't believe you're so feisty. Kinda turning me on a bit," he admits with a sly smile.

"I was pissed! The fact that she thinks I'm a jealous girlfriend or something…"

"You are," he jokes. I narrow my eyes at him, and he laughs. "I'm kidding."

"Good." I pretend to pout, then grin.

"Seems like Brittany's asking people who are close to us questions like she's trying to gather as much information as she can. I need to get with Belinda and see if she's heard anything else. I'm convinced there's a bigger plan in the works, and I'm waiting for them to strike, but I'm hoping this time I'm smarter. Now what did Loretta say?" he asks.

I let out a long breath. "She said she was moving the money because of Elliot's gambling addiction. She took it out to hide it from him so he wouldn't spend it."

Noah shakes his head, and we sit in silence for a few passing moments. Eventually, he speaks up. "I don't know if I really believe that."

"That's what I was thinking too," I explain. "I know people can relapse with addictions, but I also know how hard Elliot worked to stop gambling. Plus, no one around town has said anything about it. When he was gambling hard-core, it was all anyone talked about. Lawton Ridge would've gotten word about it by now, and we all would've known."

"You're right. People don't really tell me anything anymore, but I know Belinda would've brought it up in passing. Even Dad would've mentioned something or at least tried to reach out to him even if it wouldn't have gotten anywhere," Noah explains. "It seems like she's using that excuse to cover up the real reason."

I nod. "She wants to see Owen, and I told her I'd think about it. I don't feel comfortable letting him be around her."

"It's your decision, Katie. You have to do what's best for your son," he encourages.

I give him a smile. "I won't allow him to see her, and I won't stop asking questions until I figure this out."

He winces, and I reach for him, placing my hand on his thigh. "You okay?" I ask.

"Yeah, just every once in a while, if I sit in one position too long, my muscles freeze up." His mouth turns up, and he slightly relaxes. "I'm fine, baby, but it's cute to see you worried about me."

"I'll always worry about you, Noah." I press my lips against his. The kiss deepens, and our tongues tangle in a slow dance. By the time we pull apart, I'm breathless but also greedily want more. I change the subject as I squeeze my legs together. Noah notices but keeps his comments to himself. "Owen was pretty upset that our *Star Wars* night was canceled."

"I was bummed out about it too," he admits, and I love how genuine he is when it comes to hanging out with Owen. "Let's plan another night soon. I promise I'll make it worth the wait."

"He'd love that so much."

Noah gives me a wink, then looks at the clock on his wall. "You should probably get going. I don't want you driving around so late."

"You're right. Wish I could just take you home with me. But I need you to fully recover first. Don't want to break you." I waggle my brows, and he chuckles.

"Break me? Sweetheart, you haven't seen anything yet. Once I'm better, I'm gonna bend your body in unimaginable ways," he purrs against my ear.

"Stop it, or I might not leave," I tell him.

"Well, considering my dad's downstairs…"

I snort. "Yeah, might be a tad awkward because I'm not quiet."

"No, you're not, but I love it when you scream my name." He tucks loose strands of hair behind my ear, then stands. I steal one last kiss before we leave his room. Jerry's snoring in the recliner with the TV blaring, and Noah laughs as we pass him.

"Might've gotten away with it after all," he teases, and I shake my head as we go to my car.

"Promise to text me when you get home?"

I nod. "Promise."

"Love you," he says, leaning forward and sealing it with a kiss.

"Damn, I'll never get tired of hearing that," I admit with a cheeky grin. "Love you too."

"Always and forever," he says as I climb inside and reverse out of the driveway, smiling like a fool.

CHAPTER TWENTY-FIVE

NOAH

It's been two weeks since the accident, and I'm feeling a million times better. I'm happy to return to work on Monday, even if my life feels out of sorts at the moment. Between trying to figure out what Brittany and Loretta are up to and recovering, things have been stressful and chaotic. I booked a mini vacation at a bed and breakfast for Katie and me, and I hope a weekend away will be good for us. It will be a much-needed reset and give us an opportunity to be alone.

Before I can surprise her, I meet with my parole officer. After my accident, we rescheduled my appointment for today. It will be the first time I've met with him, and so far, he's been understanding. Since my truck was totaled and I haven't had the chance to replace it, my dad let me borrow his.

"Noah, hey," Dean gives me a warm welcome, and I shake his hand. "How're ya feeling?"

"Hey, I'm doing much better, thank you." I sit across from him as he looks at his computer screen.

We chat about my job, being back home, and my personal life, then I have to pee in a cup. Though I have no record of drug use, Dean makes all his parolees do it. Too many turn to drugs or alcohol and find trouble, which usually lands them back behind bars.

"So therapy…have you decided if you want to talk to someone?" he asks.

Scratching my cheek, I hesitate to answer. I'd thought about it, but that was before Katie and I started dating, and now I want to spend all my free time with her and Owen. Last weekend, we had our *Star Wars* watch party with a marathon of *A New Hope*, *The Empire Strikes Back*, and *Return of the Jedi*. There was unlimited soda, candy, and popcorn. Just thinking about spending more time with Owen and Katie like that brings a smile to my face. Katie's my everything. She's the light that keeps the dark days from taking over.

"Actually, I think I'm going to wait," I admit. "I don't have that internal drowning feeling anymore, especially when I'm with my girlfriend. I'm not taking it off the table completely, but I don't think it's a priority for me right now."

"Alright, that's fair. It's always an option if you change your mind."

I nod, agreeing. I'm not against therapy by any means. I think about how much has changed since I got home, and truthfully, returning to civilization is not what I'd expected. I don't tell him the details of what led to the accident or how I'm on someone's hit list. He'll make a big deal, and that's the last thing I need. The added stress is already making me tense, but Katie and being able to go back to work are keeping me distracted.

Dean's been doing this for years, probably over a decade, and I can tell he's not just here to collect a paycheck. He cares and seems interested in me. However, I'm not comfortable sharing everything with him yet.

We agree to meet in two months, shake hands, then say goodbye. I'm ready as hell to get back to town so I can tell Katie to pack her bags.

Katie's mother agreed to watch Owen, so we'll be able to relax and spend the weekend with just the two of us.

Before I drive out of the parking lot, I send Katie a text.

Noah: Just leaving my PO's office. Meet at the diner for lunch?

I smile wide when she responds.

Katie: Hmm. I guess I could squeeze you into my very busy schedule ;)

Noah: Don't sass me, woman. I've spent the past two weeks tempted to bend you over and smack that ass. I'm all healed, and my hand is just aching to do it.

Katie: Excuse me, sir? You're breaking the rules!

I play dumb.

Noah: What rules?

She sends me an eye roll emoji.

Katie: No sexting while I'm at work! I can't be all hot and bothered when I'm trying to talk to a customer about their mortgage rates.

Noah: Soooo, go to the restroom and finish the job there. Slide your fingers in your panties and rub your clit while imagining it's me...pleasuring you.

Katie: Goddammit. You just wait!

I chuckle, knowing she's definitely worked up.

Noah: See you at the diner, my love :)

Less than an hour later, I'm walking into the Main Street Diner and find Katie reading a menu as she waits for me.

I dip down and bring my lips to hers. "Hey, beautiful."

"Hey, *trouble*." She glares at me as I slide into the booth seat across from her.

"Me? I'm certain that was *your* nickname in school."

"More like Everleigh's." She snorts. "She was a bad influence on all of us. Or rather, her spontaneous personality was. Swear she could talk us into doing anything."

Before the waitress walks over, I take the opportunity to tell Katie my news.

"Speaking of being spontaneous, I have a surprise for you."

She lowers her menu and makes eye contact with me. "A surprise?" Her timid voice tells me she's unsure if she's gonna like it or not.

But oh hell yes, she will.

"I'm taking you to a bed and breakfast for the weekend. We leave tonight."

"Are you serious? What about Ow—"

"Already taken care of. All you need to do is pack a bag and be ready by six sharp."

She looks at me wearily, narrowing her eyes as if she's trying to find a reason she can't.

Reaching over, I grab her hands and weave her fingers through mine. "You deserve some time off to relax, unwind, and enjoy yourself. We'll eat, hang out, and walk along the river and downtown. Perhaps some other things…" I waggle my brows, and she immediately blushes.

"The river? Where are we goin'?"

I smirk. "Magnolia Springs."

"What?" She gasps, releasing my grip and blinking hard. "Really?"

Nodding, I smile at how excited she is. "Yeah, it's beautiful this time of year." Booking a room was a freaking miracle, but they had a last-minute cancellation that I happily took.

Katie bites her lower lip as she gazes lovingly at me. "You remembered."

"Of course. I'd never forget that."

At six o'clock, we pack Katie's car and hit the highway. It's just over an hour away. Her grandma lived there before she passed, and Katie would spend almost half her summer there during elementary and middle school. Once she was in high school, she'd only spend a few weeks there because she'd rather spend time with her friends.

The summer before my senior year, she invited Everleigh, Gemma, and me to visit her for the weekend. Gabe was supposed to go, but he got stuck working at the last minute—or that's what he claimed anyway—so I decided to drive down with the girls.

Once we arrived, I immediately saw why Katie loved it so much. Magnolia Springs is a quaint and charming small Southern town with old Victorian homes, delicious seafood, and a beautiful sunset off the river. I overheard her telling Everleigh and Gemma she wanted to get married in the same little white church as her grandparents. However, considering they got married in Lawton Ridge, something tells me when she told Gabe what she wanted, he was less than enthusiastic about it.

Katie lets out a sigh, and I interlock my fingers with hers. "What's wrong?"

"Nothing." She shrugs, then continues, "Just thinking about Loretta and Brittany. I'm just afraid they're following us and are waiting for their opportunity to pounce while we're away. Hurt you when we least expect it. I don't trust them, Noah. This whole thing is consuming me. Why did Loretta withdraw that money?"

"Baby…" I squeeze her leg to gain her attention. "I'm hearing your concerns, and I have them too, but I promise I won't let anything happen while we're away. Owen's safe with your parents, and we're together in a tourist town. Coming after us would be stupid because too many people are around. We're safe and are going to have fun."

She looks at me and releases a deep sigh, then smiles. "You're right."

"This weekend is about us. I just want you to relax and have a good time, okay?"

She nods. "This was really sweet of you."

"I might've had some selfish intentions…" I arch my brow with a smirk and laugh when she blushes.

I'm relieved when she recalls a memory from high school that involves Everleigh being pantsed at the school assembly. The thought has us both cracking up laughing.

"I haven't been here in five years," she admits as I drive through downtown. "After the funeral, it just seemed sad and pointless to visit." Katie takes my hand again.

When we park at the Magnolia Springs Bed and Breakfast, a huge grin meets her lips. A white wraparound porch surrounds the old house and beside it is a garden in full bloom.

"Thanks for bringing me here. I love making new memories with you."

I bring our hands to my lips, then kiss her knuckles. "Thank you for joining me." Winking, I lean in and thumb her chin until our mouths collide.

As we enter, my eyes trail over the unique décor. It's a mix of rustic and floral. It's a typical Southern bed and breakfast, and by the way Katie's beaming, she's excited to be here—which makes me extremely happy.

"Welcome, welcome. I'm Dolly. I'll be glad to sign you in this evenin'." A middle-aged woman finds our reservation, then asks if we're celebrating an anniversary or birthday.

"Nothing specific, just a weekend away," I explain.

"Oh how lovely. You two seem like you've been together for years." She smiles, then leans in closer to Katie and loudly whispers, "I can tell by the way he looks at you."

I grab our bags as she leads us to our room, sharing the history of the place and the generations of families who've owned it. I can already see the stress melting off Katie's shoulders as she takes it all in with a smile.

"I haven't been here in ages," Katie admits. "My mom and I stayed here once when I was a kid and we were visiting my grandmother. Honestly, I don't think much has changed."

"Probably not." Dolly snickers.

When she shows us our room, I step inside and spot the champagne and vase of red roses. From our balcony, the trees and river make for a perfect serene view. I hope being here allows Katie and me to reconnect and unwind.

"This is breathtaking," Katie says as Dolly gives a short tour, showing off the loft area with a loveseat and coffee table.

"We're definitely using that," I whisper in Katie's ear from behind as she stares at the soaking bathtub in the master suite.

She giggles and nods.

"Breakfast is served every morning from eight to ten, and there's the dining room or outside patio seating. Please let me know if you need anything. "

"Thank you so much," I tell her as she walks to the door.

"Hope you two enjoy your stay." She grins, then leaves.

I wrap my arms around Katie's waist and pull her into me. "Oh we will…" I muse before closing in on her mouth and tasting her lips.

"It means a lot to me that you planned this."

"I'd do anything for you," I tell her, cupping her face and slowly kissing her. "And as much as I want to do *very* bad things to you…" I groan at the willpower I have not to peel off her clothes. The past couple of weeks of not being able to touch her the way I want while I recover have been torturous. "We have a dinner reservation at Jesse's."

Her eyes light up. "We do? Oh my gosh, I haven't been there in ages."

"I hear they have great steaks and seafood."

"The absolute best," she confirms. "How long do I have to get ready?"

My gaze scans down her body, admiring every gorgeous inch. "You look great just how you are. What're you talkin' about?"

"Jesse's is fancy. I can't go like this."

I chuckle, then check the time. "Alright, we gotta leave in twenty if we're gonna make it."

"Shit." Katie grabs her bag and takes out a black dress. "Luckily, I packed this just in case."

"Hope you know it's comin' off later, though." I flash her a wink before she grabs her makeup tote and hurries to the bathroom.

Deciding I better change too, I put on a sleek black button-up and dark wash jeans. Eighteen minutes later, Katie emerges, and I nearly lose my ability to speak.

"Fuck me," I growl. Her hair is curled, and dark eye shadow accentuates her eyes. "You're tryin' to kill me."

She spins, showing me how perfect she looks.

"Screw it, we're skipping dinner." I pull her into me. "I'd much rather eat *you*."

Katie giggles, pushing against my chest. "No, sir. You promised me dinner. Plus, I like the idea of you wining and dining me first."

I lean down and kiss her ruby red lips. "I'd spend forever doing just that if it meant taking you home afterward."

She smirks, and we leave.

"Can you imagine if we dated in high school?" she asks as we drive to the restaurant. "You tryin' to impress me with your old beat-up Ford." She chuckles.

"Rusty Ray? He was the shit!"

Katie snorts. "We had a lot of fun, though. I bet you hooked up with a ton of girls in the back seat."

I raise a brow. "When? Between hanging out with you and working?"

She shrugs and nervously fidgets.

"What? I can tell you wanna ask me somethin'," I say as I find a spot to park.

"Alright. I guess I'm just wondering how many women you've slept with."

I chuckle, amused as hell that she'd be scared to ask. "You really wanna know?"

She briefly contemplates before nodding. "You don't have to tell me. I was only curious."

I scratch the back of my neck. "Well...including you, three."

Her eyes go wide. "Three? No way. You must've forgotten a few."

"Katie, I spent the last decade in prison."

She sighs slightly as if she'd forgotten. "I know, I meant before that...like high school and after you graduated. Plenty of girls wanted you."

"Well, there was the one I lost my virginity to. Then the girl I'd randomly hook up with. And now...you. So yeah, three." I shrug.

"Wow...now I feel stupid."

I reach for her hand and interlock her fingers with mine. "Don't. I only ever wanted it to be you. The only thing that matters now is that it'll only *ever* be you—at least if I have anything to say about it."

"You're too sweet for your own good, Noah Reid." She reaches over and kisses me, then pulls away with a contagious smile.

"Hold that thought because I plan on being anything but sweet after dinner."

Our evening at Jesse's is fantastic. We talk, eat, and laugh for almost two hours.

"Thank you," she says as we walk hand in hand to the car. "That was just what I needed."

I lead her to the passenger's side and wrap my arms around her waist. "It was. Our first date out in public."

"Does that make us official now?" she taunts.

I cup her jaw and smirk. "You've been mine since the moment we met. We just hadn't known it yet." I bring our mouths together for a heated kiss before breaking apart. "But for the record, we were *official* the night of your birthday when you were screaming my name."

"Feel like making me scream tonight?"

"Fuckin' hell. Let's go." I say.

As soon as we're back at the B&B, we tiptoe inside since it's almost ten. However, as soon as we get into our room, I don't care about being quiet.

After Katie drops her purse, I spin her until her back is to my chest.

I feather my finger along her bare shoulder and watch her shiver under my touch. As I press my lips to the hollow of her neck, I slide my hand underneath her dress and inside her panties. She's so goddamn wet.

"Baby girl," I murmur, taking her earlobe between my teeth. "You're ready for me."

"Mm-hmm," she purrs as her head falls back.

Sinking a finger inside her tight cunt, I squeeze her waist and cause her breath to hitch. "Come on my hand, baby. I wanna taste you."

I thrust in and out as she releases little whimpers. My heart beats erratically at the intense love I feel for her. The insane desire to please her takes over. Katie's always been the one for me, and I'd stop at nothing to make her the happiest woman alive. Touching her—deeply and emotionally—is the best kind of pleasure I could've ever imagined.

Bringing my fingers to her clit, I rub circles and suck on her neck. Katie's breathing picks up as I increase my speed, but I keep a steady pressure. Soon, her back arches as an orgasm takes over.

"Good girl," I muse, bringing the two fingers to my mouth and tasting her release.

"Should we check off a fantasy from your list?" Katie asks.

"My list?"

She turns and faces me, her beautiful face red and flushed. "Yeah. You had so many I started making a mental note of some of them."

I smirk, thumbing her chin and bringing her lips to mine. "Hmm…which one should I choose?"

"How many are there?" She arches a brow.

"Too fucking many."

She steps back and shimmies out of her dress, giving me the greatest view on Earth.

"No bra and red lacy panties. Is it *my* birthday?"

She giggles as I sweep my arms under her knees and pick her up. "Leave those on," I say before she can kick off her shoes. "I'm about to bend you over in those fuck-me heels so you can come all over my dick."

CHAPTER TWENTY-SIX

KATIE

Noah angles me on the side of the bed until I'm bent over, and my pussy desperately aches for his touch. As soon as he tears off my panties, I widen my legs and arch my back.

"So fuckin' ready for me," he hisses when he kneels between my thighs and slides his tongue over my slit. "God, I've missed tasting you."

My knees nearly buckle at how good he feels.

"I missed you too. Even had to bring out Channing a few times," I admit.

"'Scuse me?" He smacks my ass. "This pussy is mine now."

"Don't be jealous. I thought of you the whole time," I tease.

Noah squeezes my cheeks before separating them and diving in. He sucks and licks, then flicks my clit—driving me wild until I can hardly breathe. I've never been touched or worshipped like this before, and I focus on every sensation. Noah makes me feel things I've only read about in books.

While I try to lose myself in the moment, my thoughts take over. The fear of someone hurting him sends a painful ache to my stomach, and I worry I could lose him all over again.

Hell, I almost did two weeks ago.

"Get outta your head, baby. You're tensing. It's just you and me tonight, got it? No outside noise."

Even after spending years apart, Noah still knows me better than anyone.

I look over my shoulder and bite my lip. "Just me and you. Always," I confirm.

Noah stands and pulls me up, then leans in and presses his lips to mine. I taste myself and smile.

"I know this is probably too soon to say, but I plan to marry you someday, Katie Walker. My feelings for you are endless. We're gonna get through this, no matter who tries to come between us. I'll never stop fighting to have you and Owen in my life."

"I love you," I whisper. "More than I ever thought was possible, and it scares me. It also scares me to think something else is going to happen to you."

"I know you're worried, but I promise, I'm not going anywhere." He wipes my cheeks where tears have fallen. "I love you so much. We'll figure this out together."

"You're right. My emotions are bubbling over because I still can't believe this is real. It's you. And me. I—"

"Trust me, I know. I pinch myself every day."

My cheeks heat. "Even though I should've made you grovel more, I'm certainly enjoying the rewards."

"Is that so? You wanted to play hard to get?" he asks, popping a brow in amusement.

I playfully shrug. "Maybe…if it wasn't for Gemma begging me to let you stay at the house, who knows how long I would've made you suffer."

"Tsk tsk…you don't mean that." Noah spins me around again, capturing my waist and pressing his erection against my lower back. "You'd be missing out—" His fingers press into my clit as he whispers in my ear. "On all the benefits of—" He lowers his hand between my thighs and thrusts two fingers deep inside me. "The best sex you've *ever* had."

Moans roll out of me as my body unravels for him again. His touch, his *everything*, captivates me.

"Oh my God, don't stop," I beg as I lean against his chest and feel how hard and ready he is for me. "I want you. *Please*."

"You want it deep and rough, baby girl?" he taunts, sucking under my ear. "Or slow and sensual?"

"Hell," I breathe out. "Is both an option?"

"Whatever you damn well please." His deep voice sends volts of pleasure through me. I can barely contain myself when he pushes me down on the bed, then bends me over in front of him. He unbuckles his jeans and kicks off his boxers. When his shirt hits the floor, I know he's about to send me straight to heaven.

"Your cunt is so wet." He slides his cock up and down my pussy, teasing and torturing me at the same time. "You're gonna turn me into a fucking animal."

I widen my legs and lower myself on the mattress, giving him full access. When Noah lines up our bodies and thrusts inside, I lose my breath. With every hard pump, our skin smacks together, and I moan at how deep he goes. I fist the sheets with a tight grip as he slams into me harder.

"Shit, baby. You feel so goddamn amazing." He grabs a handful of my hair and moves my head to the side so he can suck on my neck. "You have any idea how many times I dreamed about bending you over? In my bed, over the couch, against my truck. I wanted to fuck you from behind so badly while playing with your swollen clit so I could feel the moment you lost your mind. I've lost count of the number of times I jerked off to those images. It had me coming in seconds."

My body shakes, and I can't hold back any longer. Lowering my hand, I moan at the overwhelming sensation of touching myself.

"That's my girl," he encourages. "Get it ready for me. Rub that clit nice and hard."

"Oh my God...it's too intense." I squeeze my eyes and scream. Noah captures my mouth as I release the most intense orgasm of my life.

"Holy..." I manage to breathe out.

"Move your hand," he orders.

I reposition myself so he can slide his arm between the bed and me.

"Fuck, you're throbbing."

I rock my hips with his as he continues to pound into me, alternating hard and fast with slow and gentle.

"I can't get enough of you," he says, pressing a kiss to my back. "I want to live inside you all goddamn day, Katie. Fuck you, make love to you, eat your pussy for every meal." He presses his fingers firmer against me. "I can't stop."

"Oh God, please don't." My ass bounces as he increases his speed. "Your dick feels so good. I'm addicted."

Emotions burst through me as Noah fucks me with fierce tenderness—a complicated combination but one he's mastered. Even when my body is ready to give out, and I'm gasping for air, I want *more*. More of him, more of us, more of everything.

I'm hooked on him in every way possible.

After an amazingly endless night with Noah, he holds me against his chest. He trails his fingers down my arm, soothing and caressing me as we talk about Owen. I love my son very much and miss him when we aren't together, but I needed this time with Noah. However, one of our shared concerns is how much to tell Owen about Noah and Gabe's relationship and the events surrounding the night his father died. I'd rather he never find out. It won't bring Gabe back, and it won't take away what happened between us. Owen looks up to Noah so much, and I don't want to taint the memory of Gabe with the facts of what he was doing at the bar that night. So we decided not to share that story with him. If he somehow finds out, then we'll deal with it when the time comes, but for now, he never needs to know.

I wake up to the sun beaming through the window and smile at the hard body next to me. We fell asleep late into the morning hours, talking and laughing about old memories. I feel like my true self when I'm with Noah, like I did when we were kids. He makes me stupidly happy, and I still can't believe after all these years, this is where we ended up.

Since Noah's eyes are still closed, I carefully crawl under the covers. He may not be awake, but the tent he's sporting says otherwise. I gently fist his erection before licking my tongue up his hard shaft. Noah stirs and moans, encouraging me to keep going.

Wrapping my mouth around his tip, I suck hard, then lower myself down. Noah releases another guttural moan as his hand searches for me. I smile as he fists my hair and shows me the pacing he wants. As I suck and stroke him, he moans and rocks his hips.

"Baby girl, get up here and ride me right now," he demands. "I wanna come inside you."

I whip off the blankets and lick my lips as I straddle him, then lower myself down.

"Oh shit," he hisses, grabbing my breast as my pussy tightens around his cock.

"You like me on top?"

"Fuck yes. Keep goin'."

Noah grips my waist, and our bodies move together until I

can no longer take it. An orgasm rips through me as my pace increases, and I feel him stiffen beneath me. He lets out an animalistic growl as he releases inside me, and I collapse on his chest.

"Oh my God," I pant.

"Best way I've ever woken up." He chuckles, pushing my hair off my face so he can kiss my lips. "Good mornin'."

I laugh with a blush. "Morning."

After we clean up, we head downstairs and grab breakfast from the buffet. After last night's and this morning's festivities, I'm starving.

"How y'all doin'? Enjoying your stay?" Dolly asks after we take our seats with full plates.

"Yes, it's been amazing. This place is so beautiful," I say, grinning at Noah who's nodding in agreement. She chats with us for a moment, then leaves us to eat.

"So what's on the agenda today?" I ask.

"Well as much as I want to keep you in bed all day…I've made arrangements for an in-room couples massage."

My eyes widen. "You didn't! Really?"

"And then after dinner, we'll take a two-hour sunset cruise down Magnolia River, Weeks Bay, and Fish River. It stops at Big Daddy's for drinks and to watch the sunset before we come back."

My emotions bubble over just thinking about the lengths he went through to plan this romantic weekend. No man has ever done anything like this for me. "I love you. That sounds perfect."

"I love you too. And it will be perfect…after we make use of that tub tonight." He winks.

I snort, beaming with more excitement than I've felt in a long time. Though we're in our thirties, it feels like we're teenagers again. Hanging out, making each other laugh, and finding ways to enjoy each other have been the highlight of my weekend.

I only wish now we didn't have to worry about someone trying to kill him.

The couple's massage nearly had me melting off the table. I'd never felt so relaxed in my life and having Noah close made it even better.

"My entire body is butter. You could fold me in half, and I wouldn't feel a thing," I say as I collapse on the bed.

"Is that so? Maybe I should take advantage of this newfound flexibility." Noah grabs my ankles and pushes my knees to my chest. "Hmm...yeah, I could work with this."

I giggle and stretch my legs, rolling away so he can't snap me in half. "Nice try. You promised to wine, dine, and cruise me first."

"I most definitely am...but also..." He stands next to me and undresses. "We're using that tub before we leave. Strip, woman."

Noah fills it and adds some bubble bath. Next, he lights candles and closes all the curtains. "Even though it's not dark outside yet, we're going to improvise."

The champagne, the rose petals on the floor, the relaxing music—he's thought of every little detail. I didn't think it was possible to love this man more than I already do but every day, he proves to me why we should be together.

"Alright, baby. The tub is full, so let's go." He grabs my hand and helps me step in, then slides in behind me.

"Oh my God, it feels so good," I say with a sigh as I relax

against his chest. His strong arms wrap around me as he feathers kisses on my neck.

"You deserve it, sweetheart. I want to give you everything," he whispers.

I look over my shoulder and meet his eyes. "You're all I want, Noah. You're all I've ever wanted. This getaway is just a bonus."

He smiles, then leans down and captures my lips.

"Even though I don't deserve you, I'll spend the rest of my life proving to you how special you are to me."

"You deserve more than you give yourself credit for, Noah. I just want you to be happy," I confirm.

"Trust me, I've never been happier."

After our relaxing afternoon, Noah and I leave for dinner. We had seafood at Orange Beach and talked and laughed for hours. I almost suggested we skip the cruise and spend the rest of the evening naked under the sheets, but I could tell how excited Noah was to take me.

"It's so beautiful, such a natural thing we take for granted," I say as we watch the lazy sun sink below the horizon. Bursts of yellow and orange with slivers of pink fill the sky, and I can't stop staring at the sky. Noah holds me close as I lay my head on his shoulder, and we admire the view.

"You don't realize the things you take for granted until they're taken away from you. Basic human rights. Simple leisures. A home-cooked meal. Everything," he says.

"You can always talk to me about it, Noah," I assure him. "But only if you want to."

Just because he cut me out of his life during his time in prison doesn't mean he needs to keep it from me. I want all of him—even the parts that haunt him.

"As much as I appreciate that, I want to erase those memories from my life as much as possible. You're all I want to focus on now. You, Owen, and my family and friends."

"A new chapter," I confirm with a smile. Though he's decided not to go to therapy right now, I have hope that someday he will. I wish I had after everything happened, but Owen helped me cope. Between taking care of him and working, there wasn't much time to really think about anything else anyway.

"Are you ready to go back to work Monday?" I ask as we make our way to the B&B.

"Hell yes. I feel like shit for leaving Tyler hanging, once again." He groans.

"Tyler understands."

"I know he does, which I'm grateful for, but I don't want to take advantage. After the gym is done, I hope he'll hire me until I can find something else."

"What are you wanting to do?" I ask once we're inside our room.

"I think something with my hands, fixing or building stuff. It's what my dad did in his spare time when he wasn't at the garage and what I helped him with during my school vacations. But beggars can't be choosers either, so I'll take anything."

I wrap my arms around his neck and pull him closer. "You'll find something. You're talented, hard-working, honest, and really good in bed."

Noah chuckles, securing his hands on my waist. "Is that so? Think I can add that to my resume?"

"Put it under...*special skills*." I chuckle.

He slides his hands to my ass and lifts me. "Hmm...can I use you as a reference?" he asks, throwing me on the mattress. Pushing my legs apart with his knee, Noah towers over me.

"Before I agree to that, I'm gonna need to see how proficient your oral skills are."

"Is that so?" He arches a brow, sliding his hand underneath my shirt.

"As well as your expertise on proper etiquette and the ability to learn new techniques."

"That is quite the list of imperative qualities," he muses, pinching my nipple, causing my breathing to grow rapid.

"Well, it's all about having the right credentials," I say, my eyes fluttering closed as he presses his knee harder between my thighs.

"And self-confidence," he adds.

"Mmm...definitely. Dependability, drive, power..." I gasp when he increases the speed over my pussy. "All what it takes to really stand out from the rest."

Noah continues teasing me until I'm breathless and reaching my climax—all before he's even undressed me.

The man has superpowers.

Before I come down from my high, he unbuttons and tosses my jeans aside, then yanks off my panties before sinking his face between my legs. He sucks my clit and thrusts two fingers deep inside me. Every time I get close, he backs away, then does it again and again, driving me insane with desire.

"Noah!" I scream. "I'm about to forcefully hold your head there if you move one more time."

He licks his lips and chuckles. "Just trying to give a thorough oral exam."

"If you don't finish me off, then I'll do it myself," I threaten as I slide my hand down.

He playfully nips at it, but I quickly remove it.

"No, ma'am. You come when I tell you to. Got it?" He flashes me an arrogant wink, and I equally hate and love him for it. My body is on fire, and if he stops one more time, I'm going to cry.

"Now let's test your physical stamina," I say with a lifted brow.

Noah slides off the bed, a cocky grin plastered on his face as he removes his clothes. His erection springs free, and the urge to take him in my mouth nearly takes over. I love the taste and smell of him. Everything about Noah turns me on.

"Lie on your side, baby girl," he demands, crawling into bed behind me.

He lifts one of my legs, then positions himself at my entrance. Sliding in slow, he pushes in deep and fills every inch of me.

"Fuck, you're so tight in this position," he hisses into my neck. Snaking a hand between my thighs, Noah circles my clit and increases his pace.

"Oh my God," I murmur, surrendering to every glorious inch of him. The sensation of him pounding into me and rubbing slowly has the buildup surfacing quickly.

"You like that?" he asks in my ear.

"So good," I mutter.

"You want harder?"

"God, yes."

Every stroke, every caress, every lick, suck, and kiss—Noah cherishes me in a way I never knew existed.

CHAPTER TWENTY-SEVEN

NOAH

I wouldn't have been opposed to staying another week tangled in the sheets with Katie at the B&B. I'm pretty sure I've had a permanent smile on my face since we got home yesterday afternoon. The morning comes quickly, and I'm looking forward to going to work.

Instead of taking Dad's truck today, he offered to drop me off because he had a few errands to run. On the way to town, we stop and grab a dozen donuts, then make our way to the gym.

"Did ya have a good weekend?" Dad asks as the brick building comes into view.

"Yeah, it was great to get away and relax," I tell him. "You and Belinda should go visit that B&B. Would be a nice weekend getaway, and the food around town is really good."

Dad nods. "That might be an idea. Belinda's birthday is coming up soon. Might have to plan somethin' special."

He slows in front of the gym, and I grab the donuts. "Want one while they're still warm?"

With a big grin, I open the box.

"I'm about to have breakfast at the deli. Better not tell Belinda," he says, taking my offer.

"Your secret's safe with me," I tell him before getting out of the truck and waving goodbye.

I laugh and walk inside, where Tyler and Gemma are standing at the front counter. They turn and look at me then Gemma sees what I'm holding.

"You spoil me," she says, moving closer.

"You? These are for Tyler," I tease.

He chuckles as Gemma smacks my arm.

"Okay, you win," I say, handing them over.

After opening the box, she looks at me. "Did you get a dozen?"

"Yeah," I tell her. "Why?"

"They shorted you," she says. "I might call down there and—"

"I didn't get shorted. I gave one to Dad." I shake my head.

She snorts. "I'm blaming my instant rage on hormones."

"You only got a handful of months left to use that excuse," I say, taking a donut for myself and looking around at what they've accomplished while I was out.

"It looks incredible in here," I say, moving through the main area.

"Thanks," Tyler says just as Smith walks through the door. "The grand opening is in four weeks, and we still have a fuckton of things to do."

"I'm ready," I say with a grin, and Smith greets me with a nod.

Tyler pats me on the shoulder. "Great. I've made a list, but mainly all the equipment that was delivered on Friday needs to be assembled."

When I turn around, I see the stacks of boxes leaning against the wall. I'm surprised I didn't notice them when I entered. "Wow."

"We're only waiting for a few more things to arrive. Smith,

today I'd like you to finish working on the juice bar. Noah, if you can start assembling the equipment, that would be great."

He hands me a piece of paper. "This is the floor layout showing where each one needs to go."

A smile hits my lips. "Looks like a good plan."

"If you have any questions, let me know. I'll be working on the boxing ring."

"And I'll be micromanaging," Gemma says around a mouthful.

Tyler presses a kiss on her lips and laughs. "While looking as pretty as ever."

It causes me to chuckle as I move toward the equipment. I'm thrilled to have something to keep me busy. Considering there's so much, I imagine it'll take me all week to get everything put together. I move the boxes closer to their final place to make it easier. Some of it is heavy as hell, and I have to ask Smith to help me a few times.

"You been doin' okay?" he asks after we set down a rack of bench press weights.

"Yeah, feel like my old self again, but it was a struggle not being able to do basic things."

He nods. "Can't imagine. Must've had an angel lookin' over you, based on what Gemma said."

"I did. Grateful to be alive right now," I admit, knowing just how lucky I was to walk away from that accident.

After everything's moved, I read the instructions and begin the assembling process. Katie texts me a few times, but we're both so busy, we can't talk much. By the time I lift my head, Tyler's asking me if I'm going on lunch break.

"Yeah, I was thinking about getting a burger and fries. Want me to get you something'?"

"No thanks. I brought leftovers because Gemma will blow a gasket if we waste any food. Do you know how hard it is to cook for just two people? I've been eating meatloaf for four days straight." He lifts a brow and grins. "Married life."

"Can't wait," I say with a laugh reminiscing on how it felt to hold Katie through the night and wake up with her next to me.

Tyler's expression softens, and he looks down at his cell. "Better get that burger before the lunch rush ruins it."

"You're right," I say, then go and wash the grease from my hands. On the way to the diner, I text my girlfriend.

Noah: What're you wearing?

Katie: Wish it were you.

Noah: Damn girl, gonna make me stop by that bank for a loan, if you know what I mean.

I fantasize about bending her over her desk and listening to her soft moans as she tries to hold back her screams.

Katie: So...what are your plans tonight?

Noah: Was hoping to devour you.

I enter the diner and order a combo to go. As I wait for it to cook, I step outside and soak up in the warm sunshine.

Katie: That sounds like a solid plan. Owen was asking when he'd get to see you again, so I was wondering if you'd like to join us for dinner? :)

Noah: Honestly, I'd love that.

Katie: Good! He'll be really excited about this.

The thought warms my heart. I'd be lying if I said I didn't miss seeing him. Though they visited a lot while I was taking it easy, I've already grown attached to him. There's an internal desire to protect him and Katie from the world because I've seen how ugly it can be.

Noah: Great! I'll pick up a cake for dessert. And ice cream. Maybe we can watch a movie after dinner? I did promise to watch the first *Avengers* with him.

Katie: As long as he's in bed by 9pm at the latest.

Noah: Deal. It's a date!

After I'm given my food and pay, I walk back to the gym. I quickly eat, then spend the rest of the afternoon bolting things together. By the time my shift ends, my muscles are sore, but it feels good. Dad picks me up on time, and I ask him to take me by the bakery and the grocery store on the way home. I run in and grab a half-gallon of vanilla Blue Bell ice cream, then we go to the bakery.

It's almost closing time, but Jackie still greets me with a smile.

"What's the special occasion?" Dad asks when I return with a big ass chocolate cake.

"Owen invited me over for dinner," I proudly tell him as we make our way home.

"You can use the truck tonight. Belinda's gonna come over when her shift ends, so I don't need it."

I thank him, and soon, we're pulling into the driveway. I put the ice cream in the freezer, then jump in the shower to wash off the day. Once Katie texts me that she's picked up Owen, I get dressed and make my way over.

"Noah!" Owen's face lights up the moment he sees me.

"Hey! How's it goin'?" I ask, and he fills me in on his

schoolwork, basketball, and how he wants a dog as Katie cooks.

"A dog?" I ask, and Katie shakes her head.

"We're not getting a dog yet. Maybe when we move into the house."

Owen pouts. "That's never going to happen."

Katie nearly pins him to his chair with her glare. "It *will* happen."

"Bud, it's gonna happen," I assure with a grin. "Maybe by the end of the year," I tell him.

Katie's mouth curves up into a smile. "That would be a miracle."

"It could happen," I say, wanting to wrap my arms around her waist and kiss the softness of her neck as she stirs the noodles.

Owen grabs my attention. "Mom said we could watch *Avengers* after dinner!"

"I know! I'm excited to see it with you and even brought cake and ice cream," I say, setting everything on the counter.

Soon Katie's piling plates full of spaghetti and passes around garlic bread that's fresh out of the oven. My stomach growls and I nearly inhale it as we chat about the chaotic day we've had.

"So work went okay?" Katie asks.

"Yeah, it was great. My muscles ache from lifting all the weights, but I'm happy to be back. We have four weeks until the grand opening. It's gonna fly by."

"Yeah, it will," she tells me. "I'm sure they're glad to have you back."

"Oh yeah, Tyler was thrilled with how much I was able to do."

"That's amazing," she says just as we finish eating. Once the three of us are done, I grab our plates and rinse them off.

"Do y'all want dessert now or after we start the movie?" Katie asks Owen, then glances at me.

"Now!" Owen exclaims, and I laugh.

"He's the boss," I say as she passes me and slides her hand across my lower back. As she stands next to me, my body instantly aches for her.

"Please cut mine small. Might have to roll me outta here after that amazing meal," I admit.

"I'm feeling the same way," she tells me with a laugh. Katie serves the ice cream and cake, and we make our way to the living room. As we start the movie, Owen sits on one side of me and Katie's on the other. At this moment, with them both so close, I feel a deep sense of family. I love them so much that I can barely contain it, and I already know I want to spend forever with them. As I think about our future, I wrap my arm around Katie, brushing my fingertips along her skin. She leans into me, and I hold her close.

When the credits roll, Owen yawns, and Katie tells him it's time for bed. He doesn't argue, but he gives me a tight hug before he goes to his room.

"Thank you for coming," he says as he squeezes me. I hug him back.

"Anytime."

"Tomorrow then?" He raises his eyebrows, but before I can answer, Katie interrupts.

"Come on, Owen. Bedtime." She grins.

After he's tucked in, she meets me on the couch. I can see how tired she is, but it doesn't stop her from leaning over and kissing me.

"Baby," I whisper against her mouth. "I'd join y'all for breakfast, lunch, and dinner every day of the week if that's what you wanted."

"I know," she admits. "He's getting attached, and I don't want you to feel obligated."

I run my hand under her T-shirt and touch the softness of her stomach. "I'm already attached to you both. There's nothing you can do about it."

A blush hits her cheeks, and our mouths crash together. "I need to taste you," I plead.

It takes no convincing. Katie stands up and quietly leads me to her bedroom. When we walk in, she locks her door and slowly undresses. I study her, drinking in her curves, and move her toward the bed.

She lies down, her hair splashing across the stark white blanket, and I feather kisses from her collarbone down to her inner thighs. Being the greedy little thing she is, Katie opens her legs wide, giving me full access. As soon as my mouth touches her, she hums and writhes. She sinks against me, covering her mouth with her hand, and moments later, the orgasm takes over.

"Baby," I say, dipping my tongue inside, fully tasting her before pushing away.

She props herself up on her elbows. "I think that's the fastest I've ever…" Her words trail off, and she pats the mattress next to her.

"It's because I know what your body wants," I murmur against her lips as she undoes my pants and takes control. She teases the tip before taking all of me into her mouth. Using her hand, she strokes and sucks, making me feel like a fucking king.

"Yes," she mumbles. "Come in my mouth," she says when my body tenses. I keep my moans buried deep inside but find it nearly impossible as my orgasm builds. She smiles and picks up the pace until I can no longer hold back.

"I love the way you taste," she says as she swallows every drop, then lies next to me. We get under the blankets, and I hold her tight. My body fully relaxes as I lie next to her, and my eyes grow heavy. I know if I don't get up now, I'll stay the night, and I don't think we're ready to explain that to Owen yet. Though he knows we're dating, he doesn't know the full extent of Katie's and my relationship. We've been careful about how much affection we show one another in front of him.

Before I fall asleep with Katie wrapped in my arms, I kiss her good night, then force myself to get up and get dressed. It's not too late, just a little past ten, but we're both exhausted after our weekend together and working all day.

"See you tomorrow, sweetheart," I say.

"Mmm," she responds with a sleepy smile. She looks comfortable and content.

"I'll lock up," I tell her. After her house is secure, I drive home, feeling tired but also elated. I pull into the driveway and park beside Belinda's car.

When I walk in, they're sitting at the kitchen table drinking tea.

"Hey, Noah!" Belinda says.

"You want some Earl Grey and cookies?" Dad asks.

"Nah. I'm probably gonna go to bed. I've had a long day," I admit with a yawn.

"Night!" Belinda and Dad say at the same time.

"Good night." I offer a smile and go upstairs.

As I'm sitting on the edge of my bed, removing my shoes, I can hear them talking. While I'm not trying to eavesdrop, the moment I hear my name, my attention zones in on their conversation.

"I'm just worried about Noah," she tells him. Her voice lowers, so I move to the top of the staircase.

"When Loretta came to the deli right before close, she had a crazed look in her eye. I sat her at a booth, then went to my office to start closing duties. When Brittany came from the back, Loretta started screaming at her."

"Really? It takes a lot to push Loretta to that point. She's usually good at holding her emotions in and staying calm," Dad says with a concerned tone, and it's true. When I was a kid, she never raised her voice.

"I've never heard her so angry, and I've known her for over twenty years," she says with a sigh.

"What was she saying?" Dad asks.

"She yelled about the money she had given Brittany and asked why she was still in town."

My adrenaline spikes, and I try to recall what Loretta told Katie. I knew it wasn't being hidden from Elliot because of his gambling issue. She flat out lied to Katie, which angers me. Thankfully, there's a long pause before Belinda speaks up again because it gives me time to process this revelation.

"And then Loretta mentioned Gabe and said she knew her son better than Brittany ever did, and that they weren't even together that long. Then Brittany said something in return, but I couldn't quite make out all of her words. Something about her son, Anthony."

Another long pause. My mind reels as I try to figure out what the hell is really going on.

"Brittany knew Gabe?" Dad asks.

"Apparently so. Loretta asked her again why she was still in Lawton Ridge. Brittany mentioned Noah and said there was a change of plans. After that, I walked out of my office into the dining area, and they got eerily quiet. Brittany's face was beet red, and Loretta's eyes were nearly bugging out of her head. I tried to defuse the situation and asked Loretta if she'd be ordering anything before we closed down the kitchen. Instead, she glared at Brittany like she was ready to strangle her, then got up and left."

"This is odd," Dad says. "Do you think—"

"Loretta and Brittany are responsible for Noah's accident?" she asks. "I don't have a doubt in my mind."

"Did Brittany say anything to you once Loretta left?" Dad asks exactly what I want to know.

"No. She didn't even try to explain herself, but there was something dangerous behind her forced smile. I can't quite put my finger on it, but I don't trust her."

"Best to keep an eye on her then," Dad suggests.

"I'm not letting her out of my sight," Belinda snaps.

CHAPTER TWENTY-EIGHT
KATIE

I WAKE up with a permanent smile on my face. Being with Noah has been a dream come true, and I love how caring and compassionate he is when it comes to Owen. Last night was incredible, and for the first time in a long-ass time, I feel complete. My son has a man in his life that he genuinely looks up to, and Noah's more than willing to be a father figure to him. Seeing how they interact with each other makes my heart swell because I can see the special bond they share. It's almost like this is how it was meant to be—Owen, Noah, and me. *My family*.

Though we're taking it slow, I can't help but imagine our future together.

After Owen and I finish eating breakfast, he brushes his teeth, then grabs his backpack, and I take him to school. Once I'm at work taking my first sip of coffee, my phone buzzes.

Noah: Hey, baby. Good morning.

Katie: Morning! Sleep okay? ;)

Noah: Actually no.

My face contorts as I read his message because I wasn't expecting that response. Moments later, he calls me.

"Hey," I answer. "Everything okay?"

"I don't know..." He hesitates. "Last night after I got home, I overheard Belinda talking to my dad. I've tried to ignore it, but some of the things she said...Katie, they're working together," he abruptly says.

"What? Who?"

"Loretta and Brittany. I want to tell you everything, but I'll wait until later tonight when we're alone," he says with a lowered voice. "I don't want anyone to overhear at the gym."

"That's fine. Not a problem," I tell him.

"We can chat after dinner tonight. My treat," he says, and I know he's smiling by his tone.

"Owen would love that," I admit, just as Missy enters and says my first appointment of the day is in the waiting room. I wave to her to bring them in.

"I'm sorry. Gotta go," I say.

"No problem at all. Love you," he tells me.

"Love you too, bye."

Unfortunately, the day passes by at turtle speed, and I've looked at the clock more times than I can count. By the time I pick up Owen from my parents' and Noah comes over for dinner, I've thought of every possible scenario known to man. My mind has been in overdrive, wanting to know what was said.

Noah brings fried chicken, mashed potatoes with gravy, and a pile of buttered biscuits. We devour the food like we haven't eaten in a week. Owen yawns, and I notice he's struggling to stay awake, probably because I let him stay up a little later last night.

"Time for bed," I finally say, and he sticks out his lower lip.

"But I wanted to hang out with Noah some more."

Noah grins wide. "I'm gonna be around a lot, bud. Get some rest, and maybe we can hang out this weekend?"

Owen's eyes light up, and it makes me smile. "Deal," he tells

Noah and holds out his hand to shake on it. I lead him to his room, and after he changes into his pajamas and brushes his teeth, I tuck him in, then tell him good night.

On the way back to Noah, my body buzzes with the prospect of what he'll say. I sit next to him on the couch, and he leans forward, painting his warm lips across mine. When we break apart, he meets my eyes. "Are you ready to hear this?"

"I don't know. I guess it's best to just pull off the Band-Aid. Tell me what kept you up all night."

Noah sucks in a deep breath, then begins, and after he explains what Belinda heard, I feel queasy.

"What're you thinking?" he asks, studying my face. "You okay?"

"All of this makes me sick to my stomach and puts me on edge. I've hardly been able to eat or keep anything down."

He grabs my hand and kisses my knuckles. Sad eyes meet mine. "I'm so sorry to put you through this, baby. I hate that it's affecting you so much."

"It's okay. We're going to get through this and prove they're responsible."

Noah lets out a long breath. "There's more."

"More?" I ask. "Seriously?"

"I have a gut feeling she's the woman Gabe was with the night of the accident," he barely whispers. "And I think she was pregnant with his baby."

A chill rushes through me as I remember what Owen said about Anthony not having a father either.

"I don't remember the woman's name who testified against me or what she looked like, but I'm almost certain it was her. I also think Loretta knew about the baby and has tried to keep it hidden. I believe that's what all of this is really about. It's the only thing that seems to make any sense."

I try hard to understand, but some of this still doesn't line up. "So why would Brittany want you dead?" I ask.

"Revenge," he simply states.

My head spins. "The stress of it all is weighing so heavily on me because I'm so worried about you. I was hoping we'd have a fresh start together."

"I'm not gonna let anyone or anything get between us. Not Loretta. Not Brittany. No one. I'm so sorry I brought this trouble to you," he states matter-of-factly.

"It's not your fault, Noah. I just know we have to be careful because you're being watched. Keeping you safe has to be our priority."

He lets out a sigh. "Based on what I heard in the hospital and the lengths Brittany's already gone to get back at me, you're right. She won't stop until she gets what she wants—me dead."

"I'm still convinced Loretta is the ringleader of all of this, especially since she asked Brittany why she's still in town," I say.

"She could be, but Brittany has skin in the game too. Can't trust either of them."

Noah pulls me into his body and holds me. I lean my head against his shoulder and inhale his scent.

"We need to tell Tyler," I tell him.

"You're right. He might have an idea or some sort of solution, considering he kinda went through something similar. Even if I tried to make a police report, it would be useless at this time because we have no proof." He chuckles. "When I say it out loud, it sounds like a major case of paranoia."

"A handful of people have witnessed all this go down from the beginning, so we know that's not the case. We need to figure out how to keep you protected."

"Maybe I should leave town?" He looks at me with sad eyes.

"No. If you leave, they win. We have to beat them at their own game so they can be prosecuted for all the wrong they've done," I say.

"I know leaving isn't an option, Katie. There's too much I love here. Mainly you and Owen." He smiles, and I place my palm on his cheek and kiss him.

"We'll figure it out," I promise. "Together. Maybe you can talk to Tyler tomorrow? See if he can come over so we can fill him in on what's going on?"

"I'll chat with him first thing in the morning."

After work, I pick up Noah from the gym. He spoke with Tyler, and he said he'd stop by tonight. We pick up cheeseburgers on the way and eat them once we're at my house.

"What do you think he'll say?" I ask, dipping a fry in my ketchup.

Noah shrugs. "He has more experience dealing with crazy people than any of us, so I'm praying he has some sort of solution."

Though it's true, it still makes me laugh. After we've finished eating, Tyler arrives without Gemma. He looks at us and smiles, but he's mainly all business. Noah explains what has happened so far and all the information we've learned over the past few weeks. He goes over what he heard at the hospital, the vandalism, what Belinda said, and even the large sum of money Loretta withdrew from the bank.

"I'm certain Loretta and Brittany are trying to kill me," Noah finally says. Silence fills the room.

Tyler keeps a straight face, but his jaw is clenched. After another minute, he clears his throat and speaks up. "You need a bodyguard immediately. Someone to watch things when you can't. If Anthony is Gabe's, then she'd have some sort of relationship with Loretta, even if it was a broken one. Loretta needs to be confronted, and the sooner, the better. She could stop this if she's the one in control of the situation."

"Where do we find a bodyguard? Online?" I ask, not knowing how any of this works.

Tyler chuckles. "Not quite. I know a guy. Eric Hudson. When I was having issues with Victoria, he came down here. He's always willing to help a friend out, especially when it comes to crazy women. I'll call him and see if he has time, and if he does, I'll book him on the first flight here."

I let out a sigh of relief as Noah nods.

"In the meantime, until we can figure out what to do with Loretta and Brittany, I need you to be overly cautious. Keep your eyes on your surroundings, always have people around you, and don't leave town. Makes it too easy for them to run you off the road. I'll call Eric on my way home." Tyler looks at us before standing. "I'll let you know what he says."

While it's settled for now and the conversation is over, I feel better knowing we'll have help. After we say our goodbyes, Noah walks Tyler out. Five minutes later, he returns to the couch where I'm sitting.

"You okay?" he asks.

"Yeah, just trying to take it all in."

Noah stares off in the empty space before looking at me. "I know Tyler will do anything to protect us. A bodyguard, though? Never thought I'd need one of those."

"Where's Eric gonna stay?" I ask.

"I didn't even think about that," he admits. "Maybe a hotel in Mobile?"

"He'd need to keep a close watch on you, almost like he's your shadow. You two could always use the house now that it's not so cold outside," I suggest.

"Are you sure?"

A smile slides across my lips. "Of course. I know you miss those high ceilings and country aesthetics."

Noah tries to hold back his grin but fails. "I kinda did miss it and seeing you at lunch."

I lean against him and wish none of this was happening. "You have to tell your dad what's going on if Eric agrees, so then he at least knows. With all of this going on, it's best not to hold anything back because I know he's worried too."

He nods in agreement. "I'm gonna try to keep my life as normal as possible so no one's suspicious of anything. That way, if they do have something planned, Eric can help stop them."

"I think that's a great plan." I glance up at the clock and toward the window. "It's gonna get dark soon, and not that I want you to leave, but you should get going."

Noah stands up and pulls me with him, then places a soft kiss on my lips. "Love you, sweetheart. So much."

I wrap my arms around his neck, and he squeezes my waist. "I'll never get tired of hearing that," I admit.

A car door slams, and I peek outside to see Owen and my mother. Owen's talking her head off as they walk down the sidewalk toward the front door. Seconds later, I open it, and as soon as my mother sees Noah, she lights up.

"Hi, Noah," she says, and he greets her in return.

"Hello, Mrs. Walker. You look nice today."

I think I see my mother blush, and I shake my head at him when he passes her. "I'll text you when I get home," Noah tells me with a smile and a wink before saying goodbye to Owen.

"Bath," I tell Owen, and he listens.

"You two look good together," Mom tells me, and I feel like a shy twelve-year-old girl again.

"Thanks, Mama," I say as she turns. "Be careful out there."

"You too, honey." She gives me a smile, then leaves.

After his bath, Owen does his homework, and I text Everleigh. I fill her in on the plan involving Eric.

Everleigh: Eric? Oh, I remember him! How could a girl forget?

She always has a way of making me laugh, even when I don't need it. Almost immediately, she sends another text.

Everleigh: All jokes aside, Eric's a good guy. He'll keep y'all protected. I trusted him with my brother's life.

Katie: Thank you! That's exactly what I needed to hear.

Everleigh: You're welcome. Also, I miss hanging out with you!

I smile because I know she's being genuine.

Katie: We need to get together and plan Gemma's baby shower!

Everleigh: Yes, we do. The sooner, the better.

Katie: I'll shoot some dates over to you tomorrow.

Another text comes through, and I see it's Noah letting me know he made it home. I release a sigh of relief and tell him good night. An hour passes, and I start yawning. I get up and tuck Owen in before going to bed. I fall asleep instantly with hope in my heart that everything will work out for the best.

CHAPTER TWENTY-NINE

NOAH

A FEW DAYS after talking to Tyler and devising a plan to get Eric to Alabama, I decide it's time to tell my dad and Belinda. Since I won't be staying here, they'd know something was up, and I don't want them to worry.

I didn't hold back and told him about everything I knew. I even admitted to overhearing their conversation about what Belinda heard at the deli between Loretta and Brittany. Then I mentioned our theory on Brittany being Gabe's mistress and having his son. Though I've had days to process this, it still feels unreal.

"You sure about this?" Dad asks once I finish. "Having a bodyguard?"

"Yeah, he's trained and can help keep us safe until whoever the man they're working with is caught."

"Trained in what exactly?" Belinda furrows her brows.

"He protected people in the mafia in Vegas," I say truthfully. "Last year, he helped Tyler and Gemma too. If they trust him, then I do too."

"The freakin' mafia?" Belinda gasps. "Are you sure that's

necessary? I don't even know where Brittany is, so she may not be a threat anymore."

"What do you mean? She's not workin' at the deli?"

"Actually, no. I fired her a few days ago. She got an attitude with a regular and *accidentally* spilled a large Coke on him. Plus, she showed up late. It was like she didn't care anymore. Though I'd had a bad feeling about her for a few weeks, I needed the help. However, that was my last straw. I haven't seen her since, and from what his teacher said when she came in this afternoon, Anthony hasn't been in class either."

"So you think she ran?"

She shrugs. "Or she's hiding."

"You think she's working with Loretta?" Dad asks.

"We think Loretta funded a hit man, and Brittany hired him. From what I remember overhearing at the hospital, Brittany paid him twenty grand, the exact amount Katie said Loretta withdrew the day of the accident."

"Son of a..." he mutters, his face turning red with rage.

"I know. Which is why Eric is coming tomorrow, and we'll stay at Katie's farmhouse. There's no room for him here, and I don't want you two to feel uncomfortable. Hopefully, it's only temporary, and this will be resolved sooner than later."

Dad stands and gives me a hug, then whispers for me to please be safe. "You may be in your thirties, but I'll worry about you till the day I die."

"I know, Pops."

"Has anyone confronted Loretta?" Belinda asks.

"Katie asked her about the money, and Loretta lied about why she withdrew it. She asked Katie to let her see Owen, but she hasn't because she doesn't trust Loretta. No one has asked her about the conversation with Brittany at the deli yet."

"She loves her grandson more than anything. She's not just gonna accept that she can't see him," Belinda says.

I shrug. "Katie won't back down until she knows the truth and we're all safe. I know Owen's probably confused about it, but for now, it's what has to happen."

After we finish our conversation, I go upstairs and immediately fall asleep. It's a relief that all of this is now out in the open, and we're all on the same page.

I can't believe it's already Saturday, and Eric's flying in from Vegas today. Tyler and I go to the airport to meet him, and while I'm anxious and nervous, I'm also grateful he's agreed to help. Although he was here last year, it's nearly impossible to give accurate directions. Most of the country roads don't have street signs, and GPS will lead you to the middle of nowhere, so it was just easier to have him follow us.

When he approaches us, Tyler does introductions.

"Nice to meet you." Eric shakes my hand.

"You too. Sorry it's under these circumstances."

"Don't worry about it. I live for this kind of excitement." He smirks, then looks at Tyler. "You've gotten fat."

Eric chuckles, obviously giving Tyler a hard time.

"It's the sympathy baby weight," I chime in. "He's eating for two so Gemma doesn't feel bad."

Tyler rolls his eyes, but a smile hits his lips.

"Just playing with ya, man. You look great. Marriage suits you." Eric nudges Tyler's shoulder, then we walk to baggage claim.

Instead of heading back to Lawton Ridge after he gets his rental, we meet at a restaurant to talk and give him the details.

"I swear, something's uncanny about your small town," Eric muses as we eat.

"You're tellin' me." Tyler snorts. "It's starting to feel a little cursed."

"Only if you're an ex-con, though." I sigh, taking a sip of my drink.

"You're sure it's a hit man they hired?"

I nod. "Pretty certain. Had to be a pro to leave the scene of the accident before the ambulance arrived. I'm positive Brittany picked him up. It was evident she wasn't happy I survived."

"And this Loretta…" He perks a brow. "She wants you gone too?"

"We think she funded the hit man," I confirm.

"So essentially, we're looking for three people?" Eric asks.

"Four, if you count Loretta's husband, Elliot. But I haven't seen him since I arrived. I think it's mainly those two plus the guy they hired."

"If he's a pro, he's probably equipped to take you out from a distance as well. I'm gonna need to do perimeter checks and go everywhere with you until I find him."

"Gonna put a damper on your private time with Katie." Tyler snickers.

Eric shakes his head. "If you're in her house, I'll keep watch from the car. Don't get blue balls on my behalf."

I snort. "Appreciate that."

Tyler drives me back to Lawton Ridge. Katie's with Owen until her mom can watch him this afternoon. We've been so preoccupied that we haven't had much time to work on the house, and it makes me feel bad. I hope to eventually help her get to the point where she can move in. Even though she's too stubborn to admit it, she's struggling to pay her rent and mortgage on top of purchasing the materials needed for the remodel. I want to do everything in my power to take some of the stress off her.

When we arrive at Katie's, Eric gets out of his car and meets us on the porch.

"Couldn't spring for a hotel?" He chuckles when we walk inside.

"There aren't any here," Tyler says.

"This is my girlfriend's place we're fixin' up."

"I'm just messing with you. It's fine. I'm not picky." Eric smirks, looking around.

"We'll be roomies for a while too," I taunt.

"I really appreciate you coming here," Tyler says as I lead Eric to the master room where we'll be staying.

"No problem, man."

Two air mattresses are set up with blankets and pillows with a little side table Katie brought over. I plan to bring a mini fridge with drinks and snacks as well.

"So I never got the full story of what happened last year with you two," I say as Eric unpacks some of his things. "Care to give me the CliffsNotes version?"

"About Victoria? Or as I preferred to call her: Crazy Bitch?" Eric spits out.

"We're gonna need a few beers for this convo." Tyler sighs.

"Let's go to the pub," I suggest. "Then we can show Eric around."

Tyler drives, and once we're inside and seated with our drinks, they tell me the story of the first time they met. It's a whole side of Tyler I never knew, and I'm shocked as hell when he spills all the details.

The drama that went down with Tyler and his two friends Liam and Maddie is insane. Eric used to work for mob boss daughter, Victoria O'Leary, who framed Tyler for drugs and illegal guns. After he did time in prison for a crime he didn't commit, Eric asked him to be a character witness in a deposition for his girlfriend's death. Victoria wasn't happy when she found out Tyler helped in the murder case against her, so she came to Alabama to get back at him. Some shit went down, and she ended up dead.

Just hearing about it gives me chills.

"You know that sounds fake as fuck," I taunt afterward.

"Oh, shit was crazy even before Tyler got involved. Victoria was a level-ten narcissist and psychopath."

"Maybe she's related to Brittany."

After two days of Eric following me around and sleeping at Katie's farmhouse, I return to work. It feels weird to be watched, but according to him, he's had "worse jobs," and this is nothing compared to what he typically does. He's over six feet tall, built like a linebacker, and enters a room like he's ready to kill the next person who dares to speak. I definitely wouldn't cross him.

"Mornin', Noah," Gemma sing-songs when I walk through the front door. Her smile immediately drops when she spots Eric behind me. "Whoa, is that Eric?"

"Hey, Gemma. Nice to see you again."

Gemma rounds the front desk and gives him a side hug. "You too...I think?" She places a hand over her belly, then looks at me. "What's goin' on? He didn't fly all the way down here just for a quick visit."

"Hey, guys." Tyler waltzes in from the back office.

"You care to explain some things to me?" she asks Tyler with her hands on her hips. "The last time Eric was here, shit hit the fan."

"I'm hurt," Eric says, resting a palm on his chest over his heart. "I came here just to see you, of course."

Gemma rolls her eyes. "Nice try. I know my husband and

brother well enough to know that's a bunch of bullshit. You're here because of Brittany, aren't you?"

"Yes, ma'am."

Gemma releases a long, agitated breath.

"Thanks for *not* telling me." Gemma grits her teeth as she stares at Tyler, then at me.

"I didn't want you to stress, especially since your blood pressure is already high," Tyler explains. "The baby needs you to relax."

"The baby needs its mother to be in the loop so she doesn't stress out!" Gemma argues.

"I'm, uh…gonna walk around and check out the area," Eric offers, stepping back. "I'll be out of the way, though, so go about your day like normal."

Tyler flashes him an apologetic look before Eric goes outside.

"Alright, Smith has the list of tasks that need to be done today so we stay on track for the grand opening in three weeks," Tyler tells me.

"I'm on it, boss," I say, then give Gemma a hug. "Don't be mad, sis."

"Don't give me a reason to be then," she snaps.

Tyler mouths, "Hormones," while shaking his head, and I snicker before walking away.

The workday goes smoothly, and Eric's right, I barely noticed him. He walked around, making a note of the emergency exits, then he checked the alley and the other stores on the block. Since the gym is near downtown, several taller buildings would give a hit man a perfect bird's-eye view of the area. Eric came prepared, though, and won't hesitate to shoot this guy if the time comes.

"Ready?" I ask Eric once I say goodbye to everyone.

"Yep. Secured the perimeter and the whole damn block. Now I just need this guy to show up so I can—"

"Arm wrestle him," Tyler quickly interjects.

Gemma scowls. "I'm not an idiot. I know exactly what Eric's planning."

"G'night, sis." I give her a side hug.

"Be careful. I mean it," she orders, squeezing me in return.

"Don't worry. I'll keep him out of trouble." Eric winks.

Once we're at the house, I take a shower and get dressed.

"I'm gonna have dinner at Katie's tonight. You're more than welcome to come eat with us, or you can grab something on your own if you'd rather."

"Nah, I ate only a couple of hours ago while I was at the deli. I'll drive you there and stake out from the car just in case there's any suspicious activity. Forgot to mention earlier that I'm running a background check on Brittany and Loretta. I also have a friend in Vegas who's digging into their financials and cell phone history."

I raise a brow, shocked he's able to do all that. Instead of asking questions and getting answers I don't want to know, I change the subject. "Alright, well, text me if you get hungry. I can bring you some leftovers."

Eric smirks, patting my shoulder. "Not my first rodeo, Noah. I'll be fine. I'll text you if I see or need anything."

Before we leave, Eric walks around the house, then lets me know it's safe to come to the car. The drive over is uneventful, and admittedly, I do feel safer with Eric close by. As soon as Katie answers the door, I pull her in for a hug, and her body molds to mine.

"Hey, baby. I've missed you." I press my lips to hers. We've texted and talked on the phone all weekend, but I haven't seen her in person since last week.

"I missed you more," she whispers, moaning against my mouth.

"Noah!" Owen's voice breaks us apart, and we realize we almost lost control.

"Hey, bud. How's it goin'?" We bump fists, and he smiles.

"Good. Did you see another *Star Wars* movie was released on Disney Plus?"

We all walk to the kitchen, and I inhale the smell of Katie's food.

"No, I didn't. Guess we'll have to watch it this weekend." I grab the plates from the cabinet and set the table as Katie takes the casserole from the oven.

"Yes!" Owen cheers. "I'll make sure we're stocked up on popcorn."

"Alright, time to eat," Katie announces. "Owen, grab the silverware please."

"I'll get some glasses," I say.

Once we're seated, we dive in. Owen does most of the talking while Katie and I sneak glances at each other. As much as I enjoy hanging out with him, I'm dying to be alone with my girl before I have to leave. Though I'd much rather sleep over, it's best if Eric and I are in the same space.

"But Mom, I'm not even tired," Owen whines around a yawn.

"Oh really?" she muses, then reminds him to go brush his teeth.

Once he's tucked in for the night, I help Katie pick up around the house and wipe down the counters.

As she rinses the dishes, I wrap my arms around her from behind and nuzzle my face into the softness of her neck.

"You know what sounds *really* good right now?" I whisper in her ear.

"A hot shower, a pint of Ben & Jerry's, and binge-watching Netflix?"

I chuckle. "I could get on board with that. Perhaps we should start with the first and go from there?"

Katie dries her hands before turning and wrapping her arms around my waist. "I know exactly where it'd go."

The corner of my lips tilts up. "Only if you seduced me."

She giggles, tilting her head so I can capture her mouth.

"Hmm...might be a good chance of that happening." She lowers her hand to my erection. "Though, I think you've made my job easy."

"Mmm...don't tease me, woman. I've been dreaming of your mouth on me for days."

"Take me to the shower, and perhaps I can help make that a reality." Katie smirks, and I immediately lift her and walk us to the bathroom, where she most definitely *helps* me out.

CHAPTER THIRTY

KATIE

Even though Eric's been in town for five days, I still find myself looking over my shoulder and waiting for Brittany to appear. Since she's been MIA, I'm paranoid as hell about what she's planning next.

My mother has been picking up Owen every day after school, so I decided to tell her what was going on with Loretta. I spared her the details she didn't need to know and wanted to make sure she didn't mention it to Owen or speak to Loretta. I have no doubt she'll eventually reach out to Mom because after learning she lied to me about the money, I've sent her calls to voicemail. I'm pissed because for a moment, I believed her.

"Hey, you heading out? I'll walk with you," Missy says, poking her head into my office.

I check the clock. "Not yet. I have about ten more minutes of stuff to do."

"Okay, see ya tomorrow then! Thank God it'll be Friday!" She releases a *whoop-whoop*, and I chuckle, waving goodbye.

Once I've cleared my inbox and tidied my desk, I grab my bag and lock my office door behind me. I check my texts and smile when I see Noah's name on the screen. Just as I'm about to unlock my car, I notice Loretta standing next to it, waiting for me. My adrenaline spikes, and I go into overdrive as I check my surroundings.

"Katie." She wears a defeated expression.

"What're you doing here?" I ask, keeping my phone tight in my palm just in case.

"I wanna see my grandson," she states.

Arching a brow, I place a hand on my hip. "Which one?"

She narrows her eyes. "What do you mean? The only one I have."

I scoff, resisting the urge to roll my eyes. "You sure about that?"

"What on God's green earth are you talkin' about, Katie?"

"Well, seeing as Anthony is Gabe's son, I was just wondering which grandson you were talkin' about."

"Wha-I have no idea what you're—"

"Don't insult me, Loretta," I interrupt. "I've put the pieces together. Brittany was one of Gabe's mistresses, wasn't she?"

She inhales a sharp breath as if she's debating on coming clean or not. If she knows what's good for her, she better.

"*Yes*, she was. He got her pregnant, but Elliot and I didn't know until after Gabe passed."

"So that's how you knew her and why you teamed up with her to kill Noah?"

She balks. "What? Of course not."

"Explain the twenty grand then. And don't you dare lie to me this time."

"Katie, let's sit down somewhere and talk about this," she pleads.

I look around the parking lot. "I'd rather not. There are cameras back here just in case."

"You really think I'd try to hurt you?"

"I'd say never until someone started coming after Noah, and then you withdrew the same sum of money that Brittany paid a hit man. It's not hard to figure out what's going on. He's responsible for Gabe's death, and you and Brittany aren't happy he's back. He took away your only son and Anthony's father."

"Katie, I really don't know anything about someone trying to kill Noah, but yes, I did give Brittany that money. Years ago when she gave us proof that Gabe was her son's father, we paid her to keep quiet and leave town, knowing how it'd look and all."

"How it'd look?" I raise a brow, knowing it was to save Gabe's image.

"I knew it'd break your heart even more. You didn't deserve learning the news of that after everything you'd already been through. It'd tarnish your memories of Gabe and would be a constant reminder of what he did to you. Elliot and I thought we were doing what was best for everyone."

"By ignoring a child who was your blood relative? Of course I would've been hurt, but what he'd done couldn't be changed."

"Brittany's extremely unstable and would've made your life hell, Katie. I did it for both of us," she exclaims.

"Seems like she's dead set on making Noah's life hell. She's behind everything, and when I saw you withdraw that money, I thought you could be too."

"I assure you I only gave her that money so she'd leave town again. She was blackmailing us with rumors and said if we gave her the cash, she'd take Anthony and move away."

"And you believed her?"

"Well, she did last time, so I was hopeful. When I saw she returned, I reminded her of our deal, and she said she had unfinished business."

I think back to what Noah told me was said at the deli and what Loretta's saying seems to match. While I have no reason to believe Loretta since she made up a tall tale previously, Belinda heard this exact conversation, so I know she's telling the truth. "You knew she was coming after him then?"

"At the time, I didn't realize what she was capable of. It wasn't until things started happening that I put it together."

"Noah had to hide for weeks to keep Jerry and Belinda safe," I nearly shout. "Since no one knew it was her at the time, he couldn't risk it."

She pins me with a stare. "I'm a little surprised you're defending him so much. You sure forgave him quickly. I know Gabe wasn't perfect, but Noah—"

"I love him," I blurt out, my cheeks heating at the confession I've hidden from her for so long. "We're together."

"Oh." She swallows hard. "Can't say I'm entirely shocked, considering how close you two were before the incident. Does Owen know?"

"Yes. But not about that night. And I'd like it to stay that way," I clarify. "He's too young to understand."

"What's goin' to happen if he finds out from someone else?"

"I'll figure that out when the time comes, but for now, there's no reason he needs to know. It was a very unfortunate accident."

Loretta huffs, and though this is a hard topic for her to discuss, she keeps her opinions to herself.

"I would never hurt Owen or put him in harm's way," she says softly. "I miss him, Katie. Please let me see him."

As much as my heart goes out to her, I can't agree just yet. "I'm sorry, Loretta. Until Brittany is caught, he's staying close to my mother and me."

"I love him more than anything. It's why I wanted Brittany out of town. I don't want him finding out about his dad's affair any more than you do."

"Of course I don't, but he has a half brother. I can't keep that from him forever." As much as I don't want Brittany near any of us, Anthony's an innocent child who's suffering from this too.

"Brittany wants Noah to pay. Gabe promised her this whole fantasy life, and she blames Noah for ripping it away from her. From the sound of it, she'll stop at nothing to make that happen."

I scowl at the thought of Gabe promising the world to another woman. "Exactly what did he tell her?"

She lowers her eyes and is reluctant to speak. "After she told him she was pregnant, he promised to leave you. Gave her this whole speech about being a family and giving her everything she ever wanted. She was sleeping with him, so he probably fed her whatever she wanted to hear, but either way, she believed him. When she provided us with a DNA test that proved Anthony was his, we were adamant about you never knowing. So she blackmailed us to keep her secret."

Hearing that is a punch to the gut, but I'm not entirely shocked either. If he was capable of cheating on me when I was pregnant, then he was capable of leaving me too. If he would've been up front about not being happy in our marriage, the fight that resulted in his death might've never happened.

Or rather, I should've confronted him months before that and left him. I stayed because I wanted our son to have a family, but that takes a lot more than two people being married.

"And I'm guessing the money ran out pretty quickly, and she knew she could score the cash to help take out Noah if she blackmailed you again."

"Yes," she confirms. "That's my best guess."

"I want to believe you had no idea what she had planned, but I have to keep Owen safe. Until she comes out of hiding and can be caught, protecting my son is my priority."

"I understand that more than you know, Katie. I wanted to protect my son too. His image. His wife and child. I wish I knew why he cheated on you, and I don't want to believe he told Brittany those things, but regardless, I love him no matter what, just like you love Owen. Whether it was a mistake or he really planned to leave, I'm not sure. Just know my intentions were pure."

"I believe you, Loretta," I say, meaning every word. She's been there for me since the moment Owen arrived, and I'd never second-guess her love for him. However, since I don't know what Brittany has planned next and how she involved Loretta, I won't take any chances.

"Thank you. I understand you have to do what's best for Owen, but please let me see him soon. We miss him terribly."

I nod. "I'll consider it, okay?"

"For what it's worth, I like seeing you happy. I hope Noah realizes how amazing you are." She grins.

"I appreciate that." I smile, feeling the weight melt off my shoulders now that it's no longer a secret. "Owen really likes him too."

"I'm sure he does. I wish I could forgive and forget like you, but as a mother—"

"You don't have to explain anything to me," I interject. "I can't imagine that kind of pain. It hurts too much to even think about how I'd cope if I lost Owen. I'll never put that kind of pressure on you, and Noah will never push those boundaries either. But now you know where I stand and that Noah is in our lives now. *Permanently.*"

"Thanks for telling me. And thank you for taking the time to speak to me. I was going crazy after you stopped answering my calls."

"I better go and pick up Owen before my mom starts to worry," I tell her, reaching for my keys.

"Alright, dear. Drive safe. Give him a hug and kiss from me, okay?"

I flash her a small smile. "Will do."

Loretta walks back to her car, and then I get into mine. My heart races, and my brain buzzes. I can't believe that conversation just happened, but I'm relieved as hell. It's believable that she'd pay Brittany to get out of town to protect Gabe. Image is everything to the Reids, especially when it comes to their only son. The question now remains: where the hell is Brittany and who is she conspiring with?

ONLY US

As soon as I get to my parents', I wrap Owen in a big hug.

"Mom!" He wiggles. "You're suffocating me!"

I giggle, then kiss his cheeks. "I missed you!"

My mom chuckles. "He got hungry, so I fed him some mac 'n cheese."

"Thanks. Guess that means you'll have extra time to take a bath," I muse, ruffling his greasy hair. "Because you definitely need it."

"Mom!" He groans, rolling his eyes, then walks away.

"I'll see you tomorrow," I call out as we head out the door.

On the way home, Owen tells me all about his day.

"Speaking of school, have you seen Anthony in class lately?"

"No, the teacher said he's sick. He's been out all week."

Hmm…well, that confirms my suspicions then. She might've taken him out of school so people thought she left, but I'm not convinced this is over. And the thought scares me to death.

Since Belinda fired her, who knows where she could be now.

"You go wash up, then put on some clean jammies," I tell him when we go into the house. "Clean underwear too."

"I know!" he bellows.

"Excuse me? Wanna lose that attitude?"

"I don't have an attitude," he snaps.

"Sounds like one to me," I counter.

When he's finally in the bathroom, I call Noah.

"Hey, baby. I was wonderin' where you were," he says, which reminds me I never read his text message from earlier.

"Sorry, Loretta ambushed me after work."

"What?"

"Yep, she was waiting for me at my car," I tell him, then continue to explain what we discussed.

"Do you believe her?" he asks when I'm done.

"Yeah," I say honestly. "She loves Owen too much to jeopardize their relationship. She knows she'd lose the only person connected to her son if she tried to harm you."

"So she knows about us then?"

"She does," I confirm. "She wasn't that shocked, though. It was actually a good conversation and one we needed to have, but I told her I wasn't ready to leave Owen with her yet."

"How'd she take it?"

"Uhh...she understood but was still upset."

"Well, I guess it's nice to know she's not trying to kill me, but it's still worrisome that Brittany's MIA."

"Anthony hasn't been in school either, so something is definitely up. I still think she's planning something."

"It'd have to be something really good with Eric around."

"Hopefully, she'll give up and just go away," I say, but it's wishful thinking.

"So besides that, how was your day?"

Noah has me smiling and laughing in seconds as usual. We talk about work and what we hope to do this weekend at the house.

"Mom!" Owen calls.

"Oh shoot, I better go. Owen's yelling for me."

"Alright, baby. I love you. Text me before bed so I can say good night, okay?"

"I will. Love you too."

Once we hang up, I walk to the bathroom and peek inside. "What is it?"

"I forgot a towel."

I chuckle. "Hold on."

After Owen is dried and in his pajamas, we curl up on the couch with a bowl of popcorn and watch one of his favorite cartoons. As he's sucked into the screen, I decide to group text Gemma and Everleigh to give them an update.

Everleigh: She WHAT?

Gemma: OMG...the audacity!

Katie: Put down your pitchforks…let me explain.

After several long messages, I finally get out the whole story about Loretta and what happened with Brittany and Gabe. It feels like Deja vu as I've now repeated this twice in just a few hours.

Everleigh: I'm just gonna say it. The rat bastard is lucky he's dead for not only cheating on you but for knocking up another woman and promising to leave you.

Gemma: Everleigh!!!!

Everleigh: What? You're thinking it too!

Katie: Trust me, I know…but I could've left too. We were young and stupid.

Everleigh: Don't you dare make excuses for him!

Katie: I'm not, but it takes two people to break up a marriage.

Everleigh: Yeah, Gabe and his whore.

Gemma: ANYWAY…so we know Loretta isn't trying to get Noah killed, but we still don't trust her.

Katie: I do, but I'm just not ready to fully let her back into our lives, at least not until Brittany is taken care of. If she sees Loretta with Owen, it might make him a target. I don't know, but I'd rather be safe than sorry.

Gemma: Yes, use your mama instincts!

Everleigh: I'm about to hire my own hit man to find this bitch.

I snort.

Katie: Don't worry, Eric's here and is doing everything he can to find her. He's not gonna let anything happen.

Gemma: He's really good at what he does.

Everleigh: Pretty hot too.

Rolling my eyes, I send a reply.

Katie: Don't even think about it, Everleigh Blackwood.

Everleigh: I'm just admiring the way the man looks in a tight black T-shirt and combat boots, okay?

Gemma: That's her weakness.

I chuckle in agreement.

Katie: She definitely has a type. The bad boy vibe.

Everleigh: They're the best in bed. What can I say?

She sends a tongue sticking-out emoji.

Gemma: You have daddy issues.

Katie: Or mommy issues.

Everleigh: Let's be real, I have both.

Though I know we're just teasing, it's true. Tyler helped raise her due to their junkie mother and nonexistent father. When he left for the military, she moved in with their grandparents, and neither of them has had a relationship with their mom. Everleigh didn't let it define her, though, and neither did Tyler. She worked her ass off, started her own boutique, and is thriving.

Katie: I gotta get Owen to bed and then myself soon, so I'll talk to you guys later. Can't wait for the grand opening next weekend!

Gemma: OMG, I'm so nervous but excited! I'm so ready for it to be here.

Katie: I have no doubt it's gonna be amazing!

Everleigh: There's an open bar, though, right?

Gemma: Good night.

Everleigh: What? I'm just asking!

My face hurts from smiling so much.

Katie: Night!

I read Owen a chapter from his book, and he quickly falls asleep. Once I double-check that the windows and doors are locked, I make myself a cup of tea, then crawl into bed. Though it's just past nine, I call Noah and talk to him for an hour before falling asleep.

CHAPTER THIRTY-ONE

NOAH

It's the day the entire family's been waiting for—the gym's grand opening. I arrive early with Dad to help set up the tables with the treats Belinda made for the hundreds of people expected to stop by. Eric joins us too, but he stays out of sight. I've almost stopped noticing him around because he's stealthy as hell. The past nine days have been quiet, but Eric's convinced this is the calm before the storm. He's still been keeping watch on Loretta, though she's not as suspect as she was before. There's been no sign of Brittany or Anthony, and I'm hoping that means she's given up and dropped her vendetta. Katie doesn't believe that's the case, though, and neither does Eric, so we've been extra careful.

Within the hour, most of Lawton Ridge and some of Mobile will arrive to congratulate Tyler and Gemma. Opening a new business around here is a big deal because it doesn't happen too often. Gemma went all out and hired a DJ, a hot dog truck, and set up arts and crafts booths for the kids. She's also giving away a ton of prizes, from yearly memberships to big-screen TVs. It's been the talk of the town all week.

Before the excitement fully commences, Katie arrives looking as gorgeous as ever with her hair pulled to the side. Her lips are ruby red, and she's dressed in some tight jeans and a top that shows me the softness of her neck. When she comes closer, I pull her into my arms. Owen smiles, and though I'm hesitant to let her go, I create some space between us.

"Sorry," I whisper, leaning in just so she can hear. "Can't help myself. You're so goddamn beautiful."

When I push away, she laughs and grins. Today's a big deal for more than one reason. This is the first time we've been seen together in a public setting, and I interlock my fingers with hers so everyone knows she's my girl. Many haven't forgotten what happened with Gabe, and I'm sure we'll be fueling the rumor mill until something else gets their attention, but neither of us cares. We no longer want to keep our relationship a secret, so we thought this was a good time. That way, there's no doubt she's mine, and I'm hers.

People begin arriving in packs, and the band starts playing a country song. Soon, it seems all of Lawton Ridge is here and in full celebration mode. Some stare while others whisper when I wrap my arm around Katie's shoulder or hold her hand, but it doesn't bother us. We're not ashamed to be together. Anyone who doesn't agree can fuck off because I don't care about their opinions. For once in my life, I'm happy and so is Katie. I finally have what I've always wanted—*her*. And I want the whole damn world to know.

"Mom, can I get my face painted?" Owen asks as we pass the booth that has a line of eager kids waiting.

"Sure," she says, and we go to the end.

"Do you know what you're gonna get?" I ask Owen. There are at least fifty designs to choose from, way too many for indecisive kids.

"Captain America!" he confirms with a fist pump.

I nod. "That's a great one!"

Soon, he's plopping down in the seat, and Katie and I watch

as his entire face is covered in red, white, and blue paint. After it's finished, I give him a high five, and Katie pulls out her phone.

"You two get together. Let's take a picture."

Before she can snap it, someone walks by and offers to take one of the three of us. Katie happily stands next to me, and we smile wide.

"It turned out great," the woman says, handing Katie her phone back.

With a smile, Katie turns the screen around and shows us.

"Our first family photo," I say, and I think I see her emotions take over for a brief second.

"It's perfect," she says.

We stop and grab a hot dog, slathering on the mustard like there's no more left on the planet, and eat at the picnic tables set up in the parking lot. The sun beats down on us, but honestly, the weather is perfect. A few lingering clouds and a constant breeze help so we don't bake.

Tyler and Gemma walk around as calm as can be, and they greet everyone who passes them. When they come closer to us, I ask if they need anything, and Tyler shakes his head.

"You're off the clock today," he says with a grin, then glances at Katie. "Y'all enjoy yourselves."

"Yes, sir," I reply just as Katie's parents walk over. Owen runs toward them and gives Katie's mom a big hug. Face paint smears on the side of her shirt, but her smile never fades. It's obvious how much she loves Owen.

"Hey, kids," Mrs. Walker says to us.

"Mom, can I hang out with Memaw and Papa?" Owen asks without hesitation.

Katie scrunches her face and looks at her mom for approval.

"Yeah, I'd love to take him around. All the arts and crafts like sand art and necklace making, and I think I saw a dunking booth too," she says.

"A dunking booth? I must've missed that one. Gemma really did go all out," Katie replies, and I agree.

"Sometimes, she can be a *little* extra," I say with a laugh.

"Call me when you're exhausted," Katie tells her mother and gives her dad a hug. Soon, Owen's leading them through the crowd back toward the kids' activities.

After the mayor gives a speech about new businesses and the Lawton Ridge community, Tyler's handed the giant pair of golden scissors and cuts the ribbon in front of the door. The crowd cheers with excitement, and he thanks them all for coming. Soon, Gemma gives people a tour of the inside of the gym.

"This is amazing," Katie leans into me and says. She's seen the progression of what we've done, but now, all the finishing touches have been added.

"I'm actually impressed by how well it turned out, though I had no doubt it would be anything other than great," I admit. One of Gemma's new employees is whipping up samples from the juice bar and passing them out to people. Katie and I stop and try a few flavors.

"Well, hello to you," I hear a woman say from behind.

Immediately, Katie's face splits in half. "Ruby! Stephanie! Y'all came!"

"Wouldn't miss it. Actually, I think Tyler would've divorced me as a friend if I didn't show up," Ruby admits and pulls Stephanie close.

"You're damn right," Tyler says from behind.

"Told ya," Ruby says with a wink. "How've you been, Noah?"

"Great," I admit, and she smiles wide when she notices my fingers are interlocked with Katie's.

Moments later, Everleigh meets up with us, and Gemma comes over too. Soon, we're all trying to talk over each other, laughing and cutting up. When I glance at Katie, she takes the opportunity to pull me to the side.

"I think the juice bar got to me. My stomach is kinda messed up and gurgling. I'm gonna run to the car and get some Pepto," she says.

"Okay, I'll come with you," I tell her.

She shakes her head and looks around at everyone. "No, no. It's fine. I'm only parked a few blocks away by the deli, and plenty of people are around. I'll be right back. Have fun. Enjoy yourself," she says, then walks away before I can protest.

"The juice bar is fucking fantastic," Ruby says, grabbing my attention when she rubs her hand across the countertop.

"Right? Noah did all the cabinetry work." Tyler eagerly gives me credit, showing her the other side with all the storage space.

I smile. "I actually really enjoy building things, so I had a good time. The top is a live oak edge. Smith did that part," I admit.

"The workmanship is incredible. You should start a business," she suggests.

A small chuckle escapes me. "That's what they all say."

"I'd hire you," Ruby admits.

"Yeah, and I would too," Everleigh tells me. "I've been wanting to redo some cabinets in my kitchen for *years*. I'm imagining it now."

"He's expensive," Tyler says. "And you're too cheap."

Our group of friends bursts into laughter.

"I am *not* cheap. I'm just smart with my money. Well, unless it comes to shoes, purses, and wine, then all bets are off."

"Nice save," Gemma tells her before she's pulled away by someone asking about memberships. Tyler excuses himself too, and I check the time on my phone. It's been at least fifteen minutes since Katie left, and I begin to grow concerned. I tell everyone I'll catch up with them later and walk outside to call her. It rings and then goes straight to voicemail, so I try again.

Immediately, I walk through the crowd and start searching for her. When I pass Mrs. and Mr. Walker painting ceramic jars with Owen, I ask if they've seen Katie. They shake their heads, and I force a smile though I'm internally freaking out.

After her phone goes to voicemail another five times, I start to lose it, and Eric rushes toward me, noticing there's an issue. "What's wrong?" he asks.

"I can't find Katie. She's not answering her phone. She was going to her car to grab some medicine, but she's been gone for at least twenty minutes now."

Eric's calm as we walk toward the deli where Katie said she parked. The entire time, I keep calling her phone, not giving up hope. I keep telling myself that maybe it died or something else happened, but I also can't stop from thinking the worst. Eric abruptly stops, and when I see Katie's car, anger floods me. All four of her tires have been slashed, and immediately, I know something terribly wrong has happened. She's nowhere to be found.

"There are cameras," Eric says, pointing up at them. "We might have some hard evidence if there's foul play."

"Fuck," I whisper-hiss, calling Katie again.

"She might be back at the gym. We should look around one last time to make sure," Eric suggests, and I agree but also don't want to waste any time.

As soon as we return, I spot Gemma and Everleigh eating snow cones. I rush over to them. "Have you seen Katie?"

They both shake their heads. "Is everything okay?" Gemma asks, concern filling her tone. She makes eye contact with Eric, and though he doesn't say anything, Gemma knows what it means. I watch as she drops her cup and bright red ice splashes across the concrete.

"I don't know," I tell her truthfully. "I—"

Before I can get any other words out, my phone rings, and rage fills me when I see Brittany's name on the screen.

I walk away from all the noise with Eric hot on my trail and answer.

"Noah," she purrs. "How are you?"

"Cut the shit," I snap.

"Ah. Okay. Playing hardball. Got it. Well, as you've probably figured out, I have your girlfriend."

I put her on speakerphone so Eric can hear what she's saying. My hand trembles with fury, but I try to keep control before I say something that could get Katie hurt.

"If you touch her—"

"We're not playing macho man today, Noah. You're not in control here; I am. Now you're gonna listen to me very carefully and follow every fucking one of my directions, or I'll kill her. And trust me when I say it would satisfy me beyond belief to end this cunt's life."

My heart races.

"So if you want your precious girlfriend back, I need you to meet me alone at the storage units outside of town," she says. "You know which ones."

Eric immediately starts walking and waves me to follow him.

"Why are you doing this?" I ask, trying to stall her for just a little longer.

She's so quiet I think the call dropped. "Because I want you to suffer for murdering the love of my life. This is only fair, Noah. There are consequences to every action, and this is yours. You took away the only man I loved, so I'll take away the only woman you've ever loved. At first, I wondered how I'd be able to pull this off. Honestly, you made it too easy."

It's obvious she's using Katie as bait. She's not her main target. I am. I've always been. "So if I show up, you'll let her live?"

"I'll tell Nicolas to let her live," she says.

"Who the fuck is that?" I ask.

She laughs. "Don't worry about it."

"How can I even trust you?" I seethe.

"Oh, I'd much rather see you bleed out than her. You have thirty minutes. If you arrive a minute late, she'll have a bullet in her head. And I won't stop until you do too."

The call ends, and all of our conspiracies about Brittany make perfect sense.

CHAPTER THIRTY-TWO

KATIE

I DON'T KNOW why those smoothies would affect me like that, but I'm assuming it's all the fiber. The last thing I want to do is leave because I'm not feeling well, so the best solution is to grab the Pepto pills I have in my glove box for these types of emergencies.

A smile fills my face as I leave the celebration and walk toward my car. It's only a few blocks away, and I can still hear the band playing in the distance. As I get closer, I unlock my phone and scroll through the few pictures I have of Owen, Noah, and me together. Earlier, when he said it was our first family photo, I nearly cried. My emotions bubbled over, and I lost my words. It's been only Owen and me for so long that when he said that, it felt right. We *are* a family, and I love him with all my heart.

When I turn the corner, I see my car, and as I move closer, I notice all four of my tires are slashed.

"What the actual fuck?" I say out loud just as I'm getting ready to call Noah. Before I can, I'm grabbed, and my arms are secured behind my back. I struggle, trying to break free, but the man holding me is too strong. A few seconds later, I'm peering into dark brown eyes.

Brittany.

"Let me go!" I scream. All I want to do right now is claw out her eyes.

A maniacal laugh escapes her dark red lips. "No."

Taking another step forward, she grabs my cheeks and squeezes hard, digging her nails into my skin. "I never understood what he saw in you."

I glare at her, wishing she'd drop dead.

"Gabe never had the best taste in women," I throw back.

Her fist connects with my stomach so fast that she knocks the wind out of me. My pain only causes her to laugh. As I suck in air, she tells the guy who's holding me to bring me to her Suburban.

"Why are you doing this?" I croak.

She opens the back door, then crosses her arms and stares at me. "Isn't it obvious? You're the ticket that will lead Noah directly to me. Honestly, I should've taken this route a lot sooner."

"You don't have to do this, Brittany. Just let me go, and we can pretend none of this happened," I say, thinking about Noah and how Owen's with my mother. They'll all be looking for me if they aren't already.

"Don't think so. There's no turning back now." She reaches into the back and grabs a roll of duct tape.

The sound of her pulling it from the roll nearly pierces my ears.

"Please," I beg again. "My son is with me."

"I don't give a fuck about your kid." She rips the tape and slaps it hard over my mouth. I struggle to break free, but it's no use.

"Nicolas, don't you fucking let her get away."

Moving behind me, Brittany tapes my wrists together, then wraps it around my thighs and ankles until I can hardly move. I try to scream, but it's so muffled no one would ever be able to hear me. Tears stream down my face as I come to terms with what she's done. Adrenaline courses through my veins, and I wish I would've let Noah accompany me like he wanted. But I was stupid and insisted he stay.

My phone buzzes in my back pocket, and Brittany grabs it and smirks. It's Noah. She turns it off, then slams it on the pavement. The screen immediately shatters, and she picks it up and throws it in her vehicle.

"I'm gonna kill him," she seethes. "Then this will all be over."

Sweat forms on my brow as I try to scream through the tape. My stomach is so upset, and I'm scared that I'll throw up with my mouth secured closed. This is the worst possible time to be sick.

"We need to get going," she tells Nicolas. "They'll be looking for her soon."

With all her strength, Brittany punches me in the stomach again and brings her knee in too. "That's for being a bitch toward me."

I lose my balance and fall to the ground, where Brittany kicks me until I nearly lose consciousness.

"And that's for fucking the man who killed Gabe."

After a minute of her physically taking her anger out on me, Nicolas grabs me by the hair and throws me in the back of her SUV. After the doors slam closed, the engine rumbles, and we're quickly speeding away.

I wonder how long it'll take Noah to realize I'm gone. After I didn't answer the first time, I know he's already searching for me. I just hope to God he has Eric with him because I don't doubt Brittany's words for one second.

She speaks to Nicolas in a high-pitched tone, like she's happy about what she's accomplished. I try to turn my body to see out the window but can't manage to twist around. My eyes burn with hot tears, and I try to take myself out of the situation until I hear Brittany tell Nicolas she's calling Noah.

A lump the size of Texas forms in my throat as I hang on to every word she says.

"Noah," she purrs. "How are you?"

I can only imagine what he said to her and wish the phone was on speaker.

"Ah. Okay. Playing hardball. Got it. Well, as you've probably figured out, I have your girlfriend."

She's silent for a moment. "We're not playing macho man today, Noah. You're not in control here; I am. Now you're gonna listen to me very carefully and follow every fucking one of my directions, or I'll kill her. And trust me when I say it would satisfy me beyond belief to end this cunt's life."

I wish I could see her reaction, but based on her tone, she's unamused.

"So if you want your precious girlfriend back, I need you to meet me alone at the storage units outside of town," she says. "You know which ones."

For a second, I think she's ended the call because she's quiet. All I can hear is the hum of the tires against the road. She eventually speaks up and forces me back to this reality. "Because I want you to suffer for murdering the love of my life. This is only fair, Noah. There are consequences to every action, and this is yours. You took away the only man I loved, so I'll take away the only woman you've ever loved. At first, I wondered how I'd be able to pull this off. Honestly, you made it too easy."

The tears begin to fall again. I never wanted to put Noah in danger, and now, I'm the reason he'll go straight to Brittany.

"I'll tell Nicolas to let her live," she says with a laugh, then continues. "Don't worry about it."

I try to scream and tell him to stay away.

She speaks up again. "Oh, I'd much rather see you bleed out than her. You have thirty minutes. If you arrive a minute late, she'll have a bullet in her head. And I won't stop until you do too."

She hangs up, and I can only imagine the satisfied look on her face. "It will all be over soon," she confirms.

"It will," Nicolas agrees. "I told you it'd all work out."

Eventually, the SUV makes a hard turn onto gravel, then comes to an abrupt stop. Brittany and Nicolas get out, and I'm convinced they're going to leave me in the hot vehicle. It's already hard enough to breathe, but the heat seems to make it worse.

A long time seems to pass before the back opens. Nicolas grabs my arm and drags me across the gravel toward a storage unit.

I'm thrown into a metal chair, and I try to adjust my body the best I can without slipping off it. I glare at Brittany, wishing my internal anger could magically strike her down. By the grin on her face, I know she's enjoying this a little too much. *Psycho bitch.*

The large garage door of the storage building is closed to a crack. Nicolas flicks on the overhead lighting that seems to buzz with intimidation as they load their guns.

Right now, I'm more scared than I have ever been in my life. The last thing I want to do is bring any attention to myself, but it doesn't matter because her beady eyes zero in on me.

Brittany stands before me and shakes her head with disgust. Another step forward is all it takes for her to grab a fistful of my hair and pull it as hard as she can. I nearly slide off the chair, so Nicolas finds a way to secure me to it as if the duct tape isn't enough.

I wish I could tell her to go fuck herself. Excitement seems to roll off her.

With great exaggeration, she sticks out her bottom lip, mocking me. "Poor baby is upset. She didn't get to hang out with the murderer all day."

I let out a muffled scream as she paces in front of me, playing with her gun.

"We've got twelve minutes," Nicolas says before stepping outside and closing the garage door again.

Brittany acknowledges his words with a nod but keeps her focus on me.

"I know you're probably wondering why I want to kill your boyfriend," she says, randomly pointing her gun at me to try to scare me.

If I could talk, I'd tell her I already know why. Instead of giving her any sort of response, I keep my eyes forward, not acknowledging her because that's what she wants.

She doesn't like me ignoring her, so she grabs my cheeks and forces me to meet her cold gaze. "Gabe loved me. He loved me so damn much, more than he could have ever loved you." Her voice shakes with anger, or maybe it's pain. I can't tell.

"The night of the accident, he met me at the bar so we could come up with a plan for him to leave you. You disgusted him, Katie. It's why he fell in love with me so hard. I was your opposite in every sense. He promised me we'd be a family and move away from Lawton Ridge to start a new life together. Him, me, and our son, Anthony."

I try to stay calm, but my breathing increases, and I feel red-hot anger. Though Loretta told me most of this, it hurts coming from Brittany.

"We were together for over a year, sneaking behind your back. There were plenty of times I fucked your husband in your bed. The same one you woke up in that morning and made before you went to work." She smears it in my face.

"I pleased him in ways you never could, and he had said the only reason he married you was because he felt obligated."

I don't want to hear anymore, but she continues.

"Gabe was going to hand you the divorce papers the next week. I'd taken money from my savings so he could hire a lawyer to do it. But all of that was ripped away from me the night your fuckhead boyfriend killed him. Noah stole my happily ever after, and I'm ready to take that from him."

I want to tell her it was an accident, and Noah never intended to hurt Gabe, but it's not like she'd believe me anyway. Brittany paces, then she puts the gun to my temple. Though the metal is cold, it feels as if it's burning my skin.

She's a loose cannon, and I don't doubt that she'd kill me. I slam my eyes shut and say a prayer that Owen will be taken care of if something happens to me. Tears spill down my cheeks as I imagine him not having me in his life. It's bad enough he's growing up without a father—losing me would destroy him. And Noah too. Everyone would be devastated, and the truth is, I'm not ready to die. Not yet. Not when I feel like my life has just begun.

"You wanna know the reason Gabe wanted to start a family with me? He said he wasn't convinced you'd keep your baby full-term." Her words stab through me as I relive the devastation of the miscarriage and how worried we were about Owen surviving.

"But you did," she says with a snarl. "And our boys are the same age. In the same class. Who would've ever predicted such a thing? He's a sweet kid and has the same mannerisms as Gabe, but then again, so does my Anthony. Too bad they'll never know they're brothers."

She forces herself under my skin with her words.

Brittany laughs as if she finds something funny about this situation. "Loretta knew the whole time and never told you, did she? Guess she planned to take it to her grave until I showed up again."

With every passing second, I grow angrier. Pissed that Gabe would do this to me, would lie, but then again, he had a way of promising things without delivering. I'm sure Brittany hadn't seen that side of him yet, but he would've done the same thing to her as he did to me—because a tiger can't change its stripes. Not that any of that matters now.

Nicolas knocks on the metal door. "He's here."

Brittany tucks the gun in the back of her jeans and walks outside, closing me up inside.

"Is he by himself?" I hear her ask.

"From what I could tell when he pulled in." Nicolas grumbles.

For a moment, while I'm completely alone, I let the elephant-sized tears fall. They're not caused by sadness but by deep-rooted anger.

A car comes to a stop, and moments later, Nicolas speaks. "Put your fucking hands up," he demands, and I wish more than anything I could warn Noah.

"I need to see Katie to make sure she's okay," Noah says.

The door lifts, and I see the panic in Noah's expression. All I'm concerned about is Brittany murdering him and forcing me to watch. I think that was her plan all along.

Noah takes a step forward, and Brittany points the gun directly at me. "I kept my end of the deal. She's alive…but soon won't be."

"Brittany," he hisses. "I knew your word was shit."

"That night at the bar, I had to bear witness to you killing the love of my life. Now I finally get to return the favor," she says.

I keep my eyes on Noah, hoping he understands how much I love him. I wish this wasn't happening, and we were back at the grand opening eating hot dogs and listening to music. Today was supposed to be different. It was supposed to be our day.

Brittany steps closer to me. "Any final words you'd like to say to her?"

She places the gun to my temple, then turns and looks at him. Noah yells and rushes forward, giving Brittany enough time to turn her body and pull the trigger.

It happens too fast.

The shot.

The ear-piercing sound.

Then watching Noah fall lifelessly to the ground.

I scream out and try to break free as Brittany's laughter echoes throughout the space.

"It's over," she says with a relieved breath. "It's *finally* fucking over."

CHAPTER THIRTY-THREE

NOAH

The shot goes off, and immediately, I feel pain as I fall to the ground. Brittany's laughter rings in my ears as more gunshots are fired.

I stay still, not wanting to draw any attention toward me.

"Put the gun down," I hear Brittany say. She's breathing heavily as feet shuffle around me.

"Not happening," Eric tells her, loading another round. Though my head is turned the other way, I know he's killed Nicolas. There's not a doubt in my mind.

"Put your fuckin' gun down!" Brittany screeches.

Eric chuckles, completely unfazed by her. "You first."

"I'll shoot," she says, and I open my eyes as she moves farther away from me. Eric's using the car as a shield while Brittany steadies her shaking hand.

I hear Katie crying, and I want nothing more than to go to her, but I can't move.

"If you know what's good for you, you'll get in your SUV and drive the fuck away," Eric warns. "You have no idea what you've done."

"Fuck you," she hisses. "I'll finish what that bastard started.

This has nothing to do with you," she screams and pulls the trigger.

Based on Eric's laughter, she misses. "Shoulda probably gone to the range for some target practice before trying to act like a badass. Pathetic."

Brittany points her gun again, and I hear a revving engine accompanied by tires squealing.

Then I watch as a silver Toyota slams into Brittany from behind at a high speed. Her body flies over the hood, and she lies in a crumpled hump on the ground.

Seconds later, Eric comes into view. He walks past me and goes to Katie. I manage to roll over on my side, my chest burning, and she comes to me after she's free.

"Noah, Noah. Baby," she says, moving my body around, frantically sobbing.

"Katie," I say, grabbing her wrists and trying to sit up. "I'm fine, sweetheart."

Eric comes over and gives me a hand, and I help Katie up, then wrap my arms around her. I smell the scent of her hair, kiss the softness of her skin, and take her all in.

"How are you alive?" she asks, confused. "I watched her shoot you."

I smile and nod toward Eric. "It was his call on the bulletproof vest."

I unbutton my shirt and show her. Katie runs her hand across the entry point.

"Just gonna be sore for a few days." I wince, knowing it's already bruising.

Eric gives us a moment, and I hold Katie tight. Tears slide down her cheeks, and she squeezes me like she's never going to let me go.

"I was so scared I lost you," she says. "So fucking scared."

"I felt the same. I didn't really think she'd pull the trigger," I say. "I'm just happy you're okay."

"She has a faint pulse!" Eric yells.

Katie's eyes go wide. "Brittany's still alive," she whispers.

I have no concept of time because the passing moments seem to rush by and slow down all at once. But when I see Loretta get out of the car, my mouth falls open.

"Loretta?" Katie asks with confusion in her tone because I've lost the ability to speak.

She walks swiftly toward us, wrapping her arms around us. "Oh thank God, you're okay."

This is the closest I've stood next to my aunt in the past decade. She looks like she's been to hell and back.

"I've already called 911," she tells us. "An ambulance is on their way."

Eric kicks away Brittany's gun, then goes to Nicolas. "He's dead."

I don't have it in me to turn my head and look.

"What're you doing here?" Katie finally asks Loretta.

"Well, honey, I knew Brittany was up to something, so I did some investigating. When I saw Noah and this young man leave so quickly, I knew something was going on, so I followed them. When I saw Brittany had a gun, I didn't know what else to do. I had to protect you," Loretta says, then she meets my eyes. "I owe you both as much," she admits, and I feel like I'm living in the twilight zone.

"Thank you," Katie says and then immediately bends over and empties her stomach on the gravel.

"Are you okay?" I ask, noticing her cheeks are still red from where the duct tape was and see scratches on her cheeks.

"I think it's all too much. My body's going into shock," she admits, and thankfully the ambulance arrives. As she takes a step forward, Katie nearly passes out, so they decide to take her to the hospital to get her checked out. After Brittany is put on another ambulance, the police rope off the area and start asking questions.

Loretta and I have more than enough evidence, and I'm grateful as hell she doesn't hold back. After they've gotten everything they need and get our contact information for later, Eric and I walk to the car. Before we leave, I turn to Loretta and thank her. Something I never thought I'd be doing.

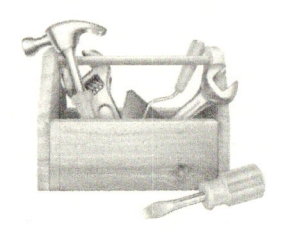

On the way to the hospital, I call my dad and Gemma. I also reach out to Katie's parents and let them know what happened. By the time I arrive, Katie's already in a room being pumped full of fluids. Her parents arrive with Owen, who's immediately upset to see his mom lying in a hospital bed.

"I'm fine," she coos, trying to calm him. "Mama's gonna be okay."

Owen leans across the bed and lays his head on her stomach. The stress of it all has gotten to him, and it's written all over his face, but he keeps it tucked inside. A typical Reid reaction.

I move closer to him and place my hand on his shoulder. "I wasn't gonna let anything happen," I admit. Owen turns around and gives me a hug. I squeeze him tight, wanting to protect him just as much.

Katie smiles as she watches us, and I see a twinkle in her eyes. Her mom fills the empty space with a rundown of how the rest of the celebration went. My old friend guilt visits again when I realize I've thrown another wrench in Gemma and Tyler's happiness.

Before I can say anything, my dad and Gemma rush through the door with panic written on their faces.

"Oh thank God," Gemma says when she sees Katie and me. "I was worried sick."

Dad greets the Walkers, then pulls me into a hug. "You had me worried, kid."

"I know. Hopefully, this won't be an issue anymore," I admit.

"What the hell happened?" Gemma finally turns and asks me. "One minute, you're searching for Katie, and the next, she's in the hospital."

"It's a long story," Katie says, giving everyone a very brief summary of what happened, without all the detail because Owen's in the room. I can tell she's being careful with her words, but Gemma gets the gist of it.

"Loretta?" Gemma whispers, then looks at Dad and me.

"Forgiveness heals the heart," Katie's mother finally says. "She did the right thing."

I nod, keeping my opinions to myself.

Eventually, we're told Katie will be kept a few more hours because she was so dehydrated. Everyone says their goodbyes. Her parents offer to take Owen with them, so I stay with her. Eric's doing recon in the hospital, keeping tabs on Brittany, and texting me when he learns something new. Apparently, a police officer has been stationed outside her door to keep guard. As soon as she's released from medical care, she'll go straight into police custody.

I pull my chair next to the bed, wanting to be as close to Katie as I can.

"The thought of losing you nearly destroyed me," I admit. "I wouldn't have been able to continue without you."

Her soft eyes meet mine. "I felt the same. I thought…" She chokes up again. "I thought you were dead, and for that ten minutes, I didn't want to be alive either."

I stand and lean over the bed, needing to brush my lips

against hers. Before the kiss can deepen, the door opens, and the doctor enters. He smiles and stands at the end of the bed.

"Katie Reid?"

"Yes," she confirms.

"We've gone over all the test results, and once you get the rest of those fluids in you, we'll release you. Your vitals are stable."

She lets out a relieved breath.

"Oh, and the ultrasound showed the babies are fine too."

My heart rate increases, and I give the doctor a confused look.

"Babies?" she asks, sounding just as surprised as me.

With a grin, he confirms. "Yes, I'm positive it's twins. And they're doing just fine. I'll just ask you to start seeing your doctor soon so they can keep watch. Other than that, do you have any questions for me?"

"No sir," she says with a tremble in her voice, and he leaves.

I turn to her, waiting for an explanation. "Did I hear him correctly? Or am I dreaming?"

A blush hits her cheeks, and she tucks her bottom lip into her mouth and nods. "Yes," she whispers. "Noah, you're gonna be a daddy."

My emotions take control, and my eyes begin to water. "He said babies, twins, as in more than one."

She laughs as a big smile fills my face. "I'd just taken a pregnancy test yesterday because I realized I was late. I didn't want to say anything until I had blood work done because I don't trust those plastic sticks."

"What did I do to deserve you?" I ask as a few tears of happiness roll down my cheeks. "You're pregnant with *my* babies. We're going to have a family together." I try to take in the moment and enjoy it. Sitting on the edge of the bed, I kiss Katie with so much passion, we nearly lose control.

"I'm so happy," I admit.

"Me too," she whispers. "Seems as if it's real and confirmed then. Apparently, I'm nine weeks. The estimated due date is in December."

I grin. "Guess I better light a fire under my ass to get that house finished well before then."

Katie chuckles. "That would be a dream come true."

"All of this is." I run my fingers through my hair and softly touch her cheek.

"I think I've experienced every emotion on the spectrum today," she says when I tuck loose strands of hair behind her ear.

"Me too, sweetheart. But right now, I'm on cloud nine. I never thought I'd have the opportunity to be a dad, especially with you."

She meets my eyes and hesitates. "I was scared to tell you too soon just in case I miscarried."

Her admission has my heart cracking into a million pieces. "Katie," I hum, forcing her to meet my gaze. "We'll take it one day at a time, and no matter what happens, I'll be right beside you the whole way, okay?"

"I don't want to take this happiness away from you," she admits. "I'm worried, especially now that I've learned it's twins. I knew there was a possibility I was pregnant, but with two babies? Noah," she says. "It's even riskier to carry multiples."

I move as close to her as I can. "First of all, you've already given me so much, *too* much. Your love is enough, Katie, and there are days when I feel like I don't deserve you. I don't expect anything else. What's supposed to happen will happen, and we'll take precautions along the way to make sure you're safe, and the babies are too. And if something does happen, I wouldn't be upset with you or think you're taking anything from me. You're the most important thing in my life. I love you with every ounce of my being, every inch of my heart, and I'll stand beside you through thick and thin. We're doing this together." I interlock my fingers with hers and press my lips against her knuckles.

She leans back against the pillow and slightly relaxes. After placing her hand on her stomach, Katie grins. "They're going to have the best dad in the world."

"And so will Owen," I say, and don't have to explain myself any further. I plan to be in their lives permanently, and I'll do whatever I can to provide for them both.

"I love you," she tells me. "So damn much."

"I love you too. You're my everything." Leaning over, I lift her shirt and kiss her stomach. I don't fully understand how our lives will change, but I'm welcoming it with my entire being.

CHAPTER THIRTY-FOUR

KATIE

AFTER I WAS RELEASED from the hospital yesterday evening, Eric drove us home. On the way, he discussed returning to Vegas in a few days, considering Brittany's no longer a threat. For the first time since all of this started, I felt like the stress has finally dissipated. Until he leaves, Eric's staying in Everleigh's spare room because there's central air and the basic essentials. I owe Eric so damn much because I'm not sure Noah or I would be alive without his help.

My mother brought Owen back after dinner, and he was *very* clingy, not that I minded. He's never seen me in the hospital, and I think it scared him. I've tried to assure him I'm fine and everything is okay, and I stayed with him in his room and held him until he fell asleep.

Noah even spent the night with us. He slept in my bed for a bit and held me, then went to the couch before Owen woke up. Because the doctor was so adamant about me resting, Noah wanted to make sure I did. The stress and trauma combined with dehydration could've resulted in tragedy, but I try to push those thoughts away. I'm overwhelmingly grateful we're all okay.

It was shocking to learn I was having twins, but to see the

amount of pride and excitement radiating from Noah made me so happy. I'd been nervous to tell him, trying to find the right time, wanting to be certain it wasn't a false alarm. Now that he knows, things feel different between us. In a good way, though, in the type of way where I know we'll always be together. I'll do anything to protect these babies, and I pray nothing happens. I'd be lying if I said the thought of miscarrying again hasn't plagued me, but Noah is gentle and understanding, and it's only been twenty-four hours.

I sleep in and wake to the sound of my bedroom door opening. Noah enters with a tray full of food, and Owen carries a glass of milk and orange juice. Sitting up, I rest my back against the headboard and smile.

"Good morning," Noah hums, setting the tray on the bed as I brush fallen hair from my face. My eyes go wide, seeing biscuits and gravy, sausage patties, bacon, and a fruit bowl.

"Happy Mother's Day, Mom!" Owen says, handing the drinks to me.

"Thank you, sweetie," I tell him, meeting Noah's eyes with a soft smile. "I totally forgot."

"We've been just a little preoccupied," he reminds me, and I nod.

"One second," Owen says, then runs off. Noah takes the opportunity to lean in and steal a kiss.

"You're so beautiful in the morning," he whispers against my lips before pulling away.

Owen rushes back with something in his hand. When he gets to the edge of the bed, he passes me the item wrapped in pink paper.

"You got me a gift?" I ask.

With a big smile, Owen nods, eagerly waiting for me to open it.

I tear off the paper, and I'm instantly in awe. Owen drew a

picture of him, me, and Noah standing in front of the new house. I swallow hard, hoping I don't cry.

"You like it?" He smiles wide.

"I *love* it, baby. It's incredible."

Noah leans over and looks at it. I watch his eyes soften as a grin touches his lips. "This is awesome!" Noah encourages.

"Last week, my teacher let us make gifts for Mother's Day, and I asked if I could draw a picture instead. I've been practicing a lot with my comics."

I open my arms, and Owen falls into them. I squeeze him tight. "Thank you. I love it so, so much."

"You're welcome, Mama!" We break apart, and he snags a piece of pineapple from my fruit bowl with a laugh.

"Are you hungry?" I ask, offering more.

"We already ate," Noah tells me with a wink. "Enjoy your breakfast and meet us in the living room when you're done," he adds.

"Breakfast in bed. I can't remember the last time I've done this," I admit, taking a big bite of eggs. Noah and Owen leave, and I nearly inhale the food. After I'm done, I get dressed and walk into the living room that's full of balloons and several dozen roses.

Owen eagerly yells, "Surprise!"

I gasp. "You two spoil me too much."

Happiness streams through me, and the only thing that pulls me away from the moment is my cell phone ringing. I see it's Loretta and decide to answer.

"Hey, Katie," she greets. "I just wanted to check and see how you're doing."

Noah meets my gaze as I sit on the couch. "I'm okay, was told to rest and drink plenty of liquids." I don't dare tell her why, at least not yet. That's not the type of conversation you have over the phone anyway.

"Good. I've been thinking about you all morning and wanted to know if you'd mind if I came by after lunch so we can talk."

I owe her at least that much, considering what she did for us. "Sure, that'll be fine."

"Thank you," she exhales. "I'll see you then."

The call ends, and I stay quiet for a second.

"Everything okay?" Noah finally asks, taking a seat next to me as Owen goes to his room.

"Yeah, Loretta wants to come over later and talk. I wonder what she's going to say." My voice trails off when Owen comes back with his tablet. I force a grin, and he turns on the TV.

"She probably wants to explain herself," Noah suggests, and I know he's right.

We watch TV and play games for a few hours until it's lunchtime, and Noah whips up some quesadillas. Owen hasn't left my side all day. Eventually, moments like this will be few and far between, so I try to enjoy them. After we finish eating, I sit at the table and watch Noah clean up.

"Do you think we should tell him?" I ask Noah when Owen excuses himself.

"Only when you're ready," he says, walking over and pressing his soft lips against mine. I tug at the hem of his shirt, needing him more than I need air.

"Mmm," I moan against his mouth before he pushes away.

Owen returns with his iPad and plops down.

"Hey," I say to him, and he looks up at me. "There's something I need to tell you. Well, *we* need to tell you."

I glance at Noah, and he sits at the table beside me and across from Owen, who glances back and forth between us. "What?" he asks.

I lick my lips then grab his small hand. "Do you remember when you were little, and you always asked me for brothers or sisters?"

Owen nods. "Yeah."

"What if I told you that you're gonna be a big brother?" I ask, and Owen's eyes go wide.

"Seriously?"

I nod with a smile. Owen gets up and wraps his arms around my neck. "I'm gonna have a little brother or sister?"

"Actually..." Noah says. "Maybe both? Your mom is having twins."

"Two babies?" Owen giddily asks.

"Yes," I say, loving how excited he is.

"Does that mean you're staying around forever?" Owen asks Noah.

"I'm not going anywhere, bud," Noah says, then grabs and squeezes my hand.

"So you're moving in?" Owen asks Noah.

"Uhh," Noah hesitates. "That's kinda up to your mom."

I don't answer his question. The last thing I want to do is put pressure on Noah, though I'm sure he'd do it in a heartbeat. "There's one more thing, Owen. You can't tell anyone yet because it's still really early."

He grins. "Don't worry, Mom. I'm really good at keeping secrets," he says, then glances back at Noah. "I'm a pro!"

Another hour passes, and I know Loretta will be here soon. Noah and Owen don't let me leave the couch for anything and wait on me hand and foot. While I wait for Loretta, I get a group text from Everleigh and Gemma.

Everleigh: Happy Mother's Day, mamas!

Gemma: Thank you! Happy Mother's Day, Katie! How're you feeling today?

I smile because this Mother's Day is more special than any of the others I've had.

Katie: Thanks! I'm feeling okay! Just enjoying being spoiled today.

Everleigh: Yay! You deserve it. I was super worried about you, but thankfully, Gemma kept me in the loop. I'm glad you're alive. Otherwise, I might've had to avenge you.

Gemma: Everleigh! You're terrible. Katie, glad you're doing good. Noah's being on his best behavior then?

I snort, and Noah glances over at me and shakes his head, knowing we're talking about him.

Katie: I had breakfast in bed, balloons, flowers, a yummy lunch, and I've been told I'm not to get off the couch unless I have to pee. I feel like a queen.

Everleigh: Cause you are!

Gemma: After everything that's happened lately, you deserve it.

Soon, a knock taps against the door, and immediately, my heart hammers in my chest. Noah gets up and opens it. Loretta gives him a soft smile. It's a much better reaction than the sneer she typically throws when his name is mentioned. Though yesterday she seemed relieved to see us both. It's proof things are changing for the better.

"Hi, Noah," she politely says, and he steps aside, allowing her in.

Owen sees her and immediately runs over to give her a hug. It breaks my heart that I've kept them apart, but my intentions were good. "Mimi, I've missed you."

"Missed you too, baby," she says, then meets my eyes, and I think I see a tear fall.

"Hey, Owen, wanna go shoot some hoops while your mom and Mimi talk?"

He grins and nods, then runs to his room to change. I mouth, "Thank you," to Noah before they go outside.

Loretta moves to the couch and sits a cushion's width away. At first, I'm tense, and the whole situation is awkward, but then she speaks.

"Katie, I'm so sorry for keeping the truth from you," she says. An apology from the beginning is a good start.

"Thank you," I say, genuinely meaning it. "I hope you understand why I wouldn't let you see Owen. A mother's intuition never lies."

"You're absolutely right," she admits.

"With that being said, I'm grateful that you were there. I don't know if I'd be sitting here right now or if Noah would be alive. There was a lot at stake, and you risked so much. I appreciate you."

She grabs my hand and squeezes it. "I knew Brittany was going to try to pull something. She had called me and was rambling on about how I won't see her again after today. Immediately, I got in my car and drove to the grand opening. When I was getting ready to park, I saw Noah and that man frantically searching around, and I knew something had happened. So I followed them from a distance, not wanting to be suspicious but also hoping I didn't lose them. Noah never noticed me, and when they pulled into the storage, I stayed parked on the side of the road where I could kind of keep watch. I sat there contemplating what I needed to do, but then I heard what sounded like gunshots and acted." The tone of her voice changes, and I can see how much this has affected her.

"Thank you," I whisper.

"I knew I wouldn't be able to forgive myself if something

happened to you, Katie. I felt responsible and should've gone to the police the moment Brittany started her threats. But I couldn't. All I ever wanted was to protect Gabe, but he had chosen her, and she was willing to destroy everything I loved. How could my son love a monster? I'm sorry I didn't raise him better."

My eyebrows furrow. "You raised him the absolute best way you could. Loretta, none of what he did was *your* fault. I understand wanting to protect him. I loved him, and I know somewhere inside he felt the same about me. But he loved Brittany, and there's no telling how many other women he *loved* too."

She looks at me with understanding. "My son had issues, and there's no denying that. I'd like to think he would've grown out of all of this and turned out okay. When I found out he had cheated, I was so disappointed and sad. The boy I raised would never do that to a woman. There were a lot of realizations and mistakes made on my part. I'll always love Gabe, but he did things that I'll never understand or forgive."

"I feel the same way, but neither of us can change the past, Loretta. All we can do is try to make a difference and hope to change the future, our future, for the better." I grab her hand and squeeze, hoping she knows I mean every single word.

Moments later, Noah comes inside grinning. "Owen's playing with some of the neighborhood kids. He's destroying them."

"I'm glad you're here, Noah. I kinda need to chat with both of you about something."

Noah swallows and sits on the other side of me.

Loretta looks back and forth between us. "Brittany's going to jail once she's released from the hospital and will wait for a trial."

"We heard," Noah speaks up. "She needs to be behind bars."

Hearing him say this causes a chill to run up my spine, considering he knows what's in store for her.

"I won't be charged for anything." She lets out a relieved breath.

"What about Anthony?" I finally ask. All I can think about is that sweet kid not having any parents, living in a toxic environment with a mother obsessed with seeking revenge.

Loretta lets out a long sigh. "That's what I need to discuss with you. Child Protective Services contacted me after Brittany explained Elliot and I were Anthony's biological grandparents. We're the only relatives he has, considering her parents passed away years ago, and she has no brothers or sisters. They said if we didn't take him, Anthony would be sent to foster care."

"No." I gasp and cover my mouth. I turn to Noah, and he interlocks his fingers with mine.

"Apparently, he had been in a hotel alone, and they were supposed to check out yesterday, but Brittany never showed up. The hotel manager called CPS, and they immediately opened an investigation. Anthony had no idea where his mom was, and he hadn't eaten since the night before. Poor thing was basically abandoned. After they searched for her, they learned she was hospitalized and would go to jail until she went to trial. When she woke up, she gave them my info, and they called me."

My thoughts take over, and I can't stand the thought of this. "Loretta, you can't let that happen," I whisper.

"I know. I talked to Elliot and prayed about it. I called them an hour later and told them I'd take him. I wouldn't be able to live with myself if I allowed him to be placed in the system. We'd already rejected him so much growing up, and I felt guilty. No telling what kind of damage she's done to him. It's almost enough to break me."

I place my hand over my heart, relieved but also shocked considering what she went through to keep him a secret. "Thank God. You're doing the right thing."

"I know. I tried so hard to hide the fact that Gabe had another child, and now I'll be raising him. Guess that's karma's way of getting me back. Funny how it all works out in the end, isn't it?"

"You've always had a huge heart," Noah confirms. "You'll

give Anthony a good life. Right now, he needs love and stability more than anything."

I see Loretta trying to hold back her emotions, and as she nods, tears fall down her cheek. "I know Gabe wasn't perfect. It's been difficult for me to accept what happened. Deep down, I know you didn't mean him harm, Noah. I know you didn't. You were always a good kid. Your parents taught you the difference between right and wrong, and you never had a violent bone in your body. I understand how upset you were with what he was doing because I was just as angry for what he did to Katie when I found out the truth."

Noah sees the tears streaming more rapidly and grabs some tissues for her. We sit silent, giving Loretta the time she needs to finish what she came to say. As she grows more emotional, I wrap her in a hug. It's hard to see her like this, considering she's always so put together and composed. "I'm sorry for not telling y'all the truth as soon as Brittany came to town. I'm not sure if I'll be able to forgive myself."

"We forgive you," I say softly, trying to comfort her. "In a strange way, I understand why you did it. Sometimes it's easier to pretend something didn't happen than to acknowledge the truth. I'm kinda guilty of it too."

When we pull apart, she sucks in a deep, relieved breath. "I guess it's time to turn over a new leaf. I'm really glad you two found each other again. You deserve to be happy."

I never thought I'd *ever* hear her say those words. Ever. But a smile touches my lips because I know she means it. "Thank you. I really appreciate that."

"I hope that Anthony will get to spend time with Owen, and they'll know the truth about each other one day. I'm aware they were friends in school, but I think their bond is much deeper than that."

Noah nods. "I'd love to have Anthony around. And I'm sure

Owen would be happy to get to spend time with his half brother."

I chuckle to myself, and Loretta tilts her head at me. "Sorry, I'm just laughing at how odd all of this is. Owen went from having no siblings to…" I trail off for a second and turn and look at Noah, asking for silent permission. As if he reads my mind, he places his hand on my shoulder and gives me a head nod. "To having *several*," I continue.

I notice the confusion on her face. "Several?"

Noah gives a soft laugh, and I can feel the warmth of his breath on the back of my neck, which causes goose bumps to form. "I'm pregnant," I happily say.

"With twins," Noah adds. "But we're not making any announcements anytime soon."

I turn to her. "Oh yes, please don't tell anyone. My parents and Noah's dad haven't been told yet. You're actually the only one who knows outside of us."

Loretta grins wide. Standing, she gives Noah a hug and then pulls me in for another. "Thank you for telling me. I'm so thrilled for you two. I'll always consider you my daughter, Katie. And I hope you two allow me to continue to be in Owen's life and the babies' lives too."

"We'd be honored," Noah confirms, and I'm in awe at how easily he speaks with her after how she's treated him. It feels as if our lives are finally moving in the right direction, and everything's going to be just fine.

CHAPTER THIRTY-FIVE

NOAH

The gym's busy for a Friday afternoon, but it makes the day pass faster. Though I enjoy working with Tyler and my sister, it's not as fulfilling as it was to renovate. For now, I'm managing the front desk, so I mainly register new members and scan others in. Occasionally, I answer the phone and do random tasks as needed. Basically, I'm a glorified receptionist, but I appreciate having a job until I find something permanent.

If someone had told me I would have a gun pointed in my face and the life of the woman I love threatened, I would've called them a liar. The very moment I thought I could lose Katie for good, I didn't hesitate to rush toward her. I'd take a bullet for her any day but thank God for the vest that saved my life. It's been a month since that happened, and we're finally getting back to normal.

Noah: Hey, baby. How're you feeling today? How's work?

I've never been more excited in my life to be a dad and start a family with Katie. Finding out she was pregnant was a huge shock, but we're excited about this next step in our relationship. I love her more than I could ever express and can't wait to make her my wife. Though I wish I could take away her sickness, she's taking it like a champ.

> **Katie: Great and great! Gonna leave work early and grab Owen before heading home. How about you?**

> **Noah: Fine, it gets busy, then slows down for a bit. Hoping to leave early too.**

> **Katie: YAY! Can't wait to see you!!**

I smile at her enthusiasm.

> **Noah: Love you, see ya soon!**

Though I know Katie's a strong woman, and she acts fine, I worry about how she's handling the incident—or rather, her lack thereof. She didn't have much time to process it before it was confirmed she was pregnant, and I'm worried she's suppressing her feelings. It was a tragic event for everyone involved, and I know I've pushed away my pain and bitterness by focusing on other things like our relationship. Compartmentalizing emotions isn't a new concept for me, though. It started when my mother passed away, then continued when I went to prison. I worked through the different stages of emotions the best I could.

First, I experienced denial that I had killed Gabe and was being charged with his murder. Then I felt intense anger and took an unfair plea deal instead of risking being sentenced for longer. Next came the bargaining, depression, and eventually—acceptance, which took years. It didn't mean I was fine with what happened or the outcome, but rather, I accepted I'd lost ten years of my life for an unintentional crime.

The only reason I didn't spin out of control afterward was because redemption became my focus. I felt so damn guilty for putting my father and sister through that while also not being there for Katie. I didn't give myself time to obsess about how I had to start completely over or how my life would never be the same. I pushed through the fear and worked hard, which miraculously resulted in the outcome I wanted.

However, not how everyone deals with life-altering events like that. Katie hasn't really talked about it, and I don't want to force her until she's ready. Instead, she's focused on being pregnant more than anything. I just don't want her spiraling later on because she's ignoring what happened a month ago. I'm supporting her the best way I know how and will continue to do so. Since I wasn't around after Gabe passed and refused to see her once I went to prison, I don't know if this is how she deals with things. But if it is, I'm going to respect that.

After the accident, I bought a new truck. Thankfully, my dad agreed to cosign on the loan so I could get a reliable one with enough room for our growing family.

"You gonna make me one of those juice drinks?" I tease Gemma when she comes wobbling over.

"I might...if you ask nicely." She smirks.

"*Please*," I exaggerate. "Would my favorite sister in the whole world make me one?"

She rolls her eyes. "With a side of spit? Comin' right up."

"Last I checked, that wasn't on the menu, so you can hold that."

"Noah givin' you a hard time again?" Tyler asks before kissing Gemma's cheek.

"More like the other way around," I counter.

"Oh, don't be a baby," she pokes.

Speaking of baby...

"Hey, make sure y'all aren't late for dinner tonight. Katie's been eager about it all week."

ONLY US

We're finally ready to tell our friends the incredible news, and I know they'll be ecstatic and surprised. Katie planned a dinner so she could announce it to everyone at once.

"I wouldn't dare." Gemma beams. "And I can't wait. It's been too long since we've all been together."

"Better remind Everleigh. She'd be late to her own funeral." Tyler snorts.

"Already did." I wave my phone. "Speaking of which, is it okay if I leave a little early? I wanna help Katie get everything ready."

"Yeah, go ahead. I can manage the front until Caleb comes in for his shift."

Now that more people are working out in the evenings, the gym stays open till ten.

"Thanks, man. I'll see you guys in a bit." I pat Tyler's shoulder before heading out.

I drive to Katie's and smile when I see her car in the driveway.

"Hey, buddy," I greet Owen when I walk in. He's in the living room watching something on Disney Plus.

"Hi, Noah!"

"Where's your mom?"

"She's taking a shower," he tells me.

Perfect timing.

I kick off my shoes and pull off my shirt as I walk to the bathroom. Then remove the rest of my clothes before opening the curtain.

"What're you doin'?" she exclaims, then slides her eyes down my body.

"Thought we could conserve water since I needed to rinse off too." I grab her waist and carefully pull her closer to me. "I missed you." Then I place a palm over her baby bump. "Missed my babies too."

She wraps her arms around me and leans in, whispering

against my lips. "I missed you too. Are you excited to finally tell everyone? I'm waiting for them to freak the fuck out when they hear it's twins."

"Not as excited as I am right now." I waggle my brows, and she giggles.

Katie wraps her hand around my shaft, and my breath hitches. "I can see that."

I groan as she strokes me a few times, then circles the tip.

"Too bad we gotta get ready," she taunts, removing her hand.

"Ohh, you're a cruel woman." I cup her breast and gently squeeze. "You're gonna pay for that later," I whisper in her ear.

"Hmm, yeah? Tell me all the ways you're going to punish me."

Fuckin' hell. She's going to make me lose my goddamn mind.

"Oh, baby girl…" I growl hoarsely, then bring my hand between her legs and rub her clit. "You have no idea how hot you make me. Your round stomach, perky tits, and luscious ass. I'm gonna bend you over and tear you apart."

Her head falls back with a throaty moan. "Okay, screw the party. We'll text them the news instead."

I bring my fingers to my mouth and taste her juices. "Nice try. You wanted to play this little game, sweetheart. Now you gotta wait your turn."

She sticks out her bottom lip and pouts.

"Don't worry. Later, I'll eat that pussy until you're coming on my face." I flash her a wink.

"Be careful…that's how you knocked me up in the first place," she teases.

"Not like I can get you any more pregnant." I shrug. "Hell, I hope to knock you up before you leave the hospital."

"Noah!" She chuckles. "I don't think you quite understand how giving birth works. We'll have to wait six weeks after labor to have sex again."

I pop a brow, unamused. "Six weeks? Like…in a row?"

She snorts, pushing the curtain back and stepping out while grabbing her towel. "Yes. Longer if you keep talking about knocking me up again. Two newborns will keep us *plenty* busy, trust me."

My heart hammers in my chest because although I've had time to process the fact that we're having twins, it cements the fact that I need to get a better-paying job. The last thing I want is for Katie to have to take on most of the financial burden on top of everything else. I need to figure it out sooner rather than later. Ideally, I'd love for her to be able to stay at home while I'm working, but I'm not sure how that would be possible. Right now, I'm spending my free time on the house so it will be finished in the next three to four months. I haven't had much time to look for something else, but I need to.

"Okay, fair enough," I say, grabbing the soap. "I just love the idea of you carrying my child. So goddamn stunning."

"As sweet as that is…" She grins. "It also comes with weeks of morning sickness, body aches, back pain, and pretty soon, you'll be putting on my shoes. And the waddling." She sighs.

"You're a cute waddler. Plus, it tells everyone who sees your precious belly that you're *mine*." I move the curtain back so I can see her, and she blushes.

"Alright, caveman. Finish your shower. Imma try to find something to wear and get dressed."

Once I've cleaned up, I head into Katie's room and watch her dig through her closet. Since I've practically moved in after finding out she was pregnant, most of my clothes are here so I find a clean pair of jeans and a black T-shirt.

"Would you mind checking on the pot roast? I gotta blow-dry my hair and put on my face still. Oh!" She spins around before walking out. "Can you also make sure Owen's ready? He was supposed to change out of his school clothes and into his new shirt."

"I got it, baby. Go do your thing." I move behind her and

wrap my palm around her throat. Carefully, I squeeze, making sure I only press on the sides of her esophagus so I don't hurt her. "Just know that whatever you're wearing, I'll be thinking of removing it," I whisper in her ear, then kiss her neck.

She shivers with a moan. "You're such a tease."

I chuckle, then release her. "Just giving you a teeny tiny sample of how I felt during my youth. Blue balls for *years*."

She turns around with an eye roll. "Don't even get me started on whose fault that was."

"Both of ours," I quip, flashing her a wink as I walk backward toward the door. "I think I made up for it, though." I point my head toward her baby bump.

"Times two," she taunts before I go to the living room.

"Hey, Owen. Did you change out of your school clothes?"

"Not yet," he says with his eyes glued to the TV.

I walk in front of it, crossing my arms. "Okay, can you please go do it now? Everyone will be here soon."

Owen leans to one side, then the other as he tries to see behind me. "I will."

"No, now please."

Finally, he looks at me and huffs. "You aren't my dad. I don't have to listen to you."

My brows shoot up in shock. He's never talked to me this way before, and I'm not really prepared for how to respond.

"I didn't say I was, but your mother asked you to change, and since you haven't, now I'm telling you. So you either do what you're told or you lose TV privileges all weekend."

"You can't do that." He scowls.

"I sure can." I stand my ground, keeping eye contact with him. Owen and I have a great relationship, but there have been so many changes recently, and he's not been taking them as well as we'd hoped. Between the news of the babies, me being here a lot more, and talking about moving soon, he might not be getting enough attention.

"Whatever." He rolls his eyes, slams the remote down, then walks away. I contemplate stopping him so we can sit and talk about what's going on, but I promised Katie I'd finish getting dinner together. However, as soon as it's just the two of us again, I'm going to make sure we discuss everything.

"Is it done?" Katie asks as soon as I take the pot roast out of the oven.

"Looks done to me." I set it on the counter. "Smells delicious too." Katie rounds the counter and stands next to me to look. "So do you."

"Thank you." She rises on her tiptoes and merges her lips with mine. "I overheard you and Owen."

"You did?"

"Yeah, I'm a mom. I hear everything." She smirks. "You handled it well, by the way. I'm sure you weren't expecting that."

"No, I really wasn't. I feel bad I had to put my foot down." I frown. "I don't want him to hate me."

"He's testing you, well—*us*. Owen's never had a man live with us before, and if you don't set boundaries, he'll walk all over you. He's ten, going on sixteen and is trying to see what he can get away with. When he realized he couldn't talk back to you, he did what you asked. But don't worry, he won't hate you. Owen's always adored you, Noah."

"He said I wasn't his father," I say softly. "Does he think I'm trying to replace him?"

Katie shrugs, opening the fridge. "Possibly, but I'll talk to him. I've been so busy and not spending as much time with him so—"

"I'd like to talk to him first, if possible."

"Sure, that's fine. Or we can talk to him together if you want?"

"I think we need to have a man-to-man chat beforehand."

The last thing I want Owen to think is that I'm taking the role of his father. Though he never met Gabe, it doesn't mean it's easy to just accept me being here all the time. I'm content with just being in his life, but respect has to go both ways.

"Sure, babe. Just remember that he's full of hormones and will probably have an attitude and rebellious side for the next eight to ten years."

I snort. "Considering he's your kid, probably longer."

"Excuse me!" She swats at me, but I capture her wrist and pull her into my chest.

"Which I loved, by the way. Always gave me something to look forward to."

Just as I slide my lips against hers, the doorbell rings.

"Oh my God, they're here!" she squeals. "I'm so nervous."

"Don't be. They're going to be over the moon." I give her a quick kiss. "Let them in. I'll grab the plates."

Thirty minutes later, everyone's seated at the dining room table. Katie bought gifts for both couples and plans to hand them out before dessert. I can tell how anxious she is and hope the conversations about other things calms her.

"Speaking of which, Archer called today and said he's finally eligible for parole," Tyler says, and Gemma's eyes brighten.

"Oh my God, yay! That's great news," she exclaims.

"Wow, that's sooner than he thought," I say. Tyler told me about Archer weeks ago. He was Tyler's cellmate back in Vegas, and they became good friends. He's hoping he'll move here and work at the gym since he wants a fresh start. From what Tyler's told me, Archer's obsessed with working out and boxing. He could probably be a trainer and keep a steady flow of customers.

"It might be a few months before he's released, but he's scrambling to figure out what he'll do, and I keep telling him to come here. The only problem is…" He hesitates for a moment. "He needs somewhere to live until he has enough money to get his own place."

"Isn't the apartment above the grocery store available for

rent?" I say. "Maybe you could talk to the landlord to give him a deal for a few months?"

"It was rented out last week." Tyler sighs.

Since he and Gemma live in the cottage behind our dad's house, I know they don't have any extra room. Most of it's covered in baby gear now that Gemma's due soon.

"What about Everleigh's? She has a spare room," Gemma suggests.

Tyler shoots her a glare, but Gemma shrugs with a grin. "You needed ideas."

"Yeah, but not living with my sister!"

"I'm right here," Everleigh chimes in. "I can have whoever I want in my bed."

"*Spare. Room,*" Tyler emphasizes.

"Oh my bad, I thought you said…" She glances over at Owen, remembering we have little ears in the room. "Something else."

"Mm-hmm, sure you did." Tyler groans. "I'll come up with a different plan."

"Just because a man lives with me doesn't mean I'll jump his bones, okay? I have willpower…*mostly*," she mumbles under her breath.

"Does he have tattoos?" Katie asks.

"Uhh, yeah," Tyler responds.

"Oh okay, then yeah, she's doomed." She laughs. "Bad boys with tattoos are her kryptonite."

Everleigh waggles her brows with a smirk. "I'll be callin' him daddy in no time."

Katie clears her throat, eyeing Owen, but he's not even listening.

Everleigh shrugs.

"Plus, I wouldn't even charge him rent. He could pay in other ways, though…" Everleigh taunts.

"Absolutely not," Tyler barks. "You're the last thing he needs the minute he gets out of prison."

"What's that supposed to mean?" she asks, offended, and it takes everything in me not to laugh at their antics.

"It means he needs to focus on rebuilding his life, not getting mixed up in a relationship."

"Who said anything about a *relationship*? We can be friends with benefits."

He points at her. "Exactly. No."

"What's friends with benefits?" Owen asks, and we all turn toward him.

"Thanks, Everleigh," Katie deadpans.

"Sorry," she mouths.

"We'll talk about it later," Katie tells Owen.

"I'm gonna grab dessert," I interject, hoping to shift the conversation since everyone's finished eating.

"While he's doing that, I have a couple of gift bags for you guys," I overhear Katie tell them.

I take the peach cobbler out of the oven, then find the scooper and grab the ice cream. Once I have everything, I bring it all to the table and set it down in the middle.

"That smells heavenly." Gemma inhales deeply. "Baby agrees."

"What are these for?" Everleigh asks when Katie hands her one of the bags.

"I didn't know we were exchanging gifts." Gemma takes hers.

"Stop worrying, it was a surprise." Katie smiles wide as she takes her seat. Her knee bobs under the table, and I place my hand over it to calm her. "Anyway, open them up!"

The first item they take out is a candle.

"Oh my gosh, I love the smell of baby powder." Gemma sniffs and sighs. "So fresh and clean."

"Well, I'll just light this to scare off Archer. Most men run at the hint of babies." Everleigh snorts. "Problem solved, brother."

Tyler shakes his head, not amused.

The next thing they remove is a tin.

"Cinnabuns!" Gemma immediately takes a bite. "Ohmagawd, these are so good," she says around a mouthful.

"And cookies!" Everleigh grabs the next thing. "Y'all tryin' to fatten me up or what?"

"Oh, what cute pink and blue hearts. Did Mrs. Wright make these?" Everleigh asks.

"No, Mom and I did," Owen says, and seeing his face light up brings me hope that he's just as excited as we are. "They're sugar cookies."

"Mmm...delicious," Gemma says, shoving half of one into her mouth.

"Are you gonna share with me?" Tyler chuckles.

Gemma glares at him. "I'm already sharing with your child so..." She stops mid-sentence and looks at Katie. "Wait. Baby powder candle, cinna*buns*, and pink and blue cookies..."

"Are you pregnant?" Everleigh shouts.

On cue, Owen stands and removes his zip-up hoodie. Underneath is the T-shirt Katie and he made.

"Only Child Expiring Soon..." Everleigh reads in a high-pitched squeal.

"Oh my God, no way!" Gemma jumps out of her chair.

Owen spins around so they can read the back of his shirt.

"Reid Twins coming November," Everleigh continues as her voice goes an octave higher.

"TWINS? Shut the front door!" Gemma rushes over at the same time as Everleigh, and they completely lose their minds.

Soon, the three of them are teary-eyed and squeezing the hell out of Katie.

"Be careful, my babies are in there," I tease.

"Congrats, man," Tyler says.

"Thank you." I smile.

"You too, Owen. Are you excited?"

Owen shrugs. "Yeah, I guess. It's probably gonna smell bad in here, though."

We all laugh.

"I totally called it," Everleigh says moments later.

"Called what?"

"That you'd be knocked up in no time. The way you two..." She quickly stops herself, remembering Owen is in the room. "Anyway...congrats. I couldn't be happier for y'all."

"We get to be pregnant together!" Gemma beams. "How far along are you?"

"Just turned thirteen weeks today."

"You're three months?" Everleigh shouts. "You hid this for that long?"

"We wanted to wait until we had our scan and knew they were healthy. Plus, we needed some time to process it ourselves," I explain.

"We only found out a month ago after the *incident* when I was already nine weeks," Katie adds.

"Wow...I'm still in shock you're having twins," Gemma says.

"You and me both," I muse, wrapping my arm around Katie and pulling her in for a kiss. "But we couldn't be happier."

"Are you gonna find out the genders?" Tyler asks.

"Yeah, at our twenty-week scan," Katie says.

"What are you hoping for?" Gemma asks Owen. "I bet you want brothers, huh?"

He shrugs. "Maybe one of each. That way, I can have a brother and a sister, but I guess it doesn't matter either way."

Katie smiles at him. "You'll be the best big brother regardless."

"For your sake, I hope it's boys. I grew up with a sister..." I tease.

"And I was an angel," Gemma declares.

The four of us laugh.

"It doesn't matter to me," Katie says, smiling at me. "I'm already the happiest woman in the world to have my amazing son and you in my life."

ONLY US

She has no idea how much that means to me because only months ago, I was hoping to have a place in her life at all. Now here we are—madly in love and expanding our family.

I'll do anything to keep her this happy and will continue to prove to her how much I adore her and Owen, but my biggest fear is disappointing her. I worry about not being able to get a better-paying job and not being a good enough partner or parent, but I'll always try my best no matter what. After all these years of wanting and wishing to be with her, I'm giving *us* my all.

CHAPTER THIRTY-SIX

KATIE

"I don't think I can hide this bump anymore," I tell Everleigh over the phone. "Hell, I already need more maternity clothes."

"I'm shocked no one at work has noticed. Your face is puffy, and you're exhausted all the time."

"Wow, thank you." I groan. "Remind me again why we're friends?"

"Because I tell you the truth and don't sugarcoat shit," she replies, and I can hear the smile in her tone.

"Okay, fair enough. I'm gonna tell them today. Plus, I need to let my manager know about taking maternity leave and the possibility of delivering early."

"Fifty bucks they already know. Better pay up if I'm right too."

"And I'm hanging up now."

"Alright but don't forget about our plans tomorrow evening," she says, reminding me about our girls' date to plan Gemma's baby shower.

"I'll be there," I sing-song.

"'Kay, love you. Bye!"

I hang up and look down at my baggy shirt. I'm almost out of flowy tops I can hide underneath, and at seventeen weeks, it's obvious I've gained some weight. After I told our friends last month we were expecting twins, I've kept the news hush-hush at work. But since we'll be learning the genders in a few weeks, it's time they know the good news.

"Hey, Missy. Stop in on your lunch break. I gotta tell you something really quick," I say on the way to my boss's office.

"Ooh...juicy gossip, I hope."

I smirk. "See ya in a bit."

My heart hammers in my chest as I knock on the door, and Dana waves me in. I don't know why I'm so nervous, but instead of tiptoeing around it, I just blurt out the words.

"I'm pregnant, so just letting you know I may need to go on leave in a few months."

Her eyes widen with a smile. "Congrats, Katie! That's wonderful. I didn't even know you were seeing someone..."

I blush. Though it's not been a secret, we haven't blasted the news either. I guess not as many people saw us together at the grand opening holding hands like I thought. "Yeah, Noah and I've been together for a while now."

"You deserve it. And I'll do whatever I can to help make sure you have the time off you need."

"Thank you, I appreciate that. I'll likely go early since it's twins."

She nearly shrieks. "Holy...I guess double congrats are in order then."

I laugh with a shrug. "Yeah, we were pretty shocked too."

After a few minutes, I excuse myself and go back to my office, where Missy anxiously waits.

"It's not your lunch break yet."

"I told Monica to cover for me because I couldn't wait."

As I shake my head, I walk behind my desk and decide to show her instead. Placing my hands over my belly, I tighten the fabric of my shirt and show off my bump.

"Shut your mouth!" she exclaims, jumping to her feet. "You're pregnant?"

"Mm-hmm."

"I knew you were getting dick'ed! Totally called it." She does a fist bump in the air. "Apparently a little too well…"

"Oh my God, you're obnoxious." I snicker, sitting down.

"Do you know what you're having?"

"Twins…" I snort.

She smacks my desk. "You're lying."

"Nope. Not sure about the genders yet. Soon, though."

"Dare I ask who the father is?" She arches a brow. "I mean, I've heard rumors but…"

I relax my shoulders and proudly tell her. "Noah Reid."

Missy's smile widens, and it's obvious she already knew. "No wonder you've been so happy these past few months."

"It's been amazing," I agree. "Never been happier."

She tells me how happy and excited she is for us, and I feel lighter for the rest of my shift. Now, everyone knows. After work, I pick up Owen from my mother's. Now that school's out for the summer, I drop him off at her house or Loretta's in the morning. Since basketball season is over and I wanted him to stay busy and active, he signed up for baseball. So they take him to practice and youth group. Loretta has temporary guardianship of Anthony until Brittany's trial, so Owen's getting to play with him as well. Though Owen doesn't know the full story of why Anthony's living with Loretta, the time will come eventually, and I'll have to figure out how to have that conversation.

"How was your day, sweetie?" I ask when he jumps in the back seat.

"Fine."

"Anything excitin' happen?"

He shrugs. "Not really."

"How was practice today?" I question as I drive us home.

"Good."

Lord, it must take a witch's brew to get more than one-word answers from him.

"What do you want for dinner?" I look at him through the rearview mirror, and he shrugs.

"I don't care."

"Noah found a new movie on Disney Plus he thought you'd like. Could make some popcorn and snuggle up with blankets," I say enthusiastically, hoping he'll budge. He's been in a mood for the past two months, and I don't know why he won't talk to me about his feelings. I won't push him, but I want him to know he can open up to me.

"Maybe." He shrugs again, staring out the window.

By the time I pull into the garage, I give up on getting him to talk. As soon as we walk inside, he rushes to his room, and I remind him to take a shower since he's all sweaty. Instead of responding, he slams his bedroom door.

"Hey," Noah says, coming from our room. "What's that about?"

I inhale sharply. "Who the hell knows."

Noah wraps his arms around me and pulls me in for a kiss.

"He used to be so clingy and loved hanging out with me. Now it's like he doesn't want anything to do with me at all." I pout.

"Give him time. He's still adapting to all these changes. Plus, he's almost eleven and probably going through preteen hormonal changes."

"Well, I wasn't ready for this yet. It seems way too early."

"Want me to talk to him?" Noah offers.

"You're sweet, but somehow, I think that might make it worse. Maybe it's best we just let him know we're here if he wants to chat and let him can come to us whenever he needs to."

"Sounds like a solid plan."

Since finding out we're pregnant, we've tried to include Owen in all the excitement and house planning, but he hasn't seemed interested. I know a lot of changes are happening at once, but I hoped he'd come around by now and would want to be a part of it.

The following morning, I stay in bed later than usual and catch up on sleep. So I can have a peaceful morning to myself, Noah takes Owen to the new house with him. I hope they'll be able to bond or at least have a conversation that consists of more than one-word answers. Noah's trying so hard not to overstep his boundaries while still wanting to be the role model Owen craves. I never seriously dated anyone after Gabe, so I didn't know what to expect when I finally did. I hadn't anticipated that Owen would feel like Noah was trying to replace his dad. I can't help but feel guilty about not only adding a man to our lives but also two siblings.

Everleigh: You should come shop for some maternity clothes before the end of my shift. Then we can go to the Coffee Palace together!

I read her text after inhaling a big bowl of pasta and feel more bloated than ever.

Katie: Hope you have extra, extra, extra large. I look like a whale.

Everleigh: We have everything from petite to whale size ;-)

Katie: Har har. Fine, I'll come around four.

Everleigh: Perfect!

After a shower, I squeeze into a pair of maternity shorts that won't last another week. It's almost the middle of July and hot as hell, so I'm extra miserable. Finding a shirt that doesn't squeeze my belly or my breasts is another annoying task.

Once I finally find something that doesn't show off everything and doesn't suffocate me, I put a headband in my hair to keep it off my face. It's not long enough for a ponytail without loose strays falling, so I opt for the next best thing.

When I'm satisfied with my makeup, I grab my purse, slip on my shoes, and drive to Everleigh's boutique, *Ever After*. After my nap, I was bored, so I got ready and arrived thirty minutes early.

"Katie!" she squeals the moment I walk through the doors. "You look so cute!"

She rushes over and hugs me. "If cute means swollen and chubby, then thank you."

"You're being silly. This baby bump is adorable!" She rubs her palms over the fabric of my shirt. "Any kicking?"

"Not right now. Usually only when I'm exhausted and trying to sleep," I muse. It's too early to feel any kicking, but things seem to be happening sooner since this is my second pregnancy.

"Your belly popped out since the last time I saw you," she says as we walk around.

"Sure did. Though I don't look huge yet, I feel huge."

"Well, you aren't twenty years old having a baby. You're thirty-two having twins. Your body isn't going to respond to pregnancy the same way," she says.

"Well, aren't you the expert," I tease.

"I'm around a lot of pregnant women." She shrugs. "Plus, with Gemma's daily updates, I feel like I've gone through her pregnancy myself."

We both laugh as I search through the maternity racks. "You better hurry up if you want our kids to be around the same age."

"I haven't found a man worthy of being the father to my baby. I'm getting old, though, so maybe I should host a bachelor auction."

"Highest bidder gets to rent out your uterus?" I snort.

"Ha! No, it'd be the best applicant. Must have a good job, not living with his mother or ex-girlfriend…"

I arch a brow, wondering if she's already experienced these circumstances.

She continues, "Must have his own vehicle and be somewhat mentally stable."

"Somewhat? Sounds like you have some high standards," I taunt, chuckling at her list. "Though if you're gonna go through the work of having an auction, you might as well make sure you're getting the best out there."

"Either that or I'm going to a sperm bank. Then I can be as picky as I want without having to deal with a man's bullshit."

Everleigh chooses at least a dozen items for me to try on. I end up buying three tops and bottoms even though I'll be lucky if they fit me for more than six weeks.

"Hey, Gemma," Everleigh greets.

"Are you having a shopping day without me?" she immediately scolds.

Gemma's been working part-time at the boutique ever since Jerry retired, but she's down to only once a week since the gym opened.

"No, I stopped in early before Everleigh and I met for coffee. I'm out of cute things to wear," I explain.

"Well, we do have the best maternity clothes. Also, I'm insulted y'all planned a coffee date on the one night I work." She pouts with her hands on her hips.

"It's a coffee date to plan *your* baby shower," Everleigh tells her. "So that means you can't be there."

"Aw…you guys! I can't wait to see what you two come up with!" Gemma beams.

"It'll be nothing if you keep whining about it," Everleigh teases.

"Don't worry, we have the date already set and the venue reserved. Just need to plan the little things," I reassure her.

"Okay, well don't forget that I love, like really love cake."

"There will most definitely be plenty of that." I smirk.

After checking out and saying our goodbyes, I drop off my bags at my car and grab my binder of notes. Then we walk to the Coffee Palace and find a cozy spot in the corner.

"Alright, before we dive in, I have to ask…" I say, sipping on my chai tea latte. "Are you seriously considering letting Archer move in with you? A guy you've never met before?"

Everleigh nods. "Yeah, I mean, I'm at the boutique all the time anyway, and he'll be working at the gym, so it's not like we'll be around each other that much. Tyler said he's a good guy and very protective. Sounds like someone I need in my life anyway."

"Gemma says he comes with *a lot* of baggage. Hope you're prepared for what's to come after he's served his time."

"Well, not any more prepared than you or Gemma were," she says with a casual shrug.

"Gemma and I both had a history with the guys we ended up with. You've never spoken to Archer."

"No, but it'd only be temporary. If he wasn't Tyler's friend, then I would think twice about allowing it, but he needs help just like Tyler and Noah did."

"Yeah, I'm sure he'll appreciate it."

It's not that I don't trust her instincts, but neither of us knows Archer.

"Tyler told me why he's in prison," Everleigh states. "And it's not what you think."

"All I know is that he went to prison for killing his sister's abusive boyfriend. His lawyers were able to prove self-defense, which helped him get a shorter sentence," I say.

"His sister actually shot her boyfriend, and he took the fall. Fabricated the evidence so his fingerprints were on the gun instead of hers."

My brows shoot up in shock. "Wait, really?"

"He walked in right after she shot him and didn't think twice about it. A few weeks later, she found out she was pregnant."

"Oh my God. That's...*crazy*."

"I know. So even though he's rough around the edges, he's a decent guy. Anyone who would do that for their family has to be," Everleigh says.

"Well, just please be careful. I know the damaged kind is just your type," I tease with a smirk.

"Damaged, mommy issues, tragic past...sign me up." She waggles her brows, and I burst out laughing.

"I think you have your own issues, girl. I should be warning *him* instead," I tease.

"Probably should." She winks. "But anywho, let's plan this baby shower."

Everleigh looks over my notes. "Cupcakes, streamers, and a male stripper."

I snort. "That's not what it says. Nice try, though."

"No, but it should," she grumbles.

After we chat for a couple of hours and plan everything from the food to the games and guest list, I head home. I'm exhausted but excited to see my boys.

"Hey," I greet Noah as soon as I find him in the kitchen alone, loading plates into the dishwasher. "Well, if that isn't the sexiest thing I've ever seen."

"There's my beautiful baby mama."

I arch a brow. "Excuse me?"

He smirks, pulling me against his chest. "Wanted to hear what it sounded like. Sixteen-year-old me is still shocked you're having my babies."

Wrapping my arms around his waist, I smirk. "Me too, but I wouldn't have it any other way."

Noah tilts my chin up and presses his lips to mine.

"Owen crashed already. So I guess that gives us some alone time..."

I giggle. "You must've kept him busy today."

"We worked hard. I think he had fun, though."

"Good, I'm glad to hear that after how moody he's been lately."

"We chatted a little, and I mainly just listened," he explains.

"You're amazing, you know that?" I pull him down for another kiss. "Wanna come to bed with your baby mama?"

"Fuck yes." He growls, biting my bottom lip. "I'll meet you in there after I finish up in here."

He smacks my ass as I walk away.

"Don't bother wearing clothes either."

CHAPTER THIRTY-SEVEN

NOAH

"Have you seen my shoes?" Katie asks, frantically walking around the bedroom.

"Which ones?"

"The black strappy ones."

I raise a brow. "The ones in your hand?"

She stops and looks down, sighing. "Oh my God. I swear, this baby brain…"

"You're freaking out, sweetheart. You need to calm down." I embrace her, hoping to comfort her. "It's supposed to be an exciting day."

"I know, and it is, but I'm just so nervous."

I palm her cheeks and bring my lips to hers, tasting the sweet tea she drank earlier. "Don't be. The babies are healthy, and today, we get to find out what they are. No more calling them olive and pea."

She chuckles. "I can't believe I'm over halfway through this pregnancy. It's flying by. What if we aren't ready by the time they arrive?"

"Don't stress about that. We will be," I try to reassure her. My goal is to have the house move-in ready by the end of

August, which gives me another month. The upstairs is finished, and I plan on surprising her this weekend with the bassinets I built.

"Okay, you're right. It just feels like I'm starting all over again as a brand-new mom."

"It's my first time, so I expect you to guide me through this whole parenting thing," I tease.

Katie snorts, sliding on her shoes. "I'll give you the CliffsNotes as soon as I figure it out myself."

"Mom!" Owen yells from the living room. "Memaw is here."

"Crap, where's my purse?"

"You left it on the counter. I'll grab it," I tell her, rushing to the kitchen.

"Hey, Noah."

"Hi, Mrs. Walker."

She flashes a warm smile. "I think you can call me Dianna since we're family now."

"Alright, sure." I grin.

"Can I call you that? I'm your family," Owen asks.

"Absolutely not," Katie interjects. "She'll always be your memaw."

"You'll always be my little jelly bean." Dianna boops his nose.

"I'm too old to be called that." He groans.

"Okay, I'm ready to go. I'll drive," Katie says, grabbing her keys.

"Everyone excited to find out what the twins are?" Dianna asks cheerfully. "We should all take our guesses."

She sits in the back seat next to Owen, who looks less than thrilled about going to the appointment, but Katie wanted him to experience it.

"I think it's boys. You'll get two brothers," I say, looking at him over my shoulder. "Wouldn't that be cool?"

He shrugs, staring out the window. "I guess."

"I have a feeling it's girls," Dianna says.

"I think it's one of each," Katie chimes in. "But I'll be happy either way."

"Me too." I smile.

"Have you thought of any names yet?" Dianna asks.

"A few but nothing that has stuck," Katie admits.

"Maybe Owen has some name ideas he likes?" I say, hoping to engage him.

He ignores me and continues gazing outside.

Katie squeezes my hand and gives me a sympathetic smile. I know Owen will eventually come around, but it kills me that he's feeling left out and isn't the same bubbly kid as before.

He opened up a little when we worked on the house a few weekends ago and mentioned his dad when I asked him what was wrong. Instinctively, I froze but just listened so I could support him. He mentioned how many of his friends have their dads at baseball games and to practice with and how he wishes he had that. It makes him feel left out. Then he said he was jealous the twins would have a father. I almost told him I'd always be here for him in the same way, but I chickened out and didn't want to overstep my boundaries.

The sad way he looked broke my heart, and I didn't have the courage to tell Katie about our little chat. I told him he can always talk to me about anything and that I'll keep it between us unless he says otherwise.

The situation with Anthony being at his mimi's has been confusing for him too, and I wonder if it's time we tell him that Anthony is his half brother. Surely, he'll have more questions, but if I were him, I'd want to know.

Brittany was charged with attempted murder, kidnapping, and conspiracy to commit murder, so Loretta and Elliot have full guardianship rights. All Owen knows is Anthony's mom got into a lot of trouble and has been in jail.

We arrive in Mobile, and soon, she's parking at the clinic. I take her hand as we walk inside and sit in the waiting room.

"Did you know I was going to be a boy?" Owen asks Katie.

"Sure did, and I couldn't have been more excited about it!" She beams at him.

"What about Daddy? Was he happy too?"

Katie cups his face. "Of course he was. He even picked out your name."

Owen's eyes light up. "He did?"

"Yep, and when you were born, I chose his name for your middle name so he would always live with you."

Owen squeezes his eyes as if he's trying to hold back tears. I remember when I lost my mother around his age and how devastated I was, knowing I'd never see her again. I have ten years' worth of memories, though, where Owen only has the stories other people share.

I try hard not to get choked up, especially since today's already an emotional day, but luckily, Katie gets called back before that happens.

After Katie gives Owen a hug, we all follow the ultrasound tech to a dimly lit room. I can tell Katie's getting anxious by how fast she talks and nods at the instructions.

Ten minutes later, she's lying on the table with her shirt up. The tech explains all the measurements she needs to get and says she'll print us some pictures. The two babies on the screen already have my whole heart, but the love I feel at this moment is so damn intense.

"Wow," I whisper, sitting next to Katie and squeezing her hand.

"Baby A is sucking their thumb," the tech says with a smile. "I think Baby B is sleeping, but if you want to know the genders, I can wiggle around a little bit."

"Yes, please. We want to know," Katie says.

The tech moves around to get where she needs to go. "Alright, ready?"

"Yes!" Katie and I say at the same time.

"Baby A is a boy!" she announces.

"Yes, I knew it." I grin.

"And Baby B…" She narrows her eyes, moving the wand around before she says, "Another boy!"

"Oh my gosh," Dianna squeals. "A houseful of boys."

I glance over and see Owen smiling. Relief floods through me that he's excited to witness this. Katie wipes the tears off her cheeks, and Dianna is over the moon.

"Twin boys, sweetheart. Can you believe it?" I lean over and kiss her.

"I think we should name one Darth Vader," Owen says. "Or Anakin." He shrugs as if it's the best idea ever. "Or one Darth and one Vader."

"Well, it would continue with the *Star Wars* theme." I chuckle, flashing him a wink.

"How so?" Dianna asks.

"Owen was Luke Skywalker's uncle's name," I explain.

"Okay, that I didn't know." Katie sighs. "But Luke is cute."

"Funny enough, Walker is close to Skywalker, which is one of the most famous last names in the films. So it's almost like we have to continue with it," I say, teasing her about her maiden name.

Owen grins. "See? I was right!"

"Perhaps a different name than Anakin, though," Katie muses as the tech hands her the printed ultrasound pictures.

"Okay, I'll look up names on my tablet when we get home and make a list," he says eagerly, and honestly, if he picked Darth Vader, I wouldn't even care because I'm just happy he wants to be involved.

"No peeking," I whisper in Katie's ear as my hands cover her eyes. "Keep walking." I do my best to guide her into the nursery. It's a room I haven't let her see in over a month, which hasn't been too hard since I've taken over most of the remodeling.

"I'm not! Can I look now?" she begs.

"Just one minute." I position her in the doorway and click on the light. "Okay, baby. Go ahead."

I remove my hands and watch as her eyes flutter open. "Oh my God," she gasps. "Where did all of this come from?"

"My dad and I built the bassinets. Belinda restored an old rocking chair and dresser."

"I-I can't believe y'all did this!" She walks deeper inside, running her fingers across the wood pieces. "It's so perfect."

Katie wraps her arms around me, and I pull her into a hug.

"The flooring and paint are beautiful. I can't wait to decorate."

"I have direct orders to tell you it needs to be a *Star Wars* theme."

Katie chuckles. "I'm never getting away from that, am I?"

"I don't think so. Though he said if we don't like Anakin, he'd accept Finn or Ben."

"Duly noted." She groans, placing a hand over her belly.

After giving her the nursery tour, she talks about what we still need.

"My sister said she and Everleigh want to throw you a

shower since it's been so long since you've had a baby. We could register for anything else we need."

"They do?"

I nod. "Of course. Any opportunity for Everleigh to drink."

She chuckles. "Well, my mom mentioned wanting to throw us one too, so I guess the three of them could plan it together. I just feel bad because I had one with Owen."

"Over ten years ago," I remind her. "If your family and friends want to do this for you, I think you should let them."

"Alright," she agrees. "But can we *please* not have a *Star Wars* theme?"

I laugh, bringing her lips to mine. "I don't think either of us has an option anymore."

After I show Katie everything else I've worked on and what still needs to be finished, we go back home, and I can tell she's getting tired.

"Sweetheart, go take a nap. I'll pick up Owen and hang out with him for a bit. Actually, I'll take him and Anthony to the park. We'll play baseball and burn off their energy." Since he's at Loretta's, it'd be easy to take them with me for the afternoon.

"You're the sweetest man on the planet, Noah Reid."

"Hold that thought…there's something I wanted to discuss with you."

Katie leans against the headboard and rests her arms over her belly. "Okay…"

I bring up my idea about telling Owen the truth about Anthony and sharing just enough so he understands they're siblings. Since Anthony's not going anywhere anytime soon, it'd only be a matter of time before he finds out. I don't want him to be disappointed he didn't hear it from his own mother.

"I agree with that, but I want to be the one to tell him," she says.

"Of course." I smile, grabbing her hand and pressing my lips to her knuckles.

"I just hope Anthony doesn't tell Owen anything he doesn't need to know. I have no clue what Brittany shared or what he could've overheard," she states.

Nodding, I sit beside her on the bed. "Let's just take it one day at a time, okay? You need to rest and take it easy."

She groans. "Yeah, yeah."

Chuckling, I give her one last kiss before leaving to pick up Owen.

"Hey, Noah." Loretta greets me with a smile. "Congrats on boys! I heard the news."

"Yes, thank you. Gonna be a rowdy house." I shove my hands in my pockets. "I wanted to take Owen to play some ball at the park. Any chance I could take Anthony with us?"

She gives me a suspicious look before her face breaks out into a grin. "I'm sure he'd love that. He and Owen play so well together."

I can tell Loretta's still adjusting to all of this too. She could've let Anthony go to a foster home for the next eight years, but she took responsibility and accepted him into their lives.

Loretta calls for the boys while packing up Owen's things. "I know you're busy with fixin' up Katie's house and working, but I'm looking for someone to redo a bedroom. Would you be interested?"

My eyes widen in shock that she's asking me. "What are you lookin' to get done?"

"New carpet, paint, light fixtures, and putting together new furniture. I want Anthony to feel at home here, and I think giving him a brand-new room might help him get a fresh start."

"That's a great idea, and I'd love to help." I grin.

It's perfect timing too because I've been working less at the gym to finish the house. I've been thinking about pursuing carpentry jobs for more money but also because I enjoy it.

"Hey," Owen says when he runs into the kitchen.

"Hey, bud. You and Anthony wanna go to the park for a bit?"

A loud echo of screaming entails, and I take that as a yes. "Alright, let's go!"

Four hours later, I'm drenched in sweat from chasing the boys and fetching balls. I've never seen Owen laugh so much, and it brought me so much joy to see him being a kid.

"That was fun," he says once we walk out of Loretta's house after dropping off Anthony.

"Good, I thought so too." I smile at him. "Looks like you and Anthony get along really well."

He nods, then frowns. "I feel sad for him, though."

"Because of his mom?"

"Yeah, and he never met his dad either. Guess we have that in common."

I suck in a breath. If only he knew…

"Hey, wanna go to Ma & Pop's Ice Cream Shoppe before we go home? Surprise your mom with some frozen yogurt?" I ask as we reach my truck.

"Yeah! Sounds good to me."

Owen takes me by surprise when he wraps his arms around my waist and hugs me. I return the gesture and smile like an idiot. Though I'm not his father, I'm blessed to be in his life, and I'll never take that for granted.

CHAPTER THIRTY-EIGHT

KATIE

IT'S BEEN a couple of weeks since Noah surprised me with the nursery and new furniture. I'm eager to finish decorating it, but today is finally Gemma's baby shower, and I couldn't be more excited to see everyone. Yesterday, Everleigh, Belinda, and I decorated the event room we rented. We hung streamers and balloons, and set up all the tables to make sure everything would be perfect for today.

Since Loretta and my mom will also be there, Owen's staying with Elliot and Anthony for the afternoon while Noah works on the house for a few hours.

"Hey, we're leaving soon. Got all the stuff you wanna bring?" I poke my head into Owen's room and scowl at the dirty clothes on the floor. "It's amazing how you manage to get your shirts right next to the hamper…" I walk in and struggle to pick them up. At over five months pregnant, bending down is a daunting task I'm sure will only become impossible in the next coming months.

"Sorry…" He gives me his cute puppy eyes. "Yeah, I'm ready. But—"

"What?" I ask, turning to face him once I've picked up his floor.

He lowers his eyes and shakes his head. "Never mind."

I sit down on his bed next to him. "What is it, sweetie?"

Shrugging, he stays silent, but I can tell something is bothering him.

"What's wrong?"

"I overheard Mimi talkin' to Pawpaw the other day, and he said something about Daddy and Anthony." His voice lowers when he mentions his father.

"Okay…" I linger, prepared for what he's going to say. "What'd you hear?"

Owen swallows hard and blinks before meeting my gaze. I try to stay calm so he doesn't see the nervousness written all over my face.

"That my dad was also Anthony's dad," he blurts out. "Mimi said something about how Anthony's mom told him."

I stare at him, waiting.

"Is it true, Mom?"

I flash a small smile, taking his little hand in mine. "Yes, sweetie. You and Anthony share the same father."

He's silent for a moment and furrows his brows as he tries to figure out how that can be.

"But we have different moms?"

"Correct. So you're half brothers," I explain.

"How come we don't have the same last names then?" he ponders.

"Well, that's because Anthony's mom decided to give him her last name, and we gave you Daddy's. But that doesn't mean you aren't related. It just means you have different last names."

"Was Daddy married to Anthony's mom too?"

Oof. I contemplate how to answer without making Gabe sound like the piece of shit he was for cheating on me.

"No, honey. He was only married to me. He and Anthony's

mom got together before I was pregnant with you," I say, hating that I'm not telling him the whole truth, but he's too young to understand an affair or cheating. Even though Gabe doesn't deserve my kindness, I don't want to taint Owen's thoughts about him. Someday, he'll realize it, but he doesn't need to know now.

"Oh okay," he says. "So we share the same dad but not the same mom."

"Correct." I smile.

"Does that mean Anthony has to come live here with us since his mom is gone?"

"No, he'll live with Mimi and Pawpaw."

"But my friends all live with their siblings," he states, though I know it's an exaggeration. Some are blended families and share custody between the parents.

"Every family is different and unique, honey. It's okay that you don't live with Anthony because he gets to be with his grandparents now, and you'll get to see him at school and anytime you're over there."

"That's true. It's kinda cool saying I have a brother." He grins. "And soon, I'll have two more."

My smile grows wider. "That's right. Two little baby brothers who are going to adore you and look up to you."

"Well, that's because I'm taller."

I laugh and pull him in for a hug. "I hope you realize how much I love you. Nothing will ever change that."

"I know, Mom. I love you too."

"There have been a lot of changes this year, and it hasn't been easy, but I'm proud of the young man you're becoming," I tell him honestly, hardly believing he'll be eleven soon. "I wasn't prepared for you to grow up so fast."

He giggles and rolls his eyes. "I'm almost taller than you."

"Ugh," I groan with a laugh. "Don't remind me."

Noah pops his head in and grins. "You guys ready to go?"

"Yep. Everleigh will probably be late, which means I can't be." I snort.

The three of us pack into the car, and after we drop off Owen, Noah drives me to the town hall.

"Owen knows about Anthony," I say once we're alone. "That's what we were talking about in his room."

Noah's brows shoot up. "How'd that happen?"

"He overheard it at Loretta and Elliot's. Honestly, I'm kinda relieved. He and Anthony could have a genuine brotherly relationship. I never wanted to keep that from him, but I'm worried about what Brittany told Anthony about Gabe."

"You mean, about how he died?"

"Yes. I have no doubt she fed him some bullshit story, and if so, it's only a matter of time before Anthony repeats it to Owen."

"What do you wanna do? If you want me to tell him, I will."

A small smile appears on my face. "I know you would, but I think he should hear it from me. That way, he can ask me questions right away if he has any, and you'll be close by if he wants to speak to you."

"I'll support whatever you wanna do, sweetheart." He takes our interconnected hands and kisses my knuckles.

"That's why I love you." I smile wider, then sigh. "There's never a right time for that sorta conversation, so I'm not sure when. Perhaps after we move, so it's not one stressful thing after another?"

He nods in agreement. Though I hadn't planned on *ever* telling Owen the details of what happened, I also don't want to risk him finding out from someone else. If he easily overheard about Anthony, it'd only be a matter of time before he hears about this too.

"Don't forget you have to come back and help us load up everything," I remind him when he parks in front of the building.

"I won't. Just call or text when you need me." He leans in and cups my face, pressing his lips to mine. "And I know you won't listen anyway, but please take it easy. Belinda, your mom, Loretta, Everleigh, and Ruby will be there. Let them do the work."

I grunt. "I'm the co-host. I can't just sit on my ass."

"But you're supposed to be staying off your feet," he reminds me.

"I know." Groaning, I nod and grab my purse from the back seat. "I'll be careful."

A couple of weeks ago, after my ultrasound, my doctor called and said that due to having high blood pressure, being over thirty, and carrying multiples, I'm at risk for developing preeclampsia. To avoid swelling up like a balloon and gaining too much weight, she advised me to elevate my feet, drink a lot of water, and get more rest. Seeing as I have a mortgage, rent, bills, and a family to support, I can't risk being put on bed rest. I don't want to waste my maternity leave lying in bed before they're born because I only get twelve weeks.

"Love you," he calls out.

"Love you too," I say through the window. "Have fun at the house today. It's hotter than hell and half of Georgia."

He smirks with a wink. "I'll be fine. Stay off your feet."

Once I'm inside the hall, I find relief with the cool air conditioning. Considering Gemma's due in a month, I don't know how she's surviving in this heat. I remember being so miserable at the end of my pregnancy, especially since Owen was born in August, the hottest month of the year.

Belinda's catering the lunch, and I find her in the kitchen getting everything ready.

"Everything looks delicious!" I exclaim as I steal one of the rolls. Taking a bit, I double-check my list to make sure I didn't forget anything. With my baby brain, I've had to write everything down, or I simply don't remember.

Mrs. Wright made cupcakes, and Alessandra delivers them just as Everleigh prances in.

"It's party time!" she shouts.

"Finally…" I scold.

"What? We said noon. I'm fifteen minutes early."

"Noon for the guests, eleven for the *hosts*," I clarify.

She shrugs. "Potato, *potahto*."

"At least you're here before Gemma," I say just as Gemma strolls in, beaming.

We all exchange hugs and smiles. "You look gorgeous!" I tell her, admiring her adorable pink sundress. "We have a crown and sash for you to wear too."

"Oh my gosh, you didn't!" she squeals. "Okay fine, I'll wear it."

"And since you two bitches can't drink, I'll be drinking for tree." Everleigh smirks, holding up a bottle of vodka.

"Everleigh!" Gemma scowls. "It's noon."

"Ever hear of *mimosas*…?"

I snort. "You're a handful. Gonna pray for the poor man you end up tying down someday."

"Oh, he'll be tied down alright…rope, handcuffs, cable ties…"

"Not the kind I meant, Ev." I chuckle.

Once the guests arrive, we chat and mingle until it's time to eat. Everleigh was in charge of the games, and after the first one, I realize what a mistake that was.

"Baby Advice Mad Libs," she sing-songs. "Fill out the card, and whoever has the most creative answer wins this lovely gift basket of lotions and bath bombs." She holds it up. "You'll get twenty minutes while you eat, and then I'll read them aloud."

"How're you feelin', sweetie?" Loretta asks as I chug water.

"I'm great. Constantly tired and I still get nauseous a few times a day, but I honestly can't complain that much."

"It's going to be so nice having so many little babies." She smiles.

"Imagine if Everleigh gets pregnant next," my mom chimes in.

ONLY US

"Imagine if I had a girl, and she falls for one of your little boys," Everleigh adds, waggling her brows. "Or both."

"This sounds like a naughty Hallmark movie." Gemma snorts.

"Your children aren't allowed near my boys." I place a protective hand over my belly. "*Especially* the girls."

"I take offense to that!"

The group of us laughs.

When the twenty minutes are up, Everleigh collects everyone's cards and begins flipping through them.

"Alright, I think we have a winner," Everleigh announces with a shit-eating smirk.

"My advice for the mom-to-be is 'no matter what he says, anal is not permitted after giving birth.'"

"Oh my God, I think I peed myself." Gemma laughs. "Who said that?"

"There's no name on the card," Everleigh says, flipping it over. "Alright, you dirty birds, who wrote this one? You can't get your prize if you don't come forward..." She rocks the basket back and forth, trying to entice them.

Finally, someone raises their hand. "Mrs. Florence!" Everleigh announces with a gasp.

Everyone's heads turn, and I snicker at the way she's blushing. *The librarian.*

"It's always the quiet ones, y'all..." Everleigh giggles, bringing her the basket.

After games and food, Gemma opens her gifts, and I write down every item while Everleigh takes pictures. Watching her excitement makes me so happy for her and Tyler, and it makes me even more eager to hold my babies. Since they're waiting to learn the gender, most of the clothes are yellows, greens, teals, and purples.

Once they're all opened, Belinda announces it's time to count the clothespins to see who won the grand prize, which is a hundred-dollar gift certificate to the deli.

The door opens, then slams with a loud bang. Eyes stare at the woman marching in with a deep scowl on her face. I don't recognize her, and by the looks of everyone else, they don't either.

"Hello, can I help you?" Belinda asks nicely.

"I'm looking for Everleigh Blackwood," she sneers.

Oh shit, this can't be good. The woman's flaming red hair is perfectly curled at the ends, and her green eyes pop against her pale skin. There's a big shiny rock on her left ring finger, and I have a gut feeling I know where this is going.

"I'm Everleigh," she announces next to me. She stands and waits for the woman to stalk over.

Before any words are exchanged, the woman slaps Everleigh across the face. Gasps echo through the room.

Just as I'm about to yell at the woman, she speaks up.

"You homewrecking whore! You slept with my husband!"

Yep, that's where I thought this was going.

Everleigh holds a hand to her cheek and furrows her brows. "I did not!"

I lean over and ask, "Who's your husband?"

"Eric Hudson," she replies.

My eyes widen in shock as I direct them toward Everleigh. "You slept with the bodyguard?"

Everleigh shrugs with a guilty expression. "Well, yeah. But he wasn't wearing a ring. I didn't know he was married!" she defends.

"Well, he is!" the woman exclaims. "Perhaps you should ask a man before jumping into bed with him."

"Perhaps he shouldn't be sleepin' around then," Everleigh counters.

The woman lowers her eyes up and down, then scoffs.

"Perhaps you should cover your body, and you wouldn't be temptin' a spoken for man."

I snort at her sexist comment, and she scowls at me.

"I think your anger is directed at the wrong person here," I say kindly. "Eric should be to blame."

As much as I'm grateful for his help, he's not innocent in this.

"Don't worry. He'll get what he deserves," she spits out, then storms out as fast as she entered.

"Everleigh!" I scold again.

Gemma waddles over with frustration in her eyes. "How could you do that?"

Everleigh shrugs. "I was bored."

"Then knit a sweater!" Gemma grits between her teeth. "You don't sleep with a married man."

Everleigh clears her throat. "I didn't know he was married, y'all," she announces to the room of onlookers. "Totally not my fault. He should've said something."

"To be fair, I don't think any of us knew," I say. "He never mentioned it to Noah or me."

Gemma's shoulders relax. "Me neither. After the death of his girlfriend last year and how devastated he was, I'm surprised he jumped into another relationship so quickly."

Yeah, that is kinda odd.

I make a note to ask Noah and Tyler about it later.

"Okay, back to the game, everybody…" Belinda claps her hands, drawing people's attention back toward her.

Three hours later, the shower finally comes to an end. Noah and Tyler arrive to help load all the gifts into their car and pack up everything.

"You ladies have fun?" Noah asks, wrapping his arm around me. "Did you stay off your feet?"

I groan with an eye roll. "Yes, I behaved."

"She really did," my mom adds with a grin. "I made sure of it."

"Well, thank you, Dianna." He flashes her a charming smile.

"I don't know how you managed it, but I swear you have my mother wrapped around your finger," I tease as he leads me to the car.

"It's the Reid charm, baby." He leans in and tilts up my chin. "Took a while to work on you, but…" He lowers his eyes to my stomach. "Worked eventually."

CHAPTER THIRTY-NINE

NOAH

THE FURNITURE we ordered arrives today, and I can't wait to get it set up. For the past couple of weeks, I've been carefully packing everything at Katie's place since she's on light duty. Though I moved in after we found out she was expecting, we haven't formally discussed me living with her in the new house. She'd probably freak out if I didn't, so I don't think it's needed at this point. While I've loved staying here, this was always Katie's space, and it never really felt like home to me. I'm just glad we'll be able to have a clean slate and make the new house ours together.

Now that I'm getting more side jobs to fix or build things and work less at the gym, I'm making more money and can finally contribute to the mortgage and everything else. It feels great knowing I can take some of the burden off Katie, though it still doesn't seem like enough.

Katie's been staying off her feet at work as much as possible, and I make sure she rests when I'm home. I've loved being on this journey with her and watching her belly grow. Feeling the babies' movements and kicks have been the greatest joy I've ever experienced.

"Excuse me? Sit your cute ass down, woman." I wrap my arms around Katie as she stands at the kitchen counter, mixing pancake batter in a bowl. "Let me make breakfast," I whisper in her ear. "Then feed it to you naked in bed."

She smirks, shaking her head. "I'm allowed to stand to make food," she tells me. "Plus, you've been doing so much. I feel useless."

"You're anything but that, sweetheart. You're carrying twins and taking care of Owen while working a full-time job. It's the weekend." I playfully smack her ass. "Go relax."

Katie huffs with a sigh. "I'm tired of relaxing. It's boring."

"Read a book, watch TV, take a nap. I'll even rub your feet." Grinning, I spin her around and cup her face before leaning in and pressing my lips to hers. "Everleigh's gonna stop by this afternoon when she's done with work."

Katie scowls her disapproval. "I don't need a babysitter."

"I know, sweetheart. But knowing you aren't alone will help ease *my* mind. I'm not sure how long Owen and I will be gone, and I don't want to worry about you," I tell her genuinely. "Plus, I'm sure she'll keep you *plenty* entertained." Considering Everleigh never stops talking, Katie will be begging for boring alone time.

"Fine, but if you come home and I'm drunk on virgin margaritas, you have no one to blame but yourself."

I snort, licking my lips. "Alright, deal."

"Noah!" Owen strolls in. "Are we leaving soon? I've got my tool belt!"

He shows it off around his waist, and I smile. "Yeah, buddy. As soon as you eat breakfast, okay?"

I take over making the pancakes so Katie can hang out with Owen for a bit. Though I've enjoyed working on the house and making it perfect for her, I'm glad it's almost done so I can go back to spending my free time with them.

After we eat, I kiss Katie goodbye, then press my lips against her stomach. It's become my ritual anytime I leave.

"Love you."

"Love you too, sweetheart."

Owen bounces in the back seat as he looks out the window toward the freshly painted house. "Whoa, what's that?"

Grinning, I park on the street so the delivery driver has room to back into the driveway later when they bring the furniture. "It's your early birthday gift."

"A basketball hoop?"

I hop out of the truck, then walk around to open his door. "Yeah, I thought we could play together and invite Anthony over to play with us too. What do ya think?"

Owen crashes into me, hugging my waist and burrowing his head in my stomach. "I love it. Thank you."

"You're welcome, buddy. Wanna go check it out? There should be a basketball in the garage."

"Heck yes!"

As he runs toward the house, I click the garage opener, and he grabs the ball. I meet him in the driveway as he bounces it around.

"You know how to play one-on-one?" I ask, knowing he played in a youth league earlier this year.

Owen shrugs, keeping his eyes focused on what he's doing. "Kinda. What are the rules?"

"I'll teach you," I tell him, effortlessly swiping the ball from under him. "First one, don't let the other person steal it from you."

"Hey!"

I laugh, then dribble out of his reach before shooting it into the hoop. Owen runs after it, and I give him pointers as I try to block him from the basket.

"Now, pretend you're going right but fake and go left instead," I instruct.

He does what I say and actually gets around me to take his shot.

"Nice!" I cheer for him.

"Can we do that again?" The excitement in his voice has me grinning ear to ear.

"Sure."

We set up the play again, but this time, the ball bounces off the rim and goes flying down the driveway. "I'll get it!" he announces and takes off before I can stop him. Just as he runs toward it, I realize the delivery truck has arrived and is backing up into the driveway.

"Owen, wait!" I shout, but he doesn't hear me over the truck's beeping. There's no way the driver can see him, and since Owen isn't paying attention, I run toward him. "Owen, move!"

He finally turns around, and I grip his shirt, yanking him out of the way. "You tryin' to get hurt?" Owen blinks as if he just noticed the truck. I pull him in for a tight hug and sigh. "You scared me. You could've been hit."

"Sorry, I didn't know."

Inhaling a sharp breath, I try to calm my racing heart. "You gotta be more careful, okay?"

He nods and grabs the basketball, then we walk back to greet the driver and his colleague. Though the new furniture is finally here, we aren't officially moving in until next weekend. Katie's lease on the rental ends at the end of the month, which gives us more time to pack and clean before handing over the keys.

"Well, whatcha think?" I ask Owen once the couch is set up. "Think your mom will like it?"

"Oh yeah. She's wanted a sectional *forever*!" he tells me dramatically.

I chuckle because he's right. Though she was determined to stay within the budget, I splurged and ordered what she truly wanted, along with a coffee table, end tables, and a new dining room table. We're moving the beds and dressers last, then each room will be complete.

"Are you excited this place is finally finished?"

"Yep! It's nice and big, which means enough room for a dog!" Owen adds with a grin. He's been asking about getting a pet, and we keep telling him maybe after we move since we'll have our hands full with infants soon.

"Well, you aren't wrong." I flash him a wink.

As a surprise, Katie's parents, Jerry, and Belinda purchased two cribs for the nursery. I was saving up to buy them when they told us they were ordered and on the way. Their bassinets will go into our bedroom, and once the twins grow out of them, they'll move to the cribs. Today, Owen and I are putting them together.

"Do you think you'll like being a dad?" Owen asks as we sit on the floor and look over the instructions.

"Yeah, most definitely. Though a little terrified," I say honestly, chuckling. "But I know that being a dad is one of the greatest gifts in the world."

Owen frowns, and before he speaks up, I already know it's going to be about Gabe.

"I know how my dad died."

Okay well, maybe not that.

Blinking, I try not to be too expressive as I wait for him to elaborate. As far as I know, Katie told him he got hurt, and that was it. We haven't really discussed in detail what he knows.

"What do you mean?" I finally ask.

He fidgets for a moment before responding and looking up at me. "Anthony told me what his mom said."

My heart hammers in my chest as I anticipate his next words.

"He said *you* punched him."

And I've officially entered into panic mode as my chest tightens.

"Well..." I clear my throat, trying to buy some time. "We did have a fight that night."

"Anthony said he hit his head, and it caused brain damage. That's how he died. Is that true?" His voice is level and doesn't sound angry, but I know I need to tread lightly. He's asking me without his mom present, so it's not like I can dodge the conversation and let her take over.

"Yes, that's right." The words barely come out, but I can't lie to him. It was only a matter of time before he found out.

"Is that why you were in prison?"

I nod. "Yeah. Getting into a fight that caused his death was a crime, so I had to pay the price."

"What were you fighting about?"

"Um, well…" I brush a hand through my hair, contemplating how to answer. "We were arguing about your mom. I thought he should be home with her because she was pregnant with you and having some issues. He had a lot to drink that night and didn't agree. We ended up arguing and fighting when he wouldn't listen."

"Oh." Owen lowers his eyes. "Anthony said his mom was there too."

"Yeah, she was," I confirm. "I didn't realize it was her, though."

"I think she's mad you got out of prison," he says. "But…" He shrugs with a small grin. "I'm not. I'm happy you're here."

My brows pop up in shock. "You are?"

"Yeah. You make my mom really happy. She doesn't know this, but…" He hesitates before continuing, "I used to hear her cry at night. Now, she smiles and laughs all the time. I like that much better."

My heart swells, and I pull him in for a hug. He'll never know how much his words mean to me.

"I hope you know how much I love your mom and how truly sorry I am for what happened to your dad." I release him. "I love you too, ya know. I'll always be here for you no matter what."

He nods with a smile.

"Actually, I have something I wanted to ask you."

"What's that?" he asks.

I hadn't planned on talking about this with him just yet, but it's the perfect opportunity.

"You think you can keep a secret for a while?"

He beams. "I'm a great secret keeper, remember?"

I chuckle, agreeing. "How would you feel if I asked your mom to marry me?"

His jaw drops. "Really?"

"Yeah, I wanna marry her and for us to be one big happy family. What do you think?"

"Does that mean you'd be my dad?" he asks eagerly.

"I can be whatever you're comfortable with, Owen. You friend, your stepdad—"

"Can I call you Dad?"

I blink, shocked by how well he's taking all of this. "Of course, if that's what you want."

Smiling wide, he nods. "Well, it might confuse the twins if I call you Noah and they call you dad, so…"

I smirk. "Right, that's very true."

"When are you gonna ask Mom to marry you?"

"Um, well…I wanna make it really special, so that takes some planning. It might not be for another month or so."

"Did you get a ring?"

"Kinda. My mom died when I was your age, and she had two wedding rings. Gemma has one, and I was hoping to give the other to your mom."

Dad gave Tyler my mom's original wedding ring, and when she thought she lost it years later, Dad bought her a new one. Shortly after, she found the other, and that's how she ended up with two. It works in our favor, though, so Gemma and I both have a piece of her to share.

"I bet she'd like that."

"I hope so...It's a very special ring, and I need to make sure it'll fit. But remember, no telling her."

He zips his lips. "I swear."

I'm on cloud nine as we continue building the cribs. Owen talks about ideas he has for baby names and how he can't wait to hold them. A part of me wishes Katie was here to experience this magical moment with him too, but I appreciate getting this alone time. For a while, I thought he was upset about all the changes, but now I see he just wants to be involved and informed.

"We did it, kiddo. They look great." We stand back and look at our accomplishments. "Just need a changing table."

"And *Star Wars* stuff!" Owen adds.

"Of course. Darth and Vader need it," I tease, and Owen giggles.

I check my phone for the first time in hours and see a dozen text messages from Katie.

Katie: Everleigh is here.

Katie: She's making us watch *Bad Moms*.

Katie: Now she's rapping to Cardi B. Please help me...

Katie: Noah! Stop ignoring me.

Katie: Everleigh just told me double-dick penetration is her favorite position, and I've never wanted to bleach my brain more than I do right now.

Katie: You better not be dead.

Katie: OMG...Everleigh just shoved half a pizza in her mouth, and the smell is making me nauseous.

Katie: S.O.S.

Katie: You owe me the BEST foot massage of my life, you hear me?

Katie: And a back rub.

Katie: Plus an orgasm.

Katie: I'm hungry.

I don't know whether to laugh or cringe at the images she put in my mind. Instead of replying, I call her.

"It's about goddamn time," she snaps with a huff.

"Sorry, sweetheart. Owen and I were busy, and I forgot I put my phone on silent. It'll never happen again," I assure her. "Is Everleigh still there?"

"Back that ass up, b-b-back it up." I hear Everleigh chanting in the background.

"Guess so."

"I swear, she's freaking high or something," Katie whispers.

"High on life, baby!" Everleigh says. "Just tryin' to entertain my bestie."

"Please tell me you're on your way home?" Katie groans. "Preferably with food."

"Yes, we're just cleaning up, and I'll grab something or stop at the store. What're you hungry for?"

"Well, *not* pizza..." she exaggerates. "Cheesecake and seafood gumbo."

I nearly gag at the combination. "Alright, I swing by the deli and see what Belinda has."

"And the bakery," she tells me.

"Sure, got it," I say, holding back a laugh. "Be home soon. Love you."

"Love you, too. Please hurry…" she deadpans.

The call ends, and I tell Owen our plans. He jumps into the truck, and when we arrive at the deli, I order the gumbo and a couple of different sandwiches to be on the safe side. Katie's infamous for changing her mind at the last minute.

Then we head to the bakery, where I pick up some desserts. When we walk into the house, Everleigh's loud ass is the first thing I hear.

"Hey, baby daddy," she muses when I set the bags on the counter.

"Ha! You wish. Not *your* baby daddy," I taunt with a wink.

"Oh please. You're too wholesome."

"Everleigh prefers the rugged, damaged, and toxic type." Katie saunters toward me, and I immediately pull her in for a kiss. I can't wait to tell her about my conversation with Owen, minus the proposal and ring parts.

"Even better when they use all their anger issues in bed." Everleigh waggles her brows, then realizes Owen is next to her. "Pretend you didn't hear that."

"He's heard you run your mouth all his life." Katie scoffs as Owen walks away, unamused. "I expect you to be the one who gives him the birds and the bees talk," Katie directs to Everleigh.

"Just tell me when…he'll know everything by the end of the convo." She smirks.

"That's what I'm afraid of…"

"Alright, lovebirds. I'm out. Got me a hot date tonight." Everleigh hugs Katie before rubbing her belly. "Be good for Mama, boys."

"Bye," I say as she steals one of the sandwiches.

"Thank God you're home. I've missed you." She leans up and captures my mouth again. "How'd today go?"

I can't contain my smile. "Really well. Can't wait to tell you about it later."

"Awesome. I'm about to stuff my face, then take a bubble bath."

"Go ahead, sweetheart. I'll get Owen to bed."

It's on the tip of my tongue to tell her what he said, but I'd rather wait until later when Owen can't overhear.

"You're too good to me." She sticks out her lower lip, which always melts my heart.

"Just wait till I can be *really* good to you later," I whisper in her ear.

She giggles, and I playfully smack her ass before she grabs her food and takes it to the living room. Though I keep saying it, I can't believe how far we've come. I've finally got my girl, and I never imagined we could be this happy and content together.

Loving and being loved by her is the best feeling in the world.

CHAPTER FORTY

KATIE

I WAKE up with a smile on my face because I've been waiting for this day for months. The house I've put my blood, sweat, and tears into is finally going to be our permanent home. It really feels like Noah and I have invested so much of ourselves into this, which makes it even better. I'm proud of what it's become and can already envision raising our little boys under that roof and making plenty of memories.

The past seven months with Noah have been a dream come true. Our journey back to each other started so rocky, and now we're six months pregnant with twin boys. Noah shared with me some of the conversation he had with Owen last weekend. Though I was nervous to learn Owen brought up Gabe, I was also relieved by his reaction. It warms my heart even more to hear Owen call Noah dad. He beams every time, and I adore how close they've become.

"Mm...I love it when you hold me like this." I snuggle deeper into his arms as we lie in bed.

"I'll hold you close forever, baby."

"It's moving day!" Owen knocks obnoxiously on the door. "I repeat..." he shouts louder. "MOVING DAY!"

I groan. "Thank God his new room will be upstairs."

He chuckles, bringing his hand to my stomach. "It won't matter because soon there'll be three boys, and we'll be outnumbered."

"Fuck." I snort, admiring how sexy he is first thing in the morning.

Noah tilts up my chin and brings his lips to mine. "Glad my morning breath no longer bothers you. In a few months, you'll be seeing more of me than you've ever wanted, and if I don't scare you away by then...you're definitely a keeper."

He arches a brow. "I've been smelling your morning breath since freshman year when I'd pick you up every day for school, and you'd ask for a piece of gum."

My eyes bug out, and I playfully smack his chest. "I brushed my teeth before school!"

"So the gum was for me? Hoping it'd finally be the day I kissed you?" He flashes a cocky smirk.

Pushing against him, I roll to the edge of the bed and, after struggling, finally pull myself up. "I think you were hoping that's what it meant."

"Don't reverse psychology me, woman. You'd ask for a piece of gum every single time I drove you to school. If you brushed beforehand, why'd you need the gum?"

I stand and face him with a scowl. "We're really having this conversation? I'm close to poppin' out two of your children, and you want to talk about something that happened fifteen years ago?"

Noah stands, facing me. "As a matter of fact, I do. Especially if I'm right," he muses.

Rolling my eyes, I grab the clothes I set out the night before. Everything else is packed, minus the bedsheets and blankets we slept on.

"Alright fine," I say defeatedly, knowing this will make me sound super obsessive. "The first few times were because I was worried I had bad breath because I was going through puberty. My mom had made it very clear I was to wear *extra* deodorant. After a week or so, it felt special, like you were only buying gum for me, and you looked so excited when you handed me a piece. I didn't stop asking because I thought you'd think something was wrong, so I just quit drinking orange juice at breakfast. The combination of cinnamon and citrus was horrible, but I liked that you bought gum for me." I shrug, feeling even stupider now that I've admitted it aloud.

Noah closes the space between us and cups my face. "You're ridiculously adorable."

I grunt. "I'm starting to realize now why you never asked me out. I was awkward as fuck as a teen."

"Not anymore awkward than I was, trust me. I was so hung up on you, I stocked up on enough gum to last me years. I bought every flavor I could find. I don't know, it felt oddly intimate. Like…no one else was allowed to ask me for a piece, and you weren't allowed to take any from someone else."

"Wow…we were weird." I laugh, and Noah does too.

"Young lust…" He shrugs.

"Turned into long-lasting love," I add.

"Damn straight, woman. Whatever you want, I'll make sure I've got it." He flashes a wink before crashing his mouth to mine. My arms wrap around him as I pull him tighter. Noah threads his fingers through my hair, and we lose ourselves in each other.

"Mom! Dad! The movers are here!" Owen calls out.

"Dammit," I hiss. "Can't we tell them to give us like twenty minutes?"

Noah arches a brow. "You kept me up till three in the mornin'. You're insatiable."

I blush. "I can't help it. These damn hormones are making me horny as hell."

"I'm not complainin'…" He presses his lips to my forehead.

"We'll have plenty of time to christen every room in the new house."

"We better!"

Noah quickly rushes to put on some pants and a T-shirt. He tells me to get dressed and meet him at the house since I can't really do anything other than tell the movers where to put things. Though most of the boxes are quite heavy, Owen's eager to help, so I let him stay with Noah and finish up. It puts a smile on my face at how much time they want to spend together.

By early afternoon, everything's moved into the house, and living here finally feels real. The furniture and beds are set up, but each room has a million boxes, and unpacking seems so daunting. I'm already overwhelmed just thinking about it.

"Hello..." my mom calls from the front door. I'm too exhausted to move off the couch, so I shout for her to come in. "I came with reinforcements."

She walks in with Loretta and Belinda behind her.

"And food." Belinda grins.

"Oh thank God. I'm starving."

She hands me a box, and I smile wide when I see a club sandwich and fries inside. "Thank you, thank you!"

"Thought we'd come and help you get things organized," my mom says.

"Y'all are saints. Thank you again."

"Where're the boys?" Loretta asks.

"I think they're in Owen's room putting his clothes and stuff away," I respond.

"Where do you want us to start?" my mom asks.

"How about the kitchen? Then the bathrooms? Then maybe my room and the nursery?"

"We're on it, sweetie. You just eat and rest." My mom pats my head as I mumble another thank you around a mouthful of food.

After another hour goes by, Everleigh pops in. "We need to plan a house party!"

"Well, since you mention it, we're having Owen's eleventh birthday party in two weeks. Think you can get off work?"

"I'm the boss, remember?" She grins. "I wouldn't miss it for the world."

I smile. "Great! No inappropriate gifts this time, okay?"

"What do you mean? He loved his back massager for Christmas!"

Closing my eyes with a sharp inhale, I remind myself not to get worked up because my blood pressure is already high. "That wasn't a back massager, Everleigh!" I grit between my teeth.

"Well, he doesn't know that…" She waves me off.

"You just wait till you have kids. I'm gifting them condoms, lube, and a subscription to PornHub."

Everleigh rolls her eyes. "Please, that sounds like the perfect gift."

"It won't be for you."

She scoffs.

"Mom, come look at my room!"

"Okay, hold on. Might take me a minute to get off this couch." The sectional I've always dreamed about is so damn comfortable that I sink into it. With the extra forty pounds added to my body, I can hardly roll off.

"C'mon, Mama. Let me help you," Everleigh says, pulling me up.

"Thanks. I would've been stuck there till I gave birth." I laugh.

After Owen gives me the grand tour, I check on my mom, Loretta, and Belinda. My emotions bubble over at how sweet they are for helping me, and soon, I'm full-on crying.

"I think someone needs a nap," Everleigh says.

"Sweetie, go get some rest. We've got this," my mom says.

I glare at Everleigh, who pokes fun every time I overreact. "You just wait. I'm praying you get knocked up with triplets."

"Don't you dare wish that for me! I can hardly take care of myself and my dog."

"Adding back massager to *your* birthday list this year. It's time you learn how to properly take care of yourself…" I waggle my brows as she gives me a death stare.

"Ha…oh, I can take care of myself like that just fine. But I might not need to anymore with Archer coming soon." She crosses her arms over her chest, and I swear Tyler is somewhere cursing her name.

"Who's Archer?" Loretta and my mom ask simultaneously.

"Everleigh's future heartbreak," I taunt, grabbing a glass of water.

"Future baby daddy, future boy toy, future husband…" She releases a dramatic, dreamy sigh.

My mom furrows her brows, confused. "I'll explain later."

"Don't forget my invite." Loretta grins.

"I'll bring snacks," Belinda adds, and we all laugh at Everleigh's expense.

"A puppy!" Owen screams so loudly when Noah brings him inside that I wouldn't be surprised if the entire block heard him. "Oh my gosh, he's so cute!"

Owen's nearly in tears as he holds out his arms to take the two-month-old golden retriever pup. He's been begging for one, and I finally caved for his birthday.

"What do ya think, bud?" I ask.

"I love him! What's his name?"

"Whatever you want. Your choice." I smile at how happy he is and hope to God we can keep up with the little monster. Granted, it probably wasn't the best time to get a puppy, but there never would've been with how much we have going on. So rather than making Owen wait, we surprised him at his party.

"He looks like a sweetie," Everleigh coos. "I volunteer to dog sit anytime. Sassy would love him."

Our friends and family are all here at the house to celebrate Owen's birthday. Tomorrow, he officially turns eleven, and I've been an emotional wreck about it. I don't know where the years have gone.

"Since Mom and Dad won't name the twins Darth and Vader, maybe I can name him that?" Owen asks, squeezing the furball to his chest.

"He looks too sweet to be called that," Gemma chimes in.

"Nah, he needs a good rugged name. Like Maverick," Noah suggests.

"Yeah! Maverick!" Owen exclaims, loving the idea. He brings him over to me.

"Maverick it is." I pet his little furry head. "Better be a good dog."

"He will be! I'm gonna train him to do all sorts of tricks." Owen beams.

"Well, can the first one be how to go potty outside?" I cringe at the wet spot on the floor.

"Uhh...I don't think that was Maverick," Gemma says. She holds her stomach, and my eyes lower down her sundress, then to her feet.

We're all staring in disbelief.

"Uh...did your water just break?" Everleigh squeals. "I knew you were having contractions! You looked miserable all afternoon."

"Yeah, I think so." Gemma's eyes widen in fear. "They

weren't consistent, though, so I thought they were just Braxton Hicks."

"We gotta get you to the hospital." Tyler takes her hand.

"Call the doctor first and tell 'em we're on the way," Gemma says.

"I can do that," Belinda interjects. "You guys go, and we'll follow you. I'll make sure they know you're coming."

Once I manage to stand, I give Gemma a quick hug. "Good luck. I love you."

"Love you too. I'll text or call you as soon as I can."

The party doesn't end for a few more hours as we anxiously wait to hear from Gemma and Tyler. After they admitted her, it was confirmed she was already five centimeters dilated.

"Won't it be cool if they have their baby on my birthday?" Owen exclaims as he and Anthony run around with Maverick.

"I wish I could get a puppy," Anthony says. "I've never had one before."

"You can come and play with Maverick anytime you want!" Owen offers. "Right, Mom?"

"Yes, of course. As long as you don't track mud in the house."

"We can take him for walks and teach him how to play fetch!" Owen's face lights up, and it brings me tons of joy to see him so happy. Noah also got a dog crate, bed, and tons of chew toys. I'm just crossing my fingers he doesn't chew on the new furniture.

Once the party's over and Owen's tucked in for the night with Maverick asleep next to him under the covers, I finally make my way to bed. Noah rubs my shoulders, back, and feet. Though I'm exhausted after the long day, I'm still waiting for an update on Gemma's progress. I'm dying to find out what the baby is. An hour ago, she was at eight centimeters and high on an epidural.

"Want me to run you a bath?" Noah offers. "I could soap you up real nice…" His taunting voice makes me smile.

"You're sure takin' advantage of my hormones, aren't you?"

"Excuse me, you're the one who nearly jumped me in the shower this mornin'."

"Pfft...I can barely walk. I came in to brush my teeth, and you all but caveman carried me in there."

"Can't help it if my baby mama is too damn sexy for her own good, and..." He feathers his lips on my neck, shooting a shiver down my spine.

His hands roam my body, and soon, I'm moaning his name as he touches me.

Just as I'm about to scream into a pillow, my phone goes off.

"Ignore it," he begs.

"I can't. It's probably Gemma!" I reach over and see Tyler's calling on FaceTime. "Oh my God, it's them."

Pulling the covers over my chest, I click the screen and smile widely at the precious baby sleeping on Gemma's chest.

"Oh my goodness," I whisper-squeal. Gemma looks exhausted but so damn happy.

"It's a girl," she announces, and this time, I can't hold back my excitement.

"Ahhh, I can't believe it! She's precious! When can we come visit?"

Though it's after midnight, and we haven't slept yet, I'm almost too pumped to wait.

"First thing in the mornin' if you want," Tyler answers. "After we get some sleep, though."

"Congrats, you guys," Noah says. "What's my niece's name?"

Tyler grins, then looks at Gemma. "You wanna tell them?"

"Scarlett Madelyn," she announces, and I can see emotions soaring through her.

Scarlett...after their mother.

"Madelyn is after my friend, Maddie," Tyler explains. "She and Liam named their firstborn after me, so I figure I'd shock the hell out of them and use it for Scarlett's middle name."

"I bet she'll love that," I say. "It's a gorgeous name. I love it!"

"I do too," Noah says. "Owen's gonna be ecstatic that they'll share a birthday."

"And in a couple of months, this will be you guys. Enjoy the pain meds," Gemma says with a grin.

"Times two." I snort.

After a few minutes, we hang up, and Tyler immediately sends us pictures of baby Scarlett. I can't get over how much she looks like Gemma. It makes me even more excited for us to meet our boys.

"You can't possibly be getting baby fever when you're literally pregnant with two..." Noah shakes his head, and I chuckle.

"I want to hold our babies so bad..." I stare at the photos. "But now I can't wait to hold her. She looks so little and sweet."

"Alright, sweetheart. Put the phone down and let me remind you how I plan to knock you up again by New Year's."

Noah captures my mouth, continuing where we left off and making sure I'm *plenty* aware of his intentions.

CHAPTER FORTY-ONE

NOAH

Since Gemma had her baby, life has been a little crazy. Being an uncle has been a trip, and I know life will be even crazier when I meet my boys. The moment I met Scarlett, I knew I'd never let anything or anyone harm her. Though Gemma had joked about us having kids around the same time in the past, I'm happy it worked out that way. Now they'll grow up and go to school together. Trust me when I say that Katie and I are trying to prepare ourselves for all the trouble they're going to get in as well. If they are anything like we were, we're gonna have our hands full and then some. Though I'd like to believe we're smarter than our parents were, I don't think we're prepared for what's to come.

Owen has been such a great help since we moved into the house. He seems to love his new life, enjoys calling me dad, and is delighted he has a half brother with more on the way. Anthony comes over a lot. We treat him as our own and want the boys to make up for the lost time. They both share the loss of their father, but they've found strength in having one another. It's funny seeing the two of them together because they act so much alike. Anthony's a polite kid, but it's obvious he never got the attention he deserved, and Loretta's trying her best to change that. None of us can change the past, so we're devoted to making the future better. Honestly, it all worked out better than I ever could've imagined.

Now that it's the beginning of October and the temperature has started to drop, I decided to plan something special for Katie. She's dressed and waiting for me in the living room with Owen. After I'm ready, I get a text message and glance down, seeing Tyler's name.

Tyler: Are you ready for today?

Noah: Been waiting a lifetime for it.

The thought makes my lips tilt up. Before I leave the bedroom, I grab the black velvet box and slip it inside my jacket pocket. The last thing I want her to see is the ring.

When I enter the living room, Katie laughs. "Finally! Sometimes you're worse than a woman."

I snort at her. "No, you're just Ms. Impatient these days."

She sighs. "I keep thinking about the candied apples and the warm pie at the pumpkin patch. It's making me hangry!"

"And I want to do the hayride! Mom told me y'all went when you were teens."

The memory of Katie holding my hand tight as we rode around on a lowboy stacked with hay bales nearly encapsulates me. The cool air and holding her close almost had me spilling my feelings, but I got cold feet. This time, I can guarantee that won't happen.

"Loretta and Elliot might show up too," I tell Katie, not wanting her to be shocked in case we run into them. "I invited them last minute so they could bring Anthony along if they wanted. Apparently, he's never been to a pumpkin patch before."

Her eyes soften. "Should we pick him up and take him with us?"

"Yes!" Owen yells.

"It's up to you," I say.

Owen nods his head. "Please, Mom?"

"Okay, okay. I'll call Loretta and ask."

While Katie is on the phone, Owen watches her like a hawk. Though he's only a few months older than Anthony, he's really taken on the big brother role. He doesn't let anyone make fun of his brother at school and has become very protective of him.

Katie waits, then Loretta answers, and from what I gather, they're already on their way there. I check the time and realize we need to get going too.

"Oh okay. I'll tell Owen he can meet up with y'all then," she says with a smile. "You too. Bye."

"Time to go," I say with a wink. "But don't forget your jackets. It might get cool this afternoon."

On the way out, Katie and Owen grab theirs out of the closet next to the front door, and she explains to Owen that Anthony's coming. He's giddy with excitement as we leave, and so am I. She has no idea what's planned.

The drive to the pumpkin patch only takes an hour, and it's easy to see the seasons changing based on the colors of the leaves. It's outside of Lawton Ridge in the middle of a gigantic pasture that's empty most of the year except during this time. Katie lets out a happy sigh as she places her hand on her stomach and looks outside.

We have to pay to park, but I drop off Katie and Owen at the entrance first. It also allows me to get my thoughts together while also limiting how much she walks. As I go to meet them, the leaves crunch under my shoes, and the cool, brisk breeze brushes against my cheeks. I know Owen would've complained he was cold later. I'm actually kinda getting used to this dad thing and love having him as my son.

ONLY US

When I meet up with them, I wrap my arm around Katie and Owen skips ahead of us. Though it's a pumpkin patch, booths are set up with crafts, food, and even games. Not much has changed in the past fifteen years, and I feel nostalgic as we enter.

"Mom! Look!" Owen says, pointing at a giant bubbly orange drink. It makes me chuckle.

"Do you want one?" I ask, and his facial expression gives him away.

Katie chuckles. "Oh lord. We're gonna have a sugared-up kid tonight!"

I step forward and order each of us one. Apparently, it's a pumpkin fizzy drink poured over a scoop of ice cream, and it tastes good. Even Katie's eyes light up when she takes a sip. "Make that *three* sugared-up kids."

She grabs my hand and places it on her belly, and I feel them kicking.

I chuckle. "Active little things, aren't they?"

"They're ready to come out!" Katie exclaims.

"Soon, baby," I tell her, leaning over and pressing a kiss on her forehead.

After we're done, the three of us take a stroll down one section with nothing but Fall Y'all and Halloween décor. "Oooh. I love this wreath." Katie stops and admires the straw and ribbon attached to the giant thing.

"Get it! You've got a nice big door to hang it on. Would look great on the house," I encourage.

"I'll mark it down to $75," the woman sweetly offers. "When're ya due?"

"I'm due in December, but I'm thinking they'll come next month." Katie beams.

"Oh honey, that'll be here in a blink. Summer's over, so the hard part is done," she says.

"Can I keep it here and pick it up before we leave?" Katie

asks, and the woman agrees with a nod. With a swipe of our card, the wreath is purchased and set aside.

We continue walking, and I'm trying not to focus on my plans for later today.

"I think I want one of everything here," Katie admits, just as Anthony sprints over and nearly tackles Owen in a hug.

"Katie!" Anthony says. He tries to wrap his arms around her but settles for an awkward side squeeze due to Katie's belly.

Soon, Loretta and Elliot come into view wearing smiles while eating dipped ice cream cones. "Hey, kids," Elliot says. When he leans in and hugs me, he whispers in my ear, "Everyone's in place."

I step back and give him a nod. Loretta's eyes twinkle when she looks back and forth between us. "Anthony's been loving this so much. Thanks again for inviting us."

Katie grins from ear to ear, watching the two boys together.

"He's had ice cream and a Coke. Probably gonna bounce off the walls later," Loretta tells Katie.

"Two peas in a pod," Katie says in return. "Isn't this amazing?"

Loretta nods. "Yeah, the weather is more than perfect. You want me to watch the boys so you two can take your time walking around?"

I glance at Katie and nod, and she agrees. "Sure, that'd be great."

Before we leave them, Katie explains to Owen that he can stay with Anthony and to be good for Memaw and Pawpaw. She fixes his wild mess of hair and gives Loretta and Elliot a wave before we head across the way.

We wait in line for the hayride, and when it pulls up and slows down in front of us, the workers grab a step for Katie to use. After we're settled, we sit close, and I wrap my arm around her. I lean in and place a soft kiss on her lips as the tractor pulls us around the pumpkin patch. The sweet smells of caramel and cotton candy drift through the air and mix with the earthy scent of freshly baled hay.

"This has been so much fun," Katie says.

"And just think, the day is just getting started." I give her a wink. "Remember when we came here as teenagers?"

She sweetly nods. "I do. I remember actually finding the courage to hold your hand on this very ride."

"You remembered?" I ask with raised brows. Of course she did.

She smirks. "How could I ever forget? I was nearly shitting bricks that I had made a move even though it was a childish one." Her tone drops into a whisper, and she tugs me toward her, and I lean in. "Shoulda sat on your lap and stuck my tongue down your throat."

I smirk. "Woman. You know what happens when you say stuff like that…"

She snickers just as the ride comes to a stop at the entrance of the pumpkin patch.

"Let's get off here," I suggest, and she agrees.

We step off, and she stares at the thousands of pumpkins in all different colors and shapes. People are taking pictures with them while others are decorating or carving.

"I think I need to go to the bathroom," I tell her, grinning.

She laughs. "There's one out here?"

"Yeah, just on the other side. Might take me about ten minutes," I say and lead her to some hay bales arranged as seating. "Might be good for you to rest a minute. I'll be right back."

"Okay! Bring me back a candied apple, a slice of pumpkin pie, and another one of those fizzy drinks." Katie gives me a wink.

With a laugh, I shake my head. "Yes, honey."

I make my way through the crowd of people, and it takes at least ten minutes for me to get to the area where I've asked all of our friends and family to meet. When I turn the corner, they're chatting and laughing. Excitement fills the air.

Gemma, Tyler, and Everleigh hoot and holler as soon as I come into view. Gemma's rocking the stroller back and forth, and I love that she brought Scarlett too.

Dad gives me a big hug. "You ready, son?"

"As ever," I say, meeting everyone's eyes. I'm so thankful Katie's parents, Belinda, Elliot, Loretta, the boys, and my and Katie's best friends are here to celebrate this special moment.

After everyone takes a step closer, I suck in a deep breath. "Do y'all have your letters?"

I glance around, and they nod, holding their silver envelopes.

"You do know this is gonna make her bawl like a baby?" Everleigh says, tapping hers against her palm.

"You weren't supposed to read it, Ev," Gemma whisper-hisses over the stroller.

She snorts. "I literally just peeked a little. I needed to know what she was gonna be reading so I'd be aware of how to react."

Gemma groans and crosses her arms over her chest, eyeing Everleigh. "I passed them all out and instructed them *not* to read them. Some people just don't know how to listen."

"It's fine. If anyone was gonna break the rules, it would be her." I look at her and smile.

"That's very true," Everleigh admits. "It's almost like you know me better than your sister."

Before Gemma digs in, I speak up. "Okay, so y'all know the order, right?"

Gemma steps forward. "Yes, I'll get Katie, hand her the letter, then bring her to Tyler. Then it goes Tyler, Everleigh, so on and so on. I've got this, bro. Have faith in me. I did just plan a pretty incredible grand opening and deliver a baby. I'm a pro at this point," she tells me with a lifted brow and a smirk.

"You're right." I wipe my sweaty palms on my jeans. "Just a little nervous. That's it."

ONLY US

Loretta speaks up. "She's gonna say yes. This is your destiny."

"She better!" Owen pipes up, and it makes Anthony giggle.

Everleigh snorts and squeezes his shoulder. "She will. There's no doubt about it."

I suck in a deep breath, trying to calm down, then feel inside my jacket pocket for the box. It's almost time, and I know Katie's probably growing impatient that I haven't returned with her snacks yet. The thought has me chuckling to myself.

Katie's parents give me hugs, and I can tell how overjoyed they are. I asked them a month ago after I asked Owen's permission. They were more than thrilled that I wanted to make things official with their daughter. They've always treated me like a son and respected me even after everything that happened.

"Excited to have you officially be a part of the family," Katie's mama tells me.

"I promise to always protect her and love her," I say.

"We believe you," her dad tells me.

"It's almost time, y'all. I need you to start lining up," Gemma instructs. She's a sassy little thing, and I'm glad I put her in charge of the people part. Takes a sliver of the stress away.

My sister was such a big help with planning this. When I was reminiscing about our past, all the letters we used to write to each other in high school came to mind. At that moment, I knew exactly how and where I wanted to propose.

I stand at the end of the pumpkin patch and know Katie has a long way to walk. She'll be reading each of the notes I wrote to her about our past and our future. It will take her some time, and I'm okay with that, but I know my heart will be racing until I see her, and she says yes.

I expect tears of happiness because she's been so emotional lately, but by the end of it, I hope she agrees to be my wife.

CHAPTER FORTY-TWO

KATIE

As I'm sitting on a bale of hay with my feet propped up to stop the swelling, I wonder what's taking Noah so long. Maybe that number one turned into something more serious. The thought has me snickering to myself, then I go back to admiring the pumpkins.

I've always looked forward to this little festival. Well, ever since Noah brought me here when I was fifteen. I knew I had feelings for him then, but I was also too young to really understand. I guess it's true, though—when the heart knows, it truly knows. It might've taken us some time to get to where we are now, but I don't have any complaints, and I wouldn't change a thing. I've thought about if I could go back in time, whether I'd erase some of the heartache, but I realized maybe things wouldn't be the same between us. My heart flutters thinking about it.

"What're you grinning about?" Gemma asks.

My mouth falls open when I see her, and I immediately stand to give her a hug. She's pushing Scarlett in a stroller, and I bend down to catch a peek of her sweet cheeks.

"Come on," she tells me with a wink. "Let's look at the pumpkins."

"I'm waiting for Noah," I explain, not wanting him to get worried or have to search for me.

"We're just going into the patch. Text him and let him know," Gemma says.

I snicker. "Oh yeah. Text. Forgot about that one. Baby brain."

I send a quick message to Noah, telling him that I ran into Gemma and we're gonna walk around.

He sends me a kissy face emoji back.

Katie: Hope you didn't fall in!

Noah: Haha! I'm almost done. See you soon.

I tuck my phone back into my crossbody and follow Gemma. She pulls Scarlett out of the stroller and asks me to take a picture. I snap at least ten, and when we're done, she hands me a letter.

"What's this?" I ask, confused as fuck as to why she's acting so weird.

She snorts. "Open it and read it."

I'm lost, but I do what she says. When I see the handwriting, I immediately know it's Noah's. I can recognize his scribbles from a mile away.

The words nearly fly off the page as I read them.

Katie Bug,

I wanted to take you on a stroll down memory lane and confess some things in the process. The last time we were here a little over fifteen years ago, I nearly told you how much you meant to me. I almost asked you to be my girlfriend but was too chickenshit to do it. I told myself I'd never make that mistake again, and here we are. I love you more than the number of pumpkins in this patch. And you and I both know that's a fuckton.

Tears sit on the brim of my eyes as I look up at Gemma. "What's this about?"

She shrugs, and that's when I see a grinning Tyler, holding another envelope.

"You guys! I swear!" I say as he hands it to me. While I open this one, we continue our slow stroll.

Katie Angel,

We've experienced a lot together. Some bad, but way more good. Knowing that you never gave up on me after everything that happened has kept me moving forward in life. I'll never be able to repay you for saving me, for giving me a chance, and for loving me. I'll forever be indebted to you, my love, and I wouldn't have it any other way.

Now, I'm crying. Tyler chuckles as Gemma places her hand on the small of my back, and then I see Everleigh. She's wearing a wide smile and looks at me with raised brows.

"This one's a doozy," she says, handing me the envelope.

Katie Baby,

I've tried to think back to the moment I fell in love with you, and it's nearly impossible. Loving you has always just been a part of who I am. It's like I was created for the sole purpose of loving you, caring for you, helping you, protecting you, and I swear I'll spend the rest of my life doing those things. I'm not perfect, but you don't seem to see my imperfections. I don't know what I did in a past life to deserve you, but I'm thankful for that and you.

I stop and wipe my face, then suck in a deep breath. People

passing by look at me like I've lost my mind, but they have no idea how large my heart has swelled in the past ten minutes. The emotions I feel are almost too much. Loretta and Elliot meet us, and Elliot hands me another letter, then they fall in line with everyone else.

Katie Sweetheart,

I hate that I've caused you heartache and tragedy. I hate that things happened the way they did, and I've asked myself over and over if I could go back in time, would I change them? At first, my answer was yes, but then I realized that changing the past may not bring me back to you, and that's all I've ever wanted. You, sweetheart. You're my everything. Your sunshine on dark days, warmth when it's cold, and calm in a storm. I will always be there for you no matter and be an anchor when you need it the most because you're my North when I've lost my way.

Next are Belinda and Jerry, along with another silver envelope.

Katie Love,

I remember what I wished for on my eighteenth birthday. Do you remember being there? You sat right across from me at the table as the candles were burning, and you told me to make a wish. I looked you straight in the eyes, and at that moment, I wished that I'd marry you someday. I blew out the candles and held it deep inside. Years later, I thought back to that moment and was convinced that it would never happen. But now, I'm a believer. Wishes do come true, and I know that to be the truth every morning when I wake up with you in my arms.

My parents greet me with hugs and tell me how much they love me, then lead me over to Owen and Anthony. Thankfully, neither of them was carrying a letter, and for once, I'm grateful because I don't know how much more I can read before I melt into tears.

Owen grabs my free hand and looks into my eyes. "Mama, I gave Dad permission," he says, and I can see he's growing emotional too.

"Permission for what, baby?" I ask.

Moments later, Noah steps into view, looking as handsome as ever. Even though he's been wearing those clothes all day, I can see the happiness radiating from him. He moves forward, and Owen and Anthony step aside. Behind me are all of my friends and family, watching as Noah gets on one knee.

I suspected a proposal after the first letter, but I never imagined it would be anything like this. The thought he puts into making moments special for me is magical.

He rubs his thumbs across the top of my hand.

"Katie, I'm pretty sure you've figured it out by now." He chuckles, and I nod as tears drip down my face.

"I meant every word in those letters. I love you, sweetheart, more than anything in the world. I'd do anything for our beautiful children..." He glances at Owen, then back at me. "And for you. As I mentioned, you're the only woman I've ever loved with every fiber of my being, and I told myself that if I ever had the opportunity to marry you, I wouldn't pass it up. And here we are, beautiful. Katie...will you please spend the rest of your life with me and let me make you breakfast in bed, massage your feet, and treat you like the queen you are? Will you marry me?"

The whole time I was too focused on him to even notice the beautiful ring he's holding.

"Yes, baby. Yes!" I say, and he stands and slides his lips across mine.

When we pull apart, he takes the ring out of the box, slips his hand in his pocket, and then pulls out a silver chain.

"It's sized for *after* the babies." He chuckles. "Gemma suggested it."

Gemma shrugs and meets my eyes. "Don't you agree?"

I nod. "Totally."

Noah slips the ring on the necklace, then clasps it behind my neck. I look down at the diamond sparkling in the sunshine, then pull him closer. I get lost in this kiss as his tongue slides against mine, and if we didn't have an audience or weren't in public, there's no telling where this would lead.

Congratulations are in order, and we exchange hugs and tears and handshakes galore. My senses are heightened because of my hormones, and I can't remember the last time I've cried so much, but I welcome tears of happiness any day. While we're saying our goodbyes to everyone, Owen gives me a tight squeeze.

"Thank you for saying yes, Mama," he tells me.

I look at him and tilt my head. "You thought I'd say no?"

"Well no, but I didn't know," he says with a laugh. "I'm just happy Noah will be in our lives forever."

"Forever, baby," I tell him with a grin.

Loretta approaches and says they're going to do some more activities, and Anthony asks if Owen can join them. Wanting to have some alone time with Noah, I agree.

"I'll bring him home after we're done here," Loretta says.

"Memaw, can Owen stay the night?" Anthony asks with a twinkle in his eye, and I know I can't say no to that.

"Only if Katie says it's okay."

He comes over to me and smiles. "Ms. Katie, can Owen pretty, *pretty* please stay over?"

I laugh. "Sure. That'll be fine." The boys give me a handful of thank-yous. Owen gives me a hug goodbye, and I thank Loretta for everything.

As they walk away, Noah pulls me in close. "You ready to get outta here, fiancée?"

I lift my brow at him. "I like the sound of that, but I think I'll like being called wife better. Also, does that mean what I think it means?"

He bites the corner of his lip and smirks.

"Hell yes," I say. We stop and pick up my gigantic wreath that may or may not fit in the trunk of my car, then leave. When we get home, we make love until nightfall, then fall asleep naked.

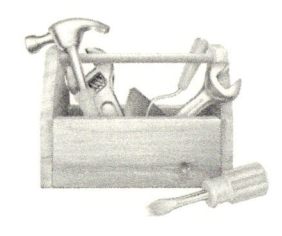

I can't believe I've been calling Noah my fiancé for two weeks. It feels like a dream, all of it. Having the house finished, the proposal, and now the baby shower for the twins. How's this my life? If someone would've told me at the beginning of the year I'd be engaged and pregnant before Christmas, I would've asked them if they had fallen and hit their head.

When I roll over in the morning and feel his strong arm wrapped across me, I almost pinch myself. It's a dream come true, and I don't dare take a damn day for granted.

"Babe, almost ready?" I hear Noah call from the other room.

I chuckle because I've changed clothes at least ten times, and now I'm exhausted. "No!" I yell back.

Moments later, I hear footsteps padding down the hallway, and the door to our room swings open. Noah grins from ear to ear. "What you're wearing looks hot," he tells me.

I lie back on the bed, not able to see over my stomach. "You'd be fine with me going naked! You're very biased!"

He laughs. "That's true, but honestly, that dress is adorable on you."

I glare at him even though I know he's being sweet. "Nothing is adorable on me. I feel and look like I've stuffed two beach balls under this dress. Do I absolutely have to go?"

"Yes," he gently says. "If you didn't, I'm not sure your mother, Gemma, or Everleigh would forgive you. Belinda would, though. I don't think you can do any wrong in her eyes."

I sigh, and he helps me up. "You're sure I look fine?"

He pulls out his phone and snaps a picture of me, then turns it around. "Cute as fuck."

A blush hits my cheek. "Maybe you're right."

Noah glances at the stack of clothes on the foot of the bed. "Done with these?"

"I guess," I say, slipping on some slides because wearing any sort of real shoe right now is torture. My body wants to burst out of whatever I put on it—shoes, bras, shirts, you name it.

Eventually, he coaxes me out the door so I'm not late to my own party, and I'm happy he did. When I show up, Noah escorts me inside, gives me a kiss, then leaves. The decorations are gorgeous, and I'm in awe at what they did. Beautiful flower displays adorn every table, along with powder blue balloons.

Gemma and Everleigh rush up to me, wearing huge smiles. Belinda gives me a nod, but she's so enamored with Scarlett that she brings all of her attention back to her. She's an adorable baby, though, so I don't blame her one tiny bit.

"Are you ready for all the games we have planned?" Everleigh asks, and I groan.

"No games," Gemma adds. "I planned activities instead because I know how much you hate them."

"Thank you." I sigh. "At least one of my friends listens."

Everleigh snorts. "I listen, but that's about as far as it goes."

Gemma laughs.

Everleigh continues. "We got onesies to decorate and set up a photo booth and a cupcake table. Oh there's also one small game. Guess the number of penises, I mean M&M's in a jar," she says, moving her arm like she's giving me a tour. "And Belinda made your favorite sandwiches!"

"Oh my goodness," I say, covering my mouth. "Y'all didn't have to do all this for me. Not at all. I feel so…"

"Special?" Gemma suggests with a side hug. "'Cause you are!"

Mom comes over and offers me a bottle of water, and I laugh because she knows me so well. "If at any point you need a break, let me know," she says with a wink. She has a way of distracting people so I can escape to the bathroom. Loretta says hello, and so does Missy, who hasn't stopped giving me shit about being pregnant and getting the D since she found out.

The baby shower is actually more fun than I thought it would be. We do the activities that Gemma had planned and open gifts for what feels like hours. I'm overwhelmed by the kindness all the ladies have shown me and by how much stuff I've gotten. When it comes to celebrating having babies in Lawton Ridge, these women are all in. After that, we eat the yummy club sandwiches and chocolate cupcakes Belinda made for the event.

As things come to an end, I stand and give a small speech, thanking everyone for coming out and loving me so much. Of course, I cry, and tears splotch my dress. The room explodes into applause, then people trickle out. While some of the ladies from church stay to clean up, I sit at a table and have another cupcake, and my best friends join me. They plop down across from me, and I'm overjoyed by how amazing all of this has been. I've got everything I need for when the babies arrive.

"You know, this party was just missing one thing," I admit with a snicker.

"What?" Everleigh asks around a mouthful, and Gemma meets my eyes.

"A woman coming and slapping you in the face for sleeping with her husband," I barely get out before I burst into laughter.

Gemma nearly chokes because she's giggling so hard.

"Oh, the thought crossed my mind," she says, totally okay with being poked at. One thing I love about Everleigh, it's often hard to get a rise out of her. If she can make herself the butt of a joke first, she will every single time.

"You know Archer got parole," Gemma eventually says.

"Really?" I ask.

"Yep. He's planning to fly here the week before Thanksgiving."

I nudge Everleigh. "Oh, you better get your place ready."

She licks her lips and bats her eyelashes. "I've been ready."

Gemma shakes her head. "Tyler isn't happy about the arrangement, but between you and me, I'm glad he's staying with you. Just be aware Tyler's been preparing his threatening speech about behaving around you."

Everleigh groans and rolls her eyes. "I'm a grown-ass woman and will do *what* and *who* I want when I want."

I snicker. "This is very true."

"Of course it is," Gemma says, then leans across the table. "And I know how you like those bad boys."

"Damn straight," she admits. "And honestly, Tyler can act like I'm his innocent little sister all he wants. He has no idea how dirty I can be."

"No, he doesn't," I say, and my eyes go wide when Tyler walks up behind Gemma and Everleigh.

"He's behind me, isn't he?" Everleigh asks, and I nod.

"Maybe I should be giving you the speech then," Tyler says as Gemma turns around and wraps her arms around his waist. He bends down and kisses her forehead. "Are we early?"

"No, you're right on time. It officially ended about fifteen minutes ago," I confirm.

Noah enters with Smith, Jerry, Elliot, and my dad. "The cleanup crew has arrived," I say with a grin as they start folding chairs and tables, sweeping, and taking out the trash. Noah and my parents load the gifts in their SUV because they won't all fit in my car.

After everything is spotless in the event center, Noah comes over to me and gives me a sweet kiss. "Did you have fun?"

"Actually, it wasn't so bad. I had a great time. It was a beautiful party, and everyone was overly generous," I admit.

He kisses me on my forehead. "Glad to hear that, baby."

On the way out, I see Tyler and Gemma standing by their car with Everleigh, who looks distraught. Immediately my brows furrow as we walk toward them.

"What's going on?" I ask, knowing something's wrong.

Tyler sucks in a deep breath and releases it. "Eric's been murdered."

A knot forms in my throat, and I'm not sure I heard him correctly even though he didn't stutter.

Noah rests his hand on my shoulder as Tyler continues. "His body was found and an acquaintance called to let me know since I was one of the last people in contact with him."

"It was probably his wife. She was livid. I just..." Everleigh's voice cracks, and she doesn't continue.

A sad expression meets Tyler's face. "I didn't even know he got married after everything that happened with Amara. He never told me."

Gemma swallows hard, then clears her throat. "You don't think... I don't even want to say it out loud."

"What?" I ask her.

"You don't think his wife would come after Everleigh next?"

Everleigh lifts her head, then looks directly at Gemma. "She better not."

"No one knows who's responsible yet, so we can't jump to conclusions. Eric had his hand in a lot of shit. Some of it I know about, most of it I don't. It could've literally been anyone."

Somehow, Tyler's words relieve my anxiety over the whole situation, but I can't help but feel a surge of guilt stream through me, knowing what he risked to help us. "This makes me really sad," I say.

"Me too," Noah confirms. "I'm really sorry to hear this."

"Yeah, me as well," Tyler says. "If I find out anything else, I'll keep you all updated."

We give our thanks, then say our goodbyes, not leaving as happy as we should.

On the way home, Noah rests his palm on my thigh as I lean my head back on the seat.

"Owen's still hanging out with Anthony," he says. "Pretty sure he's going to want to stay over there."

"Is that code for something?" I ask.

"Abso-fucking-lutely," he tells me as we pull into the driveway.

Noah leads me up the porch steps and inside to the bedroom. "Your mom and dad aren't stopping by for at least an hour with the gifts," he whispers across my neck, slowly undressing me.

"Oh this won't take me long," I say, then carefully waddle to the bed completely naked.

Noah's gentle as he parts my legs and devours me like I'm his last meal. His tongue flicks and flutters against my clit, and as I suck in air, I feel as if I'm floating into outer space. My body begs for more of him while chasing my release, and when he slips two fingers inside, I nearly lose it.

My legs tremble, and he teases and sucks me until I nearly break in half. "Please," I beg, running my fingers through his hair and tugging him back to my clit. Noah laughs against my inner thigh and presses kisses before returning to where I want him. "You're such a greedy little thing, and I love it."

"Make me come," I demand, not wanting to teeter on the edge any longer.

"Yes, ma'am," he replies, and when he places my bud in his mouth and sucks, I lose all control. "Yes, baby," he whispers as my body convulses, and I ride the wave of satisfaction.

"Fuck me," I tell him, positioning myself up on two elbows.

Seconds later, Noah's grabbing my ankles and sliding me to the edge of the mattress. "I kinda like you being all dominant in the bedroom like this. It's hot as hell."

He takes off his belt, and the sound drives me absolutely fucking wild, then he slips down his jeans and boxers at the same time. Slowly, he places the tip of his cock in my opening. "You're so goddamn wet, Katie."

"You do that to me," I admit.

Noah doesn't wait any longer before entering. He goes slow and steady, not doing any rough movements even though my body desires it more than he'll ever know. We've tried to be careful when it comes to sex even though our doctor has said it's perfectly fine and normal. I lose myself in the moment as he thrusts in and out of me and notice his breathing growing more ragged and heavier. Eventually, he's chasing his release too, and with a grunt, he spills inside me.

After we clean up, we dress in comfortable clothes and hold each other until my parents show up and unload all the gifts. I'm pretty sure the smile on my face might actually be permanent. I'm the luckiest woman alive to have a man like Noah love me so fiercely. I can't wait for him to be my husband.

EPILOGUE
NOAH

"Are you ready to meet your brothers?" I ask Owen, taking his hand as we exit the elevator onto the hospital's labor and delivery floor.

"So ready!" He's holding balloons in his other hand and proudly wearing the BIG BROTHER T-shirt Everleigh got him for his birthday.

Though Katie's expected due date wasn't until mid-December, we've known there was a high probability she'd deliver early. Four weeks early, to be exact. The boys were born a week before Thanksgiving, and their birthdays will be close to Everleigh's. She turns thirty-three tomorrow and has been going on and on about how she's going to "party it up" this weekend. I find it hilarious, but Tyler has had enough of his wild-child sister.

"Hi, sweetie," Katie whispers when Owen enters. "I missed you."

Owen leans in and gently hugs her. We've been here for over two days. After twenty-six hours of labor and keeping an eye on the boys' heart rates, they finally came at 2:07 a.m and 2:10 a.m. Katie's epidural wore off at hour eighteen, and the amount of screaming she did wasn't something I was mentally prepared for. Not being able to do much for her pain made it hard to feel useful. She had horrible backaches and cramps in her legs, so I'd rub them out the best I could. After two hours of pushing, the first baby finally arrived.

"This one is Finneas, but we'll call him Finn." Katie nods to the baby on her left. "And this one is Lucas but Luke for short."

"Finn and Luke." Owen smiles. "Like from *Star Wars*."

Katie and I chuckle. Though it was a running joke for weeks, we actually ended up liking the names and picked them anyway.

"They're so tiny," Owen says as Luke wiggles.

"Didn't feel tiny to me…" Katie murmurs.

Though they were early, both boys weighed almost six pounds and only had to be on oxygen and monitored for a few hours. They passed all their health checks and will be able to come home with us in a couple of days.

"Can I hold them?" he asks.

"Of course, buddy. Sit on the chair and put a pillow under your arm. I'll bring one over at a time."

Owen does as I tell him and eagerly waits. I grab Finn since Luke is being fussy and probably wants to eat.

Once I secure him in Owen's arms, I stay nearby just in case. I taught him all about holding up the baby's heads and being very gentle with them. Though he's eleven, he's never been around little kids before, so this is all new to him too.

"He's so cute." Owen smiles at Finn.

"They look so much like you when you were a baby," Katie tells him. "I think they have your nose."

I grin as Owen studies Finn's face. It's adorable how excited he is. Though Owen looks a lot like Gabe, he has Katie's nose, and the twins do too. They aren't identical, but it might take me a bit to tell them apart until some of their distinct features start to show. I joked around with one of the nurses and asked her to put a black dot on the bottom of Luke's foot, but Katie wasn't amused. She assures me we'll know who is who.

As excited as I am that they're finally here, I'm also nervous as hell. Being a first-time dad is like nothing I've ever experienced, and now the only thing I feel is pure fear. Katie tells me it's normal, but I feel protective and worrisome all at the same time.

After Luke settles, I switch out the babies so Owen can hold him next. It's so sweet watching him with them, and I now understand why Katie's been so emotional about it. I think of Owen as one of my own and seeing him meet his brothers is precious.

"Can I come back tomorrow?" Owen asks when Loretta arrives to pick him up.

"Of course," Katie tells him. "They just want to keep us a couple more nights, then we'll all be home together in time for Thanksgiving dinner."

"Yay!"

Belinda and Dianna are pitching in for the holidays this year and making a feast at our house. It'll be one big get-together to see the babies and stuff our faces with turkey.

I hug Owen goodbye and promise to send pictures to his tablet. Loretta guides him out, and soon, it's just Katie, me, and the twins.

"Can you believe they're going to just send us home with two tiny humans?" she teases.

"It was harder to adopt a puppy than to fill out the paperwork for the babies," I add with a smirk. "The shelter nearly wanted a background check, an annual pay stub, and urine sample."

Katie snorts, then cringes. "Don't make me laugh. I'm pretty sure I just peed myself."

"I think your boobs did too."

"Lovely. Now you'll definitely wanna marry me..." She grunts.

"Are you kiddin'? I've never wanted you more than right now..."

Katie laughs, pushing me away. "You're crazy sometimes, but I love you more than anything."

"Good because I plan to get you down that aisle at that little white church in Magnolia Springs and make you my wife...*finally*."

"The little white church my grandparents got married in?"

"It's ours. I booked it."

Her eyes fill with tears. "I can't believe you did that."

I take her hand and press my lips to her knuckles. "As I've been telling you since I was fifteen years old, I'll do anything for you, Katie."

KATIE

I'm an emotional wreck, both physically and mentally exhausted, yet I can't sleep. The adrenaline high keeps me awake as I look at the boys sleeping so peacefully. Noah's passed out on the sofa that's way too small for him. Even though I told him to go home and get some quality sleep, he's a stubborn man. I can't fault him, though, because I love that he's here with me. Unconditional love is something I never had or felt before Noah came back into my life, and I can't imagine being without it.

As much as I'm appreciative of the nurse's around-the-clock help, I'm ready to be home. After a day full of visitors from our friends and family, I want to sleep in my big comfy bed.

I see my phone screen light up and decide to check who's texting me at one in the morning.

Everleigh: Guess who's coming to live with me tomorrow!

She's either sleep texting or drunk. Perhaps both.

Katie: The grim reaper?

Everleigh: No, silly. Archer! My new roomie.

I shake my head at her obnoxiousness.

Katie: I'm surprised you're so excited about it. Thought having a roommate would put a damper on your random hookups and boy toys.

Everleigh: Nah. He can join in on the fun...

She sends an eggplant emoji.

Katie: Well Happy Birthday, you crazy lady. I hope you're being safe.

Everleigh: Yes, Mama Bear. I have a DDD. Don't worry :-)

Katie: You mean a DD?

Everleigh: That's what I said!

I snort.

Katie: You're gonna be a hungover mess when Archer comes. Go to bed and sleep it off before he arrives.

Everleigh: Then he'll think I'm old and boring. This way, he'll know from the start that I'm fun and down to get...down and dirty.

Katie: Tyler's gonna murder you. Take some meds, drink water, and go to sleep.

Everleigh: But it's my birthday!! Double-3's!! Plus, I gotta keep my rep of the cool aunt.

Katie: Okay, well please be safe and do not bring a guy home. The last thing you need is Tyler bringing Archer over, and your one-night stand is still there.

I wait for a response, but she doesn't reply. Hopefully, that means she actually listened for a change. Though it's very unlikely.

The next day, we're finally getting released, and I can't wait to go home. My mom and dad are here to help since we have more car seats, gift bags, and supplies than the two of us can carry alone. Owen's eagerly waiting for us at the house with Loretta, Elliot, and Anthony. Once we get our discharge papers, we can leave.

"Hey," Gemma says, surprising us at the hospital.

"What are you doin' here?" I smile wide.

"Scarlett and Mommy needed to get out of the house for a bit." She brings the stroller closer, and I peek inside. I can hardly believe she's two months old already.

"It's gonna be so much fun watching these three grow up together." I smile down at a sleeping Scarlett. "They'll probably get into all kinds of trouble."

"Speaking of trouble..." Gemma takes a seat. "Did you get a ton of text messages from Everleigh last night?"

"I did." I smirk. "We chatted for a bit, but then she just stopped responding."

"Well, Tyler picked Archer up from the airport this morning, and when he took him to her house, there was a guy blackout drunk on her couch."

My eyes widen at the exact words of what I told her *not* to do.

"No…" I groan, already shaking my head.

"Oh yes, butt ass naked and all," Gemma confirms. "Clothes and empty beer bottles on the floor. Tyler nearly burst a blood vessel."

"What'd Archer say?"

"I don't think anything. Probably wondering why the hell his friend is having him live there, but considering he doesn't have any other options, I doubt he's complaining much."

"I'm just envisioning the first encounter Everleigh has with him and how she's going to look like a hot ass mess. I hope she's hungover as hell too." I chuckle. "I told her to go home," I whisper.

"Yeah well, that's her problem to figure out now. She talked all this talk about Archer, and now she's made a fool of herself—a first impression fool at that."

"This is going to make for one *interesting* Thanksgiving dinner."

OWEN

I sneak into Mom and Dad's room after midnight once they're asleep. The twins are in their bassinets swaddled up like little burritos. Luke wrinkles his nose as Finn makes funny mouth movements. Ever since they came home, Mom alternates between breastfeeding and bottle feeding. I didn't even know the difference until Everleigh explained it to me, but then Mom got annoyed, and Everleigh promised to tell me more later.

Since it's Christmas break, I don't have to worry about getting up early for school and can stay up with the babies. Mom isn't getting much sleep these days, and Dad's working on starting his own contractor business. I hope to be like him someday because I like building things and getting dirty too.

It's weird to think I went from having only a mom to having a dad and three brothers, but I like having a big family. Though I wasn't sure what to think about it all in the beginning, I love it now. Noah's such a good man for Mom, and I can't wait till the summer when they get married. Mom says I get to be in the wedding with them. I'm not sure what that means exactly, but I get to wear a cool black tux.

Finn starts to get restless, and before he wakes up Luke or our parents, I take him out of the bassinet and carry him to the kitchen. He's the oldest of the twins by three minutes and usually the first to wake up hungry. I bet he'll be big like an athlete, and hopefully, I can teach him how to play basketball and baseball.

Dad taught me how to feed them, and I've watched Mom do it a hundred times now. Once the milk is lukewarm, I bring Finn into the nursery and sit in the rocking chair. He immediately takes it and starts sucking it down.

"Slow down, buddy. You'll just spit it all up if you eat too fast," I remind him. "The last time I burped you, half the bottle ended up on my shirt."

I know he doesn't understand me, but his sucking slows down, and I smile at him for listening. Luke always acts like he's starving although he eats every two to three hours. If I ate that much, I'd have a stomachache and throw up too. I have a feeling Luke's going to be the rebellious one.

"What are you doin'?" Mom walks into the nursery in a haze. "Why are you awake?"

ONLY US

"Finn was hungry…" I shrug, showing her his now empty bottle. "I wanted you to get some sleep."

"Aw…you sweet, precious boy." She palms my cheek. "Thank you."

"I can feed Luke next," I tell her. "Well, after I burp Finn. He can be stubborn sometimes and take a while."

Mom chuckles softly. "That's true. Why don't I take him, and you can get Luke's bottle ready?"

"Okay."

She takes Finn, and when I stand, Mom sits in the rocking chair. I make another bottle just as Luke starts to fuss. It wakes up Dad, but I tell him I've got it. He smiles and tells me how much he loves me, then thanks me for helping.

Anthony thought I'd be mad once he told me about the night our real dad died, but I could never be mad at the man who stood up for my mom. Noah's the best dad I could ever ask for.

Once the twins are fed and changed, Mom and I place them back into their bassinets. They're wrapped up like burritos again, and it makes me laugh.

"You're going to be the best father someday," Mom tells me.

I nod with a smile. "Just like Noah."

AVAILABLE NOW

Continue the Only One series with Archer & Everleigh's story in *Only Mine*

I'm not your girl next door.
They call me loud, blunt, and too gorgeous for my own good.
A woman who can't be tamed.

Until Archer.
The problem? He's my brother's best friend. My new roommate.
And off-limits.
Until we spend a wild night between the sheets.

But secretly dating isn't easy.
Our pasts collide with the present.
And the only man who can save me is the one I shouldn't want.

ABOUT THE AUTHOR

Brooke Cumberland and Lyra Parish are a duo of romance authors under the *USA Today* pseudonym, Kennedy Fox. Their characters will make you blush and your heart melt. Cowboys in tight jeans are their kryptonite. They always guarantee a happily ever after!

CONNECT WITH US

Find us on our website:
kennedyfoxbooks.com

Subscribe to our newsletter:
kennedyfoxbooks.com/newsletter

- facebook.com/kennedyfoxbooks
- twitter.com/kennedyfoxbooks
- instagram.com/kennedyfoxduo
- amazon.com/author/kennedyfoxbooks
- goodreads.com/kennedyfox
- bookbub.com/authors/kennedy-fox

BOOKS BY KENNEDY FOX

DUET SERIES (BEST READ IN ORDER)

CHECKMATE DUET SERIES

ROOMMATE DUET SERIES

LAWTON RIDGE DUET SERIES

INTERCONNECTED STAND-ALONES

BISHOP BROTHERS SERIES

CIRCLE B RANCH SERIES

BISHOP FAMILY ORIGIN

LOVE IN ISOLATION SERIES

ONLY ONE SERIES

MAKE ME SERIES

Find the entire Kennedy Fox reading order at
Kennedyfoxbooks.com/reading-order

Made in the USA
Coppell, TX
24 May 2023